*Jamestown*

KEEPERS
OF THE RING
2

# JAMESTOWN

## Angela Elwell Hunt

Tyndale House Publishers, Inc.
WHEATON, ILLINOIS

*For Buddy, LaDonna, Michael, and Jared Ritter*

**Library of Congress Cataloging-in-Publication Data**

Hunt, Angela Elwell,  date
 Jamestown / Angela Elwell Hunt.
    p.  cm. — (Keepers of the ring ; 2)
 Includes bibliographical references.
 ISBN 0-8423-2013-X (sc : alk. paper)
  1. Virginia—History—Colonial period, ca. 1600-1775—Fiction.
2. Jamestown (Va.)—History—Fiction.  I. Title.  II. Series: Hunt, Angela Elwell, date
Keepers of the ring ; 2.
PS3558.U46747J36  1996
813'.54—dc20                                                                                95-20605

# TABLE OF CONTENTS

Fallon Bailie

Pocahontas

John Rolfe

Kimi

Brody McRyan

Gilda

Opechancanough

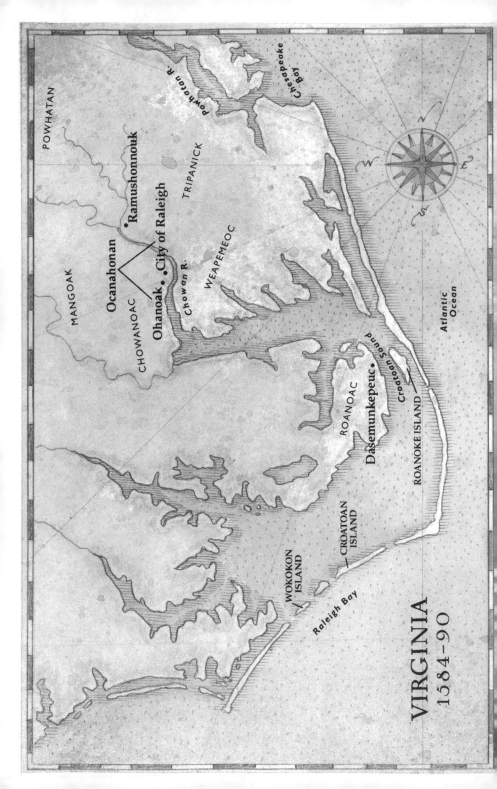

# AUTHOR'S NOTE

Yesterday my family and I celebrated the Fourth of July. After the traditional cookout and indulgence in two flag-shaped cakes (apparently cousins think alike), we gathered in the living room and debated, among other things, the current national interest in Pocahontas. No, we decided, she was too young for a romantic relationship with John Smith, but she was a peacemaker, a delightful scamp, a bright and courageous young woman willing to venture first into the camps of the unknown and then to the island of the strangers that lay far across the great salt sea.

Pocahontas lives within the pages of this story, as does her father, Powhatan, and her uncle, Opechancanough. John Smith is here, with John Rolfe. Their contributions to this tale are based upon the historical record, and I have not knowingly contradicted what historians know to be true about any of them.

Gilda, Fallon, Noshi, Brody, and Wart are fictitious characters, but they live and move and struggle through actual battles and historical situations. If they did not actually live, I like to think that they *could* have—and that bright, courageous spirits like theirs laid the foundation for this country. Because of the experiences of people such as these characters—because of their ideals, struggles, and surrender to the molding hand of God—we have a reason to celebrate.

## Fallon Bailie

*When Heaven is about to confer a great
office on any man, it first exercises
his mind with suffering,
and his sinews and bones with toil.*

*Mencius, 372–289 B.C.*

*April 1607*

The river carried them away.

The little girl woke with a sharp tingling in her arm and shifted uncomfortably between the side of the canoe and the soft, plump body of her playmate. Noshi still snored gently beside her, but Fallon lay awake, his blue eyes wide and alert under the thin grass mat that covered them in the canoe.

"I'm hungry," Gilda announced, looking to Fallon. At thirteen, he had often been entrusted with the care of the two younger children, and Gilda was accustomed to his careful authority. "Are we done with the hiding game?"

Fallon did not answer, but lay his finger across his lips and carefully stretched his long legs out toward the bow of the canoe. A shaft of bright morning sunlight fell upon his freckled face as he gingerly lifted a corner of the woven grass mat. Gilda saw him squint as he sniffed the air outside.

"Nothing," he whispered, a satisfied smile flitting across his face. "Maybe we can land the canoe here."

With the inbred caution of one who had lived a lifetime in the wilderness, Fallon turned onto his stomach and slowly rose upon his knees. The canoe rocked gently in the water and the motion woke Noshi, who opened his eyes and thrust his thumb into his mouth. "Where's Mama?" he mumbled around the thumb, his green eyes still heavy with sleep.

"You two stay under the mat," Fallon whispered, dragging his hand in the water to turn the drifting canoe toward the shore. "Don't move or say anything until I tell you there is no danger."

For the first time since waking, Gilda felt a tremor of fear. Last night her mama and papa had smiled as they kissed her and sent her to the river to play the hiding game, but their eyes had been dark and moist with tears. Fallon and Noshi's parents had been serious, too, as they hugged the boys and told them to be careful. Gilda closed her eyes and remembered her mother's fervent embrace. It was unusual for her mother and father to hug her so fiercely. And she had never been allowed to play the hiding game at night.

Gilda's chubby hand reached for the strip of leather tied around her neck. Her mother's gift to her, a gold ring, dangled from the supple leather.

"Always remember the ring," her mother had whispered after slipping the necklace around Gilda's neck. "Know that I love you. And that God will go with you always."

*God will go with me where?* Gilda wondered, tilting her head back to watch Fallon guide the boat. Why had the grown-ups sent the children away? And when would they be allowed to return?

Gilda resisted the temptation to worry. Fallon was nearly a man and old enough to take care of both her and Noshi. He would not let anything happen to them.

▼▲▼▲ Fallon Bailie—son of the late Englishman Roger Bailie, proud stepson of Rowtag, a chief of the Mangoak tribe—quietly guided the canoe with his hands until the current pushed the boat onto a sandy beach. The air was clear here; he could smell nothing but the crisp scent of pine and the earthy perfume of spring. No aromas of Indian cook fires spiced the morning air, nor was the bitter tang of destruction detectable in the breeze. The battle that surely raged at Ocanahonan lay far upstream, north of them.

The three refugees had drifted downstream all night, and as Fallon stepped out of the canoe into the shallow water, he was momentarily tempted to surrender to the overwhelming sense of loss and grief that threatened to engulf him. His mother, Audrey

Bailie, was either fighting for her life or even now lay dead beneath the enemy's war ax. What if she needed him or called his name? Tall and strong, Fallon was sure he could have defended her, but Rowtag had insisted that he take the two little ones to safety.

He glanced back at the canoe. Gilda and Noshi peered over the nose of the canoe like frightened cubs too unsure to come out of their den. Noshi was his half brother, the son of Rowtag and Audrey, and though he had been granted the handsome copper skin and dark hair of his father, his eyes were his mother's and *"as green,"* she had often declared, *"as the emerald hills of Ireland."* Gilda Colman possessed the same unusual blend of Indian and English features: golden skin, dark hair, and startlingly blue eyes. The little girl, who had yet to see her fourth birthday, had been like a younger sister to Fallon ever since Jocelyn Colman had asked Fallon's mother to be Gilda's wet nurse.

Only a few months apart, Gilda and Noshi had grown up together, and Fallon had been their constant, if sometimes reluctant, protector. Of late he had thought himself too much a man to be serving as a nursemaid for the little ones, but Rowtag had honored him last night when he placed his broad hands on Fallon's shoulders and charged him to protect Gilda's and Noshi's lives, together with his own. The responsibility he had always endured now became a solemn charge and a challenge.

After bringing his finger again to his lips to ensure the children's silence, he pulled the canoe from the water, firmly beaching it upon the sand. Crouching behind a screen of greening shrubs, he looked down the beach, then studied the sky.

Through the sun-shot leaves of the towering trees, the sky was crisp and blue; not a single cloud marred the horizon. They were far, then, from the war party that had surrounded Ocanahonan at dusk. For the moment, they were safe, but worry tormented Fallon's mind. Had the enemy seen their canoe slip away? Would the bloodlust of battle drive them downstream in pursuit?

Noshi's familiar whine interrupted his thoughts. "I'm hungry,

Fallon," he whimpered, his thumb still in his mouth. "Where's Mama?"

Fallon felt his resolve slip. If he thought about his mother and Rowtag, if he considered even for a moment that their entire world was under attack, he would not be able to do his duty. Better to pretend that they were hunting.

"We want Mama and Papa to be proud of us, don't we?" Fallon asked, turning to the young ones. "They asked us to hide in the boat, and now they want us to gather our own food. Rowtag would not want us to complain but to do our work well."

"I can make a fishhook," Noshi said, thrusting his chubby leg over the side of the boat. "Watch me."

"I can help," Gilda answered, splashing into the water behind Noshi.

"Good," Fallon said, forcing a smile. He knelt to look into the children's eyes. "Do not wander from the boat. If you see or hear anyone approaching, run and play the hiding game in the woods. Do not come out for anyone but me, do you hear?"

"Yes," Noshi answered, plopping himself into the mud at the water's edge. "I will make a hook and we will catch a fish for breakfast."

"Do that, then," Fallon said. He turned toward the woods, then paused and looked back at the children. Gilda sat in the sand next to Noshi, scouring the mud for a sharp stick. Both were occupied and, if all went well, they would not stir.

Fallon paused to whisper a prayer for success, then darted into the woods.

▼▲▼▲▼ Though European blood ran undiluted in his veins, Fallon had been reared as the son of a Mangoak chief, and he had learned his lessons well. By the river's edge he found a nest with five eggs, and he took three, knowing the mother bird would not desert the nest as long as an egg remained. Under a rotting log he found a generous collection of grubs and termites, which he scraped into the leather bag hanging at his waist. The grubs and eggs would do for breakfast. Fallon knew he and the children only had to travel near the water and they would find food. Further downstream he would lay snares and trap animals as they came to drink at the water.

He smiled in pleased surprise when he returned and found that Noshi had actually managed to make an excellent fishhook of splintered wood. Gilda had pulled long fibers from reeds growing at the water's edge for a fishing line. "Here," Fallon said, slipping one of the juicy grubs into the pointed barb of the hook. "You're ready to fish. But first, you need to eat something."

Gilda crinkled her nose at the sight of the grubs. "Ugh," she said, shaking her head. "I won't eat those."

"You've had them before in stew, you've just never had them raw," Fallon said, pushing a handful of the insects toward her. "You need to eat, Gilda, if you're going to be strong."

"I'm strong already," she said, her lower lip edging forward in a pout. "And I won't eat bugs."

"Then eat this egg." He handed her an egg, which she accepted with a dubious expression. Fallon showed her how to chip away the top of the shell and swallow the egg in one gulp. Noshi took an egg and imitated his older brother exactly. Not wanting to be bested, Gilda followed their example, albeit reluctantly.

"Rowtag said we must be strong if we are to survive," Fallon said, fixing the two children with a stern glance. "You must obey me and not argue. If I say eat, you will eat. If not, you will die."

Gilda's lower lip trembled, and for a moment Fallon feared she would cry. But then she pressed her rosebud lips together in a remarkable show of courage and walked back to the water's edge where her fishing line lay.

Fallon sighed in relief and tossed the grubs onto the ground, unable to eat the squirming things himself.

▼▲▼▲▼ They spent the morning fishing on the river-bank, then Fallon selected dark and dry wood for a nearly smokeless fire. While their five fish roasted, Fallon napped and the young ones played quietly among the bushes. As the day began to die, Fallon wrapped the roasted fish in wide green leaves and told the children to climb back into the boat.

"Where are we going, Fallon?" Noshi asked as he lay down next to Gilda inside the canoe. "Can't we go home?"

Fallon automatically looked northward up the river, but nothing stirred on the blue-brown surface of the water. If their parents had survived the attack on Ocanahonan, surely one of them would have come down the river. But not a living soul had stirred from the north.

It was time to be honest.

"We can't go home again," Fallon said, pushing the canoe off the bank. "Mama and Papa are of certain dead, Noshi. Your mama and papa are dead, too, Gilda. They wanted us to find a safe place."

Noshi stared at Fallon in disbelief, but Gilda's bright blue eyes filled up with tears. Fallon immediately regretted telling her the truth. Suppose she cried and wailed all night? He had planned for them to drift quietly downriver under the cover of darkness, but if he had to deal with a screaming youngster . . .

She did not make a sound. A sad little sigh escaped her lips as tears rolled from her eyes, and she pressed her fist into her mouth, a strangely adult gesture for one so young. Noshi began to cry noisily, and Gilda quietly slipped her arms around his neck and held him tight. Fallon loaded the fish into the canoe, then pushed it into the current. Climbing into the boat beside the children, he pulled the grass mat over their heads and dashed bitter tears from his own eyes.

Fallon could sense the youngsters' questions and fear, but he did not want to talk about the death of their village. After drifting for some time in the darkness and listening to the children squirm restlessly, he made an effort to lighten his voice. "Can't you go to sleep?"

"No," Gilda answered, wriggling against the side of the canoe. "Noshi's elbow is in my belly."

"I can't help it," Noshi protested, turning from Gilda. He lay his hands on Fallon's chest. "I'm scared, Fallon. It's dark and quiet out here."

"There is nothing to fear," Fallon said with a confidence he did not feel. He ran his hand through Noshi's thick, dark hair. "I know! Let's practice the catechism that the minister taught us. We'll say it over and over until we know it by heart."

"I already know it," Gilda said proudly. "Start it, Fallon."

"Let me get more comfortable." Fallon shifted in the narrow space until he lay flat on his back. Delighted at the change in positions, Noshi rolled over him and lay against the canoe on his left side, and Gilda snuggled under his arm on his right.

Fallon tented his fingers on his chest. "What is your name?"

"That's easy," Gilda said, giggling. "Gilda Colman."

Fallon lifted his head to look at his brother. "And you? Surely you have a name?"

"Noshi," the boy said, punching Fallon playfully in the ribs. "You know my name."

"Yes," Fallon answered, relaxing against the canoe. "And who gave you this name?"

"My mother and father," the children recited together, sitting up in their eagerness, "who wish to bring me up in the knowledge of Christ."

"Very good," Fallon said, grateful that the challenge seemed to have dispelled their fear. "Now rehearse the articles of your belief."

Gilda took a deep breath and began immediately: "I believe in God the Father, who made me and all the world."

Fallon lay his finger across her mouth and turned to Noshi. "And you, little brother? Who has stolen your voice?"

Noshi jumped in: "I believe in God the Son, who has redeemed me and all mankind."

Fallon nodded. "And the third article?"

Gilda giggled in the darkness, unable to remember, but Noshi knew the words: "I believe in God the Holy Ghost, who sanctifieth me and all the elect people of God."

"Who are the ee-lect, Fallon?" Gilda asked.

He laced his fingers again and thought a moment. "I guess the elect are the people of Ocanahonan and all other people who follow Jesus Christ, if there be any."

*But what if there aren't others?* A dark and cynical voice whispered in his mind. *And if there is no Ocanahonan, there remain only you three. . . .*

"There are other elect in lands where Jesus is worshiped," Fallon said, more to reassure himself than the children. "Mama told me of England and Ireland."

"Will we go there?" Noshi's voice was a childish treble in the darkness.

"Only God knows," Fallon answered as the canoe swirled in the darkness. "Now, let's practice again. What are your names?"

"Noshi!"

"Gilda!"

"And who has given you these names?"

"My mother and father," the children chorused.

"Soft," Fallon said, laying his finger across his lips. "Not so loud. We mustn't wake the fish."

The English ship *Susan Constant* lay at anchor in the wind-whipped waters off the shores of Virginia, and John Smith paced her deck, unable to sleep. Cursed be Captain Christopher Newport's fears! Despite the trials of the last two days, Smith would gladly have spent the night ashore, even with a nation of savages breathing down his neck. But Newport and his cronies were fearful, especially after their first landing had been met by a volley of arrows. Though the savages had been dispersed by gunfire and had not been seen in two days, Newport would not allow his settlers or seamen to remain ashore at night.

The *Susan Constant's* two companion ships, the *Godspeed* and the *Discovery*, were anchored off the starboard bow, and their lantern lights shone steadily across the dark waters. Smith could hear the sounds of relieved merriment from their decks, for despite their first harsh welcome, the euphoria of sighting the noble trees and unravished forests of Virginia had not yet worn off. The planters aboard fancied themselves explorers and were doubtless giddy with dreams of the riches they would send back to England.

Even the basest of them deserved a bit of self-congratulation, Smith admitted grudgingly to himself, for the journey across the great Western ocean had been difficult. Thirty-nine of 144 prospective colonists had died en route, victims of scurvy and other diseases. After the proper prayers for burial of the dead at sea had been read from the captain's *Book of Common Prayer,* the unfortunate ones had been hastily consigned to the ocean depths. And so tonight, like every night since they had set sail from England, every man aboard was silently grateful that he slept in the ship and not in the bowels of the deep.

The expedition had been a year in the planning. Chartered by King James in April 1606, the Virginia Company of London had been established for three purposes: to search for gold and other precious metals, to explore the rivers of the New World for a possible passage to the South Seas, and to look for the lost colony that had been initiated at Roanoke Island.

Those purposes were published and well known, but there were other, lesser-known reasons men were sent to Virginia as well: Investors hoped to gather a profit through peaceful trade with the Indians of Virginia; King James desired to install a military base to effectively defend Virginia against ongoing Spanish colonization in the New World; and clergymen felt an urgent need to evangelize the Indians with the gospel of Jesus Christ.

John Smith had not crossed the great sea for God, government, or gold. He had ventured forth for glory. Should he find gold and serve God or his country in the process, so much the better, but he had joined the expedition solely for the adventure. A professional soldier since the age of twenty, Smith had stood in imminent danger of losing his life at least a hundred times, but the hand of God—or amazing strokes of good fortune, depending upon a man's viewpoint—had thus far preserved his life.

Smith rubbed his beard and leaned on the ship's rail, savoring his recollections of danger. Because of his Protestant beliefs, he once had been tossed overboard from a similar ship en route to Italy. Picked up by a passing skipper, he had joined a corps of Hungarians who lived solely to fight Turks, and, while amongst them, he had invented an incendiary bomb that effectively dislodged enemy positions.

In a duel for his life, he had beheaded three Turkish champions, but at the battle of Rotenthurn he was wounded and carried off by the Turks. He thought fortune had cast an indulgent smile his direction when he was sold as a slave to an aristocratic woman, but she lent Smith to her bullying brother, who delighted in humiliating servants. After killing the tyrant in self-defense, Smith escaped through Russia while wearing a slave's iron collar about his neck.

Virginia had seemed a logical choice for a willing adventurer, but it seemed he and trouble could not be separated for long. Within days of putting to sea, he and the captain had been at odds. Smith snorted in derision. Perhaps he *had* voiced his opinion too forcefully on an occasion or two aboard ship, but that cursed Captain Newport was touchy beyond reason! John certainly hadn't deserved being chained below deck for most of the journey simply for questioning the wisdom of lolling around in the ocean when there was work to be done. Then there was that pompous aristocrat Edward Wingfield—he was even more intent upon Smith's demise than Newport. On the Caribbean island of Nevis, Wingfield had actually dared to construct a gallows with a noose intended for Smith's neck. But Smith had faced his disgruntled accusers and blithely remarked that they were handsome gallows, but he could not be persuaded to use them.

Smith smiled grimly, recalling the frustration on Newport's and Wingfield's faces. Only the diplomacy of Reverend Robert Hunt had calmed them enough to call the men aboard ship so the voyage could begin its final journey. And Smith had climbed the gangplank with poise, his hands still shackled behind him, his confidence unwavering.

"To overcome," Smith whispered at the ship's rail, smiling as he watched the waves strive to reach the stars, "is to live."

Yes, throughout his twenty-and-seven years, John Smith had been moved by only two things: a mild interest in money and an unshakable passion for adventure.

Surrounded by animal sounds and the stirring of dark river waters, the children's canoe drifted throughout the night. Fallon woke to see dawn brightening the sky above, and he lifted a corner of the grass mat to peer out. Several Indian canoes lined a clearing on the riverbank ahead, and in the moist, chill air Fallon could smell cook fires. The delicious aroma made his stomach cramp with sudden hunger.

Careful not to disturb the sleeping children, Fallon put his hands in the water and quietly guided the canoe to the shore. He slid noiselessly from the boat into the water, beached the canoe firmly in the sand, then flung the dew-heavy mat back over the sleeping children.

Twenty feet downstream he saw a trail leading away from the water, and as he crouched down and crept nearer, the tall timbers of a palisade rose in the distance. He closed his eyes, trying to remember which Indian villages lay south on the Chowan River. Was this Tandaquomuc? Metackwem?

His heart went into sudden shock when a painted warrior stepped out of the gloom, the tip of his spear gleaming white in the semidarkness. Fallon uttered a quick greeting, knowing his life depended upon the ease with which he spoke in the Algonquin tongue, and the Indian indicated the trail with a jerk of his head. Fallon stepped forward, his heart in his throat—he had no choice but to follow the path before him and face the village chief, the *werowance.*

The warrior called to his fellows as he escorted Fallon into the village. A crowd followed in their wake, and the werowance came out of his hut to greet the visitor. They met near the center of the village, and Fallon could feel the eyes of the tribe upon him as they remarked upon his pale skin and red hair. The warrior pointed to the chief and told Fallon that he stood before Gepanocon. He was an aging chief whose skin as well as his hair had grayed over the years. The man's head had been shaved from the crown to the eyebrows, but coarse hair hung long down his back. He wore an animal skin at his waist and an embroidered mantle over his shoulders. His chest had been painted with an intricate picture of a rattlesnake, complete with beaded rattles and sharp fangs.

Fallon lifted his eyes from the harrowing picture and met the chief's stern gaze.

"Why do you come to Ritanoe?" the chief asked, and Fallon recognized the name of the village. Warriors had often come from Ritanoe to Ocanahonan to trade.

The quick question needed a thoughtful answer. Drawing himself to his full height, Fallon answered in the tongue of the Algonquin tribes. Speaking slowly, he explained that two days ago an enemy, probably the Powhatan, had surrounded Ocanahonan to destroy it. He and two children had escaped in the night.

Gepanocon's eyes narrowed as the tale unfolded, and when Fallon had finished speaking, the aged leader held out his hands as a sign of welcome. "We will send men to search Ocanahonan for survivors," he said, nodding gravely. "You and the children with you will make a home in our village. Our women will be their mothers; our men will be their fathers."

The chief nodded as if the matter were settled, then he cast a searching look toward Fallon. "Know you how to beat copper into weapons?"

Fallon shook his head. "I have not learned a trade," he said, for the first time ashamed of his youth. "I followed in the footsteps of my father, Rowtag, and learned to hunt and fish."

"Those are good lessons," Gepanocon said, nodding. "But we will see if others yet live. Go now and bring those with you into this village." With an abrupt gesture, Gepanocon signaled to two women, who ran to Fallon's side for the walk back to the river.

His mind hummed with questions as he led the women to the canoe. Gepanocon had acted kindly in allowing Fallon and the children to remain in the safety of camp. The question about copper, however, troubled him. Why did the chief care so much about a mere metal when lives were at stake?

The canoe was waiting on the sand where Fallon had left it, and when he lifted the grass mat he could see that neither Gilda nor Noshi had moved. With their arms tossed around each other in comfort, they slept still, their dark heads nestled together as one. Without a word, the two Indian women reached into the boat and each lifted a child, nestling their gentle burdens into the soft curves of their bodies as they started down the trail back to the village.

Fallon followed. He knew he ought to feel relieved that the children had been properly delivered to safety. This was what his parents wanted, after all, and he had done his duty. But his heart twisted at the sound of the women's gentle crooning. He had been Gilda and Noshi's protector since they were weaned. What would he do now that the watchful eyes of an entire Indian village stood ready to guard and shelter them?

▼▲▼▲ Gepanocon sent out a scouting party immediately. At sunset of the second day the scouts returned from the city that had been Ocanahonan with six wounded men. Fallon sat outside in the evening shadows as the tribal elders gathered around the chief to hear the scouts' report, and he flinched when the warriors stated flatly that Ocanahonan, the great city of the clothed people, was no more. "All were dead save these six: four English and two Indians," one of the scouts said, gesturing to the wounded on the ground. "Only the gods know which of these will survive."

Fallon stood and peered over the shoulders of the assembled crowd for a glance at the wounded men, hoping that his stepfa-

ther would lie before him. But though he recognized the four
Englishmen, they were not of his family, and the two Indians
were marked with the tattoos and painted designs of the
Powhatan. Fallon closed his eyes against the storm of hate in his
heart. If God was just, those two would die!

▼▲▼▲▼ Whether from God's hand or their wounds,
the two Powhatan warriors did die before sunrise. The four
Englishmen lay in the chief's own hut, where the women
cleaned their wounds and the conjuror chanted prayers. After
three days, Gepanocon lifted his hands in victory and announced that the four Englishmen would survive and teach
them how to hammer copper into weapons. The village celebrated with a great feast and dancing around the fire, and Fallon
drew close to Noshi and Gilda, who stood apart and watched the
scene with fascination.

Despite his knowledge of Indian ways and his fluency in their
tongue, Fallon felt that he had mistakenly stepped into another
world. Ocanahonan, with its mixture of English and Indian cul-
tures, had been a thoroughly civilized city founded on Christian
principles and governed by an enlightened code of law. Women
had worn modest clothing, hands were washed and faces
scrubbed, men carried themselves with dignity and honor. The
guiding principles behind the laws, customs, and everyday civil-
ity were the codes and morals found in God's Holy Bible, and
Indian and Englishman alike had revered this sacred book.

How different was this primitive place! The women wore long
skirts of leather with no clothing at all on their upper bodies;
men danced in breechcloths around a roaring fire while their
heavily tattooed chests gleamed with coats of bear grease. The
werowance's priests and conjuror screamed and clawed the air
near the fire, begging aid from unseen spirits and gods of the
night. Watching, Fallon felt his skin crawl with revulsion.

Though the people of Ritanoe had been generous to offer shelter, Fallon knew this place could not be his home. And though

the women seemed affectionately disposed toward Gilda and Noshi, he would not leave the children in this village where heathen spirits might supplant the knowledge of the one true God.

Fallon reached for the children's hands and pulled them away from the sight of the screaming conjuror. "I want to see the dancing," Noshi protested, planting his heels into the sandy ground.

"No," Fallon answered, pressing his lips firmly together. "You're coming with me."

Gilda did not protest, but her blue eyes did a slow slide toward the fire as Fallon led her away. "Don't even look at it," Fallon rebuked her, resolutely pulling her with him. "You're not a child of darkness."

As the savages of Ritanoe danced in celebration, Fallon took his small charges into an empty hut and reminded them of what they had learned in Ocanahonan. "Your father, Gilda," he said, lowering his head to look into the girl's eyes, "was a minister, a man of God. Your mother's heart would be broken if she thought for one minute that you might forget the one true God."

Gilda blinked, and her slender brows knitted in a frown.

"And you, Noshi," Fallon said, turning to his half brother. "If our mama and papa knew that you wanted to dance with those Indians—"

"Papa was an Indian," Noshi interrupted. "And he danced. I saw him!"

"Your papa danced in praise to the one true God, not to the demons of air and wind," Fallon corrected. "Listen to the priest when he speaks and you'll hear that he speaks of evil spirits! Look at the idols in the center of the village—never did you see an idol in Ocanahonan!"

Gilda screwed up her face as if she would cry. "I want to go home," she wailed plaintively. "There are people here we know. Let's ask them to take us home, Fallon."

"The Englishmen have been very sick, and we must wait for them to get well," Fallon answered. He gentled his voice. "And there is no more Ocanahonan, Gilda. From this day unto your last, your home is with me."

She walked forward and leaned against his chest—a simple, childlike gesture of trust—and Fallon awkwardly brushed the top of her head with his hand. Noshi leaned against him, too, and Fallon embraced them both.

After a moment, the older boy squatted so that his eyes were level with those of his two charges. "What is your name?"

"Gilda Colman."

"Noshi."

"Aye," Fallon answered, inhaling their wonderful warmth. "And who gave you this name?"

"My mother and father," the children recited together, "who wish to bring me up in the knowledge of Christ."

"Very good," Fallon said. "Now rehearse for me the articles of your belief."

Ashore in Virginia, the English lifted prayers of praise for a safe journey, then erected a cross on a point of land they called Cape Henry in honor of the eldest English prince. After this ritual, the settlers returned to the *Susan Constant,* the *Godspeed,* and the *Discovery.* The three ships shed their sails like molting birds and anchored in the mouth of the wide river newly christened as the James.

Captain Newport promptly dispatched landing parties. Over a period of weeks, a half dozen small vessels loaded with men, supplies, and arms rowed up the river to explore possible settlement sites. The men's expressions were locked with anxiety, sobered by the possibility that they might meet with resistance such as they had encountered on their first excursion ashore. Though the Indians they had met since that day had been friendly, still, one never knew what lurked in the savage mind.

As John Smith stepped out of the shallop one morning and splashed toward shore, he was almost disappointed that they had not yet encountered more opposition. Apparently the savages had heard about English firepower and decided to welcome the settlers instead of resisting. He hoped the Indians would not prove to be cowardly or weak; surely a country that was itself beautiful beyond description could not have spawned an inferior people.

Steadying his impatient heart, Smith paused on the shore and waited for the other members of his landing party. Drawing his sword, he relished the heavy feel of the hilt in his hand, then took a practice swipe at a vine hanging from a branch. No English spring could match the color of Virginia, he thought as he looked into the wilderness before him. The land blazed with dogwood, honeysuckle, and wild roses. Grapes and raspberries flourished in every crevice and shadow, and in some places strawberries covered the ground so thickly that it would be impossible to step without crushing them.

He knew the woods teemed with game, too, and in days past the men of England had been alternately delighted and amazed by the myriad assortment of animals. One wiry creature, hanging by its tail from a tree, had startled Captain Newport into firing his musket, and a black-masked furry creature that scuttled across the trail had been promptly misidentified as a monkey. Deer were numerous and unafraid, watching the English progress with indifferent eyes, and huge flocks of birds rose from the woods in bright colors. One flock had flown over the river in such a vast number that the sky darkened for the space of five minutes.

A faint trail led away from the river where the colonists had landed, and Smith suspected that at its conclusion they would find an Indian village. "Arm yourselves and be ready lest the savages prove less than friendly," he called over his shoulder to the men behind him. "But let us pray God that these will be as accommodating as those we have met thus far."

Steadying their muskets against their shoulders, the English dove into the woods, and wildlife scattered around them.


▼▲▼▲▼ Miles away, Wowinchopunk, chief of the Chesapeake Paspahegh tribe, received word that small parties of clothed and bearded men had landed from great winged ships on the sea.

The chief gravely considered the news. He had heard much of these clothed men. He knew they should be handled carefully, for they carried rods of thunder in their hands and had the power to strike entire villages with sickness.

Reluctantly, he gave the order to send a welcoming party and to prepare a feast.

▼▲▼▲▼ By the thirteenth of May, the English council had decided to establish their colony thirty miles up the James River. The site was a flat peninsula three miles long and surrounded by six-fathoms-deep water that could be navigated easily by large oceangoing vessels. The spot could be defended with ease against invaders from land or sea, for the only bridge to the mainland was a narrow isthmus that lay under water at high tide. These considerations overrode Smith's concern that the land was low and marshy; indeed, the council leaders paid him scant attention when he voiced his uneasiness.

With the council's approval, Captain Newport gave the order to moor the three ships to the trees outside the peninsula where they would build a fort and a settlement called Jamestown.

The next day, all 105 Englishmen went ashore and gathered on firm ground. The colonists helped unload their stores from the ships, and canvas tents were set up for shelter as the council members drew an outline and rough plan of the fortification they would immediately build.

Though orders in a recently unsealed box from the directors of the London Company had named him as part of the governing council, Smith knew the aristocrats on the council did not hold him, or his opinion, in any esteem. So he worked quietly among the other men, doing what had to be done, and waited.

▼▲▼▲▼ While Gilda and Noshi collected wild blueberries in the field outside the palisade of Ritanoe, Fallon sat in the grass and kept a careful eye on them as he pondered what he should do. The children had taken easily to life in the village, playing with the other youngsters and joining in the work that had to be done. They would not understand why Fallon wanted to leave.

The four surviving Englishmen, though weak and dazed at first, had also adapted to life at Ritanoe. They banded together and used their knowledge of metallurgy to win Gepanocon's favor. If the chief wanted metal weapons, Fallon had heard them say, let the ore be brought from the rocks and river, and they would fashion arrowheads that would not bend and knives that would cut the toughest hide of a bear. But let the English be given a hut, and let their food be brought there, and let them work in peace.

Gepanocon, giddy with dreams of conquest, had given the Englishmen the best his village had to offer. Fallon watched his fellow countrymen with disdain, shocked that they freely made such selfish demands and guiltlessly accepted the chief's offers of women and food and furs. The Englishmen attended the tribal dances and smiled at the conjuror's black tricks. They slipped their hands around the waists of women and took them back to their hut in the darkness of night.

Why would men change their hearts solely because they had changed their home? Fallon did not understand, and he could find no one with wisdom enough to answer.

"Fallon!" Gilda called, berries tumbling from her basket as she ran toward him.

"Careful, little one," Fallon answered, putting a hand out to steady her as she rushed to his side. "You will lose all you have gathered."

"You can share them with me," she offered generously, her bright blue eyes shining toward him in a smile. "I'm thirsty. Can we go to the river?"

"We do not have to go to the river," Fallon answered. He waited until Noshi ambled up, then put his arms on his hips and surveyed his younger brother sternly. "Do you remember what our father said, Noshi? Where can you find water in the meadow?"

Noshi crinkled his nose, thinking, and after a moment Fallon shook his head in dismay. "You must learn your lessons better," he said, rumpling the boy's dark hair. "We will not always stay in this village and we must know how to take care of ourselves. Look at this." He pointed to a narrow trail in the grass. "Whether worn by animals or man, all trails lead to water. Remember that."

"Can we go to the river, then?" Noshi said, looking up. "I'm thirsty, too."

"Nay." Fallon shook his head sternly. "We will find water another way. Gilda, you find a vine, and Noshi, find a bush with stems as thick as my finger."

The children grinned at each other, eager to test themselves, and tossed their baskets on the ground as they ran to a nearby stand of trees. Fallon sighed and looked at the spilled berries, then scooped up the baskets and followed them.

"I found a bush!" Noshi cried, dancing around a weed that grew taller than his head. "Now what do I do with it?"

"Pull it out of the ground and look at the root," Fallon instructed.

Noshi wrapped both hands around the slender trunk and tugged mightily. The ground cracked and crumbled, then Noshi held the green weed high.

"The water is in the root," Fallon told him, pulling a sharpened stone from the pocket in his breeches. Kneeling, he sliced the root and handed a piece to Noshi.

Noshi tentatively put the root to his lips. "It's sweet," he remarked, popping the slice into his mouth.

"Aye," Fallon agreed. He stood and looked for Gilda who, as usual, had wandered farther and faster than Noshi. "Where are you, little girl? Have you found a vine?"

He heard only silence for a moment, then the hair on his arms lifted as a blood-chilling scream rent the air. Fallon barked an order for Noshi to remain still while he sprinted in the direction of the sound.

Gilda lay on a small pile of rocks at the base of a gentle hill. She clutched a vine in her hand, and Fallon guessed that she had lost her footing and tumbled down the slope while reaching for it. A bloody cut had opened above her left eyebrow, and one knee was scraped and bleeding. But her wide eyes were fastened upon a pale brown snake that buzzed upon a rock a few feet away.

"A copperhead," Fallon whispered, trying hard to remember

what Rowtag had taught him about such snakes. Though the bite was serious, it would not kill an adult. But Gilda was yet a child, a mere baby.

*Almighty God, have mercy! Do not take this little one from me!* The prayer flew from his heart, but he did not let his fear show on his face. "Do not move, sweetheart," Fallon called, carefully edging down the incline toward her. "He is more frightened of you than you are of him. Close your eyes, little one, and let him go home to his children."

Gilda trembled, and Fallon held his breath until she obeyed and closed her eyes. A moment later the snake turned and zig-zagged away.

Fallon knelt and caught her in his arms as she broke into honest wailing. "I was so scared!" she cried, sobbing brokenly against his chest. "I want to go home! I want Mama and Papa! I want to see Rowtag and my own house!"

"You have me now, and Noshi," Fallon murmured, lifting a prayer of thanksgiving in his heart. As he held Gilda tightly, a curious emotion rose in his chest. He breathed in the fresh scent of her hair and tried to unravel the tangled feelings her helpless dependence inspired. It was like the beginning of a new identity, as though, in that instant, he had become her father, brother, and protector.

He pulled away and lifted her chin so that she looked into his eyes. "We are your family now, Gilda. God has given us to each other. I promise I will take care of you no matter what happens."

She hiccupped a sob. "You promise?"

"I do." He drew her into his arms again and felt his heart warm as she nestled into his youthful strength.

"I love you, Fallon," she said, her voice brimming with trust.

He ran his hand over her glossy dark hair and pressed his lips to her ear. "I love you, too, Gilda."

▼▲▼▲▼ Ten miles north of Ritanoe, a hunting party of Powhatan Indians pursued a wounded deer. They had come across a trail of blood and followed the wandering track until they found the beast, a majestic buck. An arrow protruded from the animal's side; whoever had fired the missile had missed the heart and lodged the arrowhead in the buck's shoulder bone.

Opechancanough, chief of the hunting party, motioned for his braves to circle the animal. At his signal the warriors swept in for the kill, and the weary buck had neither the strength nor the opportunity to flee. Within a moment he lay dead on the forest floor.

As the Powhatan warriors whooped in celebration, Opechancanough idly walked forward and pulled the offending arrow from the carcass. The copper arrowhead gleamed in the late afternoon sun, and his eyes narrowed in suspicion. No Indian tribe had learned the secrets of shaping copper in this way. Could it be that clothed people still walked the land? If his brother, Powhatan, had failed to rid the land of the clothed people, the war club must be wielded again. The clothed people had no place in the land and they would have to die.

▼▲▼▲▼ The first maize crop was ready for harvesting when a group of Powhatan traders arrived at Ritanoe. Gepanocon's scouts had sent word of their coming, and before their arrival the chief sent the four Englishmen away from the camp to hide in a series of sacred caves in the woods. He did not consider it a sacrilege to hide men in the sacred caves, for the Englishmen were his special treasure, the key to making weapons and utensils and good magic. The presence of the English, Gepanocon warned his people, must be kept secret.

Upon entering the village the traders announced that Powhatan himself, the great chief of the united Powhatan tribes, had sent them to trade furs for copper. The name "Powhatan" sent Fallon's blood sliding through his veins like cold needles, and he kept Noshi and Gilda by his side and hid in his hut as the traders bargained. He certainly did not want his hated enemy to know that any had escaped from the slaughter at Ocanahonan. How would Gepanocon explain the children's fair eyes or his own pale skin and red hair if they were noticed by the Powhatan?

Through a crack in the grass covering of the hut, Fallon spied on the traders. "You want copper pots?" Gepanocon was saying, folding his arms as he sat in the center of the camp. "We have only those we gained through trade with the clothed men. Why do you think we have others?"

One of the visitors pulled a long arrow from the quiver on his painted back. The copper arrowhead gleamed in the sun.

"The clothed men did not use copper for arrowheads," the most fiercely painted warrior said, turning the arrow so the copper glimmered in the bright light of afternoon. "How, then, did this come to be made?"

Gepanocon grinned toothlessly. "I may know this answer later, in one or two moons. But I cannot tell you now."

"If you know of the clothed men," the painted warrior continued, purposefully tapping the arrow against his broad palm, "you should speak. Our chief, Powhatan, hates the clothed men. He wants them to leave this land."

Gepanocon's smile did not fade. "If I have news, I will tell you later," he said, lifting his hands toward the elders who surrounded him. The elders nodded in agreement as if the issue were settled.

The visiting delegation parted as an aged member of their party stepped forward. The elder's face seemed to be made of points and edges: a sharp nose and chin, high cheekbones planing down from pronounced ridges of bone. A stark white scar shone vividly upon his cheek. Though the warrior's long hair was streaked with gray, power flashed from his eyes and rang in his voice as he spoke: "I, Opechancanough, am brother to the mighty Powhatan. And I have a gift for you, Gepanocon of Ritanoe."

Gepanocon's eyes gleamed with interest as Opechancanough gestured to a warrior at his side. The man stepped forward and deposited a buckskin bundle at Opechancanough's feet. With one smooth gesture, Opechancanough unwrapped the bundle, bringing forth a cloak lined with the luxurious fur of many beavers. An audible murmur of approval and delight rose from the crowd of onlookers, and he tossed it over his shoulder and turned to display it, dark and gleaming, against the bronze cast of his skin.

Inside the hut, Fallon gritted his teeth, pained at Opechancanough's cleverness. Such a gift demanded an equally extravagant present in return, and what did Gepanocon have to rival such a magnificent cloak? To refuse the gift would be an insult to the brother of the Powhatan chief, and to offer a gift of less value would demean the werowance of the tribe at Ritanoe.

Opechancanough held the cloak toward the werowance of Ritanoe, and Gepanocon paused only a moment before accepting it. He stepped forward, flung the cloak around his shoulders, then revolved slowly so his people could admire their chief. When he had finished, he bowed his head carefully and stepped inside his hut. The anxious crowd murmured while Fallon waited to see what the chief would do.

Finally Gepanocon returned, carrying in two hands a gleaming copper pot big enough to cover a man's head. Fallon recognized it—one of the men from Ocanahonan had fashioned it from fine copper only a week ago—and presented it to the werowance. It was Gepanocon's most prized possession.

Opechancanough received the pot with a solemn bow, then handed it to a lesser warrior as the party of traders withdrew from the village. Fallon turned away from the sight and sank in a despairing heap on the floor. Gepanocon had meant to deceive, but he'd been caught in a trap. If Opechancanough had come to trade, this mission had failed, but if he had come to learn whether any of the English still lived, he had of certain accomplished his goal.

The Powhatan warriors ran through the forest like deer, hurrying northward toward the great chief's village of Weromacomico. When they arrived, five days after their visit to Ritanoe, Opechancanough told his brother and the elders that the attack upon the clothed men had failed. The English still walked the land and worked the iron. Worse yet, the Englishmen at Ritanoe made copper arrowheads and pots for Gepanocon, who would surely rise up against the Powhatan when the time was right.

"No!" Powhatan thundered, rising from his blanket on the floor of his hut. "We will destroy Ritanoe and all in it, including the clothed Englishmen!"

"We should not kill the English," Opechancanough said, taking a seat in the circle of elders around the chief. He looked around to make certain that every elder listened, then he spoke with calculated concern. "It is said that Wowinchopunk has seen more boats with big guns in the land of the Paspahegh. The clothed people continue to come; we cannot fight them all. But if you take these clothed men at Ritanoe and hold them in your village, the others will listen to you."

"We will fight them one city at a time," Powhatan said, his face flushing as his hand closed around his war club. The dark line of roached hair that ran from his forehead to the base of his neck vibrated softly in his anger. "First Ritanoe, then Paspahegh." He gestured to one of his braves. "Run from village to village and let the drums call for a war party. Any man who wishes to strike the war post with me shall be rewarded, and Ritanoe will be no more!"

Pressing his lips together to smother a smile, Opechancanough said nothing as the runner hurried to gather men for Powhatan's war party. He would let his brother strike uselessly at the Indian villages. The Englishmen would continue to come in the winged ships.

And he would wait for his vengeance. The hate within him was a living thing, demanding to feed, but he had learned how to discipline his appetite. Unlike his brothers, Opechancanough had learned that patience was an invaluable element of strategy.

▼▲▼▲▼ "What are you doing, Fallon?"

They were on the bank of the river, and Fallon gave Gilda a brief smile before returning his attention to his knife. "I'm marking this tree with an *F* for Fallon," he said, running his sharpened blade through the wounded bark of an oak. "And under it, I'll mark a *G* for Gilda. And then an *N* for Noshi."

"Why?" Gilda asked, thrusting her hands behind her back.

Fallon shrugged. "So people will know we've been here. So if anyone should happen to come here from upriver—"

"Mama and Papa?" Her blue eyes lit with hope, and Fallon felt a stab of guilt pierce his heart. It wasn't fair to encourage her to yearn for what could never be, but how were they to go on without dreams? In his deepest heart, Fallon prayed that Rowtag had survived, that he was recovering his strength somewhere and soon would come downriver to find them.

"I don't know who might come," he said, sheathing his knife in his belt. He knelt beside Gilda and took her hand. "I don't really know why I'm doing this. But if an Englishman sees our marks, he'll recognize the alphabet and know that we were here. They'll look for us, Gilda, and take us back where we belong."

She stared at him, uncomprehending, and Fallon sighed. Where *did* they belong? They weren't English—in fact Fallon had never even seen an English ship—nor were they savages like the Indians of Ritanoe. But of all the towns and cities in the world, surely there was another like Ocanahonan, where men cared for each other and worshiped God.

"Why don't you help me?" Fallon said, searching for a stone. He found one and put it in Gilda's hand. "We'll carve a cross on this oak tree, and anyone who sees it will know that we believe in the Christ and that we're not heathen savages."

"What's a savage?" Gilda said, energetically marking the tree.

Fallon shook his head and began another carving.

▼▲▼▲▼ To the villagers of Ritanoe, the heat of early summer signaled the beginning of the harvest. The first sowing of maize had yielded a bountiful crop. The corn was gathered and carried in parfleches to the village, where it was roasted over a slow-burning fire, then stored in clay pots that were buried in the earth.

Noshi and Gilda joined in the harvest, too, gathering herbs and berries. When their small baskets were full, Fallon sent them ahead to the village while he walked behind on the trail. With every day that passed he became more and more convinced that they could not stay in this place. The difference between civilized Ocanahonan and primitive, heathen Ritanoe was simply too great. His parents had charged him with the care of the children, and as a godparent of sorts he was to watch over their souls. But how could he do so when Noshi yearned to join in the heathen dances and Gilda was fascinated by the ritual chants and charms of the conjurors?

He did not dare hope that the English would come again. Throughout his entire life he had heard stories of the great man called Walter Raleigh who had sent John White to establish a colony on the island of Roanoke. John White had left for England, promising to return with supplies and additional colonists, and the remaining settlers had migrated to a safer location upon the river Chowan. A lookout had been posted on Croatoan Island, but the months of waiting stretched into two decades with nary a sign of John White or an English return. As the years passed, the English led their Indian neighbors to believe in the one true

God, and eventually the City of Raleigh became the village of
Ocanahonan.

Could the English come again? Fallon let Gilda and Noshi
scamper even further ahead while he sat in the shade of an oak
to ponder the question. Maybe, if he took the children and traveled to the sea, he could find an answer. He had heard stories of
the Spaniards, another people from across the great ocean, and
though the people of Ocanahonan seemed to hold the Spanish in
fear and contempt, perhaps their society would be better for the
children than an Indian village—

A sudden flurry of feathers distracted Fallon's thinking. A
flock of crows that had roosted in the trees above him suddenly
took flight, and Fallon turned his head and concentrated, listening intently. Someone moved in the woods. A great many some-
ones, judging by the disturbance of the birds.

Stealthily he shifted to his hands and knees, then crept behind
a fallen log and peered into the woods. His eyes widened in
stunned alarm. Under the mushrooming canopy of trees a group
of warriors advanced. They carried brightly decorated war axes
and shields. Even from his hiding place, Fallon recognized the
brilliant red designs of Powhatan warriors.

He lunged to his feet and sprinted toward the village.


▼▲▼▲▼ Breathless, he raced into Gepanocon's hut with
the news. The werowance listened with the smiling, indulgent
attention adults give children, then gestured abruptly and told
his elders to send warriors to hide the four Englishmen.

"What of the others?" Fallon demanded, ignoring the protocol
that directed he be silent until the chief addressed him. "You
must leave your warriors here to protect the women and children."

"My men will return when the English are safe," Gepanocon
answered, rising to his feet. Moving with unusual quickness, he
grabbed his war ax and pushed past Fallon.

Fallon watched in disbelief as the chief and his warriors hustled the four Englishmen from their hut and hurried them through a secret door in the palisade walls.

"That's right," Fallon remarked critically as the chief and his men fled. "Make a palisade too strong for the enemy to come in—or for you to get out. Run, Chief, and may your greed and cowardice preserve you."

Gepanocon doubtless intended to hide the men again in the sacred caves, and Fallon knew the warriors did not have time to escort the Englishmen and return. The enemy warriors were just outside the front gate; they would not wait for Gepanocon before they attacked.

Fallon left the chief's hut and ran to find Gilda and Noshi.


▼▲▼▲▼ Serving as war chief for this battle, Opechancanough did not hesitate to attack Ritanoe. Usually he and his braves hid in the woods for hours to judge the strengths and weaknesses of an enemy camp, but Gepanocon had revealed all by opening his village to the traders. Opechancanough would not waste time at Ritanoe, for he wanted most of all to capture the Englishmen, and Gepanocon would surely try to hide them.

The old men and women of the village made a futile effort to block the opening of the palisade as the enemy streamed from the forest, but the Powhatan warriors easily trampled the piles of brush and branches. Inside the village, women and children screamed and ran from the huts the Powhatan set ablaze.

Walking behind his warriors, Opechancanough searched for the clothed men and felt his anger rise as he stalked from hut to hut only to find frightened women and children. In one hut he found raw copper and tools to work it, but the grass mats spread upon the floor were empty. This maddening inability to find his quarry drove him past the point of endurance and Opechancanough ordered that all in the village should be killed.

His warriors obediently pulled the women and children forward to meet the knife, but Opechancanough suddenly held up a hand. Standing among the knot of survivors was an unusual boy, with red hair and fair skin. He wore leather breeches and a full shirt, and Opechancanough felt his heart beat faster as he walked over for a closer look. Could this stripling be one of the survivors of Ocanahonan? Surely one so young could not be the source of Gepanocon's copper weapons.

The boy stood with his hands on the heads of two dark-haired children, and, as if by command, all three kept their heads lowered before him. "Look at me!" Opechancanough commanded, and only the older boy's head rose. He glared defiantly at the war chief.

Opechancanough felt the corner of his mouth twitch in a half smile. The boy's skin was pale and pink from the sun, his nose sprinkled with the brown spots common to the skin of the clothed people. His face was clear and his body tall like a fast-growing weed, but the troubled blue eyes were those of a man who has seen thirty summers of sorrow.

Opechancanough put his hands under the chins of the two children and jerked their heads up. The little boy's eyes were green and dark with fear, the little girl's as blue as the sky at noonday. All three children were dressed in the linen clothes of the English, and each child's forearms were tattooed with tribal markings and a small sign that made Opechancanough's stomach tighten into a knot. The sign of the cross.

Opechancanough lifted his head to consider their fate. These were not children of Ritanoe. The two boys were marked with the sign of the Mangoak tribe; the girl, strangely enough, wore the symbol of the Powhatan. And though all three bore the sign of the cross, the younger ones could not possibly understand what it meant.

Opechancanough stepped away from the children and commanded one of his warriors to bind the youngsters together. They would be captives for the chief of the Powhatan.

The two young ones cried as the warrior bound their hands. Though the older boy said nothing, Opechancanough could feel those blue eyes burning through him no matter where he turned.

With fury lurking beneath his smile, Opechancanough
ordered his men to fire the village.


▼▲▼▲ Walking in the center of the long line of warriors, Opechancanough watched the children carefully. The older
boy must have spoken to the younger ones, for the children
remained silent on the journey back to Weromacomico, neither
crying nor protesting their capture. Occasionally the little ones
looked to the older boy for comfort, but the red-haired boy
seemed to speak to them through his eyes. They followed their
captors in blind faith as if they trusted their God to take care of
them, and Opechancanough wondered if the young ones understood more than he had thought possible.

The children had earned his respect with their silence and fortitude, and he wondered what thoughts ran through their minds.
Did they think they would be killed? If, as he suspected, they
had lived at Ocanahonan, did they hold bitterness in their young
hearts toward the Powhatan? If he untied the leather strips that
held their hands, would he awaken in the night to find the older
boy holding a knife to his heart?

Opechancanough understood bitterness. As his feet methodi-
cally fell into the steps of the warrior ahead of him, he slowly
submerged himself into memory. On a summer's day years ago,
as an unnamed youth, he had been forced to hide his fear and
swallow the desperation of loneliness. At sixteen, not much older
than the boy who traveled with him now, he had seen two
winged ships enter the great bay called Chesapeake. Unafraid
and ignorant of such ships, he, his father the chief, and several
warriors paddled out in their canoes to board the largest vessel.
The Spanish admiral welcomed them and, much taken with the
youth, asked permission to take him across the great ocean so
that the king of Spain might see him. In return, the admiral promised Opechancanough's father much wealth and many garments.

The boy hid his fear as best he could when the ships sailed
eastward, and by a tremendous effort he stopped the trembling

of his knees when he was presented to Spain's King Philip II as an Indian prince. The clothed men's king, with pale skin, long curling hair, and a drooping moustache, had been delighted with the boy in the same way the young Indian had been delighted when the children of his village presented him with a trained squirrel.

The young prince was powerless in the land of the clothed men. New sights, sounds, and smells assaulted him. Men and women in this strange land adorned themselves with an excess of clothing and perfume. Jewels dripped from their necks, their heads, their hands, and the people wore more garments in one day than any Indian wore in a year. But they carried the long sticks of thunder and unending swords that gleamed with silver sharper than a snake's fangs. The youth did not dare displease his hosts.

He wanted to go home, but he was taken to Seville for instruction in both the Spanish language and religion. Under the stern Dominican friars he learned to speak the lilting tongue of the Spanish men. After several years, his teachers were not only reporting that the Indian possessed a powerful intellect, but that he was also "wily and crafty."

Indeed, he had absorbed his lessons and stored them away for future use. A chameleon among the clothed people, he aped their tongue and their manners while pondering how he could escape to his father's kingdom across the great ocean. From the Dominican fathers, and later from the Jesuits, he learned an important lesson: What could not be won by force might be achieved by diplomacy. Patience and long-range planning, he came to realize, were tools of great significance.

And so, while in Spain, the young native made a profession of faith and, to all observers, became a devoted Christian. It was the only way to please the priests who labored over his mind and soul, and, he reasoned, it was the most likely way to win his release and effect his return back to the land the clothed men called America.

When Pedro Menéndez de Avilés crossed to Mexico in 1563,

the young prince was allowed to go with him. King Philip had decreed that the Indian be allowed to return to his people, but when Menéndez tried to fulfill the king's order, the archbishop of Mexico, an insecure and ambitious man, who feared that the Indian might relapse into his former devil worship, refused to give his permission. Frustrated, Menéndez compromised and left the prince with the Dominicans of New Spain, where he stayed for three years.

The chameleon adapted again and imitated this new group of monks as easily as he had the Spanish fathers in Seville. In time he became the protégé of Governor Don Luis de Velasco, who took a fatherly interest in the young Indian and gave the prince his own name: Don Luis.

Upon hearing that his wishes and vow had been thwarted, King Philip appointed Menéndez conqueror of Florida in 1565 and ordered the authorities of New Spain to remand Don Luis to Menéndez. The archbishop and governor reluctantly complied, and Don Luis was sent off with fatherly embraces from the governor and dire warnings from the archbishop. From New Spain, Don Luis traveled to San Mateo in Florida, then two friars were commanded to escort the Indian to his own territory.

Captain Pedro de Coronas and thirty Spanish soldiers joined the two friars and sailed from Santa Elena for Don Luis's homeland of the Chesapeake, but the ship missed the entrance to the bay and anchored far southward. A sudden storm forced the Portuguese pilot to consult the two friars as to their next course of action.

Like traitors, the two priests abandoned their task and told the pilot to sail for Spain. From where he stood in the bowels of the ship, Don Luis instinctively knew that he had been betrayed. The afternoon sun, which should have been in his face, lay at his back. The friars had kept him from his home once again, and rage bubbled in his soul like a living thing.

But the patience he had learned from the Spanish monks came to his aid yet another time, and he swallowed his grief and disguised his anger as the ship anchored at Cádiz. King Philip directed that Don Luis be placed with the Jesuits to help them prepare for their missionary work among the American savages, and so the young Indian learned how to read, write, and speak not only Spanish, but Latin. During this time he also received the holy sacraments of the altar and confirmation in the Catholic faith.

Once he realized how highly the Spanish regarded their missionary work, he knew he had found a way home. Cloaking his features in piety and concern, he approached his Jesuit mentors in the autumn of 1567 with a dream to convert his parents, relatives, and countrymen to the faith of Jesus Christ.

"I wish to baptize and make them Christians as I am," he said, piously folding his hands in an attitude of prayer. "I have heard that a party of friars is about to depart for Florida and would ask that priests be sent to my country to assist me in the work of conversion." Menéndez was so delighted and relieved by the missionary scheme that he offered to supply a ship to carry a party to the Chesapeake.

Menéndez and Don Luis reached Havana in November 1568 and met with Father Juan Baptista de Segura. Over the objections of his brothers, Father Segura looked into the dead black of Don Luis's eyes and offered to join the expedition as a guide and interpreter. After a delay of some months, the ship left Santa Elena and arrived in Don Luis's homeland on the tenth day of September 1570, nine years after he had been carried away.

Upon landing, Don Luis's joy was immediately tempered. He remembered the region as fruitful and beautiful, but the land he now looked upon bore the marks of famine and disease. The natives they encountered on their inland trek seemed primitive, dirty, and sickly to Don Luis's eyes. It was as if the entire realm had been cursed since his departure.

When at last he returned home to his own tribe, the simple Indians behaved as if he had come back from the dead. His father had died in his absence, and his younger brother, Wahunsonacock, now ruled the tribe of the Powhatan as werowance—and was now known throughout the tribes as chief werowance, Powhatan.

Don Luis stood in silence as Powhatan knelt at his feet and offered to surrender authority to him. He declined the offer, mindful of the watchful eyes of the Spanish friars. He quickly stated that he had not returned to his father's people out of a desire for earthly things, but to teach them the way to heaven that lay in the instruction in the religion of Christ the Lord.

His kinsmen listened with little enthusiasm and much suspicion, though the faces of the Spanish lit with delight. For a week Don Luis played the part of patient and benevolent missionary while he watched and waited for the right opportunity to avenge his blighted land and weakened people.

One night, in a deliberate, defiant choice, Don Luis stood in the glow of village campfire and chose three wives from the women of the tribe. He had lived among the celibate friars for too long and believed his unnatural abstinence to be the reason the land had ceased to be fertile. He was twenty-five years old and already should have fathered many children. He took his wives to a village on the Pamunkey River, out of sight from the religious monks who had established themselves in a small mission not far away.

After learning of his polygamy, his missionary companions were too shocked to reprimand him immediately. But days later, when Father Segura called him before the entire religious company and sanctimoniously rebuked him, Don Luis felt the stirring of angry pride from deep within.

"I renounce you," he cried, casting his Spanish mantle aside. "I am no longer Don Luis, but Opechancanough of the Powhatan, or He-Whose-Soul-Is-White. Do not send for me again, brothers, for I will never go willingly with you."

He left the missionary compound and returned to his home on the Pamunkey, determined to abandon both the lifestyle and god of the Spanish. Four months later, Fathers Quirós and Segura visited the Indian village and tried to persuade their rebellious convert to return to the mission. Opechancanough

berated them loudly, announced that he had sold his soul to the
devil, and laughed as the holy fathers trembled before him. They
fled the settlement in horror and Opechancanough followed
with a group of Powhatan warriors, determined to repay his past
suffering with bloodshed.

Under a canopy of silent oaks on the trail, Opechancanough
killed the missionary monks, burned their bodies, and scattered
their clothing. Moving on to the mission, he identified himself as
Don Luis and called a greeting. After being admitted through the
gates, he and his warriors massacred the remainder of the
Spaniards. In the quick skirmish fueled by murderous anger,
Opechancanough received a cut across his left cheek, the only
wound ever to mar his strong body. The cut eventually healed,
leaving a smooth white scar. But the hate in Opechancanough's
heart did not heal.

That bloody day was February 4, 1571, and since that time
Opechancanough chose to hate all things Spanish and all things
having to do with Christ and the clothed men's God. With the
spirits of hatred and bitterness to guide him, Opechancanough
dealt with his younger brother Powhatan as one deals with a
simple and uncomprehending child. It was under Opechancanough's guidance that Powhatan put together an empire that
grew from six original tribes to more than thirty-two. Their system of autocratic control was more complex than any other of
the Algonquin Indians, and there was no doubt that the tribes of
the Powhatan had become the mightiest in the land.

Frightened by news and ideas from across the great ocean,
Powhatan had no concept of the power of the enemy, so through
the years Opechancanough invented prophecies and dreams that
appealed to Powhatan and effectively guided the great chief's
dealings with the clothed men.

But the English were not Spaniards, Opechancanough mused,
watching the red-haired boy struggle up a hilly path with the
two children at his side. In his dealings with the English at
Ocanahonan, Opechancanough had felt strangely ill at ease.
These men did not speak Spanish, so he was unable to spy on

them, nor did they pray at the feet of statues and require priests to beg heaven for aid.

But in helping the Algonquin, the English talked of God and his son, the Christ. And they, too, carried long guns of thunder and sharp swords.

Opechancanough lifted his chin slightly. He would not underestimate the English, nor would he behave like other unsophisticated savages. In that lay his advantage.

Weromacomico, the village of the chief of the Powhatan, lay nestled against the edge of a mighty eastward-flowing river. The village was ringed with the tallest timber palisade Fallon had ever seen. His eyebrows raised; such a mighty wall surely meant that the chief inside had mighty enemies.

No gauntlet of torture waited outside the village, for the chief expected no captives from this war party. But double lines of jubilant women and children lined the path inside the village, and their shouts of victory nearly deafened Fallon's ears as he was pushed forward between the lines. Curious hands reached out to touch his clothing and hair as he stumbled along, and he endured the probing without complaint until a gnarled warrior knelt and reached out for the gold ring hanging from Gilda's neck.

Anger rose in Fallon's chest like bile and he swung an elbow into the old man's face. The brave toppled and fell over in the dust, and Fallon was certain he had sealed his doom with that reckless move. But the other Indians laughed at the man's discomfiture and the warriors behind Fallon urged him forward.

The three children of Ocanahonan were taken to the center of the camp and tied with leather straps to a tall pole. Inquisitive villagers quickly surrounded them, jabbering in a babble of confusion as they pointed at the captives with wide eyes and superior smiles. Fallon was able to pick out certain phrases through the din:

"The girl has sky eyes."

"The boys are scratched with the mark of the Mangoak tribe, long ago defeated by the Powhatan."

"The one with red hair has hot blood."

For the first time that day, Gilda began to whimper, and Fallon spoke to her in English: "Fear not, Gilda, for God is surely with us. Do not cry, for they will see tears as a sign of weakness."

For an answer, she rested her head under his arm.

▼▲▼▲▼ "Did you find the men who make copper arrows?"

Powhatan wasted no time in seeking his answers, and Opechancanough eased himself onto a grass mat on the floor and arranged his blanket about his shoulders before speaking. "No. The clothed men who beat the copper were gone. Gepanocon has hidden them."

"And the village?"

"The women and children are slaughtered. The village elders are dead. Ritanoe will not trouble the Powhatan for vengeance, for her power is gone."

Powhatan grunted in satisfaction, then folded his arms and looked at his brother. "You have brought three children."

"Yes, my brother. They . . . interested me. The older boy is of the English. He speaks the English tongue and the Algonquin; he commands the two young ones. Both he and the younger boy are marked with the sign of the Mangoak tribe."

"The Mangoak are dead."

"Yes." Opechancanough nodded, mindful of the other elders' listening ears. "The mighty Powhatan have devoured the Mangoak. But it is said that some of the Mangoak escaped to live with the clothed men at Ocanahonan. They wore the clothes of the English and worshiped the Christ."

Powhatan said nothing, but stared straight ahead.

Opechancanough went on. "The girl is Indian, but she has the blue eyes of the English. She is marked, too."

"What tribe?"

"The Powhatan."

Powhatan stiffened, then turned slowly to stare at his brother.

"How can this be?" he asked, unfolding his arms. "No Powhatan lived at Ocanahonan."

"No," Opechancanough answered, feeling his way carefully. He suspected that he knew the girl's origin, but his answer might insult the chief.

He picked up a stick and began to write in the dirt, an act that never failed to inspire awe in the others. "Do you remember, mighty brother, five winters past, when your son Kitchi hunted in the woods near Ocanahonan? The deer were plenteous that year."

Powhatan nodded, and Opechancanough went on writing and speaking. "A man of Ocanahonan had promised me a life in exchange for one of our captives. I took a young girl from that place. That night I gave her to Kitchi."

Powhatan tilted his head slightly, listening.

Opechancanough wrote in the sand silently, then put down the stick as if he had just written a message of great significance. "Later that night, the girl escaped, but not before we tortured the Englishman who had come to rescue her. It is my belief that the English girl gave birth to the child who waits outside, for no other Powhatan has had any dealings with the women of that place."

Powhatan leaned forward and peered out the doorway of his hut as if he would judge the resemblance of the child to his son, but the press of people prevented him from looking outward. He settled back and crossed his arms again.

"Her mark is genuine," Opechancanough went on, guessing his brother's unspoken thoughts. "For what Indian would betray his clan by marking a child with another clan's sign?"

Powhatan picked up his pipe and inhaled deeply for several minutes, then passed the pipe to his brother. "Let the boy with copper hair be killed," he pronounced, his voice rumbling through the stillness of the hut, "for he is old enough to desire vengeance. Let the Mangoak boy be sold into slavery to the Tripanik tribe."

"And the girl?" Opechancanough questioned gently.

Powhatan's dark eyes seemed to gentle. "Let her be given to my daughter, Matoaka. Time will tell if Kitchi will claim her as his daughter. If he does not, she shall grow up as a sister to my own Pocahontas."

▼▲▼▲▼ Fallon knew that their lives were under discussion in the hut into which the war chief had disappeared, but whether the discussion would take minutes, hours, or days, he could not guess. He knew nothing of the Powhatan but their reputation for cruelty, and if they did by some miracle choose to show mercy, he was not certain he wanted to live within the tribe who had killed his family and destroyed a civilization far greater than they could possibly realize.

The burning sun of hot June set the fair skin on his nose to sizzling, and he heard hot, dry coughs from both of the younger children. So it had come to this! He had been entrusted with their lives and had done the best he could, only to lose them to the murderous enemy who had killed their parents. They had fled, suffered, hungered, and thirsted only to be mown down by a rain of arrows. Or mayhap they were to be tortured before they died. . . .

Fallon herded his fearful thoughts together and offered them in a wordless prayer as the dignified war chief he knew as Opechancanough stooped through the low doorway of the chief's hut and came to stand before the three children. As Fallon watched the man approach, peace and confidence settled over him. He belonged to God. Nothing would ever change that. No longer afraid, Fallon raised his eyes to meet his adversary's. What he saw there startled him: The chief's dark eyes stirred with intelligence, cunning, and undisguised hatred.

Fallon involuntarily stiffened when the chief pulled a knife from his belt, but Opechancanough only cut Noshi free from the pole. He gestured to a warrior who waited a respectful distance away, then handed the warrior the lengths of leather strips that bound Noshi's wrists. As the warrior pulled Noshi through the crowd, the war chief folded his arms and spoke to Fallon in the Algonquin tongue. "You will die," he said simply, smiling in satisfaction as he stared at Fallon. "The younger boy will be sold to the Tripaniks. They are old enemies of the Mangoaks, so it is fitting, is it not?"

Fallon lifted his shoulder in an indifferent shrug even as his hands itched to cover his ears and block out the sound of Noshi's frantic cries. His mind raced for a solution to their dilemma, but there were no answers, no way out. "And the girl?" he asked, trying desperately to keep any trace of fear from his voice.

Opechancanough's smile turned nasty as his dagger slipped under the leather strap that held Gilda to the pole. "According to her mark, she is Powhatan," he said. "She will remain here." He turned and motioned toward a woman who waited near a hut, then murmured something in her ear when she approached. Nodding in respect, the woman smiled at Gilda and tugged on the leather leash that bound her hands. Gilda hesitated a moment and glanced back at Fallon with wide, frightened eyes.

"You swear by your gods you will not harm her?" Fallon said, surrendering to the overwhelming flood of emotion that forced him to beg for mercy. He stared after her small form as if he could permanently imprint her image on his mind.

The war chief smiled again, and the white scar on his cheek gleamed in the afternoon sun. "Why would I harm one of my own people?"

Fallon ignored the disquieting thought that Gilda might in any way be related to the monster before him. He forced a smile to his face. "Go in peace," he called to Gilda, straining uselessly against the bonds that held him tight. "And God will go with you."

The Indian woman put her hands on Gilda's shoulders and led her firmly away even as the girl began to cry and reach back for Fallon.

"Go," Fallon cried, feeling as if whole sections of his body were being torn away. "And forgive me, Gilda!"

He hung his head, ashamed to lift his eyes. He had been given a charge and he had failed miserably.

Once Gilda and Noshi were out of sight, Opechancanough's mood suddenly changed. He leaned forward, his rank breath blowing across Fallon's face. "Tell me," he demanded harshly, his eyes narrowing to twin slits of hate. "You are from Ocanahonan?"

Fallon hesitated and the war chief grinned, understanding. "You are. Then know this, boy, before you die." He pulled a knife from its leather sheath on his thigh and Fallon felt the sharpened blade bite into the tender flesh of his neck. "The girl, whom your people have marked with the cross of God, will remain with us. She will be taught to love the people who destroyed your city. She will come to revere Powhatan, she will worship his gods and not Jesus the Christ, and when her time comes, she will marry one of Powhatan's warriors. And if the English come to avenge the deaths of those at Ocanahonan, that girl will die with the warriors of the Powhatan."

Each word was like another log upon the fire of guilt in Fallon's heart, and he cringed before the verbal lashing. Opechancanough finished his prophecy with a swift, light swipe of his knife across Fallon's throat, and Fallon's knees buckled under him. Unable to withstand the guilt and fear any longer, he slumped to the ground, supported only by the leather thongs that held his arms to the pole behind him.

Opechancanough smiled in victory. "Take this coward away," he called to a warrior standing outside the chief's hut. "Take him outside the village and properly cut his throat. He does not deserve to die like an Indian, and we will let the animals have his bones."

▼▲▼▲▼ The warrior's spear pricked through the fabric of Fallon's shirt with every step, and Fallon heard his escort laugh as a sticky trickle of blood began to seep down his back. They were walking downhill to a clearing, and Fallon knew once they reached it he would either be speared in the back and left as carrion, or the warrior would turn him around and slit his throat as Opechancanough had suggested.

He walked with heavy, defeated steps. Had Rowtag and the others felt this same overwhelming loss as they waited in Ocanahonan for the rising sun and the renewal of the battle? Had their arms and legs ached from sheer hopeless frustration as the fateful encounter approached?

He didn't think so. Rowtag's faith had been solid and strong. He had told Fallon often that nothing came to them but through God's hand. He was as fierce a warrior as he was devoted a father, and Fallon imagined that he met death with the same enthusiasm and confidence in God he had demonstrated in life. Why, then, did his son walk to death in hopelessness?

He paused for a moment, ostensibly to catch his breath, as his mind raced. *Father God, there has to be a way out. Show me what to do.*

"The important things in battle are always simple," Rowtag's voice came back to him as clearly as though he were whispering into his ear. *"But the simple things are always hard."* Fallon knew the important thing was escape, but how to accomplish it?

Opechancanough had dispatched only one warrior to handle the execution of a scrawny thirteen-year-old boy. Perhaps therein lay the advantage. Rowtag had often said that victory could be found in knowing one's enemy, and when the sharp spear of the executioner pricked the broken skin on his back again, Fallon whirled to study the face of the man who escorted him to death.

The brave was young, probably not more than twenty-and-one. It was possible he looked upon this as a chance to procure Opechancanough's favor. Surely he did not expect trouble from a pale English boy, particularly one who walked with heavy steps while tears glistened upon his cheeks.

In the flutter of a moment, Fallon made his decision and broke into a run. It took a long second for the warrior to realize that the quarry had fled, and in that instant Fallon veered toward a stand of trees, for it was a simple matter for a warrior to spear a target in front of him.

As he had hoped, the spear flew through the air and landed firmly in the ground ahead of him. Fallon dashed behind the safety of a tree. While the warrior reached forward for the spear, taking his eyes from Fallon, Fallon dashed for another tree and began to play the hiding game he had so often enjoyed with the children.

"If a foolish plan works," he muttered to himself as he heard his enemy curse in frustration, "it isn't foolish."

The trick, Fallon knew, was to exchange places. The prey had to become the hunter.

The warrior advanced expectantly toward the trees, his eyes searching the shadows, his spear upthrust behind him in one hand, his battle ax in the other. Fallon held his breath, mentally urging the warrior closer. One moment too soon and he would feel the bite of the spear through his ribs, one moment too late and the battle ax would crush his skull.

Closer. Fallon could hear the soft crunch of last winter's dead leaves beneath the warrior's feet.

Closer. He could see the delicate tattoo markings on the warrior's forearms.

Now!

The warrior passed the spot where Fallon hid behind the tree, and his eyes widened in surprise at the sight of his prey. The spear was useless at such a short distance, and before he could swing the club, Fallon delivered a sharp, powerful kick to the warrior's kneecap and brought his executioner down, his weapons flying from his hands.

Fallon fell on him and they scuffled silently in the dirt. Fallon used his body to keep the warrior from regaining his weapons, all the while cursing the bindings that held his hands tightly behind his back. Finally he had an opening, and a swift knee kick to the groin left the young Powhatan writhing in pain upon the ground. Fallon took that opportunity to stand and place his moccasined foot firmly upon the warrior's neck.

The man froze, afraid to move. His eyes rolled back, staring at Fallon above him, and an eerie, whining song began to rise from the warrior's mouth.

"Stop the death song," Fallon commanded in the Algonquin tongue, applying gentle pressure to the man's neck. "I will not kill you unless you think it more important to retain honor than your life."

The man fell silent and regarded Fallon soberly. "You can go back to the village and tell them I am dead," Fallon said, twisting his foot on the man's neck to reinforce his intention. "No one will doubt you, for your spear is already stained with my blood. Or, you can pursue me further, but next time I will not have mercy."

The warrior's eyes narrowed in speculation, but Fallon forced a smile. "Do not doubt that we will meet again, for I am the son of Rowtag, chief of the Mangoaks at Ocanahonan. I am also an Englishman, and I know things you have not dreamed of."

The threat was enough. The man relaxed and he stared at Fallon in resignation. "Good," Fallon said, easing the pressure slightly from his prisoner's neck. "You will lie here silently until I am safely away. If you stir or move again, I will return."

The warrior's face appeared to be set in stone, and he did not move when Fallon lifted his foot and moved away. For a moment Fallon considered asking the warrior to cut the tongs of leather which bound him, but he knew he'd be pressing the warrior too far.

It was one thing to defeat an enemy and quite another to humiliate him.

And so, running as if the hounds of hell were giving chase, Fallon bolted eastward through the woods. In that direction lay the ocean, the source of his help, if help was to be found at all.


▼▲▼▲▼ Gilda understood very little of what had happened to her. Fallon, whom she loved and trusted, had taken her from her home to a place where Indians danced and children ran naked and she and Noshi played hide-and-seek in the forest.

Then other Indians came and tied their hands and marched them far away to another village. Noshi and Fallon were with her for a moment, then they disappeared.

She mourned for days with tears and temper tantrums that the women could not stanch. Then a young girl about Fallon's age came into the hut. She did not try to soothe or scold, but merely sat on a grass mat and watched as Gilda cried and beat her fists upon the ground. When Gilda finally lay exhausted, the older girl smiled. "I am Matoaka," she said, her eyes shining in friendliness. "But my father calls me Pocahontas because I like to play."

Gilda lifted her head. "I want Noshi and Fallon," she cried stubbornly, her fists still clenched. "I want to go home."

"Your home is with me now," Pocahontas said, standing. From a basket at her side she held up a garment made of rabbit skin, beautifully embroidered on one side, thick with fur on the other. "And I have made this skirt for you. I shall call you Numees, because from this day you will be my sister."

"My name is Gilda," she protested, her temper rising again. But a colorful design of houses, corn, and rain danced across the beautiful skin of Pocahontas's arms. . . .

"Let me wrap this around you," Pocahontas said, moving closer. In a moment she had lifted the dirty linen dress from Gilda's shoulders, then she carefully wrapped the embroidered fur around Gilda's waist and fastened it with a pin made from the antlers of a deer.

Gilda stopped crying long enough to take a few practice steps in the lush garment.

For eight days Fallon wandered through the woods, avoiding trails, drinking water from the roots of plants, and eating eggs he stole from nests hidden in trees and tall grasses. He had managed to find a sharp rock to cut the bonds from his hands, but the cuts on his back became infected and fever began to ravage his body.

The fever consumed him, sapped his strength, and drove away his appetite. The hours of the day blurred into a constant forward motion, and the nights were interminable as sleep did not come. He tried to remember what his mother had taught him about medicine, but though he knew the inner bark of a young hemlock tree could be pulverized and applied to oozing sores, he could not reach to apply such a salve to his own back.

He wanted nothing more than to lie in the cool waters of the river, but the river was a highway of sorts, and he would not remain alone long if he paused there. Finally, as a last resort to combat his illness, he followed an animal trail to the river and shed his shirt, wincing as the fabric ripped scabs from his back. He crawled into the river and sat upon the spongy bottom, easing his weight back upon his hands as the rippling current massaged his fevered and infected skin.

He lay back and floated upon the water easily, succumbing to his exhaustion. When he feared he would lose consciousness and drown, he pulled himself to the opposite side and let the muddy banks soothe his wounded back as he closed his eyes in weariness and slept.

▼▲▼▲▼ On the twentieth day of June, John Smith left the fractious colony of Jamestown and ventured down to the water's edge for a time of private soliloquy. He liked the river. In fact, he would have given a week's rations to be away on an expedition rather than here at Jamestown debating the problem of their salty water supply and myriad possible solutions.

Since the official founding of Jamestown Fort, the colonists' first forays into the woods had gone smoothly. They'd met savages who proved to be friendly, one of whom even agreed to act as guide and interpreter. The party had visited another tribe where the "queen" was a large, mannish woman who wore only a deerskin and copper jewelry. She had not been at all friendly until Captain Newport offered gifts, then suddenly the riches of her village were opened to the English.

But not all the natives were so forthcoming. They had visited one village on the Pamunkey River whose chief, Opechanca-nough, was apparently linked to the Powhatan confederacy. The chief was an aged warrior whose sinewy muscles were at odds with the blank look on his face. During Smith's visit, the chief regarded the English gravely and seemed to take great pains to appear stately before his visitors. The men with Smith laughed privately at the chief's affectations and pronounced him a simpleminded fool, but Smith was not certain they were right. In an unguarded moment, he had caught a darkly speculative look in the chief's eye. There was more to the man, Smith was certain, than they had seen on the surface.

Not all the Indians welcomed or even tolerated the English. While Smith and Newport were out exploring, savages attacked the fledgling fort at Jamestown and were repelled only by the use of the ships' cannon. One boy was killed, and Edward Wingfield, the pompous goat who had been elected president of the colony, barely escaped death when an arrow passed through his beard without even grazing him. As the shallops carrying Smith, Newport, and their men had returned to the Jamestown peninsula, they'd found the fort alerted, the ships' guns mounted for immediate action, and the remaining men being drilled in the use of arms.

The Indian attack finally convinced the aristocrats of the governing board to follow the London Company's nomination and allow John Smith to take his seat on the council. The careful arbitration of Reverend Robert Hunt and the good sense of Captain Newport prevailed over the natural antipathy Wingfield felt toward Smith, and, as a result, John Smith now felt himself practically in control of the colony. Whatever positions Wingfield and Newport held, Smith's was still the voice to which the majority of men would listen in a crisis.

The responsibility would have exhausted most men, but Smith thrived on the challenge. And the danger. Even now, as he made his way to the river, he knew he should have taken his musket, or at least a companion. But so what if he was captured by savages? It would be rollicking fun to outsmart a truly great chief.

The river was quiet as he knelt at the bank and gazed toward the eastern horizon. The *Susan Constant* rocked slowly against her moorings, and in the distance the sea seemed to be an enormous sheet of dull-shining metal shading off into a blurred and fragile horizon. Christopher Newport was set to sail back to England within two days; in the ship's hold lay a cargo of a shining rock the men hoped contained gold. Most important, in the captain's cabin rested a letter written to the investors of the London Company, a letter detailing the colony's good progress and making a request for specific supplies.

A sudden splash alerted Smith and set the adrenaline pumping through his veins. Someone or something stirred below him at the water's edge!

He peered carefully, then frowned. Whatever kind of creature it was, it looked muddied and ragged. For a moment he wondered if the seamen's reports of mermaids were true, but as he scrambled down the bank for a closer look, Smith realized with a gasp that the creature before him was a boy—a red-haired, freckle-faced English boy.

Smith knelt down and pressed his hand to the unconscious boy's forehead. The child burned with fever, but did not appear to be otherwise wounded. His naked chest and arms were marked with tattoos similar to those he had seen on the Indians of the region, but the boy's hair was cut short, in the style of the English, and he wore breeches, not a breechcloth.

John Smith lifted the boy into his arms and gave a hoarse cry for help.

▼▲▼▲▼ Smith sat staring at the boy's white face. Upon his return to the settlement, he had brought his limp burden to his own tent and called for Captain Newport to come quickly. When the captain arrived, Smith sat back and let Newport examine his discovery, then smiled in pleasure when the captain uttered an indrawn gasp of surprise. "A boy! Surely he is not one of us!"

"He's not one of our boys. Just look at him, Christopher! He's tattooed like a savage, but his hair and skin are as fair as any Englishman's."

"Where do you suppose he came from?" Newport's inquisitive raisin-brown eyes widened, then he gasped. "Nay! Surely not from Roanoke! That's miles south of here. . . ." His voice trailed off as he studied the boy's still face.

Smith nodded slowly. "Roanoke was abandoned twenty years ago, but I'd wager my life that this boy's parents came to Virginia with John White. How else could he have come here?"

"The Spanish?"

"Does he look Spanish to you?"

"Then what's he doing washed up here?"

"I know not." Smith studied his patient carefully. "But his fever's broken in the last hour and he'll come around soon. Have the cook bring me some broth and bread, and let's get some meat in his belly before we talk to him."

"Aye."

Newport was about to leave the tent, but Smith held up a

restraining hand. Though they had battled in the past, he felt
sure Newport could be trusted in a matter of such importance.
Smith knew without a doubt that the good of the colony mat-
tered most to Newport. "And Captain—"

"Yes?"

"Say nothing of this to anyone, especially Wingfield. Let it be
our secret, yours and mine alone."

▾▴▾▴▾ Fallon felt the smoothness of fabric under his
hands and back.

Was this heaven?

He opened his eyes. A man stood before him, a tall man with
dark hair and brown eyes that fairly snapped with curiosity.
"Ah, so the sleeping youth awakens," the man said in English,
his teeth gleaming in a careful smile through his beard. "We'll go
slowly now, son. We wouldn't want to overtax you on your first
day back in the land of the living."

Fallon blinked. He was not dead. God had saved him. Relief
and gratitude swept over him as he made an effort to push himself up onto his elbows. The exertion made his head swim, but a
delicious aroma wafting from a wooden bowl caused his stomach to spasm in hunger.

The man noticed Fallon's glance at the bowl. "In sooth, it does
smell good, doesn't it? It's good chicken soup, made fresh from
one of England's fair hens brought to Virginia by the grace of His
Majesty the king."

Fallon gazed blankly at the man, and the stranger threw back
his head and laughed. "Surely you are acquainted with chick-
ens? But they are not important. Your strength is what matters.
Eat this soup, boy, and prepare to tell me your history."

Fallon took the bowl as the man's words rang in his ears. The
language was English—he recognized it easily enough. But the
accent was more clipped and pronounced than the tongue he
had spoken in Ocanahonan.

He lifted the wooden spoon to his mouth and sipped. What-ever a chicken was, it made a delicious soup.

"Now, my boy, do you have a name?"

Fallon paused to swallow. "Your name first, sir. Though you have been kind, there are enemies in the land."

The man's eyebrows shot up in an appreciative gesture. "Good thinking, my boy. I am John Smith, here with a contingent of settlers in the king's Virginia, in particular the Jamestown col-ony. We found you washed up on the banks of our own James River."

"The James?" An alarm rang in Fallon's head. Was this man one of the despised Spanish he had often heard about? Though he spoke English, Fallon knew that the English had a queen, the *Spanish* had a king.

He lowered the spoon and pushed the bowl away. "If you're Spanish, sir, I need not talk to you," he said, clamping his mouth closed.

"Spanish?" Again Smith's eyebrows shot up. "My boy, have you ever seen a Spaniard? I am as English as a man can be and as loyal to the king—"

"What happened to the queen?"

Smith nodded slowly as the light of understanding came into his eyes. "Indeed. It was during Elizabeth's reign that John White departed," he whispered, more to himself than to the boy. "The Virgin Queen, Elizabeth, rests today in the bosom of our Savior," he said, placing his hand across his heart in a sweeping gesture. "Her heir, King James, reigns in her place. We are English, my boy, as are you. It's as plain as the freckled nose upon your face. Now tell me," Smith whispered, fingering his beard in speculation. "From whence came you? And what became of the others with you?"

Against his will, Fallon's eyes darted again to the bowl, and Smith pushed it toward him. "I was born in Ocanahonan," Fallon said, taking the bowl into his lap. "My parents were Audrey and Roger Bailie."

Smith's eyes glowed with enthusiasm. "Roger Bailie was one

of John White's assistants," he said, startling Fallon with a sharp slap on the back. "Does your father still live?"

Fallon shook his head and slurped another spoonful of soup. "He died right after I was born, or so my mother told me. She married again later, an Indian werowance named Rowtag. We all lived together in Ocanahonan, but about two months ago the forces of Powhatan destroyed the village."

"How did you come to escape?" Smith whispered, his eyes burning with mingled admiration and curiosity.

Despite his resolve to be strong, Fallon's eyes watered as he recalled that night. "My mother and father bade me take Noshi and Gilda to safety," he said. "We crept out of the city through a hole under the wall of the palisade and drifted down the river in a canoe."

Smith drew in his breath. "Did no one else survive?"

Fallon nodded. "Four men, who were wounded but nursed by Gepanocon, the werowance at Ritanoe. He took care of them because they knew how to work copper. But only a few days ago Powhatan's warriors attacked Ritanoe, and there is not much left of the village. The chief and the four Englishmen fled, the women and children were killed, Noshi was sold into slavery, and Gilda is with Powhatan."

"Who are these people, Noshi and Gilda?" Smith asked.

"My children, my *responsibility*," Fallon answered, his voice cracking. Guilt suddenly avalanched over him, burying his heart in regret. He should have fought harder, he should have protested more, he should never have lingered at Ritanoe. . . .

He closed his eyes, willing the bitter tears away.

Smith stood and patted him on the shoulder. "Here is bread and water," he said, handing Fallon a hard loaf and a hollow gourd. "Eat, drink, and rest. But do not stir from this tent until I have returned and know what to do with you."


▼▲▼▲ John Smith's head swam with conflicting ideas as he walked about the camp. One of the colony's missions was to find John White's missing settlers, and if the boy could be believed, they all were dead. Only half-breed children and pitiful creatures like the confused boy remained, and perhaps four Englishmen who were nothing but the prized possessions of a greedy Indian chief. If the boy had told the truth, and John Smith believed he had, then the chief Powhatan had not only utterly destroyed a mighty English city, but was ruthless enough to do so again. Smith had already learned enough from his travels among the savages to know that Powhatan was greatly feared and respected, and his tribal network rivaled anything the English might hope to establish in the years to come.

If English colonization was to be successful, the English would have to befriend Powhatan. But honorable Englishmen could not and would not befriend a murderer of English subjects.

Smith shook his head. For the sake of Jamestown's survival, the investors in London must not know what happened to the men and women of John White's colony.

How then could he explain the boy?

▼▲▼▲▼ John Smith had his answer by nightfall. He reentered his tent with another bowl of stew for the starving youth, then took a seat on a small stool by the boy's side.

"You, Fallon Bailie, are an Englishman," he began, watching as the boy devoured the stew. "You need to visit England and become acquainted with the land that has given you birth, to visit the birthplace of your mother and find the church where your father was baptized. These things are possible, you know, and I will help you find your way."

The boy looked up, his eyes bright. "You'd take me to England someday?"

"I can't take you myself," Smith answered, resting his elbows on his knees and tenting his fingers. "But Captain Newport, who is leaving for England in two days, will see that you're settled and have all that you need. All I ask of you, Fallon, is that you never tell anyone else the story you told me. If anyone asks, tell the truth about where your parents were born. But never shall the words *Powhatan* or *Ocanahonan* cross your lips again."

Doubt shone in the boy's eyes; Smith knew he had asked a difficult thing. He raised a hand to forestall the boy's question. "I cannot give you a reason, Fallon, but you must trust me. The English have good reason to befriend the savages now, for we are vulnerable as we seek to establish ourselves here."

"I cannot befriend Powhatan," Fallon answered, his voice sharp. "He's a murderer, and he holds Gilda! And I cannot go back to England, for I have promised to take care of Gilda and Noshi. Thank you, Master Smith, for your offer, but as long as they are lost I must find them—"

"I will search for them in your place," Smith interrupted, placing his hand on Fallon's shoulder in a fatherly gesture. The touch seemed to calm the boy. "Would it not be better for me to find them and send them to England to be with you? After all, what place have they in such a land as this?"

The boy sat back, thinking, and after a moment he lifted his eyes to Smith's. "You will search diligently? They are but four years old and cannot take care of themselves. And when you find them, you will send them to me in England?"

"Just tell me how I shall know them," Smith said. He crossed his arms and leaned back, smiling confidently. "If you leave with Captain Newport like a good lad, I'll find your little friends and send them to you just as soon as I'm able. You'll see, Fallon. All will be well."

The boy took a deep breath, resigning himself to the idea, and Smith knew the decision had been made. "Noshi has green eyes and is marked with this mark," he said, pointing to a pattern of dots upon his wrists and arm. "We are sons of a chief of the Mangoak tribe. All of our marks include the sign of the cross."

"Duly noted," Smith said, listening halfheartedly. "And the girl, Gilda? How shall I know her?"

A secret smile seemed to play around the corners of the boy's mouth. "She is with the Powhatan," Fallon replied. "She is beautiful. Her eyes are the color of a morning sky. And she wears around her neck a circle of gold."

▼▲▼▲▼ On the morning of June twenty-first, the men of Jamestown stretched a piece of sail horizontally between two trees, a rough canvas altar. Communion was celebrated according to the rites of the Church of England, and Fallon watched, fascinated, from within John Smith's tent. The sound of singing men stirred his soul; he had not heard such singing since the worship services in the chapel at Ocanahonan. Though he missed the women's voices, still the words of the hymn comforted his heart:

> *Jesus, the very thought of Thee*
> *With sweetness fills my breast:*
> *But sweeter far Thy face to see,*
> *And in Thy presence rest.*
>
> *No voice can sing, no heart can frame,*
> *Nor can the memory find*
> *A sweeter sound than Jesus' name*
> *The Savior of mankind.*
>
> *But what to those who find? Ah! this*
> *Nor tongue nor pen can show:*
> *The love of Jesus, what it is*
> *None but His loved ones know.*

After darkness fell that night, John Smith gave Fallon a suitable shirt to cover his tattoos, then led the boy aboard the *Susan Constant*. After introducing him to Captain Christopher Newport, Smith wished them both a pleasant journey.

"Don't forget your promise to search for Gilda and Noshi," Fallon reminded Smith, half-afraid he was making the wrong decision. "You'll send them to join me in England."

"I won't forget," Smith answered, waving casually. "Now get

below and keep quiet. If anyone asks, Captain Newport is prepared to say you're his cabin boy."

Fallon nodded and crept down the narrow set of stairs into
the lower deck of the ship. The sailors looked at him curiously,
but he ignored them. Restless—he'd never been enclosed this
way before—he paced for a quarter of an hour before following
the example of the other seamen and wrapping himself in a bit
of canvas, then lying down on the floor to sleep.

But sleep did not come easily. He was on his way to England,
the land of his mother's and father's birth, but he had no idea
what to expect there. As he dozed fitfully on the hard planking
of the ship, the wind whistled over the deck and through the
open hatches, and the sound reminded him eerily of Gilda's
pleading cries as she was taken from him.

# Pocahontas

*Knowledge by suffering entereth,*
*And life is perfected by death.*

*Elizabeth Barrett Browning,*
*"A Vision of Poets"*

Weromacomico, the city of Powhatan, stood on the banks of the
Powhatan River like a stalwart fortress. A many-fingered swirl of
dark smoke rose from the towering timber palisade like an omi-
nous warning hand, but inside the walls small gardens and huts
extended outward from the central fire in a neat circular pattern.

As dusk crept into the woods at sunset, the twenty huts of
Powhatan's city filled with an assortment of villagers. Young
children usually slept with their mothers. On clear, warm nights
fathers often sat by the village campfire in the circle of elders
throughout the long hours of darkness. As soon as children
reached puberty they weaned themselves from their mothers'
sides, and young women frequently filled a hut of their own,
while unmarried warriors slept outside under the stars.

The hut to which Pocahontas took Gilda was more primitive
than the two-story house in which Gilda had lived with her
mama and papa at Ocanahonan. Fashioned of the trunks of
young bowed trees and covered with silky grass mats, the sturdy
dwelling sheltered a host of young women each night. Gilda
crept to a mat next to Pocahontas and breathed in the scent of
warm femininity. The girls' easy banter wrapped around Gilda
like water around a rock, and she fell asleep easily amid girlish
giggles and the light, quick sounds of even breathing.

Just as the sweet waters of the Powhatan River merged
with the salty currents of the great sea, so Gilda blended into
village life. Known as Numees, the Algonquin word for "sister,"
she was fiercely protected by Pocahontas, the chief's favorite
daughter.

After Gilda's rough-and-tumble days with Noshi and Fallon,

Pocahontas brought a uniquely feminine influence to the younger girl's life. Forgetting her grief, Gilda studied her protector with fascinated interest. The chief's popular twelve-year-old daughter was warmhearted, sensible, and endlessly cheerful. She charmed even the most dour elders with her disarming friendliness, and Gilda soon came to adore her. Pocahontas taught Gilda how to comb the silky tangles of her hair into braids, and Gilda longed for the day when her own hair would fall to her waist in a plume of black gold, as did Pocahontas's.

And yet, there were parts of Gilda that did not adapt to her new surroundings and life. Though the other small children ran naked throughout the camp, Gilda insisted upon wearing proper garments. She had always worn clothes in the village of Ocanahonan, and since Pocahontas wore a skirt, Gilda refused to do without.

While the men of the village went about the business of hunting, fishing, and subduing enemies, Gilda learned the ways of women from Pocahontas. Together they made the woven grass mats that were an elemental furnishing in Indian huts. They wove baskets, fashioned pots out of clay, and pounded corn in mortars. The girls helped make bread, prepared the victuals the hunters brought from the woods, and, throughout the summer, planted and gathered corn.

The children of the village had many names, according to the humor and whim of their parents, and Gilda came to know each child, but she loved Pocahontas best and remained close to the older girl's side. More than once she felt the sternly appraising eyes of the great chief upon her, and she turned away in fear, knowing he had the authority to make her go away as he had Noshi and Fallon.

None of the other villagers seemed to care what she did. To Powhatan's many wives, Gilda was but another mouth to feed, another body to wash. Once Gilda looked up to see Kitchi, Powhatan's esteemed son, watching her with a flicker of interest in his brown eyes. He was a handsome warrior, not old and not young, with an angular face, high cheekbones, and dark hair that fell thickly past his shoulders. Shadowed by thick brows, his eyes studied her carefully. Uncomfortable, Gilda fled his gaze and ran back to Pocahontas.

▼▲▼▲▼ The hot breath of August set leaves to dancing through the center of the camp, and Powhatan kept his eyes half-closed against the heat as the conjuror encouraged the hunters who would soon leave the village. The mournful, whining voice of the priest rose above the rhythmic thumping of drums, and the hunters whirled and danced in an appeal to the gods that their efforts would fill the storehouses with food for the winter.

Through his half-closed lids, Powhatan studied his son, Kitchi. The young man sat near the ceremonial fire, his legs crossed effortlessly, composing his own song to the gods. Powhatan wondered how deeply his son's heart was involved in the effort. Since the arrival of the blue-eyed girl, Kitchi had seemed even more reserved than usual. Always more eager to listen than talk, he had often sat quietly in his father's hut to absorb wisdom from the elders, but now he spent his days wandering in the woods or singing in the camp while his eyes followed Numees.

Powhatan glanced toward the small knot of girls who lingered outside the circle of hunters. Pocahontas stood head and shoulders above the others, in manner as well as in form, and her eyes sparkled with merriment as she contemplated the dancers. The corner of Powhatan's lip curved upward in a smile. She was a mischievous one, that girl, but he could deny her nothing. Though he was fond of all his many children, it was she who had most thoroughly captured his heart.

Numees stood in Pocahontas's shadow, her bright blue eyes wide as she watched the gyrations of the hunters. Reflexively, Powhatan's eyes shifted from Numees to Kitchi and back again. Could this child truly be Kitchi's own daughter? Opechancanough had said so, but Powhatan found it difficult to allow the idea to germinate within him. How could he, the greatest of Indian chiefs, have a blue-eyed granddaughter?

Powhatan mentally compared the girl's golden skin, the shape of her chin, and her strong limbs to Kitchi's powerful form. By the spirits, Opechancanough's story could be true! The girl favored Kitchi in every way but those sky-blue eyes.

Powhatan grunted to himself. It was good that the girl stayed close to Pocahontas. With the chief's favorite daughter as her companion, little Numees would be coddled, protected, and cared for. And he, Powhatan, would not have to take a hand in her upbringing.

"Beshrew these evil bugs!"
John Smith slapped another biting mosquito on his neck and
cursed the day the council had chosen this marshy bog for their
fort. The peninsula that had seemed so perfect a spot in May had
become fetid and contaminated by August. And though September breezes surely blew cool over England, the miasmic conditions of summer still hovered over the low-lying fort at
Jamestown. The sweltering heat descended like a blanket to sap
the strength of even the most able of men, and the sultry humidity of night prevented solid and restful sleep.

Unbearable weather was not the only problem. The wells the
colonists had dug produced only brackish, sour water; the misty
lowlands were nothing but a breeding ground for mosquitoes;
and the saturating humidity rotted the food stored aboard the
*Discovery*, the pinnace Newport had left behind. Each man's
daily ration of grain had to be reduced, and the barley remaining
in the ship's hold teemed with maggots. If not for the sturgeon
caught in the river, Smith knew the entire company would have
died of sickness and starvation.

Still, despite the river's provision, men died by the score. By
the time the first leaves had changed to the bright colors of
autumn, the group of settlers had dwindled considerably.

But when other men fainted, John Smith thrived. He awoke
with feverish energy each morning and immediately enlisted
men to dig fresh graves for those who had died in the night.
Motivating the men to work was difficult, for his companions
seemed to walk in the twilight world of the half-alive. "If you
faint in the day of adversity," Smith taunted them, knowing a

quote from Holy Scriptures would rouse the men when all else failed, "your strength is small. Rise with God, my friends, and let us prove ourselves."

But as strength dwindled, so did the men's patience, and the smallest incidents of trouble festered into major confrontations. Not even the remaining council members were able to work together peaceably. Smith felt his antipathy toward President Edward Wingfield grow with each passing day, and only the patient Christian exhortations of Reverend Hunt kept Smith from clapping Wingfield in chains and declaring a general revolt. The tyrant allotted food unfairly, giving more to the aristocrats, who did less work. What's more, it was rumored among the men that Wingfield was a Catholic Spanish spy. Why else would he have "Maria" as a middle name?

Unless Wingfield proved able to restore order and to urge his high-minded gentlemen friends to participate in physical labor, Smith feared that the colony's days were numbered. And he would kill before he died due to another man's negligence.

▼▲▼▲▼ By the end of September, Edward Maria Wingfield awaited justice as a prisoner in the hold of the *Discovery*. With the aid of John Ratcliffe and John Martin, Smith had succeeded in overthrowing the pompous Wingfield. Ratcliffe was the new president, and Smith sincerely hoped the man would prove to be better at the job than the London Company's first choice.

Unfortunately, within a week it became obvious that Ratcliffe loved the abstract aspects of leadership far more than the daily details of survival. While Ratcliffe pondered unnecessary particulars of administering the colony's nonexistent political life, Smith took a firm hand in his own survival. He succeeded in trading worthless trinkets for maize from the Indians and oversaw work companies that felled a substantial number of trees for the building of wattle-and-daub houses. Thus far the colonists had lived only in rough canvas tents, but the canvas coverings smelled of decay and rot and would provide little protection from severe weather or cold. Sturdy, substantial houses would be necessary if the people were to survive the winter.

Smith was prepared to ignore Ratcliffe, and even, if necessary, to become virtual dictator of the colony. Already the wind blew cool enough to knife lungs and tingle bare skin, and it was too late by far in the year to sow corn. If the remaining men were to be fed through the winter, John Smith would have to beg, borrow, or steal grain from the Indians. Foraging expeditions would be necessary, which meant he would encounter savages probably as hungry and desperate as he.

Smith tightened his belt around his thinning waist and steeled himself to the necessity of the task that lay ahead.

Far across the great Western ocean, Fallon Bailie stood at the rail of the *Susan Constant*. He let out a whistle of surprise as the seamen scampered up the rigging to cheer for the purpling mass that rose against the hazy horizon. "'Tis England, my boy," Captain Newport called, grinning down from the poop deck at the stern. "My home and yours. I've seen many sights while weatherin' the ocean seas, but none so welcome as the jeweled isle you'll see rising up to greet us."

Fallon did not answer; he only continued to stare out across the sea. In the past weeks he had seen many things, wonders he could never have imagined—large, air-breathing sea creatures as long as the ship and of certain more powerful; fires that burned on boats and cooked gelatinous pottages of fish and dried, tasteless beef; oceans that stretched far beyond the horizon; and men whose love and purpose for living was found in the sea.

Now he stood ready to visit England, the country from which his mother and father had sailed to find a new life in Virginia. *How strange,* he thought, watching the quilted landscape unfold before him as the ship drew nearer, *that their land should be foreign to me, even as my birthplace was foreign to them. Still, their God guides me, and surely our worlds are mere specks to him, like dots on a map.*

The captain barked an order, the sails fluttered down, and the ship slowed to enter the English Channel. Seamen on both sides of the bow pitched lead lines overboard to measure the depth of the channel, and the ship proceeded cautiously. Fallon frowned as he watched. Why were they so careful? Hadn't the captain been here before?

He looked up at Newport, and the captain seemed to guess his question. "It never hurts to know where you're going, lad," he said, settling his elbows on the ship's railing as he listened to the seamen call out the depths. "The bottom changes after a storm, and I'd wager there have been a good many since we departed last year. It's a good lesson to remember: Always take careful soundings, for nothing ever stays the same. The shifting rocks on the bottom can bring a ship down."

The bosun approached with a question, and Captain Newport followed the man from the poop deck, leaving Fallon alone with his thoughts. He leaned on the railing, consciously imitating the captain, whom he had come to admire, and gazed with wonder at the civilization slipping by him. So many tall ships and roof-tops and cultivated fields in this place! So many people! Ocanahonan had been a large town, but there had never been more than two hundred people living within its walls. Captain Newport had told him that thousands lived in the city of London alone.

He would have been mesmerized by the marvelous panorama unfolding before his eyes, but two small images at the back of his mind haunted him, keeping him from fully enjoying the new world spreading itself in front of him. Somewhere in Virginia Noshi and Gilda were alone and unprotected, and Fallon knew he would not rest until he kept his promise to take care of them. Though John Smith had promised to find and rescue them, Fallon could not help but wonder how capable the Englishman would prove to be. He did not know the Indians or the country as well as Fallon did.

"I should have stayed behind to search for them," he whispered guiltily. But he had felt so insignificant and helpless in the face of Smith's brave bluster, musket, and armor. Fallon shook himself reproachfully. Where was his trust in his God? Besides, surely Smith could find and rescue two children. . . .

Couldn't he?

▼▲▼▲ The two ships under Newport's command docked at Portsmouth. Shortly after their docking, Fallon heard the bosun call his name. "Captain wants to see you in his cabin," the bosun said, jerking his head toward the narrow companionway that led to the upper deck. "Right now, boy."

Fallon sprinted up the stairs and crossed the deck with eager steps. He knocked tentatively on the captain's door, but was reassured when Newport's sharp voice rang through the heavy oak: "Enter!"

Newport sat at the small table in his cabin, a sealed letter in his hand. "Your future lies within this parchment, Fallon Bailie," he said, shaking the letter slightly for emphasis. "John Smith has written explicit orders about what is to be done with you once we reach London."

Fallon swallowed over the nervous lump in his throat. "Will you read it to me?"

"In a moment," Newport answered, hesitating. He suddenly leaned forward, his eyes brightening like shrewd little chips of quartz. "You are a bright lad, Fallon Bailie, and I've been watching you for weeks. What do you say to me tossing this letter overboard and let's forget it all together? Make the sea your mistress and come with me when we leave again. We'll be back to Virginia for the colony's second supply, probably leaving in a couple of months or so, and you could be my cabin boy or one of the bilge rats working below decks." He paused to give Fallon an appraising glance. "What do you say, boy? You've taken well to the sea or I'd not be asking you to consider this thing."

Fallon's gaze centered on the letter in the captain's hand and he asked God to give him wisdom. "Is there some reason why I should not follow John Smith's instructions?"

Newport's eyes narrowed, then he shook his head. "None but my own hunch. Of the men we left behind at Jamestown, none but John Smith, and perhaps the good Reverend Hunt, have the wherewithal to last a year in that place," he said. "Smith's liable to emerge the leader of that rabble, and my suspicion is that he'll not be gambling his success on what damage you might do to him, boy."

"I cannot hurt him," Fallon answered quietly. "What harm could I do to such a man?"

"Not you, but the truth you represent," Newport said, shifting uneasily on his stool. "And if the truth is not plain to you, let's not worry with it. But make your choice, son. The sea or John Smith. Which will you follow?"

Fallon looked again at the parchment in Newport's hand. He was tempted by the captain's offer, for he had loved the sights and sounds of the sea. But Newport would return to Jamestown in a few months, and John Smith had said it would be dangerous for Fallon to remain in Virginia while Powhatan's anger hovered over the colony. God had sent Smith to save his life; Fallon was sure of it. Would he not be better off to follow the wishes of the man whom God had brought into his life?

"I would do as John Smith bids," he whispered after a moment of consideration. "If you please, Captain, what does the letter say?"

With a deft stroke of a knife Newport broke the seal upon the parchment. After skimming the letter, he thrust it toward Fallon. "Do you read?" he asked abruptly.

"Yes," Fallon answered, scanning the brisk handwriting on the page. The message scrawled upon the parchment was brief and to the point:

> My ward, Fallon Bailie, of late from Virginia, is to be taken to the Royal Academy for Homeless Orphans, there to serve as a student until the age of sixteen or until he can be apprenticed to a willing master. He is to remain at the academy under the care and guardianship of the headmaster until, God willing, I, John Smith, shall call for and make provision for him. May God preserve and protect us both while we are apart.

"That is all?" Fallon asked, turning the parchment over. Smith had not mentioned Gilda and Noshi, nor when he might be expected to return. Indeed, except for the last sentence, the reader would hardly expect John Smith to return at all.

Newport drew his lips in a tight line. "'Pon my soul, I expected Smith would do better than this," he muttered, his words barely reaching Fallon's ears. "A home for orphans! Indeed!"

"Is that not a good place?" Fallon asked, feeling a rock settle in the pit of his stomach.

"It's fine," Newport said, standing. He took the letter from Fallon and held it aloft near the open window in his cabin. "It's not too late, y'know. You might still be my cabin boy."

Fallon slowly shook his head. If he chose to follow the unpredictable sea, he might never meet John Smith or Noshi or Gilda again. And since God had used John Smith to save Fallon's life, was it not better to follow what seemed to be the hand of the Almighty and obey Smith's direction?

The boy lifted his eyes to meet the captain's gaze. "There's no gainsaying that you're more than kind," he whispered. "But I will do as John Smith has directed me."


▼▲▼▲▼ Captain Newport hired a coach to carry him and Fallon from Portsmouth to London, and in a paralysis of astonishment Fallon kept his face swiveled toward the window of the vehicle. He had never seen a carriage, a horse, or men in so much fine clothing. As they left the bustle of the docks and moved into the countryside, Fallon felt his jaw drop at the openness of a land wiped clean of forests. The region near the shore lay as flat as stretched buckskin with the sharp, gray chimneys of little villages poking up from it like clinging cockleburs. As they rode north, the land rose and fell, but still the landscape lay quilted into neat fenced pastures where cattle and horses grazed next to carefully plowed fields. Window boxes gushed red with geraniums on small, tidy cottages that stood guard over these pastures. In the distance, gradually rolling hills provided a pretty scalloped border to the horizon.

The alien beauty of the countryside faded as the coach neared London. The pointed roofs of tall city structures leapt up from the horizon, dragging up a cluster of other buildings brushed to a uniform sooty gray that reminded Fallon of the charred ashes upon his mother's hearth. The road upon which they traveled grew crowded and filled with ruts, and soon the coach jostled through a narrow cobblestone street encumbered with carriages, laden with smells, and packed with surging crowds of humanity.

Fallon had never seen so many buildings or people together in one place. He sank back into the cushions of the carriage, overwhelmed. There were a thousand things to be identified, a thousand faces to evaluate, a thousand dangers of which to be wary. In the forests of Virginia he had never imagined that such a barbaric, crowded place could exist. The reeking fog of sewage assaulted his nostrils, and the steadily falling rain did little to wash away the layered grime accumulated from generations of confined living.

The team of horses picked their way through the muck and mire, then the coach stopped outside a building on a street that seemed more quiet than the others they had traversed. Captain Newport looked out the window, then nodded toward Fallon. "We have arrived," he said abruptly.

The Royal Academy for Homeless Orphans was a wide, two-story house with all the warmth of a mausoleum. Rain fell heavily upon the structure's windows and red brick facade as Fallon stepped from the coach. As he looked up, he saw half a dozen young boys standing at an upper window, watching him in mute appraisal. Their faces were drawn and utterly without mirth. Suddenly, they scurried away like frightened rats.

"I hope you'll find a home here," Captain Newport said, stepping from the coach to stand beside Fallon. He squinted toward the heavy double doors. "The school was established sixty years ago to honor ten-year-old King Edward VI." His mouth curved in a mirthless smile as he placed his hand upon Fallon's shoulder. "The king's long gone, but the school remains, and the headmaster has a considerably good reputation in the city. He's

Delbert Crompton, or Master Crompton to you, of course. I've heard he's a sociable, jolly fellow."

Fallon knew that Newport waited for him to reply, but he could not find words to cut through his fear and feelings of hopelessness. His lips felt as cold as his heart, and the chill wind and rain colored his entire world as gray as the rooftops of London.

Fallon lifted his face to Captain Newport's, grateful that the wetness upon his cheeks would be disguised as rain. "This is where John Smith would have me wait for him?" he asked, finally finding his voice.

Newport nodded.

Fallon took a deep breath and wiped his cold hands on the new suit of clothing the captain had provided. The shirt, breeches, and jerkin fit him perfectly, though the fabric felt flimsy and too light for Fallon's taste. He only hoped the school would prove to be an admirable fit as well.

"Then let us meet this Master Crompton," he remarked, lifting his chin in what he hoped was a fair imitation of bravery. Newport gazed at him a moment, seemed about to speak, then shook his head and stepped forward to swing open the double doors.

▼▲▼▲▼ Delbert Crompton fancied himself the most capable and resourceful headmaster in London. On the meagerest of charitable contributions he successfully administrated the Royal Academy for Homeless Orphans, and the boys housed there were fed twice a day, clothed admirably well, and apprenticed easily, for their masters knew they would work hard and expect little. Compton was a practical, observant man who made it his business to know all that went on in his domain.

The church ladies who descended weekly upon the school to do small acts of kindness for their consciences' sake thought him good-natured and sociable. But the schoolboys knew his true nature, for Crompton made no effort to hide it from them. If he was hard, the better to toughen his charges; if he was parsimonious, the better to teach boys not to expect too much from life.

And if he was inebriated, well, so was half of London on any given night. His boys had become used to the rheumy glow of his wine-reddened eyes and the smell of his bourbon breath.

He was a tall man whose chief physical attribute was an enormous stomach that protruded over his belt like a tumor. At forty-and-seven, he considered himself in the prime of life. He had lost much of his hair, but his mistress assured him that she found the ginger freckles on his head as attractive as the sharp, hawklike nose that sat above his yellowed teeth. When curled into a snarl, and coupled with the threat of a cane, that monumental nose never failed to quell the spirit of a rebellious boy.

A new student stood before Delbert Crompton now, a red-haired, freckled creature of at least thirteen. He was tall and thin, but carried himself erectly with a quiet air of authority despite the uncomfortable way he shifted in his doublet and breeches. The urchin's manner instantly aroused Crompton's ire. Something seemed to flicker far back in the boy's odd blue eyes, some secret or wisdom. Crompton squinted at the boy for the space of a full minute, then decided this one had seen too much of life's hardness in his short years.

The headmaster sniffed. Nothing unusual in that. All the other boys in this place had seen the same.

"Your name?" Crompton asked, disguising his instant antipathy with a quick, brittle smile.

"Fallon Bailie, sir."

"And you're an orphan?" He asked the question with lofty concern and a mournful expression.

"Yes. My mother and father are dead." The boy looked at the floor as he said this, as if the admission still hurt. Crompton felt the corner of his mouth twitch. Snotty little brat, coming here with the air of a conquering hero when he was obviously without any social standing whatsoever.

"Have you been educated?"

The boy tilted his head and frowned, then glanced to Captain Christopher Newport as if for advice. Newport cleared his throat. "He is a very able boy, sir, and intelligent. But he has had no formal schooling."

"I see." Crompton lifted his chin and pinned Fallon with his disapproving gaze. "So you're totally ignorant."

The boy flushed—the words had rankled his considerable pride—and Newport stepped forward in protest. "He is very learned, Master Crompton, but he has no knowledge of city life. He is . . . from the country."

Crompton perched upon the edge of his desk, lowering his eyes as he listened to the rain thrum against the roof overhead. He had seen country boys—all were humble lads with dirt under their fingernails and heads perpetually lowered from bowing to the lords on the great estates. This was no country boy. More likely the esteemed captain had sired himself an illegitimate son in some distant port and fetched the child to England after the mother's death. Still, there could be no harm in accepting the boy, for Newport had ties to royal circles—a fact that might prove useful in the future.

Crompton's eyes swept again over the young man's slender form, then he drew in his breath in an audible gasp as an anomaly caught his eye. "What is that?" he cried, spitting the words. He lifted a thick finger to a row of dark dotted lines on the boy's forearms. "Who has marked this child and for what reason?"

The captain and the boy exchanged a quick glance, and the boy hastily rolled down his sleeves. "The boy has been with me for several weeks on a voyage," Newport answered. "He was tattooed by natives in a foreign port. It is of no consequence, and I pray you not to hold it against him."

"It's devilish!" Crompton snapped. "Does not the very Word of God forbid us to cut our bodies as the heathen do? Let me remind you, sir, that the blessed children in this house rely upon the charity and goodness of the people of God. We worship God here and do not allow evil or devilish practices in this place—"

"I worship God, too," the boy said, daring to interrupt. "I have been taught of God and his holy Son since my birth. I am a Christian."

"Yet you're tattooed like a devil worshiper?"

The boy flushed to the roots of his hair. "I do not worship the devil. My markings have naught to do with whom I worship."

Crompton clapped his mouth shut. The boy answered well, and, in a small way, it was good to know of these markings. Every boy had a chink in his armor, a weakness that could be exploited if necessary. This boy's Achilles heel was obvious and Delbert could use it to keep the lad in line.

"You will wear long sleeves over your arms at all times," Crompton said, standing behind his desk. "And since you have had no formal education, you will take your lessons with the very youngest boys. I am happy to hear that you call yourself a Christian, but be forewarned, young Fallon Bailie. I will watch you more closely than I do the others, for I am responsible for your immortal soul and I hope to give a good account of it on Judgment Day."

He nodded stiffly toward the sober-faced captain. "Captain Newport, take him to the dining hall and leave him there. You may rest in confidence, knowing that he will be educated and regarded as highly as any boy in this place." He sank into his chair and picked up a sheaf of papers, a clear sign that he was done with his visitors.

Newport's hand went to the boy's shoulder as they turned to leave, and Crompton allowed himself a smug smile. The man's affection for the boy was obvious. Undoubtedly the child was his son, not an orphan, and therefore a liar, like his father.

Crompton quietly clicked his tongue against the roof of his mouth, mentally filing the scrap of information away for future reference.

In the huge, cold lobby of the academy, Captain Newport rocked nervously on his heels, then thrust a hand toward Fallon. "I'll be leaving then," he said, his eyes telling Fallon to take care. "And if I see Smith when I return to Virginia, I'll be certain to give him your regards."

"Godspeed," Fallon whispered, feeling at that moment more abandoned than he had in all the days since he had taken the children from the slaughter at Ocanahonan. "I pray you will remind Captain Smith of his promise to me. And if he returns to England—"

"I'll tell him where to find you. Never worry," Newport answered. After shaking Fallon's hand, the captain turned on his heel, opened the dark wooden doors, and strode out.

Fallon turned away, unwilling for Captain Newport to see the tears that had risen in his eyes yet again. Surely this parting was God's will, for he was in the land of his mother and father. As an English boy, it would be good for him to know things of England. And John Smith had promised to bring Gilda and Noshi once he found them, so in time all would be as it should be.

Yet these inner reassurances did nothing to dispel the lump that rose in his throat, and Fallon wanted nothing more than to run into the woods and throw himself upon the earth where soft moss would catch his tears and the murmur of forest life would remind him that he was not alone.

Sadly, there was no forest in London. And so, surrounded by a cold brick building, Fallon turned from the lobby and followed the worn path in the carpet to the dining hall, where he would meet his fellow students.

▼▲▼▲▼ The dining room lay wreathed in shadows
even at noontime, and the atmosphere was musty, as though the
air had been breathed too many times by too many boys. The
sun-bleached curtains at the gray windows hung damp and lifeless in the humidity of the rain, and a faded portrait of some
grand man hung on the far wall, as though to impress upon the
diners the yawning gap between their poverty and the man's
aristocracy.

There were six tables in the room, five of simple wood and
design and plainly outfitted. The sixth, however, sat in the
middle of the room, where all might look upon its grandeur. The
center table was covered in linen and lace. Silver goblets sat at
each of the two places, and candles gleamed from pewter stands
at the midpoint of the table. Handsome carved chairs, rich with
brocaded upholstery, crouched at opposite ends of the table.

Like poor relations, the other tables hugged the walls. Long
benches served as seats, and upon each bench five boys waited,
their eyes fastened to the plain wooden bowls before them.
Rough linen runners lay horizontally across the common tables,
and each boy tucked the end into his collar so the runners served
as a combined placemat and napkin. Fallon thought the effect
strangely comic—each boy was joined both to his supper and to
the lad across from him.

An older boy stationed at the door pointed Fallon to a vacant
place where a bowl of dark pottage waited. Fallon clumped
across the uncarpeted floor, still unaccustomed to the heavy
shoes. He slid into the spot at the bench while the company of
students swiveled their eyes to study him.

His new comrades were a scrawny-looking lot with thin, pale
faces and blank, unexpressive eyes. Fallon judged the oldest boy
to be about sixteen, while the youngest was not much older than
Noshi. There were no girls present, and not a single happy
expression.

A carved door in the far corner of the hall swung open on its
hinges and Master Delbert Crompton entered, accompanied by a
man in sober dark leggings and a black doublet. Both men

walked with their heads lifted and backs stiffly arched, and two boys sprang to pull the heavy chairs away from the table so the men could be seated.

When Master Crompton had unfolded his lace napkin and placed it in his lap, the other gentleman rose to his feet and began a lengthy prayer of thanks. Fallon opened one eye to keep from dozing as the minister—for such he surely was—intoned grace over the meal that congealed in their bowls.

When the minister had finally finished he sat down, and Fallon noticed that every boy's eye trained on Master Crompton's right hand. The assembled students drew in an audible breath as the headmaster picked up his knife, speared a slice of mutton, and slowly raised it to his thin lips. The instant the mutton had safely arrived in the master's mouth, the boys scooped up their spoons and set to work on the pottage in the bowls before them.

Fallon crinkled his nose at the taste of the stuff. It was cold and bland, a curdled mixture of flour, lard, and vegetables that had spent too many days in the larder. But he imitated his fellows and ate without conversation or complaint.

When Delbert Crompton put down his spoon and stood up, the boys did the same, whether they were finished or not, and filed in a single line through an open door and into several classrooms. Fallon lingered behind, not sure where to go, until the headmaster appeared in the hallway and pointed Fallon to a small chamber. "In here," he said, his thick finger pointing to a room where five very small boys waited in chairs. "You will begin with the ignorant ones until you have caught up with what our fine older lads know."

Smarting in his humiliation, Fallon obeyed.


▼▲▼▲▼ After afternoon classes in reading, writing, and Bible catechism, the boys lined up in the dining hall for a slice of bread garnished by a thin strip of cheese. This they stuffed into their mouths without ceremony, then exited the dining hall and climbed a creaking staircase to a long, narrow room known as the dormitory.

The chamber smelled of dust, mildew, and fifty sweaty boys. A single row of high windows along the western wall lit the room with the fading beams of sunset, and Fallon could see that scores of wooden cots were stacked one upon the other in orderly rows on both sides of the room. At the furthest point of the shadowed space was the water closet.

The boys stood motionless in the narrow chamber until the headmaster's sharp face peered around the room. After nodding in satisfaction, Crompton closed the door and Fallon heard the distinct click of an iron key in the lock. The sound was a signal, for upon hearing it, his new companions broke the mold of rigid conformity and yelped in joyful release as straw-stuffed pillows flew through the air.

Fallon ducked the soaring bags of straw and moved toward a lower bunk that appeared to be unoccupied. A dirty, rumpled pillow lay upon a thin, sweat-stained mattress, and he paused before sitting down. "Is this bed taken?" he asked, looking toward a slender blond boy who lounged on the upper cot.

The boy turned onto his stomach and rested his chin on his hands. "It was Michael O'Hara's place," he said, curiosity shining in his eyes. "But Michael's no longer here."

"Is he—dead?" Fallon asked, knowing all too well how death could steal souls from the land of the living.

But the blond boy laughed. "No, he's been apprenticed to a blacksmith over in Newham. Could you be thinking that the pox had taken him?"

Fallon shrugged, unsure of what the boy meant, and gingerly sat upon the bed. The ropes supporting the mattress creaked under his slight weight as he lay down, but after weeks of sleeping with naught but the planks of the ship and canvas beneath his bones, the thin mattress felt wonderfully comforting.

Fallon ignored the commotion of the boys around him and closed his eyes, but the boy above him had other ideas. "Faith, don't go to sleep," he said, lowering his head over the side of his bed and peering upside-down at Fallon. "This is our only time to talk. If you but open your mouth in class or the dining hall, old Master Crompton will cane you across the hand. Or worse."

"Cane you?" Fallon asked, propping himself up with his elbows. "What's a cane?"

The boy rolled his eyes and snickered. "Och, and what ship of amadons and eejits brought you in?"

"The *Susan Constant*," Fallon answered, not understanding the boy's tone. "From Virginia. We only arrived yesternoon."

The boy's mocking smile flattened. "In sooth?" he whispered, lowering his voice. "You came all the way from Virginia? But where were you before that?"

Fallon shook his head. "I was born there. John Smith sent me to England so that I might come to know the land of my father."

"Your father's dead then?"

"Aye. Killed by sickness right after I was born. But my mother married again, an Indian called Rowtag." Fallon felt himself glowing with pride, but he couldn't help it. "He was a chief of the Mangoak tribe and he taught me all that a chief's son should know."

"Go on!" For a moment Fallon feared that the boy thought him a liar, but sincere trust shone from the lad's eyes. He *wanted* to believe.

"My name is Fallon Bailie," he said, sitting up and thrusting his hand toward the boy.

"Brody McRyan," the blond answered, grasping Fallon's hand. "How old are you, Fallon?"

"Thirteen."

"I'm eleven. Born on Christmas Day, I was, and killed me mother just by being born." The boy's voice was light, but darkness stirred in his green eyes as he spoke. "Me father died when I was five and I've lived here ever since. But it's that pleased I am to meet you, Fallon Bailie."

Fallon nodded soberly. "Have you brothers or sisters?"

Brody shook his head. "None I know of. Nor aunts nor uncles nor cousins. Once you're in this place, you're cut off from the world and no one comes for you. No one leaves unless they get sick and die or are apprenticed out. Michael O'Hara, who used to sleep in that bed, went out last week and I heard the scullery maid tell the laundress that Master Crompton got ten pounds of gold for him."

"He *sold* him?" The unwelcome image of Noshi being sold into slavery flitted across Fallon's mind and he shuddered.

Brody smiled again. "Nay, he apprenticed him. You really don't know much, do you now?"

Fallon lay back on the soiled pillow and clasped his hands behind his head. "I intend to learn. And you're wrong about nobody ever coming back. John Smith has promised to come back for me as soon as he's able."

"Nobody comes, didn't I just say so?" Brody answered, hugging the side of his bed. "Who are you going to believe, some man a thousand miles away or me? I've been here six years, Bailie, and I tell you, we're lost to the world. Don't count on nobody coming for you, or nobody making things a wee bit easier for you. As sure as my name is Brody McRyan, it isn't going to happen."

"Is there anything else I should know?" Fallon asked, staring at the underside of Brody's dark mattress.

"One more thing," the answer came from above. "Watch out for Master Crompton. Don't do anything to make yourself stand out. If he notices you, you're bound to have trouble."


▼▲▼▲ Delbert Crompton dined alone at his grand table in front of his boys. He didn't mind being the focus of fifty pairs of eyes; in fact, he ofttimes explained to visitors that the boys received lessons in gentle etiquette and deportment by watching him eat at a proper table. In truth, he ate before his students to remind them that they had their place and he had his. Though he was not quite top-drawer gentry, he was as close to the clergy as a man could be without donning the cloth and memorizing the Bible. His lofty status required a certain measure of their respect, and eating at a grand table, wearing fine clothing, and entertaining the gentry were but a few of the ways he had devised to make certain he acquired it.

He also enjoyed eating in the center of the dining hall because with a simple swivel of his eyes he could apprehend any of his fifty boys in an unguarded state. Many times he had caught certain ungrateful looks or expressions of derision aimed at the bowls of cold pottage, but these disagreeable countenances were promptly corrected when he removed the offending dinner altogether. Now his boys ate with careful manners and thoroughly expressionless faces. He would have staked his life on the certainty that any of his students, from the youngest to the oldest, could have dined at the king's table without cracking a smile or uttering an untoward word.

Except, mayhap, Fallon Bailie. For seven days Crompton had watched Bailie's slender form at school and mealtimes. He found the boy oddly competent in all that he undertook. He was much too intellectually advanced to remain in the remedial reading and mathematics classes, but the headmaster was determined that Fallon should finish out the year with the younger students lest he stir up trouble among the older boys. Something about Bailie unsettled him. The lad possessed an air of propriety and knowledge, a quality like that of good breeding. But how had an illegitimate brat come by such an attitude?

It was strange to see such assurance in a mere boy, especially since it was accompanied by many virtues. Bailie was persistent in his work, sympathetic to those who could not work as quickly or as ably as he, and patient as he helped the younger children accomplish their tasks. He proved himself dependable, never sluggish or less than diligent in his studies, and seemed to fancy himself a protector of the young boys with whom he studied.

On sunny days when the boys trooped through the damp autumn foliage to take their daily dose of "air," Bailie chose either to walk alone at the end of the queue or at the beginning, where he could shepherd the younger ones along the garden path. It was in the yard, Crompton noted, that Bailie never failed to elicit a reprimand. Even in the cold of autumn the boy had a penchant for removing his shoes. No matter how stringently the tutors tried to maintain a straight line of marching boys, Fallon Bailie always seemed to slink rather than step through the autumn shadows.

Yes, Fallon Bailie was different, and Delbert Crompton did not like him. Without striving to, the lad had become a sort of leader among the boys, setting a rigorous pace by example, proving himself to be worthy of emulation. The headmaster frowned. Let those pale blue eyes even once flash in rebellion at dinner or in the schoolroom, the others certainly would follow and he, the good and noble headmaster, would face a full-scale revolt.

Bailie would have to be dealt with, and the sooner the better.

The perfect opportunity for Fallon Bailie's humiliation arose that afternoon when the boys assembled in the dining hall for their supper of bread and cheese. Crompton watched Fallon closely and had to bite his lip to keep from shouting in jubilation when he realized he had found an infraction. Fallon Bailie had neglected to button his shirt cuffs as ordered. The faintest edge of his cursed tattoos showed dark against the pale skin at his wrists.

"Halt!" Crompton roared from behind the serving table just as the scullery maid was about to place a slice of bread in Fallon's hand. "What is that upon your wrist, young man?"

Bailie's gaze lifted to Crompton's. *You know what it is*, his eyes said in silent accusation.

Crompton stepped forward and grasped the boy's thin wrist in a grip of iron. With one hand he held Fallon's arm aloft, and with the other he pushed the boy's sleeve down until the tattooed marks were clearly visible, even in the dim rushlight of the room.

"These are the marks of heathen devil-worshipers," Crompton proclaimed, turning to display the arm to the younger boys, who stood in a single file against the wall. Their mouths were filled with bread, but they were too startled and frightened to swallow.

Fallon still did not speak, but Crompton wasn't surprised. He turned the boy's wrist in the other direction so that the boys behind him might have a glimpse of the devilish tattoos. "See here, students, what marks one who worships Satan."

"He does not worship the devil!" A high and resonant protest filled the hall, and Crompton turned in amazement to see that Brody McRyan had stepped from his place to defend the new-comer.

"And what would you know of this?" Crompton asked, his bushy brows lifting with the question.

"His father was an Indian chief in Virginia," Brody exclaimed as the other boys gaped in silence. "Fallon was raised up with Indians, and those are the marks of his father's tribe. He is the son of a great chief; he's like a prince among the Indians—"

"Does this boy look like an Indian prince to you?" Crompton interrupted, his heavy voice drowning out Brody's protesting whine. "Red hair, freckles, pale skin—," He snickered, and after a pensive moment, the older boys began to laugh with him. Their pealing laughter ricocheted off the high ceiling. Even the dour face of the scullery maid cracked into a smirk.

But Fallon neither laughed nor smiled. His face flushed as red as his hair and his arm tightened in Crompton's grip until the sinews felt like steel. "You will not laugh at my father," he whispered, the intensity of his glare lifting the hairs on Crompton's neck.

Abruptly, the headmaster dropped the boy's arm and the room grew silent. "I will laugh at whatsoever I choose," Crompton replied, smoothing his voice. "You're an imaginative boy, Fallon Bailie, but I must caution you not to let your imagination run away with your senses. I don't know where you came from and I don't care, but you're an orphan, an Irish runt, probably, just like young Brody McRyan here. And if either of you say one more word about Indians and princes and kingdoms in Virginia, I'll send you to the asylum for the insane where you can spin your tales until you're weary of telling them. And any of you—" his stubby finger swept the room—"who associate with these two stand in danger of a caning that'll leave you unable to sit for a week."

He paused and glowered at Bailie and McRyan. The room stilled, and even the autumnal wind outside seemed to hold its breath. "Do you understand me, boys?" he said, his words hanging in the stillness.

Brody nodded, but Bailie held Crompton's gaze steadily. "I understand completely," Fallon said, his grip smashing the slice of bread in his outstretched hand. "And I will never, ever forget what you have said."

The bright December morning was wind-whipped and bitter cold as John Smith directed the loading of a shallop with supplies. Another foraging expedition had to be organized, for the colony was down to its last stores of food and winter pressed hard upon them. The humid mists that had hovered over the marshy peninsula all summer had dissipated, and now claws of winter wind slashed from the sea as frigid and vicious as a knife.

"So you're determined to go, then." John Ratcliffe stood beside Smith, one hand cocked upon the pistol at his belt.

Smith turned slowly from the shallop. It was difficult to be respectful to Ratcliffe, even though the man was president of the colony. Two months ago Smith had thought that Ratcliffe might make a good leader, but time and trial had proven him wrong.

"If we would eat, we must go," Smith said, making an effort to keep the edge of defensiveness from his voice. "The crops we planted did not produce. Too many men who should be hunting lie ill in the fort. And unless you have a better idea, sir . . ." He lifted a brow and waited for Ratcliffe's answer.

"Well, I, ah . . . no," Ratcliffe stammered. "It's just that we are only forty men here now, and forty men cannot hope to hold the fort in the case of an Indian attack. Small numbers have never done well in Virginia; did not John White report that the fifteen left upon Roanoke Island were massacred? If they come against us while you are gone with six men—"

"You will die only a little more quickly than if you had forty and six men in the fort," Smith finished. "Your strength, John, will lie in prayer and readiness, not in numbers. Did not Gideon rout a numberless company of the enemy with only three hundred? Surely you can hold one fort with forty men who trust in the God of Gideon."

Ratcliffe's eyes fell dejectedly, and Smith clapped him on the shoulder. "If we do not go, we will all die of starvation. This voyage is our only hope, and I pray you will not keep us from it."

Ratcliffe stepped back and rubbed his hands on his arms. "Where will you go?"

It wasn't a question, it was a fearful whine from a nosy, troublesome worrier. Smith propped one leg on a tree trunk and scratched his beard, taking his time before answering. "I have met a chief on the James River, Opechancanough, who is apparently gifted with rare foresight. It's said that he has stored provisions enough to last through two winters. If this chief is as vain as I think he is, I will bring back much grain for the price of a few trinkets."

Ratcliffe sniffed in apparent satisfaction and thrust his hands behind his back. "Well then, Smith, take care. And bring back every man alive, do you hear?"

"Mark me, John, I shall do my best," Smith said, grinning. "And I pray you hold the fort tight until we return."

Ratcliffe waved in farewell, and Smith climbed into the shallop where his men waited. He nodded to the oarsmen, who set the shallop on its way eastward toward the sea. The York and the James Rivers, known to the Indians as the Pamunkey and the Powhatan, ran nearly parallel to each other until they both flowed into Chesapeake Bay. To reach the esteemed Opechancanough, Smith would take his men to the bay, then row northward to the mouth of the James.

A chill pearl-colored mist hung in the air as the cold air moved over the warmer water, and wildlife stirred in the verdant woods as the shallop slipped past. There was no sound save the soft lap of the oars pulling against calm water and the hum of insects in the woods.

Smith hummed a hymn to fill the quiet as his eyes scanned for movements in the forest ahead. In Virginia, where life and death daily hung in the balance, a man did not take peace and safety for granted.

▼▲▼▲▼ They had traveled two days up the James river when Smith spied a sandy clearing where several Indian canoes had been beached. He sighed in relief at the sight, for only about an hour of daylight remained and he did not want to keep his men on the water overnight.

"We will land here," Smith called to the oarsmen as he pointed toward the spot. "Opechancanough's village is not far from the water. So pray, good fellows, that we find the village before night falls. I'd rather spend the night by the chief's hospitable fire than on the damp ground."

The men shouted their agreement and splashed out of the shallop. After gathering what provisions they could carry on their backs, they thrust pistols into their belts and each man shouldered his musket. When all were ready, Smith proceeded to move down the trail that led away from the water.

The wood vibrated softly with wildlife as they pressed forward along a path that pointed a curving finger through the trees. Smith felt a thin, cold blade of foreboding slice into his heart as he led the way. Why? He had met Opechancanough before and had come to believe that he was a pretentious fool; surely this occasion would be no different.

*But,* an inner voice warned, *last time you traveled with a large company engaged in peaceful trade. Now you are determined to take this man's corn, whether by trade or force.*

They traveled for the space of half an hour through the gray bones of bare trees. The trail that had been clear at the river's edge had vanished beneath the carpet of dead leaves that crackled beneath their tramping footsteps. Above the men, the sun began her relentless slide into the west. Smith paused to consult the compass he carried in his pocket. "We must make camp soon," he said, peering through the gathering darkness. "Any man who spies a palisade, make it known."

"I thought you said you've been here afore," John Clemens said, frowning as he pushed past Smith. "Just where is this poxy chief's village? Just when I thought we might get a bit of hot supper—"

Without warning, an arrow whistled through the air and lodged in Clemens's breast. The man fell back without a sound, his complaining stopped as suddenly as if someone had turned a valve in his chest.

"Take cover!" Smith yelled, flinging himself to the ground. "Find the enemy!"

While the English fumbled for their pistols and muskets, Smith cursed the falling shadows, for it was impossible to see where the enemy had situated himself. While the others aimed at nothing and fired uselessly at the leafless trees, a rain of arrows fell upon them as if from nowhere. Smith knew from the muted cries of pain behind him that several of the arrows had found their targets.

Scarcely daring to breathe, Smith crouched behind a wide oak. Arrows whistled overhead, then the sounds of struggle ceased. "Who is with me?" he whispered hoarsely over his shoulder. "Who still lives?"

The roar of absolute silence greeted him; even the wildlife had fled. Risking a single unguarded moment, Smith turned to look behind him. All six of his companions lay dead on the ground, arrows protruding from their chests, giving them the appearance of grotesque pincushions. He swore softly. At any moment the savages would come forward to gather their trophies of English heads, and yet he still lived, albeit with a musket that would fire only one shot—and that only if he was lucky. The gunpowder in the horn at his belt was damp from the river's humidity and probably unfit for use.

He flattened his back along the bark of the oak as he pulled his sword from its sheath. Let them come. He'd take two, maybe three, but he would not be dispatched to heaven without sending some of the murderous savages to the grave.

A breeze whispered silkenly through the cold woods, and

from somewhere in the distance a bird trilled a brief song as it settled down to roost. Smith gritted his teeth to keep them from chattering as he waited. A wild and improbable thought skittered through his brain: In the court of King James, men and women might pass this hour eating on golden plates or devouring the latest gossip, yet in His Majesty's Virginia, this same hour would bring him face-to-face with savage death.

After a moment that seemed woven of eternity, a twig snapped and fallen leaves whispered under stealthy feet as the attackers approached. Smith shivered with a cold that was not from the air and felt sweat bead on his forehead and under his arms. He had faced certain death thrice before and won. If God was merciful, he would do so again.

He waited until he could smell the ammoniac odor of sweat before he whirled to attack, and his sword cleanly cut the throat of the first surprised savage it encountered. The second warrior, too, fell before he could even lift his battle-ax, but though Smith labored mightily and fought with the skill of a fencing master, he was no match for the company that surrounded him in the wood.

Within moments, he reeled to face the dozen painted warriors who circled him. He watched as one pulled a loaded bowstring to his cheek. A sword was no match for a distant arrow, and in a flash of comprehension, Smith flung his sword away and laced his fingers atop his head.

He waited grimly.

The archer paused and the other savages studied him warily, doubtless afraid of some superior weapon on his person. Smith haltingly announced in the Algonquin tongue that he was their prisoner. Over and over he repeated the message until finally a tall brave with a stream of feathers woven into his hair stepped forward. With an expression as hard as granite, he wrenched Smith's hands from his head and bound them firmly. Another warrior pressed a spear to Smith's back.

Despite the language barrier, John Smith did not need to be told that his life now rested in the hands of their chief.

▼▲▼▲▼ The village of Opechancanough teemed with life. Women and children stood around cooking fires as they prepared the evening meal, and warriors who had not been involved in the ambush sat in front of their huts, their eyes strangely veiled as John Smith was brought in to face the chief.

The conquering heroes sang and shouted in victory as they carried the heads of their vanquished enemies and prodded Smith forward into the camp. The bizarre parade stopped at one of the grass huts, and after a moment, the esteemed werowance himself came out. This brother of Powhatan stood tall and carried himself like royalty despite the lack of ornamentation upon his person. He wore only a breechcloth, like his warriors, and a simple mantle of fur hung over his shoulders. Of all the Indians who stared now at Smith, only the chief's face was undisguised by war paint, and an aloof strength lay about his features. Unlike Powhatan, Opechancanough wore his hair long and tied into a long hank that fell over one shoulder. A fine white scar lay upon his taut face, and the arms that emerged from under the mantle bulged with muscle.

But Opechancanough's gaze held Smith's attention most. The chief's dark eyes seemed wary—even haunted—and for a moment Smith thought he glimpsed a fine intelligence. Then the eyes shifted into a blank stare and Smith had the eerie feeling that he stood before a statue not unlike one of the carved images he had seen gazing impassively over the bodies of dead Indian chiefs.

Smith searched his memory for words in the Algonquin language. He had practiced a little in England, for many terms and phrases had been published in the writings of Thomas Hariot and other explorers of Virginia, but in his desperation he could not recall a single word. Angry, violent men he could face with unreasonable courage, but before this inscrutable chief he felt his energy and intellect atrophy.

Of a sudden he remembered the Indians' fascination with trinkets. He held his bound hands aloft, his eyes begging for assistance, and the chief shifted his gaze to a warrior and nodded almost imperceptibly. A sharpened stone rent the bonds in a forceful stroke, and Smith nodded his thanks to the chief. If bravery and force would not save his life, perhaps a glib tongue and sleight of hand could.

In a quicksilver gesture, he pulled his pocket compass from his doublet and held it aloft on his palm. The warriors of the circle leaned forward, fascination shining on their faces. Only Opechancanough remained impassive.

"The arrow points always to the north," Smith said, smiling as he indicated north with his arm. He turned toward the setting sun. "West, sunset, yet the needle points north. East, sunrise, but the needle—" he tapped the glass covering of the compass— "will always point north."

He held the compass up again and knelt on one knee before the chief. "It is my gift to you, Opechancanough."

He waited for what seemed an interminable moment as the chief stared downward at him. Finally Opechancanough lifted the compass from Smith's hand and gave it to a warrior. Muttering a brief command, he pointed toward the entryway of the palisade. The circle of warriors closed in upon Smith, bound his hands with fresh ties, and a spear once again pressed against his back. The warriors led Smith out of the village, but whether to freedom or to death he could not tell.

▼▲▼▲▼ Opechancanough watched the procession leave with mixed feelings. He should have killed the Englishman for displaying a compass as if a silly toy would fascinate a chief into submission. Did all clothed men think the Indians stupid? That young Englishman had never considered that he might be facing a man of superior intelligence and strength, one who had lived more years and discovered more knowledge than his arrogant, youthful mind dreamed possible.

As Don Luis of the Spanish, Opechancanough had worked with compasses, sextants, and ships' maps. He knew how to find his way in any circumstance, how to plot the oceans, how to tra-

verse the wilderness. He knew about the English and the Spanish and the enmity betwixt the nations, and it was only because
he devoutly hated the Spanish that he had allowed this Englishman to live at all.

Opechancanough's eyes darkened. Powhatan, naive king of
the tribe, would be fascinated by this intrepid fool. He would
delight in the compass, exclaim over the Englishman's bright uniform, and marvel at the man's curly beard. And then, because
the Englishman had killed two warriors in the woods, Powhatan
would order the man's execution. And if other Englishmen later
objected, the blame would rest firmly on Powhatan's head.

Opechancanough was not willing to risk the future on one
solitary, brash Englishman.

▼▲▼▲▼ Scouts brought news of the stranger's
approach long before Opechancanough's warriors thrust Smith
through the palisade opening into Powhatan's village at
Weromacomico. The warriors had marched the English stranger
through the night, and though the Indian warriors were as stern
as stone, the clothed man's face was stained with fatigue.

Though only four years old, Gilda had learned much in her
six months with the Powhatan and knew what was coming. She
reached up for Pocahontas's comforting hand when the pale
stranger was thrust forward to kneel at Powhatan's feet. When
he rose before Powhatan, he seemed a remote, majestic figure in
the most splendid boots Gilda had ever seen. The stranger wore
a red coat and breeches of a matching fabric, and an empty
swordbelt hung from his slender waist. His face and head were
covered in thick, curly hair the color of a fox's fur, and a memory
stirred in Gilda's heart. Fallon's hair had been nearly that color;
her mama and papa had been as pale as this man.

"Who is he, Sister?" Gilda whispered to Pocahontas, but the
older girl's eyes were transfixed on the scene and she did not
respond. Powhatan demanded answers from the warriors who

had brought the stranger; they answered abruptly with violent gestures.

"He has killed two of my uncle's warriors," Pocahontas whispered, inclining her head toward Gilda. "Opechancanough says he must die."

The pale man then brought forth a round, shiny object from his coat and proceeded to demonstrate its uses to the great chief. Powhatan watched with undisguised interest, then took the object from the stranger's hand. And because no Indian ever accepted a gift without giving something in return, Gilda heard the great chief order that the prisoner was to be fed, washed, and warmed.

The chief and the stranger disappeared into the chief's hut, and Pocahontas squeezed Gilda's hand. "Isn't it exciting?" she asked, bending down to Gilda's level. "A clothed man here in our village!"

"They have come before," Gilda answered, remembering the parties of men who had come in previous months to trade with the chief.

"Yes, but this one comes alone," Pocahontas answered, her eyes dancing. "And this one is young and handsome. Have you ever seen a man with curled hair on his face?"

Gilda was about to answer that, yes, she had, but Pocahontas sped away toward her father's hut, lost in a world of her own imagining.

▼▲▼▲▼ In the great chief's hut John Smith ate the best meal he had tasted in months and nodded gratefully as one of the chief's wives draped him in a heavy mantle of furs. An interpreter had been found, a savage who had spent some months in the company of Englishmen, though he would not say where, and Powhatan asked searching and pointed questions about the presence and intentions of the English in the land between the two rivers, the territory of the Powhatan.

Fearing the chief's anger and future intent, Smith hurriedly

fabricated a series of lies. Through the interpreter he told
Powhatan that he had wandered into Powhatan territory solely
to flee Spanish pursuers, but from the darkly suspicious squint
of Powhatan's eyes he knew the chief did not believe the unfolding story. Smith felt his heart sink. A plague on those infernal
Indian scouts! Like eyes in the trees, they saw everything that
went on in the forest. Their ears were tuned to catch even whispers on the wind, and they reported all to their chiefs.

When Smith had finished his ridiculous tale, Powhatan folded
his arms. His eyes stirred slightly with anger and rested on his
prisoner briefly, then the chief turned to his conjuror and gave an
abrupt order.

The interpreter smiled at Smith. "The chief says you will die
when the sun rises on the morrow," he said, nodding as pleasantly as if the chief had ordered a cup of tea.

Two warriors stood to escort Smith from the chief's hut, and
Powhatan did not look at him again.

Gilda felt someone shaking her shoulder in the dim hour before dawn. "Wake up, small one. We must hurry!"

"Why?" Gilda murmured, sitting up. Pocahontas knelt beside her, a desperate look on her face.

"They will kill the bearded man when the sun rises. The holy men are already outside to sing the man's death song."

Gilda looked toward the doorway of their hut. Life did stir outside by the central fire; drums beat softly in time to the holy men's chanting.

The morning air was sharp and cold, and though Gilda wanted nothing more than to crawl back under her fur to sleep, Pocahontas would not let her rest. "Up, little sister, for we must see this thing! Do you think the clothed men really have the power of life and death? I have heard that they are gods, that they cannot be killed."

"They can be killed," Gilda answered, certainty in her voice.

Pocahontas stared at her for a moment, then caught Gilda's hands and pulled her from the pile of furs and out into the clearing. The village fire beckoned warmly as it danced in the wind with whoofs and puffs and streams of sparks that whirled off into the darkness of early morning. Bleary-eyed warriors danced slowly around the fire, still dazed with sleep, but Powhatan sat with his arms resting on his knees, his eyes intent upon the dancing flames. His conjuror stood at his left hand, his eyes closed as he earnestly murmured a chant in his nasal voice, and from a nearby hut the prisoner was led forth, his pale face streaked with sweat even in the cool of December.

The pale man's gaze swept the assembled group. For a

moment Gilda thought his eyes rested upon her with a shock of surprise, but then a pair of warriors yanked on the strings that bound his arms and forced him to kneel before a large stone upon the ground. Four warriors drew near to hold the prisoner with the points of their spears. Other warriors, armed with feathered and painted war clubs, danced around the fire and awaited the conjuror's orders.

The conjuror continued his chanting as the dancers worked themselves into an increasing frenzy, and more women and children spilled from their huts to witness the execution. One of the chief's wives, a broad woman, stepped in front of Pocahontas and Gilda. Agitated, Pocahontas yanked on Gilda's arm and led her to another opening in the circle where they could see without obstruction.

Gilda watched the dancers and tugged on Pocahontas's leather skirt to ask a question, but the older girl had fixed her attention on the prisoner. Gilda studied her friend's soft and limpid eyes, seeing there the same affection the older girl had shown a wild rabbit she had freed from a snare the day before.

Sweat poured from the dancing warriors' nearly naked bodies as their hysteria grew, and rivulets of water ran over their shoulders and down their faces. The red paint they had applied to their chests and shoulders glistened like blood in the firelight, and their delirium had reached a frantic pace by the time the first streaks of daylight appeared in the east.

Suddenly, abruptly, the conjuror ceased his chant and looked toward Powhatan. Panting with exertion and anticipation, the warriors around the fire stopped dancing and tightened their grips around their war clubs. The Englishman, who lay with his head on the stone, shifted his weight slightly as his eyes closed in resignation.

Powhatan lifted his hand, and every eye turned to face the condemned prisoner. But before the chief could lower his hand, Pocahontas broke free of Gilda's grip and flew over the sand toward the Englishman.

"Please, mighty father!" she cried, throwing her arms over the bearded stranger as she knelt by his side, "for my sake, spare this man!"

The prisoner's eyes flew open at her touch, and a smile of intense gratitude flooded his face at the sight of the girl by his side. Powhatan frowned and stood. He beheld the prisoner and his beloved daughter for a moment, and Gilda held her breath, unsure of what the chief might do. In the time she'd been at Weromacomico she had never seen Powhatan deny Pocahontas anything, but never before had she flown in the face of his order.

Powhatan's mouth gentled. "For you, little daughter, my own Pocahontas, it shall be done," he said, nodding slowly. "Let all know that the clothed man is hers. He is forever in her debt."

The serpent of jealousy struck at Gilda's heart as she watched Pocahontas lift the condemned man to his feet. The older girl gazed adoringly at the Englishman, and Gilda knew Pocahontas had found a new pet.

▼▲▼▲▼ After his initial amazement at the unbelievable turn of events, John Smith thanked God for yet another divine rescue and began to ingratiate himself with his Indian hosts. It was clear that the chief's young daughter considered him some sort of living toy, and for a few days he did everything she bid him to do: He helped her carry water, allowed her to comb his hair and beard, even cavorted with the other warriors around the fire for her entertainment. Indeed, he had been halfway through some strange ceremony of her choosing when he realized that she had arranged for Powhatan to make him an honorary member of the tribe. He went along with the ritual gladly, for peace with this mighty chief would be necessary if an English outpost was to survive in Virginia.

And so he drank bitter tea, ate pungent, unidentified meat, danced with the holy men and warriors, and allowed them to cut his hand and mingle their blood with his own. He shed his doublet and breeches and donned a breechcloth and fur mantle, and soon he was indistinguishable from his savage hosts but for his still-pale skin and the thick hair on his face and body.

While he lived among the tribe, he studied them carefully and found their lives practical, useful, primitive, and logical. They lived as a large family with the chief serving as the father figure; children ran freely from one woman to another as if all filled the role of mother. Indeed, the chief alone had so many wives and children it was impossible to tell which child had been birthed by which woman. But among the children there was one oddity: the little blue-eyed girl they called Numees.

Smith supposed Numees was Pocahontas's sister, for she lived in the older girl's shadow and shared the sharp, clear features and delicate feminine charms of the chief's daughter. Her skin was as golden as sunlight on an autumn day, her lashes dark half-moons against her cheek, her hair plaited in the same intricate pattern as Pocahontas's. On the rare occasions when the little girl laughed, she did so in the same vocal tones as her elder sister—but from where did she inherit those blue eyes?

Smith paused one night to ask Powhatan about the child, but the chief murmured only that the girl was Kitchi's daughter and Pocahontas's niece. Though Smith strongly suspected that the child had English blood in her veins, he was not certain of the fact until the night when he happened to warn the child away from the fire.

It was the twenty-fifth of December, Christmas, and a bitterly cold night. After supper, oblivious to the Christian holiday, the savage children had danced around the fire in a frenzied effort as much to keep warm, Smith supposed, as to celebrate the coming of winter. Young Numees did not seem to know the dances as well as the other children, and she had difficulty knowing when to cut in and out of the circle, so it was no wonder that she wandered too close to the fire and accidentally ignited the long streamers of the cornhusk doll she carried in her hands. Instinctively, Smith yelled, "Fire!" The child dropped the doll immediately, and her face flushed as if she had done something wrong.

A thread of suspicion wound itself around Smith's awareness

in that moment, and he edged into the lines of dancing children until he was close enough to reach out and grab Numees's arm.

She jerked in alarm at his touch, but said nothing when he knelt down to talk to her. "Are you all right?" he asked in English. He stared into those icy blue eyes. "Were you burned?"

She stood like a deer transfixed by torchlight, but gave no sign of understanding him. Sighing, Smith drew his knees to his chest and wrapped his arms around them. "It's Christmas, you know," he said, lowering his voice so that only Numees could hear him. "Oh, how I remember the songs of Christmas. Do you know them? There's one I favor—" He cleared his throat and began to sing: "Good Christian men, rejoice with heart and soul and voice. . . ." He paused. The little girl's eyes had half closed, and she hummed along with him as he continued the verse. "Give ye heed to what we say: news, news, Jesus Christ is born today. Ox and ass before him bow and . . ." He paused and let her finish.

"He is in the manger now—" She broke off and her eyes flew open as though she had betrayed a secret, but Smith smiled and reached for her hands.

"Do not fear, child," he whispered. "So you do know how to speak English?"

Stiff with fear, she shook her head.

He smiled. "Ah, so you don't understand a word of what I'm saying. Came you from the English village of Roanoke?"

She shook her head again.

"It's no matter," he said, warming her cold hands in his. "Your mama and papa, are they near this place?"

Again, the wordless head shaking.

"Dead, then?"

She nodded slowly.

"And you're alone here?"

Her eyes filled with tears, and, afraid she would cry out, Smith smiled in an effort to calm her. "I see you have a friend in Pocahontas. She is my friend, too, Numees, and I will not hurt you. For we are alike, you see; we both speak English and we both have blue eyes, though mine are not so pretty as yours."

For a moment she smiled, then the guarded expression fell over her face again. Smith glanced across the fire and saw that Powhatan watched them carefully.

He dropped her hands. "You must stay close to Pocahontas, Numees, because the chief loves her very much and she loves you. If I come again to visit, you and I will talk in English, but you should not speak it to anyone else in this place. Do you understand?"

She stared at the ground as if she hadn't heard him.

"Do you understand, Numees?" he repeated.

"My name is Gilda," she said suddenly, in startlingly clear English. "My mama and papa gave me that name."

And before he could question her further, she flew away to join the other dancing children.

*Gilda.* The memory hit him with the force of lighting. The boy, Fallon, had told him of a girl with blue eyes who had escaped with him from Ocanahonan. This, then, was the child the boy had been so anxious to protect.

Smith shifted uneasily as he recalled his promise that he would find the girl and send her to join Fallon in England. He had never dreamed he'd actually find her! He had only made the promise to get the boy safely away as soon as possible. His eyes rested again on Gilda as she danced. Clearly, it was a promise he could not keep. Removing the girl from Powhatan's camp would of certain be seen as an act of treachery. He would be fortunate to depart with his own life.

Better to leave the child in Powhatan's care. She behaved like a savage; why should she not spend her life as one? And if by some quirk of fate he should ever happen to encounter Fallon Bailie again, it would be an easy enough matter to reply that searching for one girl in the wilderness was well nigh equivalent to searching for the proverbial needle in a haystack.

▼▲▼▲▼ When John Smith sensed that his young guardian had begun to tire of his company, he approached her father and asked for permission to return to his home at Jamestown.

The chief's eyes shone bright and bemused over the low fire in his hut. "We had wondered how long you would remain," the interpreter explained. "A grown man is not a proper companion for a young girl, even one as playful as our Pocahontas."

"She is a delight, and you're a lucky father," Smith answered, bowing gravely to the chief. "And God has used her to make peace betwixt our peoples. But I must return to my fort, for my friends have need of me. And, of course, for your hospitality and the gifts you have given me—" he pointed to the fur mantle on his back—"I will arrange to have gifts sent to you, great chief. What can I send from our city?"

Powhatan smiled in pleasure when he understood the translated message, and after a moment of thought the chief relayed his wishes. The interpreter turned to Smith. "The chief wishes for a grindstone and two cannons," he said. "Those gifts, and no others, will do. We do not want beads or copper pots or ax heads."

"Very well." Smith smiled and nodded. "It shall be as you say. But there is one mystery, great chief, my people want to understand. It concerns a colony of clothed people like myself, who once lived at Roanoke. Have you knowledge of them?"

Something stirred in the chief's dark eyes, then a veil passed before them. Smith automatically braced himself for the lie that would follow. It was obvious enough that the chief had been responsible for the murder of the English at Ocanahonan. The boy, Fallon, had told the story in irrefutable details, and the blue-eyed child in the chief's village bore mute testimony to the existence of English in these parts. In addition, Smith had seen copper tools and broken bits of ironwork in Powhatan's village that could never have come from an Indian forge. Only the English were far advanced enough in metallurgy to create such items.

"We know of the clothed people," Powhatan said after casting a wary look at his brother, Opechancanough, who had come to visit and sat silently in the circle of elders. "There are two groups, one living well to the south at a place called Ocanahonan, and another living far to the north among the Iroquois. Many summers ago, clothed men in great ships captured several of our warriors and forced them to go across the great sea."

Smith held up his hands in a gesture of innocence. "I have not taken your warriors, great chief. But my king has asked that I inquire about the people who left Roanoke."

Powhatan nodded vaguely and the translator replied for him. "We know nothing of them, John Smith."

▼▲▼▲▼ The moon had gone through a complete cycle in the time the Englishman John Smith stayed with Powhatan's people, and as Gilda watched him walk through the opening of the palisade to return to his fort, she heard Pocahontas sniff. Turning to the older girl, who sat on a log by the fire, she saw that Pocahontas's cheeks were wet.

"Why do you cry?" Gilda asked, unable to understand. "You said you were ready for him to go."

"Have you never been in love, little sister?" Pocahontas asked, looking up as tears spangled her lashes. She smiled sadly and shook her head. "Of course not, you are too young. But I have thought much about it. And I do not want to love an Indian warrior like these around me." She lifted her chin proudly. "I want to marry a man of the clothed people. An Englishman."

Gilda frowned. "You would marry John Smith?"

Pocahontas sighed. "Not him, he's too old. But he said there are many men in Jamestown, the place where he lives. The men there have no wives and they all have bearded faces and speak in the English tongue. They are strong and have sharp swords and guns of thunder—" She broke off abruptly and smiled at Gilda. "How can I make you understand? Have you thought, little sister, about the man you will someday marry? Of all the boys in our village, which would you like to be your husband?"

Gilda sat on the log beside Pocahontas and looked around. Several boys scampered near the fire playing a game with a ball and sticks, but none of them appealed to her.

She looked up at Pocahontas. "I will marry Fallon when I am old," she said. "Mama told him to watch over me and he said he would. When it is time, he will come back for me and we will be married."

Pocahontas chewed slowly on her lower lip. "Fallon? The boy with red hair who came to the village with you?"

Gilda nodded, and Pocahontas placed her hand upon Gilda's head. "He will not come back for you, little one," she said, her voice heavy with regret. "The elders decided that he should die. The warrior who took him away came back into the village that day with a bloody spear."

"Fallon is dead?" Confused thoughts whirled inside Gilda's head. "Where is he?"

Pocahontas draped her arm about Gilda's shoulder and drew her close. "He is on the Other Side. He cannot be your husband, nor can the other boy who came with you. So you must marry one of our tribe, or, if the gods smile upon you, one of the clothed men."

Pocahontas sighed and dreamily rested her head upon Gilda's, and Gilda remained uncomfortably still as she struggled to make sense of what she had just learned. Dead. Mama and Papa, dead. Fallon, dead. The silent, bleeding heads the warriors brought back from battle, dead. Even Noshi?

How could everyone be dead?

When Pocahontas finally released her, Gilda slipped from the log and sprinted out of the village.

▼▲▼▲▼ Opechancanough watched the Englishman's departure with a great deal of interest. He could not deny that the red-bearded man possessed both luck and courage, for he had outwitted death in the forest and in Powhatan's village. The man was a skilled negotiator, too, for during his weeks at

Weromacomico he had managed to charm himself into Powhatan's good graces. Even now his brother's face was wreathed in a smile of joyful anticipation of the gifts that would soon be coming from the English.

Opechancanough said nothing to his brother, but slipped out of the palisade to shadow the party of warriors who would escort Smith downstream to Jamestown. Smith said little as he climbed into a canoe in the midst of the company, and Opechancanough imagined the man was trying to organize his thoughts and devise an explanation for reappearing in Indian dress after a month in the wilderness. A twisted smile crawled to his lips. Most of all, the Englishman would have a difficult time explaining why he returned home alone while six of his fellows rotted in the woods.

Opechancanough lingered in the shadows until the canoes were well away, then he emerged and knelt at the water's edge to drink. His body went rigid when the strangely musical tones of a child's voice shattered the stillness of the afternoon. Upstream, alone on a rock, the strange blue-eyed Numees sat with her small feet dangling in the water. She spoke to the air, and Opechancanough pressed closer to hear.

"Dear Lord and Father God," the child said, lifting her voice and heart to an unseen spirit, "you have taken my mama and papa and Fallon and Noshi. But they told me you would always take care of me. Did they tell me a lie, God? If you—"

"Be silent!" Opechancanough stepped from behind the tree where he had been eavesdropping and grunted in satisfaction when the child's head snapped around and her jaw dropped in surprise. "What god hears a child?"

The girl's face went blank for a moment, then her eyes lit and she began to speak: "I believe in God the Father, who has made me and all the world."

Opechancanough felt as though she'd hit him in the stomach. How could a mere child speak so confidently of these things? "Silence!" he barked, barely able to control his fury. "You will not pray to the god of the clothed men. He does not hear your prayers and he will not answer you."

"But Mama and Fallon said he would—"

"Did he hear your mama and the boy called Fallon?" Opechancanough demanded. "No! For they are dead. If I were to hit you now—" he stepped forward and pulled back his hand as the child flinched—"would your god hear and help you?"

She sat mute before his flashing anger, and Opechancanough clenched his fist to calm the storm of hate that had risen in his heart. "Once I prayed to this god, too, the God of Jesus the Christ," he said, his voice a thin whisper over the sound of the river's flow. "Once I gave my allegiance and my power to the priests of the clothed men's God, and they cursed my father's lands. So I turned again to the gods of my fathers, the spirits of the earth and woods, of rain and the sun."

He lowered his hand and folded his arms, and the girl's lower lip trembled in apparent relief. "If you wish to remain with the Powhatan, you will not pray to the god of the clothed men again. He will not hear you."

He waited until she lowered her head in submissive defeat, then he melted away into the woods and left her to ponder his words.

On the second day of the new year, 1608, Smith entered the fort at Jamestown amid relieved cheers from his fellow colonists. He smiled good-naturedly at his comrades' comments about his savage garb, but kept a serious face before the Indians. They would not understand the jokes that were flying about Smith's lack of proper modesty.

"We had supposed you dead," John Ratcliffe called from the doorway of his headquarters, his surprise at Smith's appearance with an entourage of Powhatan warriors evident upon his face. "What became of the men with you?"

"I alone survived the attack on the trail," Smith said, noticing that Ratcliffe's eyes narrowed in speculation. "But I have secured a peace with Powhatan and have promised the chief a grindstone and two cannons in exchange for my freedom."

"Two cannons!" Ratcliffe said, blazing up at him. "I would as lief surrender the fort! Have you gone mad?"

"Never fear," Smith answered, winking at Ratcliffe. He turned toward his Indian guides and pointed to the demiculverins mounted atop each of the three points of the fort. The entire company of warriors climbed ladders and surrounded the cannons as if they expected to carry them off, but found they could not budge the heavy armaments.

"I don't believe they'll be taking the cannons," Smith said with a wry smile, turning to his president. "They have found them somewhat heavy." Smith lowered his voice. "They will be content with the grindstone and a few trinkets. Send them home with full

bellies and garments for their backs, and the peace will be preserved."

Ratcliffe sighed in resignation, then gave the order.

▼▲▼▲▼ By January the number of men at Jamestown
had dwindled to less than forty, but those forty had the hearty
appetites of recovering invalids. They pointed long fingers of
accusation when Smith arrived—well fed, healthy, and alone—
from the wilderness. Many demanded Smith's execution, holding him personally responsible for the deaths of the six men he
had taken into the woods, but Smith managed to forestall his
hanging by promising that he would bring food to the hungry
colony if given a proper opportunity.

Confident now of his position among the English and the Indians, he took chances that certainly would have led to his death
had he attempted them a month earlier. It was with no hesitation
whatsoever that he directed a new company of men to journey
up the James River to trade with Opechancanough, the silent
chief who would not act without his brother's approval.

*He will dare not touch us now,* Smith thought, confident of
Powhatan's loyalty, *and the stored corn I saw in his village will pay
for the lives lost at the hands of his murdering warriors.*

When Smith at last stood before the towering Opechancanough, he offered a trade: Ten tons of the Indians' plentiful
corn for two copper pots, but the werowance merely shook his
head, unwilling to do business. From behind him, Smith heard
the silvery swish of steel and knew that his men had drawn their
swords. In response, Opechancanough's warriors tightened the
circle around the intruders, their eyes burning hotly as they
glared at the invaders.

Smith's temper flared in the new light of his confidence. With
his right hand upon the hilt of his pistol, he reached forward
with his left and yanked on the hank of dark hair that hung over
the werowance's shoulder. Dragging the chief forward through
the crowd of warriors to the opening of the palisade, Smith

pointed toward the river trail. "You will fill our boats with twenty tons of corn," Smith said, clearly enunciating his rehearsed demand in the Indian tongue. He glared up at Opechancanough as the nose of his pistol kissed the skin over the chief's heart, "or I will promptly load my ship with your dead carcasses."

A cold wind blew past the pair with soft moans, then Opechancanough gave a curt order to his warriors. Abruptly, the savage circle broke and began to move toward their storehouses, and Smith pulled his pistol from the chest of the werowance and settled it into his belt with a self-satisfied sigh. Now that he and Powhatan were allies, no one would dare stand against him.

▼▲▼▲▼ Opechancanough coiled himself into the flickering shadows of sunset as the English ships slipped away from the riverbank. The muscles in his face were set in a mask of rage; not even his bravest warrior had dared to approach since the Englishman had manhandled and threatened the chief. The rage in him was a living thing, but like all living things it had to be tamed, trained, and bidden to wait. The Englishman had dared to touch him, to press the iron gun against his flesh. One day, Opechancanough vowed silently, that man's flesh would be torn, and his nation would be devoured by the Indian he had so carelessly humiliated.

▼▲▼▲▼ Soon after Smith's return from the wilderness, the settlers lifted praise and thanks to God, for Captain Newport arrived with replenishments of supplies and additional settlers. The newly established peace between the English and the Indians flourished, and a brisk trade developed between the two peoples, which quickly escalated the price of corn. Trouble broke out on occasion as the Indians, accustomed to community property, "picked up" items belonging to the English. On one such occasion, four warriors from Powhatan's tribe were detained by

John Smith as hostages until a litany of stolen items had been returned. In a shrewd move, Powhatan sent Pocahontas downriver to act as ambassador to the English. The thoroughly charmed English welcomed the dancing, cartwheel-turning youth and forgave their grievances with the savages.

Throughout another long year the colonists worked and sweated out a living. In September 1608, the council formally elected John Smith president of Jamestown. The disgruntled John Ratcliffe returned to England.

Smith immediately made safety his priority. He gave orders to extend and reinforce the rough fortification surrounding the one-acre city. The original triangular enclosure grew into a five-sided fort for greater defensive strength. Smith organized a weekly military parade to train the men under his command, and his captains regularly sent out trading and fishing expeditions to deal with the ever-present threat of famine.

Smith knew that his air of command, his occasional flashes of temper, and the fact that he was a plebeian giving orders to the gentry accounted for much bitterness in his camp, but popularity was a luxury he could ill afford. During the autumn of his term of office, Captain Newport arrived from England with more settlers—including Dutchmen and Poles to manufacture naval stores—but the planners had not sent enough food to feed the newcomers. Once again Newport carried letters containing orders from the London Company that Smith's men should work to find gold, Raleigh's lost colony, and a passage to the great South Seas. In addition, Newport carried a copper crown with which Smith was to commission Powhatan as a sovereign in alliance with James I of England.

Powhatan refused to be flattered by King James's recognition. He stoutly refused to come to Jamestown for the inaugural ceremony, so a deputation headed by Captain Newport traveled to Weromacomico, entered the chief's dwelling, and forcibly placed the copper crown on his head. Powhatan, chief of more tribes than any werowance before or since, resolutely refused to kneel for the ceremony.

Smith was grateful for any excuse to visit Weromacomico, however, because he honestly enjoyed visiting Pocahontas and Numees. He had come to look upon the older girl as a heaven-sent angel in disguise and once wrote to England that she was the "nonpareil of Powhatan's kingdom." She had grown into a lovely young woman of fidelity and courage, and with her—and her alone—he made a determined effort to be kind and solicitous.

Numees, on the other hand, fascinated him as an experiment in English-Indian relations. At five years of age, the girl was an enigma, as thoughtful and eager to please as the daintiest English maiden, but as fiercely devoted to savage ideals and customs as the most intense warrior. She was vulnerable to fits of depression, which seemed odd in such a young child. During these spells of melancholy, she spoke not a word. Rather, she would brood quietly, her hand clasped around a talisman that hung from a strip of leather about her neck. And yet, even with these dark moods, Smith saw that the child grew more lovely with every passing day, with blue eyes as wide and fair as those that gleamed brown in Pocahontas's eager face.

Smith was pleased when Pocahontas expressed an interest in learning to speak "the clothed man's tongue." Knowing how Powhatan's resentment could flare into sudden fury, Smith cautioned both girls not to speak English before the chief. Numees, who spoke fluently and with a natural rhythm, hesitated to speak English, while Pocahontas, who stumbled over unfamiliar sounds and syntax, yearned to be able to converse as freely in Smith's native tongue as he now did in hers.

Pocahontas surprised him one day with the reason for her desire to speak English. "I will marry an Englishman," she said, the words strangely stilted in her voice. "I will marry you, John Smith."

"Oh no, Princess," he said, laughing as he tore his eyes away from her loving gaze. "I will marry no woman, for I am wedded to Virginia and the work I do." His eyes narrowed in thought as he considered her outspoken proposal. Maybe a marriage betwixt the chief's daughter and an Englishman might cement the peace. "I would not discourage you completely, though," he went on, giving her a paternal smile. "There are many English-men in Jamestown who would love to be your husband, and many others will soon come. Trust in God, my dear, and let me see what I can do." He patted her hand. "Someday, Princess, you will marry. Until then, be patient and enjoy the days of your youth. And keep Numees safe, for she represents all that you might accomplish in such a marriage."

Pocahontas nodded slowly and solemnly, but there was a look in her eyes that left John Smith wondering if she truly under-stood what he meant.

▼▲▼▲▼ Smith declared the arrival of four ships in the summer of 1609 a mixed blessing. They brought relief supplies and additional able-bodied colonists to bolster the sagging strength of the men at Jamestown, but among the passengers were John Ratcliffe and Gabriel Archer, by now Smith's ardent enemies.

The two malcontents bred such complaining and dissension among the men at Jamestown that by September, Smith chose to lead another excursion into the wilderness. Ostensibly the com-pany went forth to look for additional food supplies, but in real-ity Smith sought to escape the stiflingly hostile atmosphere of the colony he had single-handedly rescued from starvation.

The peace and quiet of river travel soothed him, and Smith let the gentle motion of the boat rock him to sleep. He dreamed he was at Weromacomico, with his head resting in Pocahontas's lap. Her dark eyes were fastened upon his, her gentle fingers stroked his brow and raked his hair, and his limbs loosened and relaxed in her tender embrace.

"You work too hard," she murmured, her voice as light as the breeze caressed his cheek. "Ignore your problems and they will go away."

"You don't understand," he told her, watching his reflection in the brown pools of her eyes. "To overcome is to live. One must not surrender in the struggle—"

A sudden explosion wrenched him from his dream world. A barrel of gunpowder in the boat had accidentally ignited, and Smith smelled the acrid stench of burning flesh before he realized it was his own skin burning. A scream clawed in his throat as he flung himself into the river, and pain seared his consciousness even as the cooling waters passed over him.

The men of the second boat hauled him out of the water, and one look at the face of George Percy, his second in command, told Smith that his days at Jamestown were at an end.

Because the colony had no doctor, Smith was bandaged and placed aboard the first ship sailing for England. He returned to London in 1609, just in time for Christmas.

▼▲▼▲▼ Word of Smith's departure spread swiftly through the Indian camps, and Powhatan and his people braced themselves for an uncertain future. With John Smith gone, who would chart the course for peaceful Indian-English relations?

Pocahontas and Gilda cared nothing about politics; they felt Smith's loss personally. John Smith had been their friend and confidant, and both were grieved beyond words to hear that he had left without saying good-bye.

The morning after they heard the news, Pocahontas took Gilda's hand and led her to the top of a tall cliff overlooking a chasm cut generations before by rushing river water. The water lay twenty feet below them now, quiet and still, and Pocahontas slipped a favorite copper bracelet from her arm and held it above the yawning gorge. "In memory and honor of my friend John Smith," she said, silently letting the bracelet fall. It glinted in the sunlight as it traveled downward, then hit the face of the river with barely a splash.

Wiping tears from her face, Pocahontas turned to Gilda. "Now you must give something," she said, looking at the younger girl. Her eyes went automatically to the leather cord around

Gilda's neck, and Gilda lifted her hand in a protective gesture. "I will give this," she said, taking a beaded headband from her hair. It had taken hours to carve holes in the tiny shells and string them together, but she tossed the headband into the empty space without a thought.

Both girls stood silently and considered the void. "There will never be another Englishman like him," Pocahontas said softly, her voice mournful and quiet. "Already my father is asking if I will marry next year. It is time, but how can I marry when I have given John Smith my heart?"

Annoyed and bewildered that Pocahontas would ask her such difficult questions, Gilda remained silent. What did a six-year-old know of a fourteen-year-old's problems?

But Pocahontas did not expect an answer. After a long time of silence, she took Gilda's hand and led her home.


▼▲▼▲▼ Pocahontas was not the only person to feel John Smith's absence. Without his stern leadership, discipline at the colony of Jamestown grew lax, and the colony encountered its most dismal and harsh winter in 1609 as sickness ran rampant and food supplies were exhausted. As the English grew desperate for food, relations with the Indians deteriorated. One group of thirty hungry colonists on a bartering expedition led by John Ratcliffe was massacred by the savages who refused to submit to English demands.

Threatened by starvation and savages and forced into the Jamestown fort, the remaining weakened settlers were struck by wave after wave of crippling and killing diseases. A few men of strength and daring crawled out through the fort's unguarded gates to catch snakes or dig up roots for food. Those who remained inside the city died in droves and were piled like refuse into common graves. The survivors finally gave in to their desperation—and ate the dead.

Of the five hundred people who lived at Jamestown when

Smith left in September 1609, only sixty-five remained alive six months later.

▼▲▼▲▼ On the twenty-third day of May 1610, relief appeared in the form of two small ships aptly named *Patience* and *Deliverance*. The surviving skeletal colonists cried with joy when Lieutenant Governor Gates anchored at Jamestown, spent two weeks patching his vessels, and then ordered every man aboard.

Abandoning the Jamestown fort in wild glee, the survivors filled the holds of the ships, which set sail for England on the seventh of June.

Lacking a good wind, the ships anchored overnight a few miles downstream in the James River. By the will of God, it would later be said, on the following morning a sail appeared in the distance. Gates waited until contact with the boat was made and learned that three well-equipped ships were en route with the colony's new governor aboard.

This news was met with groans, curses, and great grief. Gates returned the bone-tired survivors to Jamestown, and three days later, Lord de la Warre the new governor, stepped from his ship, knelt, and thanked God that he had come in time to save the colony. Greeting his new subjects with a sermon of thanksgiving, he restored discipline and order and declared that the colony should be run by holy edicts. To ensure that men's thoughts did not stray too far from the God who had thus far preserved them, bells would be rung for prayers at 10:00 A.M. and 4:00 P.M. every day.

"If we are to survive, and I believe it's God's will that we do," Lord de la Warre told his astounded colonists, "we must live according to his holy principles and laws. And as long as I am governor, we will not be forgetting them."

*July 1610*

An odd, volatile feeling filled the Royal Academy for Homeless Orphans one hot morning. Turning in his desk, Fallon cast a quick glance toward Brody. "What is amiss?" he dared to whisper. Master Crompton had abruptly canceled classes at the school, and the headmaster only cut classes short when a student had committed an egregious error that would normally have required lengthy and public correction.

"I know not," Brody answered, his eyes flickering over the other boys in their cramped classroom. He rose and jerked his head toward the shelf where they stored their hornbooks, and Fallon followed, placing his supplies away.

Their tutor, a nervous, pale young man who reminded Fallon of one of the skittish rats he often saw in the hallway, twitched his nose and held up a timid hand. "The master says you are all to return to the dormitory until noon," he said, his eyes darting about the room. "There is to be a guest of some significance at dinner, and the master expects us all to be on our best behavior."

He clapped his hands and the boys rose on cue, then filed out of the room in a single line, not breaking from the formation until they reached the freedom of the upstairs dormitory. Once inside, the liberated boys lapsed into their customary horseplay, but Fallon blocked the pillows that flew toward his head and reclined on his bunk.

At sixteen, he had at last taken his place in the classes for older boys who readied themselves for apprenticeship. He was officially ready for what Master Crompton called "graduation," and as he walked through the school he was faintly conscious of admiring gazes from the younger students. He had grown tall and stood nearly eye-to-eye with Master Crompton himself. Fallon was slim but powerfully built, his sinewy muscles a fortunate result from hours of wrestling in the wild free-for-all before bed, and his hair flamed as red as ever atop his head. In a fit of flattery, Brody once told him that he'd be handsome in a girl's eyes, but Fallon wasn't so sure.

At noontime, one of the tutors knocked on the dormitory door, and the boys fell quickly into line. As they filed into their usual places in the dining hall, Master Crompton took his seat at the sumptuous center table, and a clergyman of obvious high ranking sat across from him. The clergyman said a prayer, louder and longer than usual, and the boys sat to eat. Master Crompton and his esteemed guest spoke in loud voices, the better to impress the students, and Fallon froze over his bowl in total incredulity when he heard the minister utter a familiar name.

"Captain John Smith was presented to His Majesty just the other day," the clergyman was saying. "He looked right fit, especially after that accident in Virginia. Nearly took his leg off, I hear, with an explosion of gunpowder."

"Quite gruesome," Crompton offered, carefully slicing a leg of lamb.

"Indeed," the minister continued, dabbing his lace handkerchief at the corners of his thin mouth. "Welladay, the court is abuzz with news of a letter received from our most pious Lord de la Warre. Seems he arrived at Jamestown just as the entire colony was preparing to leave, and it was only by the grace of God that he found anyone there at all. But all is as it should be, the savages meek and mildly assenting to his will, even the mighty Powhatan, whom Smith had so handily conquered."

Fallon felt his heart slam against his ribs. Though he had been absent from Virginia for years, the mere mention of Powhatan readily evoked the chief's image: the dark eyes weighing him and Gilda and Noshi, the gravelly voice that gave the order to destroy Fallon's home, his parents, his way of life . . .

And John Smith was in England! If this clergyman told the

truth and Smith had conquered Powhatan, then surely the man knew something of Gilda.

Fallon's knuckles whitened around the wooden spoon in his hand. It was folly to even *think* of interrupting a conversation at Crompton's dinner table, but if he did not speak now he would never have the opportunity.

He rose before he had even willed himself to act. "Excuse me, Reverend, sir," he said, his voice ringing loud and clear above the suddenly muted sounds of fifty boys at dinner. "But where might I find this John Smith? He is an old friend, and I must speak to him."

The moment seemed frozen in time and all the players like statues, until Master Crompton rose from the table with a look of disbelief, rage, and frustration upon his blotchy face. "You dare to address our honored guest?" he roared, blinking as if he could not believe the sight that stood before him. "You, Fallon Bailie, have dared to question this reverend minister?"

The question brought a hushed silence to the dining hall. Fallon felt Brody tug frantically on his sleeve, but he crossed his arms and turned his gaze toward the clergyman, who sat with a mouthful of food, too amazed at the turn of events to even chew his dinner.

"I'll ask again, Reverend, sir," Fallon said, nodding in what he hoped was a sign of respect. "Where might I find John Smith?"

The minister's face reddened, then he coughed into his lace napkin. In a fit of pique, Crompton thrust his chair away so that it toppled backward and clattered on the floor as the headmaster swept across the room, his thick hand reaching for Fallon's collar.

"Are you ready to be caned, Fallon Bailie?" Crompton muttered between clenched teeth as his fingers closed around the fabric at Fallon's neck. "You will go to my office and wait there until I come to you."

The headmaster's voice was a jolt of energy that propelled Fallon away from the table and out of the dining hall. He paused at the door for a moment and turned to see Crompton's baleful eyes burning toward him. "Go!" the master roared, and Fallon slunk through the doorway in the heavy silence.

▼▲▼▲▼ The ten lashes on his bare buttocks left Fallon's skin broken and his teeth chattering, but he did not cry out. He would not give Delbert Crompton that pleasure.

The rod broke on the tenth lash, and Crompton threw the mangled cane against the wall. Frustrated, he roared an oath and stomped out of the room. Fallon, who had been standing bent over with his hands on his knees, remained in place, afraid he'd be in for a worse lashing if Crompton returned to find him gone. But after a moment it became clear that the headmaster had gone elsewhere to vent his anger.

Fallon groaned as the coarse fabric of his breeches brushed his stinging, broken skin. He loosely fastened his belt at his waist. He'd sleep on his belly tonight, and he'd never speak to Crompton or one of his pious dinner guests again. But Crompton would have to beat the life out of Fallon to stop him from trying to discover the whereabouts of John Smith. God had at last provided him with a way to know what had happened to Noshi and Gilda, and he would not turn his back on this opportunity.

▼▲▼▲▼ "Brody, has anyone ever broken out of this place?"

Full darkness filled the dormitory, and Fallon lay upon his stomach, his rough sheet rumpled at the foot of his bed. It was too hot to be covered anyway, and even his nightshirt chafed against his tender skin. The room echoed with the deep, regular breathing of sleeping boys, but Fallon knew Brody was still awake. The boy had thrashed in the cot overhead for more than an hour, doubtless upset by what had transpired at dinner.

"Broken out?" Brody peered over the edge of the bed, grinning in reckless excitement. "Faith, now that's an idea! Why don't you just run away? I'll go with you, and Crompton will never hurt you again."

"I can't run away," Fallon said, pounding his pillow in frustration. "If I run away, John Smith won't know where to find me."

"The same John Smith you asked about at dinner?" Brody whispered, one eyebrow jetting upward. "Name of a name, Fallon, you can't mean the bloke who is visiting the king! What's a man like that got to do with you?"

"It's a long story," Fallon answered, gritting his teeth against the pain of his torn skin as he rolled onto his side to look up at Brody. "But if he's in London, I've got to find him."

"Sure, and didn't you just say he'd be coming to look for you?"

"Maybe. I don't know. But if he does, I've got to be here. And if he doesn't, I've got to find him."

"You talk like an eejit. How can you be here and there?"

"I want to stay here, in case he comes. But if I could leave for an hour, or an afternoon—"

"Well, naturally, it wouldn't be wise to run away," Brody pointed out. "You're sixteen and ready to be apprenticed as soon as Crompton finds a willing master. Better to be an apprentice and learn a trade than be out on the streets perishing with hunger. Life's hard on a boy in London. I've heard stories. And as hard as life is in here, it's better than begging."

"Of certain," Fallon answered, his mind racing. "So, has anyone ever broken out of here for a little while? I only need whatever time it takes to find where Captain John Smith might be staying."

"You might as well ask for a letter of introduction to the king, if you take me meaning," Brody answered, his eyes gleaming with a spark of mischief. "We'll have to think on that awhile, me friend. But if the thought is solidly into your head, I'll be wanting to join you on this great expedition."

"You might earn Master Crompton's wrath," Fallon warned, glancing up. "It isn't pleasant, that cane."

"Ah, sure it isn't," Brody answered, rolling back onto his

bunk. Cutting through the darkness from above, his voice was high with suppressed excitement. "But they'll not see our like again in this place. We'll go and we'll go together."

▼▲▼▲▼ The students at the Royal Academy for Homeless Orphans were always better behaved than usual on the day after a caning. When Master Crompton rose from his chair in the dining hall, all fifty boys stood as one, and Fallon made an effort to meekly hang his head as he followed the long single line down the hall to afternoon classes.

As an older student, Fallon was one of the last boys out of the hall, and he lingered in the corridor for a moment. With one quick, disobedient glance behind him, Fallon made certain that none of the proctors followed, then he dove into the water closet, where Brody waited with an expectant grin on his face.

The two boys pressed against the closed door, their breathing quick and light in the sour-smelling chamber. "They'll know we're gone as soon as the master sees our empty seats," Brody whispered. "We have to run for it now!"

Fallon nodded, his heart in his throat, and forced himself to move quickly despite the pain he felt every time the rough fabric of his breeches rubbed against the tender wounds from his caning. Brody moved the chamber pot from the table to the floor, and Fallon climbed onto the table, then stepped from the table to the long rectangular window. He slipped easily through the opening and rolled onto the wood-shingled roof of the porch below. Brody followed, an adventurous grin on his face, and Fallon paused before moving further.

"You don't have to come, y'know," he said, eyeing the younger boy steadily. "There'll be an awful caning when we come back. The master won't be happy."

Brody lifted his chin and thrust out his lower lip. "Can you be thinking I'd let you go alone?" he asked, raking his hair from his eyes. "Besides, what would a fellow from Virginia know about London? You'd be lost without me."

Fallon sighed in relief and gave his coconspirator a shaky smile. He looked carefully around, then skittered like a crab over the shingles until he reached the ancient rain gutter that ran from the roof to the ground. He paused, knowing his jump was certain to make noise. "We'll have to be quick," he said, looking at Brody. "The cook and the housekeeper will come running once they hear this pipe creaking."

"It's all right," Brody answered, looking down. His voice seemed smaller as he regarded the distance. "We'll be fine."

Fallon followed Brody's glance down to the cobblestones on the ground. Sharp sunlight threw broken shadows onto the road, and Fallon knew one of their bones could be broken as easily.

"No waiting, then," Fallon called. He grabbed the gutter pipe, heaved his weight out into empty air, and slid down the groaning structure until he felt solid ground beneath his feet. In another moment Brody stood beside him, his face flushed with triumph, and then they ran, adrenaline driving them up the street like condemned men who've suddenly been paroled.

When they could run no further, Fallon pulled Brody into the long shadow of a building. Leaning on the stone wall as he panted for breath, he peered around the corner. "Do you know what street this is?" he asked over his shoulder. "And how we can find John Smith?"

"If Smith has been presented to the king, we should ask someone at court," Brody said, shrugging.

"Court?" Fallon crinkled his nose. "Where is it?"

"It's not a place, it's a group of people," Brody said, struggling to catch his breath. "People of the gentry, who wait on the king. Some of them actually follow the king around wherever he goes; others merely visit him."

"So how do we find this court?"

Brody shrugged again. "We go to one of the fine houses of the gentry, I'd wager. Of certain one of the lords has news of such a great explorer as John Smith." He laughed. "Or we could find the king himself."

"Maybe." Fallon answered. He leaned against the cool stone

of the building behind him and closed his eyes, forcing himself to calm down. Rowtag had taught him how to run for hours in the woods without tiring, but he had been away from the woods for a long time now. It saddened him that he could no longer accomplish the feat.

"All right, we'll try to find the king," Fallon answered, leaning forward to peer around the corner again. "Where does he live?"

Brody giggled. "Know you nothing of our king? His Majesty James, King of England, Wales, and Scotland lives anywhere he chooses. There's Richmond Palace, and the Tower of London, York Place, Hampton Court—"

Fallon growled and grabbed Brody's arm, jerking the boy forward as he moved down the street. "All right, we'll ask someone," he snapped, moving into the stream of pedestrian traffic. "Surely the people of London know where their king is."

▾▴▾▴▾ Twenty-four hours later, they'd been laughed at, scorned, and pushed aside more times than Fallon cared to remember. Brody's stomach howled audibly for food, and Fallon felt a sense of foreboding descend over him. He had planned to be back at the school long before this, but as the sun set last night they'd had no success and no way to slip into the academy undetected. Fallon elected to keep searching, for their escape would prove useless unless they discovered some news about John Smith; he did not want to be caned again without gaining something for his pain.

So last night they'd slept in the decrepit doorway of an abandoned building near the river. In the darkness Fallon had lain facedown upon the cool stones of the street and surrendered to sleep, but through the daze of weariness he felt something brush against his cheek. He opened his eyes to see a sag-bellied rat twitching its nervous whiskers in his direction. He shouted and swatted the rodent away, then sat upright on his tortured flesh for the rest of the night and tried to rest.

*Dear God,* he prayed, a wry smile crossing his face despite

his discomfort, *have I blundered into a folly of my own making?*
*Was it your will that I remain at the school to wait for John Smith?*
*For of certain I must see him if I am to find Noshi and Gilda again.*
*So why don't you provide the miracle we seek? It would be better to*
*meet John Smith now rather than endure this much longer.*

He and Brody greeted the morning sun gladly and continued
their quest, asking each man and woman they met for news of
the king's court or of John Smith, but the search proved fruitless.

Hiding behind dull clouds as gray as the buildings and streets
of London, the sun abandoned the afternoon sky. Fallon looked
about the ancient city and slumped into morose musings. If London had been a forest, he would not be afraid, but the city was a
dismal, perverse place.

A haze of smoke hung perpetually over this urban wilderness,
fed by fresh gray streams from the rough chimneys of every
house. He and Brody roamed among buildings of one and two
stories, tired and aging structures of timber and stone where merchants of every ilk plied their trades. Entire streets had been
given over to the stalls and shops of merchants, and wooden
signs hung outside and swung nosily to and fro in an effort to
advertise whatever goods were sold inside.

Masses of people streamed all over the city. Fallon noticed
that buildings at the intersections of London streets had been
reinforced with posts and heavily curtained to grant the inhabitants some measure of privacy. At one time or another the full
tide of human existence seemed to cross the boys' path. In that
single afternoon Fallon saw deformities, beauty, drunkenness,
cruelty, filth, and opulence he could never have imagined.
Stunned by the mix of excess and poverty, he watched with
incredulous eyes as the fine silken gowns of ladies were splashed
by cattle and sheep on their way to market, and brazen pickpockets plucked purses from the velvet doublets of wealthy men.

Yet amid the wealth and the sheer wonder of a vast population, the city reeked of sewage and squalor. Rubbish was casually left in the streets to be picked up by rakers who lazily
patrolled the gutters, and at any moment an upper window

might open while a maid emptied the family's chamber pots onto the streets below. Such emptyings were greeted with curses and jeers from gentry and commoners alike, and finely dressed men and women moved through the city's avenues with lace handkerchiefs pressed firmly to their noses.

The survival skills that would have served Fallon well in the woods were utterly useless here. "All trails lead to water" was a natural law of the forest, but though all streets did eventually turn to the Thames, so did the slow-moving gutters. When Fallon first saw the river, he nearly gagged from the stench and sight of it. Along its banks the river was scummy with a greenish-brown detritus of waterlogged trash, pieces of lumber, bits of floating food, and cast-off fish heads.

Closing his mind to the corruption around him, Fallon paused outside a storefront where he and Brody contemplated a steaming loaf of bread displayed in the open window. Fallon's mouth watered at the sight and scent of food, but he was distracted when a woman passed by with her dark-haired daughter at her side. The little girl turned and stared at Fallon with unabashed curiosity, and Fallon felt his heart turn over the way it always had when Gilda had looked at him in trust and love.

What had happened to Gilda? Had Opechancanough's threats become reality? Was she a Powhatan in her heart and soul, having forgotten the God of their parents? Or perhaps she was like Fallon, living lost in a foreign wilderness and knowing she would never fit in, not if she remained a lifetime.

*Almighty God, be with her . . .* , he prayed silently.

A carriage moved toward a loud crowd of pedestrians and pressed them against the bakery storefront as it passed, and Fallon felt his temper flare as a score of people thrust themselves against him. How could anyone live in such a place?

When the carriage had moved away and the crowd abated, Fallon thrust his hands tightly inside his folded arms and turned away from the distracting sight of food. "We need a new direction," he told Brody. "We've been wandering around like a couple of blind opossums."

"I'm hungry," Brody whined, casting a surreptitious glance toward the bread.

"Don't think about it," Fallon answered, frowning. "The sooner we find John Smith, the sooner we can return to the school. Now, if we approach the problem from a different perspective—"

"The minister!" Brody said, snapping his fingers. "Sure, and why didn't I think of it before? They feed the poor every afternoon about this time. If we find a church—"

Fallon's mind blew open. "A church," he repeated, turning toward Brody. "Of course! You're on the right track. The school is run by a board of ministers, right? If we just explain why we need to talk to John Smith, surely they will help us find him. And at the very least," Fallon's smile twisted guiltily, "they can give us supper."

"What if they want to send us back?" Brody asked, raising an eyebrow. "With no help, and no dinner either?"

Fallon shrugged. "If they put us in a cart, we'll just jump out. If they make us walk, we'll run away. It will work, I tell you."

"At this hour I'll go anywhere if there's a meal waiting," Brody said, nodding in agreement. "Let's go."

Fallon stepped into the open alley of the street and lifted his eyes to the horizon. Not far away, the spire of a church loomed against the paling sky. "We'll go there," Fallon said, pointing toward the steeple.

Delbert Crompton's hand trembled with repressed anger as he sealed the letter with his ring. The two boys had been gone for more than a day, and never, *never* had a boy willingly left the Royal Academy for Homeless Orphans so close to apprenticeship. It was an insult to the dignity of the school, a slap in the face of the headmaster himself, for if the boys were discovered they might lead some softhearted silly to believe that something was greatly amiss at Crompton's school.

He had learned of Fallon Bailie and Brody McRyan's absence shortly after dinner the day before, and he waited until dark before saying anything to anyone. But he knew the other boys would ogle those two empty beds the way Eve eyed the forbidden fruit, and he wanted the boys found and returned before the idea of running away sparked ideas in any other young minds. Why should they want to escape, anyway? At the academy they had food, education, and a warm bed. He did not work them as hard as some schoolmasters did, and his discipline was not unduly severe. His pleasure lay not in humiliating his boys, but in selling them, for his dutiful, efficient charges brought a great price from men interested in young, sturdy, unambitious servants who would work without complaint.

It was that thought that galled him most of all, for Fallon Bailie was ripe for indenture and should have been sold into service weeks ago. The beleaguered headmaster had fostered Bailie for more than three years, enduring the boy's silent pride and unreasonable dignity with tolerably good humor, and now it was time to be repaid for that mental and physical effort. But just when the fatted lamb was ready for the slaughter, the creature had the temerity to run off—*and* take a shearling with him!

Crompton cursed under his breath and pulled another sheet of parchment from his desk. The boys would turn up soon, for they were but pampered children who did not know the ways of the street. Even in a city of two hundred thousand people, a tattooed boy with flaming red hair could not stay lost for long. "And when you're found, my dear Fallon Bailie," Crompton muttered under his breath as he dipped his pen into the inkwell, "I'll sell you to the smarmiest, most backbreaking master I can find in all of London."

▼▲▼▲▼ The smell of steaming meat pies assailed the boys before they reached the church, and Fallon put out a hand to stop Brody. "Breathe that air," he said, the delightful aroma making his knees weak with hunger. "Master Crompton has never served anything like that at our table."

"It would be easy enough to get one," Brody replied, his eyes skimming toward the shop from which the delicious smells came. "We'll go in. You talk to the master, and while you've taken his attention to some far corner of the store, I'll snitch us a pie."

Fallon gave him a quick, denying glance. "We'll not steal our supper."

"But it would be easy! I've heard some of the other boys talk about how easy it is to lift whatever a body needs. The shopkeepers are too busy to call for the magistrate, and we're fast, we are, and we'd be away before he could catch us—"

"We will not steal. It's against the laws of God and Ocanahonan. I'd starve first."

Brody opened his mouth as if he would protest again, but then fell silent under Fallon's unrelenting gaze. "All right then, let's get to the church," he said, snatching one last glimpse of the golden brown pies in the shop window. "But let's hurry. I'm perishing with hunger, I am."

▼▲▼▲▼ The ancient church of St. Bartholomew the Great surrounded Fallon and Brody in gray silence as they passed through the oak doors separating the church from the bustling street. Brody walked forward impatiently, searching for a clergyman, but Fallon stood back and lifted his eyes to the vaulted ceiling overhead. He had never been inside a cathedral, only the rustic chapel at Ocanahonan and the simple chantry at the academy. The sheer majesty of St. Bartholomew's stole his breath.

The wooden soles of Brody's shoes clacked in the silence as he moved away, but Fallon felt himself rooted to the spot where he stood. It seemed strange that men would erect such a building to honor God, for the Almighty's works were most clearly seen in the blue of sky and the breath of the breeze, but Fallon could not deny that the sheer height and design of the building forced him to lift his eyes to heaven and contemplate the inspired genius of the church's designer.

"It's an imposing building, is it not?" a voice interrupted at his elbow.

Fallon jerked his head toward the sound and saw a dark-robed man standing before him. The man wore a pleasant smile, but kept his hands corked firmly in the wide sleeves of his robe. "I am sorry if I startled you," the man said, a loose thatch of hair falling across his forehead. "I am Father Michael, the vicar here at St. Bartholomew's."

"It's a marvelous church," Fallon answered, lifting his eyes to the ceiling again.

"Yes, but you did not come here to examine our building," the clergyman said, amusement lurking in his eyes. "St. Bartholomew's is an old church, out of fashion at the moment, and not many come here at all unless they have some specific mission in mind. You're—" he glanced quickly at the functional dark blue breeches and doublet Fallon wore—"you're a student?"

"Yes," Fallon answered. His cheeks burned as he confessed the truth. "My friend and I have run away from school because we are seeking Captain John Smith. I know he's in London and I must see him, but we've been searching for two days and I have no idea where to find him. Perchance you, Reverend, have some idea of where we should look?"

"First we will take care of your body," the clergyman said, taking Fallon's elbow and propelling him down an aisle. "You're hungry, are you not?"

"Yes," Fallon confessed. "Terribly."

"And tired, no doubt. I will take you to Mistress Fairweather, who will feed you, give you a basin in which to wash, and a place to rest while I make inquiries. And then we shall see about finding your Captain Smith."

"Would you do so much?" Fallon said, his heart overcome with pleasant surprise. "If you could, we were right to come here. Surely God has heard my prayers when I had all but given up hope."

"God always provides for our best," the clergyman answered. He stopped as Brody crossed their path and gestured to the younger boy. "Join us, my son, and let us see what the good mistress has prepared for supper. You shall eat, rest, and trust that all will be provided for."

Too grateful for words, Brody and Fallon followed the vicar into the dining hall.

▼▲▼▲▼ Father Michael finished the letter and signed his name with a flourish at the bottom of the page. He had left the boys in the midst of devouring huge helpings of the mistress's best pottage, and unless he was sadly mistaken, they were of certain sleeping now before the fire in the hall of the rectory.

Once the boys had begun to eat, he'd had no trouble loosening their tongues enough to learn that they were students at the Royal Academy for Homeless Orphans. Father Michael had a special desire to grant a favor for Master Delbert Crompton, for certainly it would prove useful in the future to have Master Crompton in his debt.

He rang for his assistant, and when the young man arrived

Father Michael handed the letter over without a word. The recipient's name was clearly indicated on the parchment, and the vicar knew the message would be delivered within the hour.

When his assistant had gone, the clergyman leaned forward in his chair, tenting his fingers as he reflected upon the vagaries of youth and the fantastic story the boys had related while they ate. The son of savages, the redhead claimed to be, the frustrated savior of an Indian princess and a brother sold into slavery!

Safely away from the boys' bright eyes, he chuckled. He, too, had felt capable of conquering the world at sixteen, and Captain John Smith should be flattered to know that even boys in a school for orphans had heard of his daring exploits and risked certain punishment to meet him. It was a pity that the boys would be returned without having met their goal, but London had orphans enough roaming the streets without adding two others. And by returning them at once, Father Michael would keep these two safe from the dangers of pickpockets, pox, and prostitutes.

The minister sighed and went back to his work. In an hour, maybe two, an emissary from the academy would arrive to pick up the boys and this little adventure would be at an end. But how pleasant it had been! It was rather like a tale from that talented playwright at the Globe Theatre who wrote of runaways assuming fantastic disguises and making claims to kingdoms and identities far beyond the possibilities of reality.

What was the writer's name? Father Michael smiled as the answer surfaced in his mind. "Indeed," he told himself. "William Shakespeare himself would delight in Fallon Bailie's fantastic story."

▼▲▼▲▼ Delbert Crompton sent four of his stoutest teachers to escort the prisoners home, and those same four men held Fallon Bailie and Brody McRyan as the headmaster administered their caning before the entire student body at dinner the next day.

Pale and trembling, Bailie and McRyan stood, gathered their breeches about their waists, then turned to face him, their judge and jury. Crompton exulted in this small but satisfying victory as he regarded the runaways. McRyan shot his friend a half-frightened look, but Fallon Bailie stared mindlessly over the assembled company as if his thoughts had wandered far away.

"As further punishment and as a fitting part of appropriate discipline, both of you have hereby forfeited the rest of your education and tenure at the Royal Academy for Homeless Orphans," Crompton said, his voice as rough as gravel. "You will be sold into indentured service immediately, to serve your masters for the maximum term of seven years while you learn a trade and seek to become useful citizens to your king and country."

If it were possible, Fallon Bailie went a shade paler.

"You, Brody McRyan," Crompton went on, turning to the younger boy, "you will be sold to John McArdle, the blacksmith, to serve him for a full seven years beginning on the morrow. And you, Fallon Bailie . . . ," Crompton paused, and the entire body of boys drew in a collective breath. "You will be sold to another master and will serve him willingly, obediently, and freely for seven full years, until you have reached twenty-three years of age."

Fallon Bailie's gaze finally focused upon the headmaster's. "And who is my master?" he asked, his voice a tremulous whisper that echoed in the silence of the room.

Crompton smiled in pure pleasure. "It's my greatest delight to announce," he said, savoring the moment, "that you will remain at the school you were so anxious to leave. You, Fallon Bailie, will serve *me*."

▼▲▼▲▼ Fallon first thought that Master Crompton meant to kill him, but though the headmaster was severe, he was not murderous. He demanded that Fallon work quickly and well, running the boy without a pause during waking hours, but every night Master Crompton seated himself in his small chamber with a pile of books and a quart of ale. He then began to read and drink, and drink and read, and soon passed into a drunken stupor that left him insensible to whatever Fallon might wish to do.

In the first weeks of his service Fallon took advantage of those quiet hours to pray and sleep, but one night while he was dusting the master's prized library he discovered a copy of *A True Relation of Such Occurrences and Accidents of Note as Has Happened in Virginia Since the First Planting of that Colony,* a book written by Captain John Smith. The book was dated 1608, and a wonderful feeling of happiness rose inside Fallon as he read of places and people he knew. Surely God had planted this book in Crompton's library so that he could read it and be comforted! Though he had not been able to find Smith in London, at least he had the printed page to tell him of Smith's exploits in Virginia.

There were days when Fallon could almost convince himself that his childhood had been a dream, but when he read *News from Virginia* by Richard Rich, an English soldier who had been in Jamestown during the starving time of 1609, Fallon was secretly pleased that he and the children had survived so easily in the woods. Another work, a sermon called *Good Speed to Virginia,* had been published in London to promote colonization, and as he read it Fallon's heart pounded with the desire to return to the land of his birth.

From reading these books, Fallon knew that the English approach to relations with the Indians would not be effective. The English were too smugly *superior,* too convinced that English ways were right and Indian ways foolish. In his lectures before his students Master Crompton represented the attitude of Englishmen, who loved to compare the wonders of English civilization to the barbarism of the savages. But despite Crompton's lofty boasting before teachers and students, Fallon knew his master would not last one day in Virginia.

Fallon began to look forward to his master's periods of inebriation, for as the man snored drunkenly, his servant had the perfect opportunity to learn all he could about the colonization effort. As soon as the quart of ale had been drunk and the master's rheumy eyes closed in heaviness, Fallon took himself to the library to pore over Crompton's growing collection of books and pamphlets about Virginia.

Time passed. The days of Fallon's service melted into weeks and weeks into months. During morning hours, Fallon scrubbed floors in the decrepit academy building, emptied chamber pots and wash basins, and peeled vegetables for the cooks in the dining hall. After a quick dinner of whatever had been left over from feeding the academy's students, Fallon spent his time attending to Master Crompton's personal affairs: shining the master's shoes; airing the master's doublets, breeches, and cloaks; and freshening the master's bed linens. Never did Crompton ask him to run an errand, doubtless afraid Fallon would try to escape, and never did the guardedly private headmaster ask Fallon to read or transcribe a letter.

Ofttimes Fallon struggled with pride as he emptied the filthy chamber pots and cleaned up after sick students. He was the son of Roger Bailie, an English aristocrat, and the stepson of Rowtag, a Mangoak chief. As a boy he had swum in freezing rivers and stood upon anthills to prove his courage and toughen his spirit. He had seen battle and bloodshed, and he had faced an enemy and won. He had been entrusted with the lives of a young boy and girl in whom the spirit of Ocanahonan would live.

Only in that duty had he failed.

But he had not finished. Fallon prayed daily that he would be allowed to complete his task, that he would find Noshi and Gilda and marry them each to the other. He would send them into the world as the best blend of Indian and English, redeemed children of Christ who could demonstrate God's ways to the savages of the New World.

When John Smith's *A Map of Virginia* was published, Fallon pored over the text to learn everything he could about the land, commodities, people, government, and religion of the fledgling colony into which he'd wandered so many years before. Not a word could he find of Ocanahonan, Gilda, or Noshi, but he read much of Powhatan and Jamestown. With every sentence Fallon became more convinced that Gilda and Noshi still lived somewhere in Virginia.

One night, as Master Crompton snored in his chair, Fallon slipped behind the master's desk and took a pen and a sheet of parchment. Carefully uncorking the inkwell so as not to disturb his sleeping master, Fallon penned a letter:

> To Captain John Smith, London
> From Fallon Bailie, formerly of Virginia
>
> Sir:
> I have hopes that you will remember me, and that you will recall serving as my sponsor to the Royal Academy for Homeless Orphans in London. I have served my time there and have tried many times to discover a way to reach you.
> I must know, sir, what became of your promise to me. I have read in your book that you had occasion to meet with Chief Powhatan. Did you, then, find the girl called Gilda, of whom I told you? And in your travels, did you happen to find the boy called Noshi, my brother? Both children are noticeably English in the color of their eyes, and I do not think you could mistake them.
> If you should happen to venture to Virginia again, please consider purchasing my contract of service from Master Delbert Crompton, the headmaster of the school. I am bound to him for several more years, but would serve you for a lifetime if I can fulfill my promise to help these two I have sworn to protect.
> I am, your servant, Fallon Bailie.

After sealing the letter with a featureless smear of wax, Fallon slipped it into the pocket of his worn doublet and carefully put the writing utensils away. He did not know how or when he might find someone to deliver the letter, but if God had truly called him to this venture, of certain he would provide a way to contact John Smith.

*1613*

"Come, little sister, lift your end," Pocahontas fussed as the two girls struggled to carry a dead doe through the greening woods of spring. The hunters had disemboweled the creature, but it was the duty of women to bring the game home, dress it, and preserve the meat. For a moment Pocahontas wished she had asked an older, stronger girl to help.

Numees struggled to lift the two spindly back legs of the doe, but blood made them slippery. "Wait," she called, dropping the carcass on the ground long enough to wipe her hands on the wide green leaves of a nearby shrub. Pocahontas rolled her eyes in exasperation. Sometimes it was easy to forget that Numees was only ten, little more than a child.

Numees gripped the bony legs in her hands again and lifted. "I don't know why you are in such a hurry to get back to the village," she said, walking with shortened steps to avoid bumping into the bloody carcass. "When you know Aranck has invited us only so you will marry his son."

"I will not marry Matwau," Pocahontas protested, carefully leading the way through the woods. "For well is he named 'enemy'. I heard him brag that he has killed five of the English."

"Five English? That is not so many. Makkapitew has killed more."

Pocahontas sighed. She knew her father had sent her to Aranck's village because he wanted her to marry. At eighteen, she should have taken a husband at least two years before. Thus far Pocahontas had been able to stall her father by insisting that none of the men in her own village appealed to her and that

Numees needed a big sister, but Powhatan had solved both problems by announcing that Numees could go with Pocahontas wherever she wished and that Aranck, a lesser werowance of an affiliated tribe, would be honored to offer any of the sons of his village to be Pocahontas's husband.

A brilliant cardinal flew from branch to branch overhead, scolding the girls for disturbing his mate on the nest, and Pocahontas would have shaken her fist at him had her hands been free. It was possible her father knew the real reason for her refusal to marry, for it had been some months since he had allowed her to visit the English fort. He probably thought that if he kept the Englishmen from her eyes and mind, the longing in her heart would lessen. But ever since the day she had thrown herself beneath the war club to protect John Smith, she had known she would never love an Indian the way she could love one of the clothed men.

"You are thinking deep thoughts." Numees offered the observation without complaint.

"Yes."

"About the English?"

"Yes. You know me too well, little sister."

Numees did not speak again, and Pocahontas allowed her mind to curl lovingly around the thought of the men at Jamestown—fair, bearded men with hair in varying shades of gold and eyes of blue and green. And it was not only their physical aspect that delighted her, for they were wise and inventive and dangerously clever. But contemplation of her marriage to one of them would be anathema in her father's eyes, for while he talked of peace with the Englishmen, he did not trust them.

"Look ahead, my sister."

Pocahontas lifted her eyes from the trail and saw bearded men moving in the clearing beyond. Englishmen!

"Hurry," Pocahontas snapped, quickening her pace.

Behind her, Numees laughed.

▼▲▼▲▼ Aranck had ordered a great feast, for Captain Samuel Argall, one of the masters of the mighty ships that offered goods for trade up and down the great river, sat at his left hand. Argall and his men had already brought forth great amounts of beads and copper, and Aranck had his eye on one especially bright copper kettle of enormous size.

Argall dipped his hand into a platter of venison that passed by and took a generous hunk of the savory meat. He looked like a little wet bird as he sat at dinner, for he and his men had bathed in the river before reentering the village for the feast. But there was no denying that this creature with a wet beard and slicked-back hair could bring riches to the tribe if Aranck traded wisely.

"Who, mighty chief, is that girl?" Argall asked, pointing across the fire toward a group of maidens who served the visitors seated around the fire pit. "The lively one wearing many beads?"

"That is Matoaka," Aranck answered, unable to keep a note of pride from his voice. "The daughter of our great chief Powhatan. She comes here to find a husband."

"Matoaka," Argall repeated, a thoughtful expression on his weather-beaten face. Suddenly the captain straightened and the light of understanding dawned in his eyes. "Surely it's not Pocahontas?"

"Yes," Aranck answered, nodding. "Such is she called."

Argall ate his meat and said nothing more as the maidens continued to serve the guests. When all had eaten and the warriors' dancing had begun, Aranck wondered if the English captain would speak again of trading and the copper kettle.

He did not. After the dancing, when the warriors retired to their places and scattered fires dotted the darkness of the village, the chief escorted the Englishmen to the hut in which they would sleep. Before Argall could disappear into the hut, Aranck reached out and touched the captain's arm. "Do you still wish to trade?" he asked, trying not to let his eagerness show on his face. "We have many furs, antlers, and much corn."

"You have an even greater prize that you know not of," Argall answered, turning from the firelight so that his face was thrown into shadow. With an abrupt gesture, the captain pulled the chief into the darkness with him. "What is the one thing, mighty chief, that you desire most from among my treasures?"

Aranck's eyes shone as he thought of the copper pot with the gleam of fire. It was more copper than any other chief owned, and more skillfully beaten than any upon the river.

"The great pot," he said, blinking slowly before the English captain.

"Ah, and it's a most valuable kettle," Argall answered. "But it can be yours, great chief, for one small favor."

"Say it."

"Give me Pocahontas, the daughter of Powhatan. I will carry her safely to Jamestown, where her father has many friends."

Aranck pulled away, frowning, but the captain kept talking. "Do not fear for her, for I will treat her well. This will work to the good for both the Powhatan and the English, for as long as she is in my care, her father will not attack the fort at Jamestown. The peace we both desire will be preserved."

Aranck did not answer, but stared past the fire into his own thoughts. Powhatan would not take kindly to Aranck's surrender of his beloved daughter, but the English captain spoke wisely. And how was Powhatan to know Pocahontas did not join the English freely? Of course, such an action would mean that Matwau would not marry the girl, but in the two months she had been in his village she had not proven amenable to the idea of marriage.

"Leave the copper pot outside my hut at first light," Aranck said, folding his arms. "I will send Pocahontas to your ship before the sun stands overhead on the morrow. If she does not want to go with you, you must let her return. I will tell Powhatan that she joined the English freely."

"So be it," Argall answered, his mouth tipped in a faint smile.

▼▲▼▲▼ "The chief must have given many furs for such a pot," Pocahontas remarked, looking wistfully at Aranck's new copper kettle, yet another proof of the Englishmen's ultimate superiority. Already the chief's wives had filled it with hominy and were boiling the mixture over the fire. Aranck stood nearby, his hands folded across his chest, a victorious smile upon his face.

"Daughter," the chief called, and Pocahontas left the circle of women and hurried to his side. Numees, she noticed, followed reluctantly.

"Yes, Uncle?" she said, looking at the chief with new respect.

"The English Captain Argall has asked that I send someone with our peace offering before the sun rises overhead today," he said, unfolding his arms. "I would send one of the warriors, but they are preparing to hunt—"

"No, Uncle, send me!" Pocahontas said, exultation filling her chest until she thought it would burst. "I am swift, I know my way to the river, I can carry ever so many furs and Numees will help me!"

"Your little sister can remain behind," Aranck said, his eyes darting toward the girl, who stood behind Pocahontas.

"She will not want to miss this," Pocahontas answered, knowing at once she had spoken too quickly. She had made no secret of her great love for the English, but experience had taught her that her father would not approve of her feelings. A year earlier she had made her way through the dark to warn a settlement of Englishmen that her father planned to raid their farms and plantations. His resulting anger at the raid's failure was such that she no longer doubted that he would kill even his favorite daughter if he knew she had managed to thwart his plans.

"I beg you, Uncle, let Numees go with me," Pocahontas asked, bowing her head in humble submission. "We will not be gone long."

"So be it," Aranck answered. He retreated into his dwelling, then returned and placed a surprisingly small bundle into her arms.

Pocahontas stared at the parcel in surprise. "So little a gift for such a big kettle?"

"It is what the English wanted," the chief answered cryptically. He folded his arms again, and a shiver ran through her as fury blazed suddenly from his eyes. "Before you go, tell me, little sister, will you take my son as your husband?"

Pocahontas felt her cheeks flood with color. She bowed her head, knowing full well that she would insult her host by refusing. But she would not be false to herself. "No, Uncle. I will not marry him, or any warrior from this tribe."

A mantle of aloofness fell upon the chief and he unfolded his arms again. "Then away with you to the English ship. Do not keep the captain waiting."

▼▲▼▲▼ Pocahontas took a moment to rebraid her hair, slip on her most decorated tunic, and wash her face before setting out on the trail to the river. Behind her, Numees performed a halfhearted imitation of the older girl's ministrations, then sighed when Pocahontas took a leather cloak from a bundle on the floor of their hut. "Must we wear our best clothes?" Numees complained, kicking a clod of dirt onto a sleeping mat. "We will only be gone a little while."

"We are visiting the English, and they are most particular about their dress," Pocahontas replied, smoothing her hair. She turned to chuck Numees under the chin. "When you are older, little sister, you will understand."

"We must come back soon," Numees insisted. "The sick squirrel needs me. I must feed him when the sun is high today."

"We'll feed him," Pocahontas answered, exasperated. Numees had of late taken to the healing arts, and though the conjuror would not let her attend to sick people, she had worked her special magic of healing on several animals.

They left the village, walking side by side, and Pocahontas kept up a steady stream of chatter until they reached the clearing where the shallop from Captain Argall's ship lay beached upon the sand. The ship itself waited at anchor in the river, and a score of red-coated Englishmen walked upon its decks. Two men who lounged in the grass on the shore sat up as the Indian girls approached.

"I have a package for Captain Argall," Pocahontas explained gravely in the Algonquin tongue. She was not certain how much the two Englishmen understood, but they glanced at one another and smiled, then stood and waved the girls toward the shallop.

"Will you go aboard the great ship?" Numees asked, her voice quietly uncertain.

Pocahontas's blood raced, but she confidently tossed her head. She had never been aboard an English ship, and the prospect was tantalizing. The men before her behaved as though they escorted Indian maidens every day. Besides, the captain waited on board.

"We will go aboard," Pocahontas said, stepping forward. She turned to Numees and held out her hand. "Do not fear, little sister. Aranck knows where we are. We are safe. Captain Argall is our friend, and we are bringing him something of great worth."

Clutching the leather-wrapped bundle to her, she held tight to Numees's hand and climbed into the wooden shallop.

▼▲▼▲▼ Captain Argall smiled broadly at the sight of the two girls in his cabin. "Ah, Pocahontas and Numees," he said, pronouncing their names carefully. "Welcome aboard the *Treasurer.*" The girls looked quite pretty, and he thought Pocahontas might even be dressed in her best clothes. How had the chief managed that?

He greeted them in the Algonquin tongue: "How good it is to see you."

"The werowance Aranck bids us bring you this," Pocahontas said, pulling the bundle from under her mantle. "It is a gift in exchange for the great copper pot."

Argall nodded, pretending to understand exactly what she

meant. While the girls waited and watched, he unrolled the covering of leather and found that it contained a small hominy cake.

"I will enjoy it," he said, holding it to his nose in a gesture of appreciation.

Pocahontas blinked in amazement, and he understood in a moment that the old chief had tricked her. She had doubtless thought she carried something of rare value, of some import, and was as stunned as he to discover that the great trade involved nothing but common hominy.

Abruptly, he called out to his bosun in English: "Raise the anchor!" Then he turned to the two girls, who appeared to visibly shrink before his presence. "You will be my guests for some time," he said, forcing a smile upon his face. "We will not hurt you. Do not fear. You will sleep below, in your own cabin."

He paused for a moment looking at the younger girl, whose fear-widened eyes were startlingly blue. Where had this child come from? Was she truly Pocahontas's sister?

"My father will not like this," Pocahontas said, her eyes flashing as she lifted her chin.

"Many weeks will pass before your father knows that you are with us," Argall replied smoothly, extending his hand to escort the girls from his cabin. "And while you remain with us, Pocahontas, the peace will remain intact. So go below, girls, and enjoy your stay."

He waited until the bosun had led the girls down the companionway, then in a blizzard of his curt orders the *Treasurer* made sail and moved away.

**John Rolfe**

*Those who aim at great deeds must also suffer greatly.*

*Marcus Licinius Crassus,*
*fl. 70 B.C.*

The afternoon air shimmered with the warmth of June as John Rolfe stood at the dock outside Henrico. Hot, water-scented winds blew across the dark surface of the river as Rolfe nervously stroked his beard. His tobacco, the product of many months of work, waited in stout barrels, ready for shipment to England.

"Is this your cargo, then?" the bosun called from the deck.

"Yes," Rolfe answered, squinting up at the sailor. "And care should be taken that the barrels remain dry, so put them on an upper deck, will you?"

"Don't worry, Master Rolfe," the bosun said, grinning toothlessly as he came down the gangplank. "We'll take care of you just like we always 'ave."

The bosun directed seamen to roll the heavy barrels up the gangplank, and John stepped back and closed his eyes, afraid one of the barrels might fall into the water. For over a year he had been experimenting with tobacco in hopes that he might find a strain mild enough for the refined tastes of the English. The native weed so beloved by the Indians, *Nicotiana rustica*, had too harsh a bite for European standards. Through his friendship with a sea captain who regularly sailed to the Caribbean, Rolfe had obtained seeds of a broader leaf tobacco plant, *Nicotiana tabacum*. Using techniques of cross-pollination, Rolfe had blended the two plants into a new strain which, he hoped, would combine the robust toughness of the native plant with the golden taste and texture of the Caribbean native.

When the last barrels were loaded aboard, Rolfe sighed in relief and saluted the bosun who had supervised the loading.

Captain Samuel Argall's ship, the *Treasurer,* waited at anchor in the midst of the river, and Rolfe found himself wondering about the oft-repeated rumor that Chief Powhatan's daughter had traveled for over two months as a prisoner aboard that ship. Rolfe had heard that Lieutenant Governor Gates was due from Jamestown to board the *Treasurer* and see for himself whether the girl was aboard and if she was being well-treated.

Intrigued by the idea of a captive Indian princess, Rolfe decided to seek shelter for the night at the public house at Henrico rather than walk the miles to his plantation.

▼▲▼▲▼ Three days later, a pillaring thunderhead in the west marched inexorably toward Argall's ship as Rolfe paced nervously on the deck. Along with Lieutenant Governor Thomas Gates and Governor Thomas Dale, he had been selected to board Captain Argall's *Treasurer* to ascertain the status and health of the hostage Indian princess.

His mind reeled in confusion. Captain Argall had assured the governor that this move had been wisely done and according to the will of God, but John wondered how keeping a teenage girl hostage aboard a cramped ship could possibly be considered a Christian act. If she wanted to return to her father, were they not wrong to hold her? And if, perchance, she agreed to remain with the English as a willing hostage, would it not be better to give her a decent house and a woman to attend her?

He had not been in Virginia long, but he had often been struck speechless by the amazing ability of men to twist God's words and will to condone almost any situation. He had lost a baby and a wife not long after landing in Virginia, and those who expressed sorrow at his loss did not hesitate to prophesy that it was God's will that Rolfe remain unmarried in Virginia, for a wife and child would only make life in the colony more difficult. How could they acknowledge his grief and urge him to rejoice with the same breath? Perhaps they had never felt as he did, shipwrecked by grief, marooned on an island of guilt and self-doubt. If he had not insisted on venturing to Virginia, if he had not chosen the disease-laden ship he had—

His thoughts were interrupted when Captain Argall appeared on deck to welcome the three men aboard his ship. After the perfunctory and customary greetings, Argall smiled and gestured toward the companionway. A young Indian girl had come up from below and looked at them with careful, anxious eyes.

Uncommonly lovely, she wore a simple dress of buckskin that revealed her slim legs and delicate arms. Her long neck curved like a bird taking wing, framed by dark hair carefully plaited into braids and interwoven with strips of leather and feathers. Her very uniqueness was alluring: dark eyes, straight nose, determined mouth. John realized he was staring and forced himself to look away. At the princess's side stood a much younger girl, her handmaid, he supposed, who kept her eyes downcast and her hands behind her back. The princess rested her hands on the smaller girl's shoulders, a clear sign of devotion.

"Are you happy?" the governor bellowed, as if by shouting he could magically make the maiden understand English, but her soulful eyes seemed to understand. After a moment, she nodded to the governor's question.

When the three men made certain that the girls had not been mistreated in any way, they withdrew from the ship and talked with the captain on the dock.

"Of certain you cannot keep her, Captain," Rolfe said. "Surrounded by rough seamen, there's no gainsaying that such a lovely young woman has no place aboard ship."

"No harm has come to her thus far," Argall answered, his chest rising in indignation. "My men are mannerly, sir, and would not touch her or the young one—"

"It is better that she come into the fort at Jamestown, in any case," the governor interrupted neatly, putting out a hand to smooth Argall's ruffled pride. "As she is a political prisoner, she should be kept at the fort."

"In the jail?" Gates asked, aghast. "She's done no wrong, nothing to warrant putting her in that miserable place."

"Perhaps in a private home," Governor Dale said, looking closely at Rolfe. "You, sir, have a house at Jamestown, do you not? And does not your sister live there? She would be an excellent chaperon for these two."

Rolfe stiffened. He did have a house at Jamestown, built for the wife and child who died scarcely after leaving England. His younger sister, Edith, lived there now, for she had come to Virginia to help with the baby. Thus far he had spent most of his time at his plantation at Henrico, avoiding the Jamestown house and the empty dreams it harbored. Much as he might like to, he could hardly deny that he had a house with a woman to care for the Indian girl.

"Yes," he answered, finding his voice. "The princess and her maid can stay with my sister. They would be safe, and Edith could educate them—"

"But your house lies outside the fort," Gates protested. "What if Powhatan chooses to steal his daughter back? There is no guard at Rolfe's house."

"The house lies minutes from the fort and is easily defensible," Rolfe offered, his enthusiasm for the idea rising. Perhaps God would bring good out of tragedy after all. If there was some larger purpose for the house and his vanquished dreams . . .

"If you are planning to keep the girl for some time, Governor, you can't keep her on this ship," he said, folding his arms. "It's not healthy or safe. But if she is under Edith's care—"

"In sooth," Governor Dale interrupted him, "she could become one of us!" He slammed his fist into his open palm. "Name of a name, why didn't we think of this solution sooner, gentlemen? Rolfe, have your sister make plans for our guest immediately. Gates, take pains to keep this quiet. We don't want the news spreading to the savages. Argall, wait until dark, then weigh anchor and escort the princess to Rolfe's house at Jamestown."

"Tonight?" Rolfe said, his pulse quickening at the thought of facing his sister with this surprise. Poor Edith had no idea of the political firestorm that was about to descend upon her.

"Tonight," Dale answered, moving swiftly off the dock.

▼▲▼▲▼ "Here?" Edith Rolfe said, her voice cracking. "In this house? I'm to keep a pair of Indian girls?"

"Hush, Edith, and do what you must to make ready," John said, flashing a quick, disarming smile. He pulled out of the quick embrace he'd given her and glanced over his shoulder. "They'll be here any minute. I barely managed to get ahead of them to warn you."

"Welladay, then let them come," she answered, wiping her hands on her apron. "They can take me as they find me."

"It's that attitude that's kept you from getting a husband," John teased, peering through the darkness toward the river.

"It's that attitude that's kept me happy," Edith replied. She followed her brother outside and stepped into the comforting circle of light from his torch. There, just down the road, half a dozen yellow torchlights danced through the darkness like cat's eyes. So many men to escort two girls?

"Armed men, too," Edith murmured when she recognized the gleam of muskets at her gate. One of the men opened the gate and stood back as the two girls moved toward the house.

The older girl—a young woman, really—carried herself with unusual grace, her dark hair stiff and gleaming like a crow's wing in the moonlight. It was obvious that her rich, fawnlike beauty affected the men with her, for they stood at a respectful distance as she passed through the small gate outside the house and neared the front door.

Edith's mouth curled into a wry smile. Men had never been affected that way by her presence. They were wont to say that she was sweet and kind, or perhaps charming, but they never stood a respectful distance away and gaped at her with the reverence these men now accorded the comely creature who walked up the path. Edith's face was too plain, her figure too plump, her eyes too colorless for beauty.

Behind the young woman walked a younger girl, and Edith had to peer around the first girl's figure to catch a decent glimpse of the little one. The two were obviously related, for they shared the same high cheekbones and widely spaced eyes.

The small girl's hair was as dark and lustrous as the first's, but when she lifted a timid glance to take in the house, Edith drew in her breath. Even in the yellow light of the torch she could see that the child's eyes gleamed as blue as a summer sky over an English meadow.

"Welcome," Edith said, awkwardly splaying her fingers against her apron. She didn't know whether to hug the girls or curtsy as befitted a princess, but John stepped forward and held the door open as the girls passed into the house.

"Show them where they can sleep and make sure the washbasin's full of fresh water," John whispered, his brown eyes lit with an excitement Edith hadn't seen in months. "You can talk to them on the morrow, my dear. And then, if you please, we'd all be more than grateful if you could teach them to be proper English ladies."

"Turn a savage into a lady?" she gasped, grasping the sleeve of his doublet. "Me? John, have you lost your mind?"

"Who else is there to do it?" he answered, pointing out the fact that only a handful of women resided in Jamestown. "You're strong and quick, Edith, and you'll manage very well. I'll be back to check on you, and the governor will make sure a guard is posted if you need one."

"John," she protested, sputtering, but her brother gave her an abrupt wave, then turned and walked out to join the party of men who left the gate and wended their way through the darkness toward the fort.

Edith watched him go, then squared her shoulders. She hadn't expected this, but she'd been wondering what she was to do in Jamestown without a baby and sister-in-law to care for. Now it seemed that God had declared a change in her plans.

▼▲▼▲▼ Edith Rolfe stood in the kitchen of her house and crossed her arms with a sigh of exasperation. Her charges sat on a bench before her, a study in opposites: Pocahontas wanted desperately to learn how to speak English and behave as an English gentlewoman, but her very eagerness tripped up her efforts. Numees, on the other hand, seemed diffident and vaguely bored by the endless lessons in language and deportment, but she picked up the language amazingly well and spoke with excellent diction and natural phrasing.

Content that the two girls were safe and secure in English hands, Governor Dale never bothered to inquire about his visitors' progress. But John, Edith noticed, traveled in from his plantation at Henrico to visit the house every weekend. He would often sit in the front chamber on a bench, a pipe of tobacco in his hand, his eyes intent upon Pocahontas as she struggled to read. The idea of "talking from books" was totally foreign to Pocahontas, but Numees picked up the concept with ease. Within three weeks of her arrival at Jamestown she could find and read elementary words in Edith's Bible.

"I think Pocahontas ought to have religious tutoring," Edith confided to her brother one night. The two girls were in the kitchen reading hornbooks at the board while John and Edith watched from the front chamber. "For how can we make her one of us unless she understands the God we serve? She is not far removed from heathenism, John, despite her refined looks and character."

"I will see what can be done," John answered, closing his own book. "Perhaps the minister at Henrico would enjoy this challenge." He winked at her. "He is unmarried, you know."

"So is every other man in this place," she said, casting him a disdainful look as she rose from the bench. Hiding her face from her handsome brother, she felt her heart twist as she deliberately hardened her voice. "And I have yet to find a man worthy of me."


▼▲▼▲▼ Pocahontas thought the Reverend Alexander Whitaker's ideas strange at first. How could one God rule so vast and varied an earth? But as the minister explained more about the mighty eternal God, Pocahontas realized that the God

Reverend Whitaker talked about was the great spirit known to
the Indians as the "manitou." Once she had grasped the concept
of one mighty God, the minister went on to say that the spirits of
wind, rain, and fire she had long worshiped were only manifesta-
tions of God's power. She had, the reverend explained, been wor-
shiping the creation, not the Creator.

She and Numees sat silently on a bench in the front chamber
of the house as Reverend Whitaker told them about sin, God's
love for man, and Jesus the Christ. As he spoke, a light slowly
dawned in her heart, and Pocahontas realized that his words contained simple and profound truth.

"Man is a noble ruin," Reverend Whitaker said, his large
hands cradling the leather-bound Bible that King James's schol-
ars had recently released. "We were made in God's likeness with
dignity and authority over creation, but sin opened the door to
death, decay, and suffering."

"I know about suffering," Pocahontas said, recalling the misery that rose in her heart when John Smith told her he could
never be her husband.

Reverend Whitaker lifted an eyebrow. "You do? Then give
your pain to God, Pocahontas. If you surrender the grief you
carry, it will be as a clean wound that God can heal."

"I would be a Christian," she said, falling on her knees before
the clergyman. "What must I do to surrender to this God?"

"Repent of your false gods and be baptized," he said, his eyes
wide with wonder as if the sight of a savage girl on her knees
surprised him. "Follow Christ and take a new name to signify
the change in your life."

Smiling through tears, Pocahontas nodded. "It is right; we
Indians have many names," she whispered, clasping her hands.
"Can you suggest a new name for me, Reverend Whitaker?"

The minister paused a moment, then placed a hand upon her
head. "Rebecca," he said, smiling. "It's a Bible name for one who
was beautiful. It suits you, my dear."

Pocahontas twisted her head to steal a glimpse of Numees,
hoping the girl would join her in belief and obedience to this

God of the English. But Numees sat stiffly upon the bench, her blue eyes burning toward the clergyman, her fists clenched at her side.

▾▴▾▴▾ "'And God said, let there be light.'" Flushed with a smile of victory, Pocahontas looked up from the Bible. Edith, John Rolfe, and Reverend Whitaker applauded her enthusiastically, while Numees gave her aunt a grudging, momentary smile.

"You've made wonderful progress," John Rolfe said, looking fondly toward the young woman. "Reading already!"

"Numees reads, too," Edith said, tilting her head in Numees's direction. "Will you read for us, little one?"

"No," Numees said, wishing the floor would swallow her up. Pocahontas reveled in attention; Numees hated it. Under the scrutiny of four pairs of eyes she frowned and snatched up another piece of bread, smacking noisily to demonstrate her deplorable manners. If they would only declare the girls barbarians and send them home! Pocahontas would become her old self and things would be as they had always been.

"I've always wanted to know, Numees, what is that you wear around your neck?" Reverend Whitaker asked, ignoring the crust of bread that dangled from her mouth as she chewed.

Numees debated whether or not she should answer, but Edith jumped into the conversation. "It's a gold ring, Reverend. She has worn it always, Rebecca says."

"A gold ring?" The minister's eyes narrowed as he smiled. "That is strange for the Indians, is it not? I have heard of copper in these parts, but not gold." He looked toward his prized protégée. "Where did she find it, Rebecca?"

"I don't know." Pocahontas blushed demurely and lowered her eyes as John Rolfe looked her way. "She's worn it since the first day she came to our village."

"Interesting." The minister reached toward Numees, and she

reflexively pulled back. "I'm not going to hurt you, my dear, I only want to see the ring—"

"No!" Numees leaned far back over her bench, in real danger of losing her balance.

"Don't be silly," Edith chided. "Let the good reverend have a look at it."

"No!" Numees cried. The ring was hers, had always been hers, had never left her neck. It was wrong for this Englishman to touch it.

She lost her balance and fell upon the hard-packed earthen floor. Laughing, the reverend hurried forward and picked her up, but before he released her he held the ring between his fingers and lifted it to the light. "Name of a name," he whispered softly. "There's an inscription inside. In Latin. *Fortiter, Fideliter, Feliciter.*"

Numees whimpered softly in frustration, and Reverend Whitaker dropped the ring and stepped away. She felt his eyes burning toward her in curiosity.

"Where'd the child find such a thing?" John Rolfe asked. "The Indians have no use for Latin."

"The Spanish," Reverend Whitaker murmured, taking his seat on the bench next to Edith. "It's rumored that they sailed up these rivers years ago. If, perchance, they insinuated themselves among the Indians, mayhap to spy out English fortifications—"

"Would that explain her blue eyes?" Edith asked.

"The Spanish are not fair like the English," John pointed out. "At least, no Spaniard I know of."

"It's a mystery," the reverend said, resting his chin in his hand. "But I pray the Spanish are not still hidden in the wilderness."

"But what does it mean?" Pocahontas asked, her eyes wide with genuine fear. "Are the words a curse?"

"No," Reverend Whitaker answered, smiling at her. "It's Latin for 'boldly, faithfully, successfully.' " He looked across the table to Numees. "What, dear child, are you supposed to boldly, faithfully, and successfully do?"

▼▲▼▲▼ Numees tossed in her bed, troubled by dreams of a God-man with holes in his hands and feet. She stood before a cross on the wall of a building and loving faces surrounded her. A woman with fair skin and dark hair whispered a song about Jesus, and as the woman affectionately squeezed Numees's hand, a ring pinched her finger.

"Mama!" The veil between sleep and dreams ripped abruptly, and Numees sat up, drenched in sweat. Panting in fear, she looked for a sign of assurance that she had been dreaming. On the other side of the room, Pocahontas slept peacefully, her hands under her cheek. She looked like an angel, her long dark hair spilling as a lovely contrast over her white nightgown.

Numees pressed her palms to her eyes. The dreams would not stop! Ever since the minister's first visit she had been haunted by dreams of a place she knew but did not recognize, of faces and voices that called to her, but they did not call her Numees. One night the dream had been colored with blood, the loving faces had mouths that opened in silent screams, and hands pushed her into a canoe where she fell, sobbing, until the river carried her away.

And Pocahontas wanted her to accept the God that inspired such dreams? She could not!

Silently, Numees pulled the soft blanket from her English bed and slipped to the floor. She was less troubled by dreams when she slept as an Indian.

She looked toward Pocahontas again and frowned. The love and admiration she had once felt for the older girl had begun to evolve into a reluctant disdain for the Indian princess who too-readily accepted the ways of the clothed, soft English.

▼▲▼▲▼ Henrico, January 3, 1614

John Rolfe to Sir Thomas Dale, Governor of Jamestown
Most Honorable Governor:

I hope this letter finds you well, sir, and I have but one request on this day. I have repeatedly examined my conscience to assure myself that to espouse myself to a creature whose education has been rude, her manners barbarous, her generation accursed, and so different, discrepant in all nurture from myself, will be acceptable to God and for the good of the colony. I propose to marry Rebecca, once known to you as Pocahontas, to whom my heart is and best thoughts are, and have a long time been, so entangled.

I have sought to meet with my lady's father, the chief Powhatan, but he has refused to admit me into his presence. But others of the tribe have assured me that the chief does so only out of pride. He is said to favor this marriage, and so all that remains is your consent, Governor, and the consent of the lady herself. She has not been yet asked, for I wait for your reply, and hope you will grant it speedily.

Sincerely,

John Rolfe

▼▲▼▲▼ A messenger delivered a letter to the house one night after supper and Pocahontas watched John Rolfe open it with trembling fingers. His eyes scanned the page for a moment, then lifted to meet her curious gaze.

"A letter from Governor Dale," he said, his voice husky and warm as the summer sun.

"Come, Numees," Edith said, tugging on the younger girl's sleeve. "We have work to do."

Numees followed Edith outside, but Pocahontas had eyes for no one but John. Something in his face held her to the bench on which she sat, and suddenly the pounding of her heart sounded loud and fierce in her ears.

"What does the letter say?" she asked, hoping though far

from certain of the business that had moved John to write the governor.

"Thomas Dale has written that I must follow my heart," John answered, letting the letter slip from his fingers as he moved to stand before her. In a gentle, graceful manner he dropped to one knee and reached for her hand. "And my heart has beat only for you in these last few months, my dear Rebecca."

Her heart reacted immediately to his intense gaze, quickening in its tempo and rhythm as a tingling delight began to flow through her. For the first time in her life, Pocahontas could not think of words to say. But John seemed to expect something, for still he knelt before her, his hand clasping hers, his emotions clear upon his face.

"It is customary for a woman to answer when a man asks for her hand in marriage," John whispered at last, a smile tipping his lips and lighting his eyes. "I don't know how it is done among your people, Rebecca, but in England a man promises his love to a woman and waits to hear whether or not she will become his wife."

"Your wife?" she breathed, scarcely daring to believe she had heard correctly.

"My most precious wife," he answered, giving her a heart-stopping smile.

"Yes, John Rolfe," she cried, leaning forward to throw her arms around his neck. He stood, drawing her up with him into a warm embrace as she pressed her lips close to his ear and said, "It would be the greatest honor of my life to call you husband!"

▾▲▾▲ One month before the proposed wedding, John Rolfe took his intended bride with him up the Pamunkey River to meet with Opechancanough, who had agreed to negotiate a peace between Powhatan and the English. When Pocahontas had originally been taken hostage, Governor Dale had demanded that in exchange for her release, Powhatan should return several runaway Englishmen as well as certain stolen goods and firearms. In addition, the Governor asked that Powhatan pledge five hundred bushels of corn as a guarantee to conclude a firm peace.

Throughout the year of Pocahontas's captivity, Powhatan had refused to either meet the terms or parley with the enemy. But now that the chief's daughter had freely chosen to marry an Englishman, Governor Dale hoped that Powhatan's pride would allow him to forgive the kidnapping and confirm the peace as his blessing to the union. Everyone involved in the prenuptial journey trusted that the presence of the princess, so obviously in love with the handsome Englishman who held her hand, would sway the aged chief's heart toward a permanent peace.

When runners reported that Powhatan refused to join the gathering or meet with his daughter and her prospective husband, Pocahontas wept against John Rolfe's shoulder, feebly wretched. But Opechancanough received the envoys into his village and promised to do all he could to meet the English terms for peace.

"Tell Powhatan this," said Robert Sparkes, an assistant to Governor Dale. He strode forward into the center of the gathering before Opechancanough, his face flushed with anger. "Unless peace is reached by harvesttime, we will come upriver again, kill your people, and destroy your homes and crops."

Pocahontas felt a shiver of terror run through her. How dare this man make such a threat when her wedding and future happiness depended upon her uncle's willingness to negotiate a peace?

But Opechancanough's granite expression did not change. When Sparkes had finished speaking, the great chief stood and pointed toward the shallop waiting at the river's edge. "Go," he said simply, his dark, impassive eyes sweeping over Pocahontas as if for the last time. "We will send word of our chief's wishes."

Dashed dreams and disillusionment raked at Pocahontas's heart as she took her place in the boat. Robert Sparkes and his fierce English pride had undoubtedly ruined all chances for peace, and she had come to know the English well enough to recognize their undeniable sense of superiority. *There are some things you English cannot conquer,* she thought, swaying slightly as the oarsmen pushed the boat from the sand into the water. She placed her hands on the sides of the vessel to steady herself, then lifted her chin. *And the pride of the Powhatan is one of them.*

▼▲▼▲▼ A week after their return to Jamestown, Opechancanough sent word that Powhatan had agreed to Governor Dale's terms. Pocahontas was free to marry John Rolfe as she so ardently desired.

On the fifth day of April 1614, the Revered Richard Buck married the widower John Rolfe to the Indian Princess Rebecca, née Matoaka, daughter of Powhatan and known with great affection as Pocahontas. The great chief did not attend the wedding, but sent his brother, Opechancanough, and his sons, Kitchi and Keme, to represent him at the wedding.

Every soul present in the small chapel at Jamestown hoped that the marriage might seal the peace between the Indians and the English forever. The marriage, and the peace it represented, brought an end to five years of intermittent war.

As Numees watched the strange blending of English and Indian customs at the wedding, her only feeling was a heavy, sodden dullness. Pocahontas was her sister no longer, for now she belonged to John Rolfe. Powhatan cared nothing for Numees; indeed, the chief seemed to have forgotten all about her. And though Pocahontas often said Numees would always have a home in her house, still, the younger girl felt not unlike a forgotten bead from a broken string, an eleven-year-old, half-loved child who was nobody's daughter.

*Is it possible?* she wondered, watching the glow of love light the face of the woman who had just become Rebecca Rolfe. *Will I ever know love like that?*

*1616*

The days fell like autumn leaves from an oak tree, one after the other, indistinguishable but for the passing seasons of Virginia. Within two years John Rolfe's tobacco had become the mainstay of the colony, and the fields outside his planation at Henrico and the house at Jamestown were planted with rows of the weed. Numees did not understand the plant's appeal—she cared for neither the pungent tobacco of the Indians nor the sweeter scent of Rolfe's mixed strain—but Rebecca Rolfe was proud of her husband and delighted with his success. John, in return, was enraptured with his young wife and the son she bore him.

"The tobacco is like me and John," Pocahontas told Numees one afternoon as she pressed a new skirt made of fine English silk. "A blend of Indian and English. Neither are quite palatable alone, but together we make a fine mix!"

Numees made a face and ignored her aunt's prattling. A warm kernel of happiness had occupied the center of Pocahontas's being since her marriage and motherhood, and the older girl's happiness stuck like a thorn in Numees's side. At twenty-one, Pocahontas was still as lighthearted as a child, and in comparison Numees felt like a staid, quiet toad next to a butterfly.

"I hope you'll consider going to England with us," Pocahontas said as she worked the iron over the fabric of the new kirtle John had imported for her. Her English had improved tremendously, and she loved to practice speaking in her new tongue. "As soon as Governor Dale is recalled to England, we'll be free to leave. We're sailing on the *Treasurer*—do you remember the long days

and nights we spent there? And after we arrive in London, John
is to write a report for the king."

"I don't want to go," Numees said slowly, waving her hand in
front of the baby's watchful gaze. He paused, eyes wide as he
crouched on his hands and knees, then dimpled for a toothless,
drippy smile. Numees shook her head and gently teased him in
Algonquin.

"At least a dozen of Opechancanough's people are going with
us," Pocahontas inserted.

"I won't go," Numees said stubbornly, lifting the baby onto
her lap. "Who would stay with Edith? I won't leave her alone."

"Edith is a grown woman; she doesn't need you," Pocahontas
answered, her voice light. "Come with us, little sister. You can
help me with the baby—"

"You want me to hold him while other people gawk?" A flood
of pent-up frustration burst forth from her, emotions she had just
begun to understand. She turned the baby so he couldn't see the
storm that darkened her face. "You want me to stand by while
they say his eyes are English and his skin is Indian? While they
poke and prod him and wonder if his blood is red like theirs? I
won't do it. I'll stay here."

Pocahontas stopped ironing and folded her arms in a defiant
gesture. "Is that my thanks, then? For keeping you with us, for
offering you the best England has to give?"

"Who said I wanted England's best?" Numees asked, lifting
her head. "I have never asked to go anywhere with you, my
aunt. It is you who always wants company. You wanted me to go
with you to Aranck's village, to Captain Argall's ship, to Jamestown. You are brave, you love the English, but you won't go anywhere alone. And now you want to go see England itself; you
would pinch their king and see if he's real. I have no such desire.
Go without me. And do not ask me to go again."

Numees waited for Pocahontas's response, but the older girl
seemed preoccupied, as if a premonition or memory had suddenly surfaced and overshadowed her awareness of the conversation they were having. "Sister?" Numees called softly, her

anger fading at the sight of Pocahontas's stricken face. The young woman jerked, startled, and rearranged her troubled expression into a pensive smile.

"It's a long way, isn't it?" she whispered, arching her brows into triangles. "Of course, I'll have John, but . . . ," her voice faded, then she threw Numees an anxious glance. "What if I never come home again, little sister?"

Numees pressed her lips to the soft hair on the baby's head as the question hung between them, unanswered.

In the halcyon days of late spring, John and Rebecca Rolfe sailed with their infant son and Governor Thomas Dale to England. After their arrival in London, John Rolfe wrote a treatise for the king entitled *A True Relation of the State of Virginia, Left by Sir Thomas Dale, Knight, in May last, 1616*. Some months later, a copy of this report fell into the hands of Delbert Crompton, headmaster of the Royal Academy for Homeless Orphans. As soon as his bleary eyes fell closed on the evening in which he had received the narrative, his servant, Fallon Bailie, fell upon its pages and did not look up until the candle sputtered out and he was forced to search for another.

Fallon's brows lifted in pleasure as he recognized the rivers and landmarks of his memory. Though a different cast of characters moved through the landscape, Fallon could see the beloved land stretching before him in wild and terrible majesty.

In October, talk at Master Crompton's monthly meeting of learned intellectuals soon turned to the king's court and the presentation of the Indian princess. Though Fallon had been wont to hide in his corner as soon as it was obvious the master had no further need of him, at the mention of Powhatan's daughter he lost all custody of his eyes and ears. He bent his lanky form into a darkened corner of the great hall and listened intently as the men smoked the fashionable new tobacco and told of the charming princess who spoke English fluently and carried herself as the daughter of a king.

"I hear she is highly respected," one portly gentleman muttered around his pipe, "not only by the king's company, but in particular by clergymen in their hopeful zeal that she will advance Christianity. The lady is a true Christian, no doubt, and in her lies our best hope to win the continent to the Savior."

"May it be so," Master Crompton muttered, doubtless missing his quart of ale, for by now he was usually asleep.

"I heard that certain of the king's court reintroduced the lady to Captain John Smith," another man offered. "He could not believe that the child who saved his life before Powhatan had grown into an affable and beautiful young woman."

*A young woman.* Fallon felt a curious, tingling shock. His mind had often formed questions to ask John Smith about the children Gilda and Noshi, but surely they had grown now to be . . . He figured quickly. If they still lived, Gilda had to be thirteen, and Noshi was only a few months older. Name of a name! Noshi was at an age when most Indians underwent the rites of manhood, and Gilda was not far from marriage. The next few months would bring the greatest trials of their lives, and he was powerless to help them!

A harrowing headache pounded his forehead as he slumped to the floor. Bowing his head, Fallon rested his hands on his knees and lifted his heart to heaven. "Father God," he prayed, not caring if the men in the room beyond heard his frantic whispers, "be where I cannot be. Remain close to the side of my Gilda and my Noshi, and bring our paths together. Guide me so that I may find them, and keep them safe until we meet again."

He opened his eyes and stared at the dancing shadows in the rushlight. The baritone voices of Master Crompton's guests rose and fell as they congratulated each other on their collective wisdom, and rain blasted against the leaded panes of the windows. Fallon was so far from Virginia! Of certain only the power of God could reunite him with the children.

▼▲▼▲▼ Hope came in the form of a severe ague which afflicted Master Crompton and forced the headmaster to send his servant on an errand to the apothecary. Fallon stepped into the busy London street and went straightway to the druggist, who promised to bring the prescribed herbs to the school as soon as possible. With a reassuring pat upon the crinkled parchment in his doublet pocket, Fallon walked toward the smithy, stopping to ask for directions several times along the way.

The narrow cobblestone street was encumbered with traffic and clogged with pedestrians, but Fallon finally found the barnlike structure that housed the smithy. A full moment passed before he recognized Brody McRyan, for the boy of his schooldays had grown into a handsome man. The softness of youth had completely left his face, and the slender arms had hardened with muscle and sinew from the demanding work of a blacksmith.

Brody stood with his forehead buried in the sweaty side of a mare, her hoof balanced betwixt his knees. He glanced toward Fallon for a moment, sweat dripping into his eyes, and muttered, "Be with you in a moment, sir."

"Brody."

The smith's apprentice abruptly dropped the hoof, and the mare snorted in disapproval. "Fallon?" Brody's eyes widened in delight. "Fallon Bailie!"

The friends embraced, then parted to look at one another again. "Ah, no, I never would a'knowed you," Brody said, his eyes snapping at the sight of Fallon. "How goes it at Master Crompton's? Are you counting the days?"

"Aye, and you?" Fallon answered, taking a seat on a bench beside the mare.

"My term will be done soon enough," Brody answered, tossing a searching glance over his shoulder. He winked at Fallon. "The master doesn't like me talking too much. Docks my dinner a bite for every word I say, he does."

"I won't keep you. I have to get back myself, for Crompton still believes in working from dawn till dusk," Fallon answered, grinning. He fell silent and studied the ground. "But I can't leave the house, you see, and I wondered if you could do a favor for me. I wouldn't put you out, but I've a letter that needs to be delivered."

Brody's eyes glinted with mischief. "I see. Can it be that our Fallon has fallen in love?"

"No." Fallon felt his cheeks burning. "I haven't even seen a girl in ten years, not up close anyway. My letter is to John Smith."

"Sure, and don't I know it is," Brody answered, laughing. He scrubbed his close-cropped head with his knuckles. "I don't know how I could help you, Fallon, because gentlemen of John Smith's caliber don't usually come to the smithy themselves."

"But gentlemen *do* come," Fallon persisted. "They have horses, they send their grooms. I have absolutely *no* chance of sending the letter, Brody, and I haven't another friend in all of London."

"And why is it so urgent that you be seein' Captain Smith now? In a year or so you'll be free and able to do as you like—"

"Powhatan's daughter is in London, Brody, and she knows John Smith. Don't you see? The Lady Rebecca Rolfe has to know what happened to Gilda! I don't know how to reach her, and Master Crompton would beat me even for asking him such a question, but if John Smith knows I need to see her—"

"I cry you mercy! Enough!" Brody said, a wry smile curling on his lips as he extended his hand for the letter. "I'll see what I can do."

"Thank you," Fallon answered, relieved. He gave his friend the sealed parchment, and Brody stuffed the letter into his jerkin.

Fallon felt a lump rise in his throat as he briefly embraced Brody. "As soon as you're released, you come find me, you hear? And I'll do the same if I'm free before you."

"Aye," Brody answered, tipping an imaginary cap before bending again into the side of the mare. "That's a promise, me friend."


▼▲▼▲▼ Delbert Crompton recovered from his illness in time to watch his well-ordered and profitable world turn on its head. Reverend Paul Stacey, the old cleric who had hitherto given Master Crompton free reign in administrating the Royal

Academy for Homeless Orphans, had the audacity to die of old age. The new rector of St. Paul's, the Reverend Stephen Archer, took an unconscionable interest in the school's administration and appeared at the academy one afternoon for an unannounced visit.

Archer stood tall and straight as he entered the dining hall. Though his skin bore the pallor of desk work, his face was serious and dedicated.

Master Crompton ushered the new clergyman to the seat of honor at the center table in the dining hall. Even seated, Reverend Archer looked taller than anyone else in the room. He did not concentrate on the headmaster, but peered around, comparing his sumptuous dinner with the meager, meatless meals of the boys. After an observant evaluation, Archer promptly announced that he would not eat a morsel until the boys had meat, too, and plenty of it, because from the looks of their thin faces they had been severely deprived.

After Crompton sent the cooks scurrying to the kitchen to find meat for the boys' bowls, the Reverend Archer fixed the headmaster with an unblinking eye and ordered that henceforth the boys would have a generous meat pottage every day. A crown of gloom settled upon Delbert Crompton as he saw the profits of years past slip through his fingers. This foolishly tenderhearted minister would insist upon proper clothing for the boys, clean linens, maybe even more classes and better instruction. He would have to employ another teacher, possibly two, and give a careful accounting of the church funds that had purchased so many fine clothes and books and lovely quarts of ale over the years.

"Have you anything to say to me, Master Crompton?" the minister asked, a look of intense, clear light pouring through his eyes from across the table.

Crompton cleared his throat and shifted his weight in his chair. It would be useless to protest, for it would take only a vote by the board of overseers to toss Crompton out of his position.

And he was too old, too tired, too *settled* to find another avenue of employment.

"I was just about to suggest that we vary our menu a bit," Crompton replied, folding his hands in surrender. "And I wondered if you might like to meet the young man who serves as my apprentice. He's a product of the academy himself, a fine boy who carries himself well. If you feel we should expand our curriculum, we could use him as a tutor immediately and spare the cost of hiring another."

"His name?" the clergyman asked, eyeing Crompton steadily over the rim of his silver goblet.

"Fallon Bailie," Crompton replied, sighing.

▼▲▼▲ Fallon did not know why he was suddenly promoted to a position of authority, nor did he understand why the students around him had suddenly decorated themselves with smiles. It was almost as if the academy had transformed itself from a prison into a real school, for the boys moved easily and noisily through the halls to their classes and actually conversed at dinner with satisfied expressions on their faces. Fallon was invited to eat in the school's society, as were the other teachers. From the center table, adorned now in plain linen like the boys' tables, Master Crompton and the new rector of St. Paul's surveyed the new and improved situation. Reverend Archer, at least, saw what he had created and pronounced it good.

Crompton assigned Fallon to a class of twelve-year-olds and directed him to teach Bible catechism. Fallon had not realized how starved he was for the society of human companionship until he found it restored to him. In his small classroom he was surrounded by eager boys who looked at him with more than the grudging respect they had henceforth shown their teachers. He realized one day that their admiration sprang from the fact that he was one of them. Of all the authority figures at the school, only he had slept in the creaky rope bunks of the dormitory and squirmed under the hot gaze of headmaster Crompton.

As he led his students in the catechism of the Anglican church, their youthful voices reminded him of the many occasions he had led Noshi and Gilda to repeat the same words: *I believe in God the Father, who made me and all the world. I believe in God the Son, who has redeemed me and all mankind. I believe in God the Holy Ghost, who sanctifieth me and all the elect people of God. . . .*

One afternoon, the headmaster ushered a new student into the class while Fallon rehearsed the students in their recitations. Master Crompton seated the boy on a bench at the back of the small room, and Fallon raised a questioning brow. Small in stature and painfully thin, the boy appeared to be not more than eight years of age.

The class paused in their recitation, waiting for Fallon to say the questioner's line. "Um . . . ," Fallon said, searching his memory for the phrase. "You say that you should keep God's commandments. Tell me how many there be."

"Ten," the class responded.

"Which be they?"

The group took a collective breath and continued in their steady, even pace: "The same which God spake in the twentieth chapter of Exodus, saying, I am the Lord thy God, who brought thee out of the land of Egypt, out of the house of bondage. . . ."

Fallon left the front of the room and knelt at the newcomer's side. "Why are you in this room?" he asked, pitching his voice below the boys' chant. "This is a class for boys who have reached twelve years."

"I 'ave," the boy said, his eyes gleaming with a film of tears. His face showed a delicate dimension of sensitivity. "I am twelve; I'm just small, my lord."

"There's no need for that title," Fallon said, patting the boy's leg. "I'm just Fallon Bailie around here, though I suppose the headmaster would want you to call me Master Bailie."

The boy nodded and hunched forward, shivering slightly in the chill of the room. Fallon noticed his worn clothing and frowned. "Have you not been given warmer garments?" he asked. "Surely Master Crompton has something—"

Without warning, the boy threw back his head and released a keening wail of sorrow. His face screwed up as tears rolled from the corner of his eyes, and Fallon fell back upon the floor in surprise. The other boys turned in amazement, the catechism forgotten.

"There, there," Fallon said, picking himself up. He patted the boy awkwardly on the shoulder. "It's hard when you first come, but we've all had a first day, you know. You'll get used to this place in time, and you'll learn many things. . . ."

"Me mother and father died yesterday," the boy cried, wiping his eyes on the dirty sleeve of his shirt. "The minister came and took me away. They took me sister, too, though I know not where, and told me I have to live in this place forever!"

"Not forever," Fallon said, lowering his head to meet the boy's frightened eyes. "You won't have to stay forever. And when your time is done and God moves you away from this school, you can search for your sister. Do you understand?"

The boy nodded slowly, then brushed the other sleeve across his nose.

"Good," Fallon said, standing. "What is your name?"

"Watford Clarence," the boy answered. He hiccupped a repressed sob. "They call me Wart."

"Wart." Fallon smiled. "That name is your choice?"

"I like it," the newcomer offered, shrugging shyly. "Me father gave me that name."

"Then by all means, Wart it is," Fallon said, turning toward the class. "Boys, I'd be pleased if you'd make Wart welcome in our school."

Fallon returned to the front of the room and to the catechism, but for days afterward the eyes of Wart Clarence followed him in wordless gratitude and unabashed admiration. Wart was not the only student who treated Fallon with such respect, and one day the loving appreciation in the boys' eyes so overwhelmed Fallon that he had to leave the room and bury his face in his hands lest the boys see his tears. He feared they would think him mad if they saw him crying over nothing, but in their grateful, happy

faces Fallon had of late seen an echo of the ennobled society he
had known at Ocanahonan, where men and women, English and
Indian, had lived together in peace and contentment under the
love of God.

▼▲▼▲▼ One cold afternoon in March the Reverend
Archer stood from his visitor's chair at the center dining table
and lifted a hand. "We must pray especially today for the soul of
a dear lady I have been privileged to meet," he said, a wounded
look in his dark eyes. "All of London prays today for the Lady
Rebecca Rolfe, an Indian princess. While she and her husband
and son waited for favorable weather to return them to their
home in Virginia, the lady has contracted the pox and lies even
now near death."

Fallon sat as though fastened to the bench beneath him. Several truths hit him at once, each with the impact of a physical
blow: A ship waited in an English harbor to return to Virginia,
the lady he knew as Powhatan's daughter lay near death, and,
should she die, all news of Gilda and Noshi might well die with
her!

The minister bowed his head to pray, but Fallon could not contain his thoughts long enough to direct them heavenward. When
the meal was done, Fallon ignored his waiting class and followed Master Crompton to his office.

▼▲▼▲▼ "What the devil?" The words exploded from
Crompton's lips when he turned to see Fallon Bailie standing
behind him. What did the accursed boy want this time? "You
have a class. Go to it now."

"I have a boon to ask of you, sir. The Lady Rebecca Rolfe—I
believe I may know her."

Crompton snorted and moved to the chair behind his desk.
Thus far he had been fortunate that the lad kept these wild fantasies to himself, but if young Bailie's madness proceeded to mani-

fest itself before his students, the council would hear of it. "You know the lady in your dreams, mayhap," he said, staring down his heavy nose. "Now get to work. I'll hear none of this foolishness."

"No," Fallon said, stepping closer. "The Lady Rebecca was . . . is . . . a great friend of John Smith's, and I have a responsibility to two children who were left in his care. She may know of them, she may have even brought them with her to England—"

"I've had enough of you, Fallon Bailie!" Crompton roared, biting back an oath. He leaned across the desk and shook a thick finger at Fallon as his face purpled. "Get back to your class!"

The tutor did not move. "Sir, I must be granted leave to visit Mistress Rolfe."

"Get back to your class or—" Crompton whirled to the fireplace behind him. A spasm gripped his chest but he ignored it, reaching out to seize an iron poker from the fire. Brandishing it in front of him like a sword, he pointed the sharp end toward his apprentice and studied the resolute face of Fallon Bailie. With any luck, the young man would take a swing at him, and give him justifiable cause to beat him so he'd not soon forget it. But Fallon Bailie remained calm.

"Sir, I must respectfully ask your permission to go see Master and Mistress Rolfe. If you won't allow me to go, I shall be forced to call upon Reverend Archer—"

Crompton winced as something nipped at his heart, then the violence in him bubbled and his eyes locked upon Fallon in open warfare. "You will obey me!" he screamed, swinging the iron poker. His rage spilled over as the young man nimbly backstepped from the blow.

Bellowing in frustration, Crompton dropped the poker and rushed toward his servant. He struck Fallon with the knuckles of his hand, a short, vicious, blow, and yet Bailie would not reciprocate or surrender. "I pray you, sir," the apprentice said again, a hand to his reddened jaw, "Grant me leave to go!"

"When hell freezes solid!" Crompton spat the words and lunged forward, his hands intent on the boy's slender throat. But again Fallon stepped out of the way. Delbert Crompton felt himself falling, then his chest erupted in a spasm of blinding white pain.

▼▲▼▲▼ Trembling, Fallon stood above his prone master and nudged the body with the toe of his shoe. "Master Crompton?" he said, lifting the heavy poker from the floor. How heavy it was, and how deliberately it had been aimed at his head!

A diabolical voice whispered in his fevered imagination. *Do it,* the murmur came. *Land the killing blow and all would know it was self-defense. You have a bruise from his blow upon your cheek, and you have borne his hatred and derision and mocking scorn long enough.*

But then the master groaned and shuddered, and Fallon ran from the office to fetch help.

▼▲▼▲▼ "There was nothing you could do," Reverend Stephen Archer told Fallon. The reverend sat in the chair that had been Master Crompton's, and for the first time in Fallon's memory the eyes above the desk were kind and gentle. "The physician said it was his heart. It was a matter of his age and his drinking."

Fallon said nothing, but bit his lip.

"There are some that will be glad to see him go," the minister said, running his finger idly along the edge of the headmaster's desk. "He was a moneygrubbing miser who put his own interests above those of the boys."

"He wasn't entirely bad," Fallon whispered. "He was resourceful. And though we didn't always eat meat, we did eat every day. I've seen worse situations on the streets of London."

"Indeed, you make a good point," the minister said, smiling. "That's why I'm prepared to offer you the job of headmaster here, Fallon Bailie. After all, you were Master Crompton's apprentice, and your contract of indenture expires in a few months. What had you planned to do after that?"

Fallon nervously pulled the cuffs of his sleeves down to cover the thin lines of the tattoos on his wrists. Did he dare reveal his dreams to his man? So far, only Brody McRyan had heard his story and believed it.

"I had hoped to go to Virginia," he finally said, compromising his hopes with his fears. "I have heard there is a great demand for those willing to work on the tobacco plantations."

"Do you like tobacco so much?" the minister asked, chuckling.

Fallon laughed. "No. But I like Virginia, from what I've read of it, of course. And I firmly believe God would have me go there. In fact," he found himself leaning forward eagerly, "I had hoped to visit Master and Mistress John Rolfe before their ship leaves for Virginia."

"I'm so sorry, Fallon," the minister whispered, his eyes darkening with sorrow. "Lady Rebecca died a few days ago. Her husband is in mourning. I'm afraid it would be impossible for anyone to visit."

Fallon felt his heart sink. What form of divine interference was this? Had he misunderstood God's will? God had brought Powhatan's daughter all the way to London, even within a few miles of where Fallon lived and worked, but yet he had not been able to talk to her. What was God's purpose in such maneuvering?

"If your heart is set upon Virginia," Reverend Archer said, tapping his long fingers upon the desk, "will you take the job of administering our school until we can find a permanent headmaster? You will of certain do an able job, for I've watched you with the boys and I know you have a heart for them."

"Thank you," Fallon whispered, not able to look up. "And yes, I will be happy to continue here until . . ." Words failed him. What else was he to do?

"Good," the minister said, standing. He extended his hand. "We will be praying for you."

Though Fallon had undertaken the headmaster's position with reluctance, he soon found great joy in righting the wrongs that had galled him ever since coming to the Royal Academy for Homeless Orphans. He discovered that the school had a great wealth of funds with which to feed, clothe, and educate the boys, and only the miserly greed of Delbert Crompton had kept the place from being a comfortable, worthwhile establishment.

Fallon decided to administrate the school as if it had been founded at Ocanahonan, according to principles of equality and reverence for God and man. Upon his orders, generous and filling meals were prepared each day, and the curriculum was adjusted to meet the needs of boys who might wish to pursue something other than physical labor as blacksmiths, fishermen, or masons. Fallon personally saw to it that the rancid pillows and blankets from the dormitory were burned and fresh linens supplied.

The despised center table of the dining hall was eliminated, and Fallon ate at a table with his students, as did the other teachers and any guests who might choose to visit during dinner. Headmaster Bailie abolished the rule of absolute silence at meals and in the halls, and the building rang with the shouts and mischief of growing boys.

One month after assuming Master Crompton's desk and position, Fallon found the Reverend Stephen Archer again in his office. He greeted the minister and invited him to take a seat. "Is there news from the council?" he asked, suddenly afraid that he might already have been replaced. Making changes in the school had been so gratifying, he did not want to leave and allow another master of Master Crompton's mind-set to return the academy to dreary poverty.

"I'm afraid there is news, but whether it is of a good or evil nature remains to be seen," the minister said, pulling a letter from a sheaf of papers in his valise. "There are two matters of business. The first concerns the council of clergymen who oversee the school. They have noticed the changes you've made."

"And?" Fallon asked, alarmed by the minister's somber face.

"They heartily approve," Reverend Archer said, breaking into a reluctant smile. "Your methods are unconventional, your discipline undeniably more lax than your predecessor's, but there's no gainsaying that the boys are happier and more productive since you took the position of headmaster. Time will prove your methods, of course, but the council would like you to continue permanently. You'd be the youngest headmaster in all of London, but in sooth—" he leaned forward confidentially—"I believe you are already the most respected."

Fallon sat back, stunned. He could not deny that his work had been unbelievably rewarding and fulfilling; he had only to look into the contented eyes of Wart Clarence to know that the boys were better off under his tutelage than the prevailing "children should be seen and not heard" philosophy.

"The council is prepared to enlarge the school and increase the headmaster's salary," Reverend Archer went on, placing a sheet of parchment upon the desk. "They'd like the school to be a model for others. Of course, you'll have scores of learned academics poking about, seeking to discover how a twenty-three-year-old man has managed to instill both love and discipline in a pack of orphans, but something tells me you'll be up to the challenge."

"I would enjoy it," Fallon admitted, a smile sweeping over his face as he thought of sour-faced critics coming face-to-face with love in action.

"But before you decide to accept our offer, there is another matter," the minister said, holding up a finger. "It seems that his Majesty's colony in Virginia has gone tobacco mad. There is a demand for willing workers, including children, especially young boys. The street orphans, as you know, are not strong enough to handle a sea journey and life among the savages, so the council has recommended that we send boys from our functioning orphanage schools. And since this academy has made a name for itself in this short time, your school will be the prime source of our recruits."

The announcement was unexpected and shocking. "I don't understand," Fallon said, shaking his head.

The minister shrugged. "It is simple. The boys will work in Virginia for a term of indentured service until they are eligible to own and farm their own land."

Fallon tilted his head, amazed. "Send orphans?" he repeated, his brain slow to comprehend that the idea was not an absurd jest. "Just like that? To Virginia?"

Archer nodded. "It is quite an adventure, I'll warrant. Of course, not all the boys from the school will be sent, only those twelve years of age and older. But their places at this academy will be filled immediately with children from the streets, and a new group will emigrate each year. Virginia has what England needs, Master Bailie—wood, land, water—and England has the manpower the colony desperately needs."

"But—children?" Fallon asked. "Among the savages?" He felt a shiver pass down his spine as the minister's words opened the door on memories he'd tried to bury. One day Ritanoe had been filled with the odor of burning flesh, the agonized screams of women and children, and sights that would of certain curdle this minister's refined blood. . . .

"They won't be thrown to the savages," Reverend Archer said, pulling back as if Fallon had somehow insulted him. "They will live in a dormitory much like the one here. During the morning, they will attend language and Bible class. In the afternoons they will work in the tobacco fields. After a term of four or five years, they will be given a new suit of clothes and acreage to call their own. It is an admirable bargain."

He thrust a letter toward Fallon, who took it up with a

trembling hand. "'The Treasurer, Council, and Company of Virginia in London,'" he read, "'have taken into consideration the continual great forwardness of His Majesty's honorable city of London in advancing the Plantation of Virginia. And forasmuch as we have now resolved to send next Spring very large supplies for the strength and increasing of the Colony, we pray your Lord and the rest to bestow your favor to furnish us with one hundred children of twelve years old and upward with allowance of three pounds apiece for their transportation and forty shillings apiece for their apparel. They shall be apprentices: the boys till they come to twenty-one years of age; the girls till the like age or till they be married. Afterwards they shall be placed as tenants upon the public land with best conditions where they shall have houses with stock of corn and cattle to begin with, and afterward the moiety of all increase and profit whatsoever. And so we leave this motion to your honorable and grave consideration.'"

"Until they are twenty-one," Fallon said, reading the letter. "You said a term of four or five years."

"If they are sixteen now, it will be a term of five years," Archer said, frowning.

Fallon lay the parchment upon the desk and stared at it, thinking. Wart Clarence was only twelve. If he chose to go to Virginia he would be a virtual slave for nine years, an eternity in such a harsh environment.

"I have spent much time in the study of Virginia," Fallon said, slowly feeling his way. "The men of the London Company do not know all the dangers. It will be such a change for the boys—"

"If they had someone to care directly for them, it would be better, of certain," the minister said, sliding the letter from under Fallon's gaze and replacing it inside his satchel. He tented his hands. "You've expressed an interest in journeying to Virginia, Master Bailie, and it is the only reason I bring this news before you. The intelligent choice, of course, is to remain here as headmaster and let the council find someone else to care for the boys on the voyage."

"This caregiver," Fallon said slowly, raking a hand through his hair. "What would be required of him?"

The minister frowned. "Nothing of import. He would keep an eye on the boys during the sea voyage and get them settled under their new masters. Then he'd be free to make a life for himself in Virginia, if he wishes. If not, he could return to England and supervise another company of boys the next year."

Fallon let his head fall to the back of his chair. What was God's purpose in this conundrum? One position offered fulfillment, wealth, and security; the other a tenuous term of uncertainty, poverty, and the harshness of colonization. To any Englishman the correct choice would be obvious, but Fallon Bailie was not an Englishman.

Even so, the decision was not an easy one. True enough, six months ago he would not have hesitated to board a ship for the colony. But the last few weeks had brought peace and purpose to his life. Hadn't he done enough? Maybe his time of hoping was done; maybe it was time to settle down in England and forget Virginia altogether. He had hoped to find the answers he sought about his family from Rebecca Rolfe, but now that she was dead what answers could he possibly find in Jamestown? Finding two children lost in the wilderness nine years ago would be next to impossible. It was unlikely that Powhatan remained alive, and John Smith, the one man who might have the answers Fallon sought, lived now in London.

"Uncertain?" Reverend Archer asked, lifting an eyebrow. "I thought you might be. So I have arranged for you to visit John Rolfe this afternoon, before his ship sails for Virginia. He has agreed to answer any questions you might have, and he is most eager to gather willing hands for his plantation in a place called Henrico. Though of course," Archer said, standing, "we are hoping you will remain here with us."

▼▲▼▲▼ The man who answered Fallon's knock was slim and pale, his brown eyes shadowed by grief. Two trunks, bound and corded with locks and chains, stood in the hall of the small inn where he was housed. The strong scent of tobacco filled the room as if Master Rolfe had just finished smoking a pipe, and the odor jarred memories in Fallon's soul from their places of safekeeping. Rowtag, his beloved stepfather, had smelled strongly of tobacco, as had half the men in Ocanahonan. It was the odor of primitive and untamed Virginia, and the recollection brought a lump to Fallon's throat.

"Fallon Bailie?" Rolfe asked, his eyes briefly sweeping over Fallon's lanky form.

Fallon nodded, unable to trust his voice, but Rolfe seemed not to notice. He left the door open, and Fallon followed him into the small chamber.

Rolfe launched into an automatic and seemingly oft-repeated sermon on the virtues of raising tobacco in Virginia, but Fallon raised a hand and cut him off. "I know about Virginia," he said, taking a seat on a bench against the wall.

Rolfe lifted a brow in a silent question, and Fallon quickly shed his doublet and then rolled up his sleeve until the tattoos on his forearms appeared. Visibly shaken, Rolfe shuddered and swallowed. "My wife had similar markings," he said, his voice thick with clotted emotion. His eyes flew to Fallon's face again. "But you are not Indian."

"I am Virginian," Fallon said. He briefly told Rolfe the story of Ocanahonan, of Noshi and Gilda, of Smith's hasty move to transport Fallon out of Jamestown and into an orphanage in England. "John Smith did not keep his promise," Fallon said, staring absently into the fire. "I have tried to reach him, but I do not know how."

"It would be no use," John Rolfe said, shaking his head in wonder at the tale. "Smith never mentioned discovering any trace of the lost colony. And though I have often been among the Indians of Virginia, I have never heard the names Gilda and Noshi. But if God is for you—" his eyes met Fallon's and seemed to see through to the heart of his soul—"then you shall find them. And I will help, if you come."

They were simple words, but Fallon heard God's call in them. The challenge of his life still remained to be met in the forests of the New World.

He stood to his feet and bowed his thanks. "Then my boys and I will see you next year in Virginia," he said simply.

# Kimi

*Behold, I have refined thee, but not with silver;
I have chosen thee in the furnace of affliction.*

*Isaiah 48:10*

Numees danced through the house again, running her dust rag
over the gleaming wood of the furniture and testing the softness
of the rag rugs beneath her feet. In the year of Pocahontas's
absence, she and Edith had done many things to make the house
more of a home for Mistress Rolfe, her husband, and their son.
Edith had hired a man to build an additional chamber off the
front hall, so now there were four distinct rooms. It was the largest house in Jamestown, and Numees was quietly glad that the
tobacco from John Rolfe's plantation had furnished enough
lovely things to make the simple house shine with elegance.
Pocahontas would be delighted to be home, and Numees could
not wait to see her again.

"Do you think the baby has learned to walk?" Edith asked as
she arranged fresh evergreen limbs and flowers over the fireplace mantle. "I know so little of babies."

The scent of pine filled the room, and the delicious aroma
reminded Numees of carefree days when she and Pocahontas
had explored the woods as two young girls. "Of course he will
be walking," Numees answered, tucking her dust rag into the
waistband of the kirtle she wore. "He is my cousin, after all, and
I walked within four seasons of my birth."

Edith shot her a questioning glance. "How do you know
that?"

Numees paused. How *did* she know that? The fact had sprung
unbidden into her mind, as part of a story someone used to tell.
She shrugged away the feeling of déjà vu. "I just know, that's
all," she answered, refusing to feel anything but happy. "You can

ask Pocahontas—I mean, Rebecca—yourself. She'll tell you that I always beat her in our village footraces."

A horn blew from the direction of the sea, and Edith went to the window and parted the new lace curtains. "The ship is in," she whispered, a current of joy in her voice. "Let us pray that last courier was right and that John and Rebecca have sailed upon this ship."

Numees shivered with the special tingle of anticipation. She wanted nothing more than to run out of the house and throw her arms around Pocahontas on the dock. But that would spoil the element of surprise. More than anything, she wanted Mistress Rebecca Rolfe to see that she, Numees, had become English, with proper English clothes, an English accent, and the knowledge necessary to run a tidy English house.

In the weeks following the Rolfes' departure for England, Numees had mourned not only for the woman she regarded as a dearly beloved sister, but for their Indian way of life that had vanished like shadows at noonday. But gradually in the months that followed, Numees eased the pain of separation by adopting her elder sister's beloved English ways. She was now eager to show Pocahontas how well she had adapted to life at Jamestown and how useful she could be in a civilized household.

Perhaps, Numees admitted as she moved to stand beside Edith at the window, she had been afraid that Pocahontas would return from England and look askance upon Numees's stubbornly Indian habits. Rebecca Rolfe and her son would have been surrounded by all things English for more than a year, and John Rolfe had promised that England's best would be laid at his young wife's feet.

So now the home of Master and Mistress Rolfe shone with polish and refinement, ready to receive its family once again. New furniture had been imported, the house had been swept so that not a speck of dirt lingered in any corner, and delicate lace curtains fluttered at the open windows. Caught up in a flood of sentiment, Numees threw her arms around Edith's shoulders.

"Dear me," Edith gasped, affection shining in her eyes. "Our happiness is truly irrepressible, is it not?"

"It is," Numees answered, reclining her head upon Edith's soft shoulder. "There is nothing on earth that could spoil this day."

▼▲▼▲▼ Three hours later, Edith Rolfe paced alone in her kitchen, the heaviness in her chest a millstone that threatened to send her crashing to the floor. John had returned to the house alone, and his news stole the sunlight from the sky and smothered the light of joy in their lives. Mistress Rebecca had died of smallpox, he told them, while they waited for favorable winds to sail home. In his grief, he had left the baby with a relative in England and returned to the house at Jamestown only to share the news with Edith and Numees. On the morrow, he planned to journey to his plantation at Henrico. There he would stay, alone with his men and his tobacco fields, far from any sad reminders of his wife.

"You did not think to bring the baby here?" Numees asked him, quiet authority in her voice. "The child is the grandson of Powhatan, and I am his kinswoman. Why did you leave him in England with strangers?"

"Yes, John," Edith answered, her heart welling with emotion. "I have no children, and I could have raised him—"

"I did not leave him with strangers," John replied, his brown eyes large and fierce with pain. "They are my kinsmen. I wanted my son to be safe from the dangers of this accursed land—"

"Safe from the savages, you mean," Numees finished, lifting her chin in the proud gesture Edith had come to know well. "Have you forgotten that your wife is the daughter of the great chief? Do you not remember that this *accursed* land gave birth to your son, your wife, and the love you shared?" Her voice rose to a fever pitch and her arms stiffened as if she willed herself not to strike him. "Have you forgotten that Pocahontas is the only person on earth I have loved? God may have taken my sister, but in taking her son, you have taken all of her from me!"

Without a further word, the young girl turned and walked to her room and quietly shut the door. Edith and John sat in silence for some minutes, then they heard the first keening undulations of Numees's mourning. The girl's cries were as eerie and moving as the wail of a wild animal, and John left the house immediately, his jaw clenched in pain. Edith alternately wept and held her ears as she paced in the kitchen, unable to prevent the terrible sound from tearing her heart.

▼▲▼▲▼ John Rolfe spent the night in a public room but stopped by the house the next morning to promise Edith that he would visit whenever he had business in Jamestown. "Continue as you have been," he said, forcing a brief smile as he embraced her in farewell. "And keep Numees with you for as long as she wants to remain. I will rest easier knowing you have company."

Edith nodded and waved farewell to her brother, then sat in the kitchen and stared moodily at the freshly swept hearth. She had developed a prosperous little business by baking meat pies for the tavernkeeper, but she could not find the energy to rise and set about her work.

Numees did not stir from her room all that morning, and at noon Edith prepared a bowl of corn bread soaked in goat's milk and rapped on the girl's door. "Come now, dear, and have a bite to eat," she called, injecting a falsely cheerful note into her voice. "I know your heart is heavy, but Mistress Rebecca is in heaven with God and she wouldn't want us to mourn for her."

There was no answer, and Edith pressed her ear to the door to listen for sounds of movement. "Come now, Numees, and let me talk to you," she pleaded. "I've a strong shoulder if you wish to cry upon it, and I've an understanding about these things. She was my sister-in-law, you know. I miss her, too." She paused. "Can I come in, dear?"

"Yes," came the quiet answer.

Edith opened the door, fully expecting to see the girl in tears, disheveled, maybe still in bed with the covers over her head. Her smile jelled into an expression of shock when she saw Numees. She stood by the window, her ebony hair plaited in the Indian style she had not favored in more than a year. She wore the simple leather garment she had worn when she first came to live in Jamestown, and she had painted her cheeks, chin, and forehead with black clay. The lovely English bodice, sleeves, and embroidered kirtle lay folded upon a chest against the wall. Edith realized with a start that the girl must have spent her day preparing this costume of mourning.

"By heaven, what is this?" Edith asked, lowering the bowl to Numees's bed. "What are you doing, child?"

"I am a child no longer," Numees answered, her speech clipped like that of the savages who halfheartedly mimicked the English. "I became a woman years ago, with the flowering of my red moon. It is time I went back to my people. I can stay with the English no longer."

Even her posture had changed; gone was the relaxed grace she had developed as she waited for Pocahontas's return. Now she stood straight and firm, her arms crossed resolutely across her chest.

"Numees, dear, what are you thinking?" Edith whispered, moving toward her. She placed her hands on the girl's thin shoulders and nodded when she saw that tears jeweled her dark lashes. "I know your heart is broken, but you shouldn't talk of leaving us. What would I do without you?"

"You have lived alone before," Numees answered, refusing to look into Edith's eyes. "Your God will protect you."

"And what will God do with you?" Edith asked, struggling to contain her emotions. She placed her hand under Numees's chin and forced the girl to look into her eyes. "I am sure God wants you to stay with us. Perhaps this sorrow is a test of our faith, or maybe there is some secret sin in our lives that God wants us to be rid of—"

"What sin?" Numees cried, abruptly backing out of Edith's

embrace. "I have followed the teachings of your God. I have not worshiped the heathen idols, I have been baptized; I have learned the prayers and studied the words written in the Holy Book. Every morning and night I pray to this God of yours, and there is nothing you can tell me to do that I have not done! Yet the powerful hand of God has torn my loved ones away from me!"

Her agonized cry filled the room and Edith stepped back, stunned by the vehemence of the girl's words. This was a tender age to bear such bitter sorrow, but though Numees was undoubtedly in the throes of fresh grief, it was wrong for her to rebel against God himself.

"Turn your face from me, if you must," Edith said, joining her hands in an attitude of dignified hurt. "Turn your face from the English at Jamestown who have sheltered you. Return to the heathens from whence you came. Live in the dirt, lie with any man who approaches you, gnaw upon the fingers of the captives your tribe chooses to torture. But remember, Numees, if you turn your face from God, your very soul will perish in hell."

A wounded expression filled the girl's blue eyes. "I must go," she whispered, her eyes filling with tears, and before Edith could amend her harsh words, Numees ran past her and left the house, her braid lashing like a whip against her back as she ran.

"Numees, come back!" Edith called, her voice breaking as she watched the girl go. She leaned against the rough timber of the door frame and dashed bitter tears from her eyes. "What would Rebecca think of you now, Numees?" she cried, her voice carried forward by the wind. "What would your beloved Pocahontas say if she knew you were going back to the heathen savages?"

▼▲▼▲▼ Numees journeyed upriver with a pair of English traders who were eager to meet the great chief Powhatan, and the news of her approach reached the chief long before her arrival. When at last she landed at Weromacomico,

Numees found that a great company of warriors, women, and children lined the bank to welcome her home.

She walked immediately to the hut of Powhatan, where she knelt before the man she had known as great chief and the father of her tribe. He sat on a mat, bare-chested and painted in the black clay of mourning. Numees felt her heart sink. Had the chief already heard her sad news?

"Welcome home, little sister," he said, his voice cracking with age and weariness. "Have you news of my daughter Matoaka?"

Numees lifted her eyes and felt everything go silent within her when she saw how the chief had aged. His once-powerful body had shriveled like an overripe peach, and his copper skin had toughened into a dry hide spotted with age and disease. His face was now little more than a complex set of wrinkles with two piercing eyes at the center.

"Greetings, great chief, the Powhatan of our people," she said, struggling to maintain control of her voice as she searched for words in the Algonquin tongue. "I alone am returned from the place of the English called Jamestown. The man to whom you gave your daughter in marriage, John Rolfe, has returned from the land of King James without his wife. He has said that my sister died of the pox while waiting to return home."

Powhatan's expression did not change, but Numees saw his entire body sag as if the life force that held him erect had suddenly depleted. His dark eyes wandered away from her face for a moment, then returned. "And the child?" he questioned gently, leaning forward.

She clenched her fists to restrain her anger. It was a personal insult to her that John Rolfe had left the baby in England, for of all women in the world she and Pocahontas had been the most closely bound. She was the natural choice to raise Pocahontas's son, and yet John Rolfe had left the boy with an English kinswoman he might never see again.

"The child lives in England," Numees said simply, knowing the chief would understand her feelings.

Pain flooded his face then, for Powhatan loved children, and the tough, snakelike artery in his neck throbbed with unspoken grief. If John Rolfe had chosen to walk into the hut at that moment . . .

From the gloom in a corner of the hut, an elder raised his hand to speak. Numees bowed her head in respect and was startled to hear the powerful voice of Opechancanough. "This, my chief, is yet another insult to store away, to keep until our chest of wrongs is full. We dare not attack the clothed men for this injustice."

"The child belongs to me," Powhatan said, pressing his thin lips together.

"Even so," Opechancanough answered, and Numees felt his eyes sweep over her face as if he weighed her intentions and thoughts, "we must exercise patience."

Powhatan pondered his brother's words for a moment, then turned to the elder at his left hand. This man sat with his withered legs spread uselessly before him, and Numees recognized him as Itopatin, another of Powhatan's brothers.

"What do you say?" Powhatan asked.

Itopatin slowly moistened his underlip with the point of his tongue, then nodded toward Opechancanough. "My elder brother speaks wisely," he said, his eyes large and timid before the elder's blazing, steadfast gaze. "My heart is in agreement."

Powhatan looked back to Numees. "What is it you ask of us?" he asked, his voice again heavy with ceremony.

"To be welcomed back into the clan of my sister," she whispered, hoping she had not overestimated the chief's loyalty.

The chief lifted his hand toward her in blessing. "Go, find a place among your people," he said, closing his eyes as if her homecoming and her news had left him suddenly blind with exhaustion.

The Eighteenth of May,
In the Year of Our Lord
Sixteen hundred and seventeen

To Fallon Bailie

Greetings in the Name of our Lord:
We of the church council do accept your resignation
as headmaster of the Royal Academy for Homeless
Orphans, and we likewise accept and commend your
desire to accompany our first expedition of children
bound for the Virginia colony.

On a personal note, Master Bailie, we do not understand what forces compel you to travel to such a harsh
and heathen land, but we stand firm in the faith that you
are pursuing the path to which God has directed you. As
you go, know that our prayers for your success and
health follow, for though some have described that land
as flowing with milk and honey, more truthful tongues
have related the sickness and divers dangers that do
dwell there.

Enclosed is a note for one thousand pounds with
which you are to furnish yourself and the one hundred
boys who will travel with you to the Virginia Plantation
next Spring upon the ship *Mary Elizabeth*. Please keep
one hundred pounds for yourself as fitting wages for
your labor. If you have need of anything, send word in a

letter to my attention. I remain faithfully yours in God's service,

Reverend Stephen Archer

▼▲▼▲▼ The months passed in a flurry of preparation. Fallon's spirits rose in anticipation of the coming journey as he continued to run the academy. Now that he had signed on for the voyage, his mind filled with goals and dreams. He wanted to be a faithful guardian and able protector for the boys he would escort to the colony by seeing that they were installed in good situations with fair and honest masters. Once that task was accomplished, he planned to visit Ocanahonan and see what evidence remained of that colony. In each endeavor, he would search for Gilda and Noshi until he found and reunited them.

While Fallon labored through the final weeks of preparation, three other orphanages in London emptied themselves of select boys aged twelve years and older and sent them to the Royal Academy. Fallon housed the new boys in the dining hall, apologizing that he did not have decent beds to offer them, and interviewed each of them as to their health, age, name, and training.

With his own students Fallon shared the news of Virginia that he had gleaned from his reading, and he was not surprised that practically all the older boys wanted desperately to discover the new continent for themselves. He paused, however, when Wart Clarence entered the headmaster's office to volunteer for indenture in Virginia. Though he was of age, the boy was still very small, and Fallon doubted if he possessed the stamina necessary for such an arduous journey.

"Wart, can't I convince you to stay in school awhile longer?" Fallon asked, putting down his pen. "You can go to Virginia next year if you like, or the year after that."

"No," Wart replied stubbornly, thrusting out his lower lip. "I'll go with you, Master Bailie, or I'll not go at all."

"Then maybe you should remain here," Fallon said, smiling. "England needs men, too."

"No," Wart insisted, blowing out his cheeks. "If you don't let me go to Virginia with you, I'll—I'll . . ."

"You'll what?" Fallon asked, smothering the grin that wanted to creep onto his face.

"I'll be miserable," Wart finished. His voice took on a frank note of pleading, and Fallon feared the boy would soon drop onto one knee and begin begging. "Please, I pray you, Master Bailie, let me go with you. I have nothing to hold me in England, and my only friends will be on the ship with you—"

"It is a dangerous journey," Fallon said, lowering his voice as he studied the young boy who had earned a solid place in his affections. "Only the strong can survive in Virginia, Wart, and I have my doubts—"

"I'm strong," Wart broke in, pulling himself up to his full height. "You'll never find a boy who works harder or longer. I can do whatever the big boys do, only don't leave me behind here, Master Fallon. I couldn't stand to lose you, too."

Fallon picked up his pen and tapped it on the desk. Despite his misgivings, it wouldn't do to have children waiting for him in the New World and the Old. "So be it, then," he said, writing Wart's name on the roster. "We'll be off together, you and I."


▼▲▼▲▼ One month before the *Mary Elizabeth* was to sail, Fallon met the man who had been selected to replace him as headmaster of the Royal Academy for Homeless Orphans. Very much in the mold of Delbert Crompton, Cranston Warner was a tall man whose dark, hawkish face seemed never to have known a smile. For a moment Fallon wavered in his willingness to depart England. He had worked so hard to bring a touch of love and warmth back into the lives of these fatherless boys; how could he entrust them to the severe-looking man who stood before him?

From behind his desk, Fallon stood. "I am pleased to meet you, Master Warner," Fallon said, offering his hand. "The Reverend Archer told me to expect you."

"The pleasure is all mine," Warner replied, taking Fallon's hand in a firm grip. But Fallon scarcely heard the words, for a lovely woman with golden hair slipped into the room and slid her graceful hand through the crook of Warner's arm. Cranston Warner melted visibly at her touch, and at the sight of her Fallon suddenly found his doubts dissolving as well.

The lady beamed a smile upon Fallon and he lost himself in the aura of irresistible femininity that surrounded her. Rosy-cheeked and fresh, she was well formed, with curves in all the proper places. Fallon felt as though his tongue had suddenly thickened, so speechless was he in her presence. How long had it been since he had been in the company of a lovely woman? It was no wonder she affected him so, for he lived and worked only with men and boys.

He found himself bowing before the lady. "A-a very great honor to meet you, madam," he said, his unwilling tongue stammering over the words. "The boys here will not know what to make of you."

Her fine, silky eyebrows rose a trifle. "If God wills, they will consider me a mother," she said, her voice warm and husky. "I count it a privilege to join my husband in this endeavor."

Fallon smiled in relief. Mistress Warner would be the source of softness behind the granite strength of her schoolmaster husband. She would provide the touch of grace to the headmaster's bent to measure and dispense discipline.

He tore his eyes from the sight of her loveliness and nodded to Master Warner. "Then I am pleased to leave the school in your care and in God's hands."

▼▲▼▲▼ As the vicious and cold winds of March quieted into the gentle breezes of April, Fallon and his company of boys climbed into carts for transport to the dock at the river Thames. The boys' cries of excitement rang over the riverfront as they trooped from the carts to the dock and waited to board the ship that would carry them to new homes in the colony of Virginia.

The pitiful orphans had no personal possessions save for the clothes on their backs, so they brought nothing aboard the ship with them. Fallon had used the thousand pounds provided by the London Company to purchase barrels of provisions and goods for the journey. When they arrived, he went aboard and checked his manifest to make certain that everything had been loaded onto the *Mary Elizabeth*. Barrels filled with seeds from English plants that might do well in Virginia had been stacked in the belly of the ship, and Fallon nodded in approval to see that the seamen had not forgotten to load the chests filled with armor, bolts of cloth, bars of iron, hornbooks, writing materials, paper, books, and Bibles. Fallon was fascinated to note that several of the other trunks bulged with bells, ribbons, pieces of colored cloth, and bright beads—frivolous trinkets destined to be used in trade with the Indians.

Once the boys had filed aboard the *Mary Elizabeth*, Fallon found that he and his students were little more than cargo in the sailors' eyes. The ship had four levels, each more crowded and filthy than the one above it. The uppermost deck was reserved for the crew of twenty-four seamen who worked the sails. The captain, a one-eyed, dark-haired rogue who blustered continually, did not take kindly to human cargo upon his upper deck.

The second deck, into which Fallon and his company of one hundred boys were crowded, had only six open windows, three on each side. Unfortunately, the windows did not permit the free circulation of air, for each was partially blocked by the mouth of a heavy cannon, necessary tools in case the ship met with Spanish raiders or pirates upon the open sea.

Below the boys, the third deck housed the livestock as well as the unfortunate "bilge rats," homeless boys relegated to the lower levels for cooking and the ship's maintenance. This deck, with its preponderance of animal life, crawled with vermin. Fallon found that he could not even descend the narrow companionway without finding his doublet covered in a fine layer of fleas, lice, and other parasites.

At the deep belly of the ship lay the orlop deck, where the heavy cargo barrels and a layer of sand provided ballast. The stinking refuse of the animals, crew, and passengers eventually filtered its way through to the orlop deck, and the stench that rose from it never failed to gag even the most seasoned seaman who dared to peer into its murky depths.

The captain alone had a private cabin aboard ship, and his quarters were barely large enough to accommodate his bed and a table for his compass and navigational charts. Fallon remembered little of his first voyage over the great Western ocean, but he knew Captain Newport's ship had not been this crowded or miserable.

As he leaned against a cannon below deck and watched the stream of life on the bank of the Thames outside the window, Fallon was suddenly filled with misgiving. Was he truly doing the right thing? If God had sent him from Virginia to find a new life in England, was his return to Virginia an undoing of all that God had planned for him?

The thought rested heavily upon him for the afternoon, killing his hope, until the sight of a tall youth upon the gangplank caught his attention. A young man in a dark cloak and hat was waving papers at the bosun, and after a moment of examination, the bosun stood aside to allow the young man aboard. Fallon grimaced. Another passenger! By heaven, did the captain seek to crowd them so that not a single boy could stretch out to sleep?

A moment later the passenger's footsteps echoed on the wooden steps of the companionway, then a cry rang through the babble of boys' voices: "Fallon Bailie!"

Fallon swung away from the window, stung by surprise. The face before him looked familiar, but the clothes were too fine—

"Don't you know me? It is Brody, you ruffian! I've come to hold your hand on this voyage and see if you've been truthful in all that you've said about Virginia."

Fallon stepped forward and clasped his friend in an embrace. "Brody, how can it be you? Your term of service—"

"Finished. Seven years I worked for that smith, and I earned my suit of clothes and my cow. I'm done with smithing for the rest of my life."

"But to come on this voyage . . ."

Brody grinned recklessly. "Can you be forgetting that mine is the spirit of adventure? I asked at the school, and they told me I'd find you here. So I sold my cow for passage aboard this ship, and I'm going to Virginia as a free man." His laughing eyes swept the cabin and the busy bodies of the excited boys. "And you, are you nursemaid to this entire lot?"

Fallon nodded. "Yes. I'm to see them installed in good situations in the colony."

"And then what, me friend? Do you have to remain as a teacher?"

Fallon leaned against the cannon and folded his arms, wondering how much he should reveal to his friend. He was fairly certain Brody would not understand his desire to venture into the wilderness; the Irishman probably dreamt of tobacco plantations and gold. Finally, he shook his head. "I won't be a teacher. I'm free to stay or return to England, whatever I like." He grinned. "I served my seven years, too, remember? I'm as free as you are, Brody McRyan."

Brody clapped his arm around Fallon's shoulders. "Then after you've disposed of your brats, why don't we go into the wilderness and search for gold? Or maybe we'll find beautiful Indian princesses to marry. What say you, Fallon? Are you suited for an adventure?"

Fallon smiled at his friend in wonder. Brody had always been able to lift his spirits—and to surprise him. "I'faith, you've no idea of the adventure that's been laid before me," he said, chuckling. "And if you are of a mind to come along, well, you are more than welcome to join me."

Brody slapped Fallon's back in agreement, then turned to hustle a couple of nearby boys out of their places by the window.

Fallon turned and looked toward the docks again. The setting sun threw long shadows of the ship upon the water. The quick footsteps of the seamen, anxious to have done with their chores before the light faded, pounded overhead as the bosun called for the gangplank to be set out of the way.

As he watched the seamen pull the gangplank aboard, Fallon felt as though some part of his body was being torn away. He had never pretended to be at home in England, but he could not deny that his life had been forever changed by living there. Smith had sent him to England to learn about the birthplace of his father; Fallon had gained enough understanding to know that he was, forever and always, what the English called an American.

As winter's chill breath abated and spring laid honey-thick sunshine upon the village of Weromacomico, the great chief
Powhatan breathed his last. His children and grandchildren
knelt at his side when life left his body, and Itopatin and
Opechancanough came from their villages to aid in the chief's
funeral.

While the warriors of the tribe sat outside the chief's hut and
composed songs to honor Powhatan's greatness and wisdom,
the priests tended their leader's body. Through an incision on
the left side of his chest, the inner organs were removed and laid
to dry on mats in the sun. Once the chief had been disemboweled, the priests cut and scraped the remaining flesh from his
bones, then carefully laid the suit of skin next to the organic
materials in the sun. The bones, still joined together by liga-
ments, were dried as well, then covered with leather to simulate
the flesh as it had once been. Finally, after days of mourning,
singing, dancing, and frantic prayers, the priests stitched the
dried skin over the skeleton. The remains were hoisted onto a
high deck in a special temple where a *kiwasa*, a four-foot idol,
guarded Powhatan's body. The kiwasa, who knelt in eternal contemplation of the great chief's deeds, had been painted black as
night but for a white breast and a flesh-colored face. The idol
wore a chain of white beads and copper ornaments, decoration
fitting for a highly esteemed werowance.

While the priests lay Powhatan to rest, the conjurors and warriors danced around the fire, tossing tobacco into the hallowed
flames to delight the gods who would speed the soul of
Powhatan on his eternal journey. The warriors stamped, danced,

and clapped in their enthusiastic wish for the chief's continued success.

"Come ravens, come eagles, come sparrows," chanted the children as they marched around the fire. "Speed the soul of our chief to the place of immortality."

Numees stood apart from the other women, watching the ceremonies in a pose of weary dignity. Neither Powhatan's life nor his death had touched her directly. As a child she had feared him except when playful Pocahontas had made his somber face break forth in a rare smile, and the chief had not smiled since the news of his favorite daughter's death. Indeed, Numees sensed that the sad news she brought had gradually stolen life from this the greatest king of all Indian tribes.

A handful of women sat near the fire with ashes on their heads. They lifted their faces in mourning, a counterbalance to the braves who danced joyfully in their effort to send the great chief into eternity. Numees paused a moment. She knew enough about the one true God to reject participation in the religious rituals, but her infinitely sorrowful spirit yearned to express her grief for Pocahontas.

Without hesitation, Numees crossed to the place where the women sat, seated herself beside them, and tossed a handful of ashes over her dark hair. As they wailed in agony, her heart filled once again with the bitterness of old grief, and she opened her mouth in a wordless cry to question God's mercy and justice.

▼▲▼▲ Powhatan had declared before his death that the position of the powhatan—the leader of the entire family of thirty-four tribes—was to be shared between his brothers, Opechancanough and Itopatin. But in the same hour that the two rival brothers arrived at Weromacomico for the funeral, Opechancanough petitioned the council of elders that he not be required to relinquish any part of total command to his younger, lame brother. With a firm voice and eloquent reasoning, he convinced the elders that he, and not Itopatin, was the only logical choice to become the powhatan.

The elders announced their decision before a convocation of several tribes at Weromacomico. "The chief, the powhatan, is not a dictator, but a persuader and giver of wise counsel," the eldest of the elders announced, standing before the circle of waiting tribes. "We need a werowance of honesty, compassion, wisdom. Both Opechancanough and Itopatin are such men. Our departed chief trusted them both, they were as his right hands. But nothing will be accomplished if we are divided; we are a mighty nation, and we must stand as one."

Shouts of agreement filled the air, and after a moment the elder held up his hand for silence. "And so we have chosen Opechancanough. Though he has lived seventy-four summers, he has the strength of a bear, the vision of an eagle, and the cunning of a fox. And he has lived with the clothed men; he now speaks as one with the Spanish and the English, he knows their god and their kings. He is the man to lead us."

Again, the crowd cheered, and the elder took his place in the circle around the village fire. Opechancanough sat motionless beside him—modesty prevented him from acknowledging the favor of his people—but the crowd went wild in dancing and song.

Numees did not dance; she sat silently in front of her hut. On her face she still wore the black clay of mourning, and ashes still grayed her hair. She watched everything with clear, impassive eyes and wondered at one point why Opechancanough appeared to be staring at her.

She learned the answer a few days later. She had left the village to draw water from the river and lost herself in a happy memory of Pocahontas until a dark shadow fell across her path. Startled, she glanced up, then fell back a step when she recognized that the great chief stood before her.

Numees bowed her head in respect and felt a creeping uneasiness at the bottom of her heart when the chief spoke to her in

English. "Why did you come back?" he asked, his tone blunt and heavy.

She blinked, confused, and lowered her eyes. "Did no one tell you? I was distressed by news of my sister's death and angered because the Englishman gave her child to a woman in England."

Opechancanough paused, seeming to weigh her words. "Have you a desire to return to the English?"

"Why would I return?" she asked, meeting his flinty gaze.

"Your eyes are blue," he answered, as if a world of truth could be found in that simple statement.

Numees felt an inexpressible surge of anger rise within her, and her jaw clenched as she rejected his words. "So God has given me blue eyes!" she stormed, not caring if she roused the chief's wrath. "God has also given me the great chief's daughter as a sister and the Powhatan as my people."

"Of which god do you speak?" Opechancanough answered, tilting his head as he regarded her. "Tell me so that I may see into your heart. Is your god the manitou of the Powhatan, or Jesus the Christ of the clothed men?"

For the first time in an encounter with the warrior, Numees could not find words. Was this a test? If she rejected the false gods of her tribe, would Opechancanough cast her out? Probably, for he hated the god of the clothed men. But how could she reject the truth of Jesus Christ, when even the stars and the sunrise proved the words she had learned in the holy book?

*The heavens declare the glory of God; and the firmament showeth his handiwork. Day unto day uttereth speech, and night unto night showeth knowledge. There is no speech nor language where their voice is not heard. . . .*

"I know about the one true God who created the world, the one the Powhatan call the almighty and eternal Manitou," she said, choosing her words carefully. "I have read his words in the English holy book and I have read of his son, Jesus the Christ. I believe the words of the holy book."

A shadow clouded the chief's face. "In lands far from here I have seen men kill and enslave others in the name of this Jesus," he said in a sharp tone he'd never used with her before. "How do I know that your heart will not lead you to betray the people of the Powhatan?"

"Because God has betrayed me," she cried, the words pouring from her heart before she could stop them. Stung by the force of her own feelings, she fell to her knees in the dirt at the chief's feet. "He has taken my sister. Sometime, I don't remember when, he took my parents, for no one has ever claimed me. I am alone in the world, mighty uncle, and this God in whom I can't help but believe has given me nothing but sorrow."

She covered her face with her hands, tasting the anguish of her tears, then she felt the chief's hands under her elbows. Patiently, almost tenderly, he lifted her to stand before him.

"You shall no longer be called Numees, sister, but from this day you will be Kimi, Woman-with-a-Secret. For you must say nothing of this god to our people. If you do, you will die. Do you understand?"

"Yes," she whispered.

"And you shall live with us and marry one of our warriors and bear children of the Powhatan so that we may be long on this earth."

Wordlessly she nodded, and he touched a finger to her wet cheek, then pressed it to his face as if he shared her sorrow. "Kimi," he said again, turning away. "Do not forget what I have said."

▼▲▼▲▼ That night, as the tribe feasted in celebration of the new force in leadership, Opechancanough sat in his position of honor surrounded by his favorite wives. He had many, several of whom were young enough to be his granddaughters, and children were born to him every year. Younger men marveled at his strength; older men were openly envious of his virility. The conjurors claimed he had been gifted by the gods, but only he knew the truth behind his unusual power.

*It is well you named the girl Kimi,* a dark voice whispered in his mind, *for you carry a secret that she alone might guess.*

The corner of his mouth rose in a half-smile. Nearly fifty summers had passed since the night he had murdered the two Catholic priests who had tried to turn him from the ways of his people. No living soul watched him drink their consecrated blood and offer his life in service to the dark power that fought against all men of God. Supernatural vigor had surged through his mortal veins as he drank from the reddened chalice, and since that day he had known he possessed the gift of immortality. Already he had outlived his younger brother and now, at last, he could build the Powhatan confederacy into a force that would rid the land of Europeans for all time.

But like a moth to a flame, his eyes kept darting back toward the girl he had renamed Kimi. Strange that she, this child of English and Indian, should keep intruding into his life. Why hadn't she died in that English city of disease like so many others?

He was certain he had been present on the night of her conception, for he himself had handed the English girl to his nephew as a prize. Years later, when the toddling child had appeared before him in the village of Ritanoe, he had recognized the features of his family in her face as clearly as he read the stars. The Powhatan tattoo upon her arms was not necessary for Opechancanough to know she was of his family, for he had felt her kinship in his blood.

But even then she had smelled of God. Often he had hidden in the woods to watch the girl playing with Pocahontas, and the child had sung songs in English—pretty, melodic, alien songs, like those the Spanish fathers had sung about God and his Son, Jesus.

He had forced himself to put the child out of his mind, for Pocahontas adored her and Powhatan would deny nothing to his favorite daughter. Opechancanough had gone back to his tribe and planned for war with the clothed men, never thinking again of the strange blue-eyed child until the marriage of Pocahontas.

When Powhatan had refused to attend the ceremony, Opechan-canough had given the bride away himself. There he had seen the girl at Pocahontas's side, still lovely, still blue-eyed, still shining like a child of the English God.

Though thoughts of her had lingered just around the corners of his mind, he had not seen her again until a few short days ago, when she appeared before Powhatan with news of Pocahontas's death. By the time he saw her sitting in ashes with the other tribal mourners, she was locked into his mind. For some shapeless reason he feared the balefire in those ice-blue eyes.

Until their talk by the river. When her pain and anger had surfaced, fear fell away from the warrior like a discarded cloak from his shoulders. Her love for the English God would wither in the barrenness of suffering. Of course, he could not be certain of that, not right away. But she was fifteen, more than an age to be married, and beautiful. Once she took off the paint of mourning, suitors would approach, but he would not agree to marry her to one of them until he knew she was completely loyal. After a year or two, if all went well.

He leaned toward his favorite wife. "Do you see the girl at the fire, the one with the blue eyes?" he asked.

Her eyes sought the girl he spoke of, then she nodded.

"Spread the word to all who will hear. From this day she is called Kimi, and one year from tonight, she may marry any warrior who is willing to provide for her. I will act as her father."

"You are good, my husband," his wife answered. Then she rose and hastened toward a group of women to spread the news, and Opechancanough dismissed the girl from his thoughts.

The ten weeks aboard the *Mary Elizabeth* were among the most miserable days Fallon had ever spent in his life. Once England had slipped away from the stern, their belligerent captain emerged as a raging tyrant. The seamen on the upper deck were regularly flogged for insubordination or breaking the captain's rules, and none of Fallon's students dared to venture out of the crowded cabin on the second deck.

Restless with the natural exuberance and excitement of youth, the boys turned to mischief and pulled pranks upon each other. Fallon found himself constantly required to intervene to prevent bullying and fighting. He was almost glad when the stress of shipboard life quelled their spirits after a week, but when the boys lay sick and vomiting from seasickness, fever, and dysentery, he vastly preferred their bickering and complaining.

Nothing aboard ship was healthful or helpful. Rations were very poor and very small, and hot meals were only served three times a week. The thick black water served up from leaky barrels hoisted from the lower orlop deck was filled with worms, and though Fallon was as thirsty as a man who had walked across a desert, at first he could not bring himself to drink of it. But he thought of the boys who watched his example. If he did not drink, they would not. And if they did not, they would die.

Compelled by hunger, they gingerly nibbled at the rotten bread from the spoiled barrels below. Filled with red worms and spiders' nests, petrified, floury biscuits were handed round at every meal, and the boys listlessly gnawed on them as Fallon encouraged them to eat and keep up their strength. Added to the ship's miserable meals and lack of fresh water were odors strong

enough to knock a healthy man from his feet. The scent of dung
fires and cooking food, the ammoniacal smell of animals, and the
reek of human sewage hung thick in the air, and Fallon constantly fought nausea despite his best intentions to set an example for the boys who clamored to go home.

Then, during the first storm at sea, the boys' clamoring turned
frantic. From his window, Fallon watched the waves roil with
whitecaps until they rose up and snarled at the ship, then the
wind freshened until the gray-green gloom of the ocean was
assaulted by steel spikes of rain that pelted the boys through the
open windows. The air inside the ship, unnaturally hot and still,
grew close as the sky darkened with boiling clouds, and the wild
footsteps of the seaman thundered above their heads.

Every boy, even the bravest and loudest of them, clutched his
neighbor for comfort and strength, and Fallon made his way to a
corner where he had put the three weakest boys. They lay still,
their faces pale and pinched, as the waves rose like high moun-
tains outside to tumble over the ship.

Inside the belly of the boat, men and animals alike were
tossed from side to side by the storm. Fallon found it impossible
to walk, sit, or even lie still, and no matter how hard he tried to
shelter his sick charges, he tumbled over them and they over him
like rag dolls as the storm raged.

Water poured down upon them through the planking of the
upper deck, and as the bilge pumps failed, the stench from the
orlop deck rose steadily to assault them like a superhuman fist.
Cockroaches and rats, stirred up by the ship's motion and the
rolling water, scurried upward to find dry ground and safety.

It was truly a scene from hell, Fallon thought as he swatted a
roach from the face of a sick boy who lay next to him. In the
white light from a flash of lightning, he saw Brody trying to comfort a pair of brothers. When Brody's eyes met his own, Fallon
knew that his brave, adventurous friend was as frightened as
any of his charges. As frightened as Fallon.

Not knowing what else to do, Fallon opened his mouth and
began to pray: "Thou, O Lord, who stillest the raging of the sea,

hear us and save us, that we perish not. O blessed Savior who didst save thy disciples as they were ready to perish in a storm, hear us and save us, we beseech thee."

The familiar prayer was from the Anglican prayer book, and many boys looked up in the dim light of the hold and weakly gave the proper response: "Lord, have mercy upon us."

Fallon inclined his head. "Christ, have mercy upon us."

As one, the boys answered: "Lord, have mercy upon us."

Fallon finished the prayer: "God the Father, God the Son, God the Holy Ghost, have mercy upon us, save us now and evermore. Amen."

▼▲▼▲▼ "What are you thinking, Wart?"

The sea had calmed itself and the sun shone hot and bright at the window. Wart had crawled into a far corner of the deck and sat with his arms wrapped around his knees. He lifted his head as Fallon approached and gave his schoolmaster a shy smile. "Nothing of import," he whispered, propping his head on his knees.

Fallon sank down onto the floor beside the boy and shifted uncomfortably in his clothes. His shirt, stiff from sea spray and simple dirt, felt like sandpaper against his skin, and his breeches could have stood upright by themselves. Fallon tried not to think about his own discomfort and focused on the boy, who had always been able to take his mind from the maddening boredom of their claustrophobic quarters.

"Surely you were thinking of something, for I saw a decided gleam in your eye," Fallon answered, teasing. "What were you imagining? The forest? Indians?"

"No," Wart answered, an abashed expression on his face. "I was just wondering if it would be possible . . ."

"What?" Fallon gestured into the air. "You want to own your own ship someday?"

"By heaven, no," Wart answered, laughing. "I'd be content never to sail again."

"What, then? Perhaps you dream of a tobacco plantation or a house in the woods with livestock of your own?"

"No," the boy answered again, but a trace of sadness tinged his voice. "I was just wondering if . . . maybe . . ."

"You can speak, Wart. I won't laugh, no matter what you are thinking."

"I was wondering if maybe my new master and his wife will be a mother and father," the boy said, lifting his head. The words began to rush like a waterfall. "It could happen. It wouldn't be impossible that a man and woman might find fondness in their hearts for me if I work very hard and do very well. And I'd stay with them always, not just till I'm twenty-one. I'd work for them, and bring my wife home to live there with them, and my children would call them Grandmama and Grandpapa—" He broke off suddenly and flushed. "If they give me a proper bed in the house, I know it could happen," he said, resting his chin on his knees again.

Fallon did not answer, thinking of the miserable sack of straw he'd slept on outside Delbert Crompton's bedchamber. Indentured servants were rarely given proper beds in the master's house, but he did not want to spoil Wart's dreams of happiness. Besides, who could say what would happen to a boy as winsome as Wart? His dream of finding a family was no less impossible than Fallon's.

"Indeed, it could happen," he said finally, rumpling the boy's hair.


▼▲▼▲▼ Though none were as frightening as the first, Fallon and his students endured many storms at sea during their weeks aboard the *Mary Elizabeth.* The boys came to weather the unruly wind and rain as well as the seamen above deck, but fear soon threatened from another quarter. After six weeks at sea, many of the boys sickened to the point of death. It was for this reason only that the captain allowed Fallon to rise from the second deck into the fresh air of open sky, and each time Fallon surfaced, the captain took a withered, pale body from his arms, wrapped it in old canvas, and allowed Fallon to quote the burial service from the *Book of Common Prayer* before dropping the pitiful bundle into the sea.

"We therefore commit this body to the deep, to be turned into corruption, looking for the resurrection of the body when the sea shall give up her dead, and the life of the world to come, through our Lord Jesus Christ; who at his coming shall change our vile body, that it may be like his glorious body, according to the mighty working, whereby he is able to subdue all things to himself." After reciting the prayer, Fallon released his bundle, and with each splash, he mentally counted backward from one hundred. Ninety-nine boys remaining in his care. . . . Ninety-eight . . . ninety-seven . . . ninety-six. . . .

When at last the seaman in the crow's nest gave the jubilant call of "Land ho!" only eighty-eight boys remained alive.


▼▲▼▲▼ Fallon and his students wept for joy at the first sight of land. Crowded around the cannon ports, they watched as the shore revealed itself as solid and substantial. "Name of a name," Brody breathed, his eyes lighting at the sight of tall trees on the horizon, "I'd give my soul to feel the ground under my feet this instant!"

"Patience, my friend," Fallon cautioned, unable to wrest his eyes from the window. "We will be out of this stinking tub soon enough."

The ship left the ocean and entered the mouth of the river Fallon remembered as the Powhatan River, but which the sailors now called the James, eventually dropping anchor about fifty yards from the shore of the Jamestown peninsula. As the sun set Fallon could see a many-sided fort upon the shore, with several rows of houses outside its stout walls. Plowed and cultivated fields lay like a patchwork quilt around the houses, and tendrils of smoke rose easily into the darkening sky to give evidence of the hospitality of English hearths.

"I hear there are a few women here now," Brody ventured, his eyes alight with hope. "And the prospect of more to come. Can you imagine yourself in one of those houses, Fallon, with a bonny wife to warm your nights?"

Fallon turned reluctantly away from the open window. "Not for a long while, Brody. I have work to do before I can give thought to settling down."

"What work?" Brody demanded, following. "We could marry fine lasses and still go out and search for gold."

Fallon shook his head. "My most urgent concern is for my students," he said, sweeping his arm wide to indicate the boys crowded around the windows. "I must make sure they are positioned in service. And then I must make a search for Gilda and Noshi. I'm certain God has sent me back to Virginia to find them."

A mask of disbelief settled onto Brody's features, and Fallon gave him a rueful smile. "I won't hold you back, Brody. If you feel you must take a wife or go treasure hunting, don't wait for me. But Noshi and Gilda are my family, and I promised I'd take care of them. I won't stop searching until I know where and how they are."

Brody raised his hands in a gesture of surrender. "Faith, it is good to know some things never change," he said, smiling. "You and the Gibraltar Rock, for example. Though I think you are an eejit for wanting to waste your time, do what you must. I'll wait. But let's not take too long about it, agreed? And to speed things along a wee bit, I'll lend a hand with the boys."

"What about your wife?" Fallon asked, giving his friend a wry smile.

"Ah, she can wait, too, but not for long," Brody said, folding his arms in resignation. "So let's unload these boys and get out into the wilderness."

Fallon shrugged. "Agreed. But I daresay we'll be there soon enough. After all, how long can it take to get off this flea-ridden tub?"

▼▲▼▲▼ Since they had dropped anchor in late afternoon, Fallon expected to wait aboard the ship on their first evening in Virginia. But when the captain came to the lower deck at sunrise on the morrow and told him that no one was permitted to leave the ship unless they could pay for their passage, Fallon flushed in anger. The boys around him grew quiet and still at this announcement, waiting to see who would win the contest of wills.

"The fee for these boys has already been paid by the London Company," Fallon protested. "I have seen the letter of agreement. You were paid three pounds for each boy's transportation."

"Three pounds covered the expenses of their food," the captain snarled, his single good eye gleaming malevolently across the hold. "It is up to their new masters to pay for their passage."

"But how are they to meet their new masters if they are not allowed off the ship?" Fallon answered, his temper rising. "These boys are sick, sir, and they need fresh water and good food, the care of a willing master and mistress—"

"They'll not be here long," the captain answered, turning his back to retreat up the companionway. "The planters are already lining up at the dock. Have a party of ten boys, the biggest and strongest, ready to go at once. We'll send them to the dock in the shallop, and when they're all accounted and paid for, we'll come back for another group."

"I'll go ashore with the first group," Fallon said, brushing dirt from his stiff shirt and breeches.

"No, sir, you'll not leave the ship until the last boy's been apprenticed. I'll not have these brats running about my ship without someone to watch over 'em."

Fallon was about to protest that none of his boys had the energy or strength to cause mischief, but his words died in his throat. He and Reverend Archer had agreed that Fallon would personally interview prospective masters and place the boys in apprentice positions well suited to each boy's talents and abilities. He had not been hired to wait aboard ship, but what could he do? At sea, a captain's word was law.

He shook his head, remembering his rosy dreams for his students. This situation, like so many others he had experienced since boarding the *Mary Elizabeth*, would be orchestrated solely by the captain. Maybe it was best to get his students off the ship however he could, then meet with the masters later on shore.

Without a word, Fallon pointed to ten of the oldest and strongest boys and gestured toward the companionway.

▾▴▾▴▾ For three days the shallop carried boys to the wooden dock and returned empty for another boatload. The planters proved the captain right, for laborers were scarce in this colony, and even the small boys were readily purchased. On the morning of the fourth day after their arrival in port, Fallon and Brody lowered the last eight boys, all of them sick, into the shallop, then climbed in after them. The fresh air smelled sweet, and a warm, sunlit day opened peacefully before them.

The arc of the shallop's bow dipped and rose through the pounding surf, sending a deliciously cool splash of spray over Fallon's filthy skin. One seaman sat at the back of the boat, working the rudder, while eight others lined the sides and rowed the boat through the blue water that rippled gently toward the shoreline. A lacy white garland of foam feathered along the sides of the shallop, and Fallon reverently dipped a finger into the froth and marveled that he rode once again upon the waters of his birthplace.

Hunched on the bench before him, Wart opened one eye and squinted up toward the sun. "Is it beautiful, Master Fallon?" he asked, clutching his stomach.

Fallon nodded, his heart moved with compassion at the sight of the sick boy. He had prayed they would reach Jamestown before Wart's strength evaporated, and that Wart would find a kind master.

An impatient crowd surged forward on the docks as the shallop approached, and a dozen hands reached forward to pull the boys out of the boat. As Fallon climbed out onto the dock, he was amazed at the temerity of the men who crowded around him. "I need two more," one man said, casting a hasty glance at the pale boys, "but these are puny sacks of skin. Have you none better?"

Fallon met the man's words with a stony glare. "These are the last of my students," he said, nodding gravely. "They are fine lads, but they have had a difficult time in the crossing. With time, care, and a few decent meals, I am sure any one of them would serve you well."

"I need a boy in the fields tomorrow!" another man shouted, pressing forward. He leaned into the boat and pulled Wart forward by the lapel of his coat. "I'll take this one. I'll sign over forty pounds of tobacco for the captain, and since this lad weighs no more than that, that's all I'll be giving."

Wart's eyes widened in fear and Fallon put out a restraining hand. "Excuse me, sir, but there's been a misunderstanding."

"There is no misunderstanding," one of the seamen interrupted, cutting Fallon off with a stern glance. "That's the price the captain demands. The price of a boy's weight in tobacco, and no quibbling. They serve until they're twenty-one, then they're free to indenture some other bloke who's desperate for Virginia."

Fallon raised his hand, about to protest again, but Brody caught his arm. "Let him go, Fallon," he said, his voice a quiet murmur in the sea of men scrambling for a look at the remaining boys. "The others have been sold already, and these are not likely to live long enough to care about the morrow. You've done your best, but you are not their father."

"They are my responsibility," Fallon whispered, trying to put iron in his voice. But suddenly he felt limp with weariness, too drained to explain his feelings further. As his emotions tumbled hopelessly in his mind he was no longer sure of what he was expected to do or how he was to do it. Most of the planters who had signed contracts of indenture for his students had already taken the boys and left for their plantations. And if the remaining few were as coarse as the knave who bargained for Wart, they would of certain prove unwilling to sit for an interview in which Fallon pressed for the boys' continued education.

Unable to fight the tide of resistance that surged against him, Fallon stood silently while the sailor collected the captain's tobacco and Wart Clarence was hoisted onto a burly man's shoulder and carried off the docks.

▼▲▼▲▼ George Yeardley, the successor to Governor Dale, turned John Rolfe's Indian weed into the prime product of His Majesty's Plantation of Virginia. Governor Yeardley so fervently urged his countrymen to plant tobacco that when Fallon and Brody entered the center of the settlement known as Jamestown, they found the weed growing in the marketplace, along the sides of the streets, and even in cast-off trunks and barrels outside the fort.

"The ships took away more'n twenty-five hundred pounds in 1616, and more'n eighteen thousand pounds last year," one planter proudly told them as they sat in the public room of the inn. Pride rang in the colonist's voice as he leaned upon their table. "They say this year we'll export nearly fifty thousand pounds, for the crop is growin' everywhere, as you can see."

Brody's eyes glinted with interest as he surveyed the green tobacco fields through the window, but Fallon pressed the man for more information. "What of the corn?" he asked, remembering the long hours he and his parents had worked to grow maize, the base for nearly all their meals at Ocanahonan. "And the beans? The squash?"

The planter laughed and waved away Fallon's question. "We've always the savages to grow our food," he said, lifting a burly shoulder in an inelegant shrug. "If we get hungry, we either trade with the savages for what we need, or—" he leaned forward and winked—"we get it another way. But we're fed here and plenty, for now that England is buyin' tobacco the starving times are done."

Fallon smiled politely and took a long sip of the first decent-tasting brew he'd had in months as he looked out the window and studied the village. The few buildings in Jamestown were similar to those Fallon remembered from Ocanahonan, but not so well or sturdily built. It was almost as if men had thrown up these structures of timber and stucco with only a temporary dedication. When Fallon remarked on the transient nature of the city, the planter laughed.

"Who'd want to live in this place forever?" he asked, lifting a hairy arm to point out the window. "You see that veil of mist coming yonder over the water? It is a killer fog, that. Betwixt the mist, the heat, and the strange diseases of this place, one of every three men to land here dies within a year."

He lowered his voice and jerked his thumb toward the doorway. "There's a great pit not far from here where the soldiers at the fort quietly dispose of the dead, so as not to alert the savages to our true weakness. There are more men buried there than live here, destroyed by cruel infirmities and wars with the savages. There were never Englishmen left in such misery as in this Virginia."

"Surely it is not so bad," Brody said, attempting to lighten the mood. "I've heard the land is rich with gold."

"Aye, if you count the green of tobacco as the yellow of gold," the man said.

"Is planting hard work?" Fallon asked, thinking of the boys he had sent to the plantations.

A sly smirk crossed the man's face. "Easier than being a soldier and a target for a savage's arrow. It is hard work from March through November. Seeds are planted in March and transplanted in April to the fields. One man can tend about three acres by himself. That is the backbreaking, hot work, and that's why so many are quick to buy the contracts of indentured servants. I have ten myself."

"Ten servants?" Fallon asked, lifting a brow. "So you have thirty acres?"

"No," the man answered, grinning. "Five hundred. Of course,

it is not all planted. I'm in need of more men yet—and I want men, not these spindly boys that came off the latest ship."

Fallon clenched his fist, and Brody must have noticed his reaction, for he hurried to change the subject. "It is midsummer now," he said, pinning the planter with a long scrutiny as if he were vitally interested in the man's trade. "What work is being done in the fields?"

"Oh," the man replied, his beery breath reaching Fallon across the table. "There are caterpillars to be picked off, weeds to be hoed, plants to be pruned. The plants are cut in August and hung in the tobacco sheds for drying. In November the leaves are stripped from the stalks and ready for transport to England."

"And the profit?" Brody asked.

The man scratched his stubbled chin and grunted. "I figure one hogshead of tobacco weighs about a thousand pounds. A hundred and fifty pounds will buy a man a virgin bride, and fifty pounds will buy a boy to work another three acres, so a thousand pounds will buy whatever a man has his heart set on."

Brody's eyes lit with excitement, but Fallon stood up from the table, too weary to ponder the joys and riches to be discovered in tobacco. "Good night, gentlemen," he said, pulling his cloak about his shoulders as he retreated into the dark, hay-strewn corner where he would sleep. "I will think more clearly on the morrow."

Fallon had been under the impression that most of his students would be lodged near Jamestown so it would be a simple matter to inspect their homes and situations. He frowned in dismay when he learned that most of the boys had been immediately transported to the plantations scattered not only throughout Jamestown, but also throughout the three other English settlements of Elizabeth City, Charles City, and Henrico. The contracts of indentured service had disappeared with the planters. After making futile inquiries aboard the *Mary Elizabeth* about exactly where his boys had gone, Fallon found that he and Brody had very little to do.

They sat on a knoll near the riverbank to consider their options. "It is a terrible fate that's befallen you," Brody told Fallon, his voice faintly mocking. "You are in a land with no worries, money in your pocket, and you are finally rid of that pack of boys. Trust them to God's hands and let's join a trading expedition. We'll search for gold along the river and then we can stake a claim of land for ourselves. If all else fails, we'll grow tobacco. In a year, if not sooner, we can purchase a bride—"

"Just one?" Fallon asked, slanting the question with a lifted eyebrow.

Brody laughed and clapped his friend on the back. "Name of a name, can you be thinking I'd share me wife with you? Never! But if the tobacco grows green, there's no reason why we couldn't have two wives each, a blonde and a brunette. What say you to that?"

"I think you are treading on immoral and illegal grounds," Fallon said, tossing a pebble into the river. "Seriously, Brody, I wouldn't mind growing tobacco, but you are forgetting—there's one thing I must do first. I've family here, somewhere. I promised my parents I'd take care of Noshi and Gilda, and if they're alive, I've got to find them."

Brody lay back on the grass and crossed his arms under his head. "You know, when you told me that story about being born in Virginia and being the son of an Indian chief, I didn't think you were telling me the truth. But I wanted to believe you, so I did. And now that we're here and I see that everything is just as you said, well, sure, I know you weren't lying. But truth to tell, Fallon, I don't want to believe. I want us to find our own adventure. Those two kids—they could be dead, though it pains me to say so. If they do live, they could be anywhere. They could be in some place where no Englishman has ever been! They could have been offered as sacrifices, or eaten by some beast. You shouldn't be spending your time on impossible dreams and foolish imaginings—"

"That's enough!" Fallon interrupted, glaring down at his friend. Brody's mouth closed with an audible snap, and Fallon turned to look at the river as Brody's gloomy warnings echoed in his brain. What if Brody was right? What if he was wasting precious time and energy on a wild chase that might get them killed or maimed or lost in the wilderness?

Yet deep inside he knew that Noshi and Gilda waited for him. Maybe they lived only days away in the west, where tall green pines fringed the horizon. For eleven years he had not finished a prayer without lifting their names to heaven, and he had endured too many hellish nights on the ocean to abandon his search now. Rowtag had taught him how to survive in the forest. He could pray that, should the need arise, his survival skills would not fail. But he could not stop searching.

"I don't know where or how we'll find them, or if we'll find them at all," Fallon finally told Brody. "But my parents died at Ocanahonan, and somewhere in this forest there are Indians who can confirm my story. Powhatan, for one."

"He's dead," Brody interrupted, and Fallon felt his mouth go dry.

"Dead?"

Brody shrugged. "I heard some of the soldiers talking about him this morning. Powhatan's been dead for some time and the new chief is making them plenty nervous. His name is O-peck—"

"Opechancanough," Fallon whispered, prickles of cold dread crawling along his back. Memories ruffled through his mind like wind on water: Opechancanough standing over him as he ordered Fallon's death, Opechancanough's taunts that Noshi would be sold into slavery and Gilda would forget everything about God and her parents and all Fallon had endured for her. . . .

"May God have mercy," Fallon whispered, and Brody sat up. "What's this? You know this fellow?"

"He's the devil incarnate," Fallon answered, rising to his feet. Suddenly frantic with an unreasoning terror, he paced the riverbank for a moment, then bent down and grasped Brody's doublet with both hands. "We've got to begin our journey soon, do you understand? If Opechancanough is making the soldiers nervous, God has brought us to this place and at this time for a reason." His eyes fastened upon the spot where the river snaked into the wooded horizon. "We'll have to find guides and hire a boat."

"It will cost money," Brody said, his voice flat.

"I've got money," Fallon answered, his mind racing. "Surely it is enough to charter a boat and stock provisions for a trip inland."

"Now you are talking sense," Brody said, standing. He clapped his hand upon Fallon's shoulder as he led the way to the fort. "I think your reasons are addled, mind you, but as long as you are headed into the wilderness, I'll be wanting to join you."

▼▲▼▲▼ Fallon hired a boat and arranged for two Anglican ministers to accompany them on a journey inland. "I don't know why you want clergymen to come along," Brody fussed as they loaded canvas bags stuffed with their provisions into the flat-bottomed canoe. "A couple of soldiers would have been more useful."

"And we would have been shot through with an arrow twice as quickly. Most of the Indian tribes recognize that clergymen are men of peace, as are we," Fallon answered, relishing the warmth of the sun upon his face and hands as he loaded the boat. Despite the heat of the day, strong force of habit led him to tug occasionally at the cuffs of his long sleeves to be sure his Indian tattoos were covered. To avoid questions and curious glances from the folk at Jamestown he still wore the proper, dignified blue doublet and short breeches of a schoolmaster. He knew that to the soldiers and hardy frontiersmen at the fort, he was a laughable sight. Brody, in comparison, wore leather breeches, a white, open-collared shirt, and a hat set at a rakish angle. His dark cloak hung over one shoulder.

"You look like a pirate," Fallon said, grinning at Brody as he hefted another bag into the canoe.

"Better to look like a pirate than a schoolmaster," Brody countered, planting his hands on his hips as he struck a heroic pose in the canoe. "An Englishman's likely to shoot you before we even reach Charles City."

"Very funny," Fallon said, taking a moment to look around to see if they had forgotten anything. A bird called as it flew overhead, and Fallon drew a quick breath of surprise when he recognized the species, though he had not seen another like it in years. A wonderful sense of homecoming flooded his heart. The water, trees, and wildlife that surrounded him were part of his home, a part of him, and he realized for the first time why he had felt so imprisoned in London. This was where he belonged!

The two ministers—both dressed in unseasonable black tights, doublets, and wide-brimmed hats—approached from the fort. Each carried a canvas bag over his shoulder and greeted Fallon and Brody with a cordial handshake.

"I'm Reverend Alexander Whitaker, and my companion is the Reverend Richard Buck," the first man said, nodding to Fallon.

He smiled companionably. "I hear you gentlemen are set upon a venture into Indian country."

Fallon introduced himself and Brody. "We want to go inland, possibly to Opechancanough's village," he said, not daring to reveal his full intention. "We have heard rumors about this new chief and desire to travel with men of God rather than men of war."

"Since his brother's death, Opechancanough resides at Powhatan's village of Weromacomico," Reverend Buck said, frowning slightly. "And talk of rumors disturbs me. What tales have you heard?"

Fallon reminded himself that everyone thought him a schoolmaster who had just arrived from England. It would not be wise to reveal his knowledge of Opechancanough's character too soon.

He shrugged carelessly. "We have heard that Opechancanough may not be willing to trade. Some say he is evil and cannot be trusted."

"Bah," Buck said, waving his hand at Fallon's apprehension as if his words were but the babbling of a frightened child. "Opechancanough is an old man, a toothless lion. I myself have met him countless times, and he has assured me that the peace betwixt our people will remain as long as the heavens stand above us."

"Well then," Fallon said, not much relieved, "we've nothing to worry about on our journey. We want to scout out locations for a tobacco plantation and maybe do a little trading with the Indians."

"Have you beads?" Reverend Whitaker asked, raising an eyebrow. "The savages love them. Particularly Opechancanough's wives."

"We have beads," Brody said, confidently patting a canvas bag in the front of the boat.

"Is this your first trip inland?" Reverend Whitaker asked, seating himself inside the canoe. "You both have the pale complexions of Englishmen just off the ship."

Brody laughed as if the question were a great joke, but Fallon

silenced him with a warning glance. "It is true enough that
we've just arrived," he said, helping Brody push the canoe off
the bank and into the water. When the boat floated freely, both
men climbed in and began to paddle. From the back position,
Fallon steered the vessel into the river current and enjoyed
watching Brody splash ineffectively until Reverend Whitaker
offered to lend a hand with the oar.

For a long while they traveled upriver without speaking, the
only sound the soft lap of oars pulling against calm water. Then,
as men do, the travelers began to share their histories, and Fallon
was surprised to learn that he traveled with two noted clergymen: Reverend Whitaker had overseen Pocahontas's religious
education, and Reverend Buck had officiated at the marriage of
John Rolfe and the newly christened Rebecca.

"I had no idea we were traveling in such esteemed company,"
Fallon said, his shoulder beginning to ache from the unaccus-
tomed exertion. "We heard marvelous tales of the Lady Rebecca
Rolfe in London. The entire country grieved when she died."

"Indeed, the Indians speak of her still," Reverend Buck said.
"And poor John Rolfe has shut himself away at his plantation at
Henrico, though his business often calls him to Jamestown."

Fallon's pulse quickened at the mention of John Rolfe. A year
had passed since they had spoken in London, but maybe Rolfe
had learned something about Gilda and Noshi. If the trip to
Opechancanough's village yielded no information, he would
seek John Rolfe at Henrico.

"I'd like to meet Rolfe," Brody said, turning so suddenly that
he nearly toppled the canoe.

"You'd better learn to ride first," Reverend Buck admonished
gently, and the back of Brody's neck reddened as he turned forward to watch Virginia glide by.

▼▲▼▲▼ Scouts relayed the news of approaching strangers to Opechancanough a day before the canoe would arrive. The
great chief scratched his chin and pretended to consult with his

elders. "They say a canoe comes with four men, two of whom wear the black suits of holy men," Opechancanough said, his blood boiling at the bitter memory of the black-robed Catholic friars who had scorned and rebuked him. "They do not carry the irons that roar with the voice of thunder."

The elders nodded, impressed that the approaching visitors did not carry muskets, but Opechancanough feared a more insidious evil. Soldiers he could handle easily, for they carried weapons of war and could be attacked without provocation, but how could he convince his elders that men of God were just as threatening?

He impressed a frown upon his forehead and stared at his elders with penetrating concern. "As you know, I can read the talking books and papers of the clothed men," he said, shrugging modestly as if this ability was a special gift from the gods. "And not many moons ago I was given a book filled with the words of one who wore the black suit of a holy man. He said that the English will give the Powhatan such things as we want and need, things which are more excellent than they take from us."

"They give us copper," an elder interrupted. "Such things we want and need."

"But they do not give us their sticks of thunder," Opechancanough gently pointed out. "And such a weapon would be useful when we hunt. But this holy man went on to say that the English wish to make the Powhatan become like the English. They wish to give us their God and take away our own. They want to take away the kiwasa and the temples with the bodies of the dead chiefs. They want to remove our villages and our wives, for the Englishmen have no wives. A few of them have one wife, but to have more than one is an abomination to their God."

"Only one wife?" an elder asked, his mouth hanging open at the thought.

"Yes." Opechancanough nodded. "In this way, the holy men of the English are more dangerous than the soldiers who come with swords and weapons. Furthermore, this holy man of the talking book went on to say that the English wish to make us men, and to make us happy men."

The import sank into their consciousness without his belaboring the point. After a moment, Itopatin raised his head to speak. "Do they not think we are men already?" he asked, his dark eyes searching Opechancanough's. "Do they not think that we are happy?"

The chief lifted his shoulder in an expressive shrug.

"If we are men and happy, we should prove it by killing these holy men," another elder said, and soon the council was agreed.

Opechancanough hid his thrill of victory behind a stony face of resolution as his warriors raced to strike the war pole and began the dance that would work them into the frenzy of bloodshed. Askook, a brave and powerful young warrior, volunteered to serve as chief of the war party, and he danced particularly vigorously whenever he ventured close to Kimi, the blue-eyed girl who remained unmarried.

Opechancanough felt his favorite wife slip under his arm as she took her place at his side. "It is good you have promised Kimi to Askook," she whispered as she watched the dance. "Kimi is skilled in healing, so they will have strong children. Even the conjuror has come to respect her gift."

Opechancanough's eyes narrowed as he watched the girl ignore her dancing suitor with studied indifference. Such coy behavior was common among the women and considered properly modest. But was she yet of the same heart and fiber as the others of the Powhatan, or did loyalty to the English God yet remain in her heart?

▼▲▼▲▼ A dull malaise choked Kimi's heart and voice at sunset as the war party gathered their weapons and streamed through the tall gate of the palisade. She did not cheer them, for some part of her had always dreaded the sight of war clubs and the shriek of battle cries. It was her nature to heal wounds, not cause them.

When the warriors had gone, Opechancanough and his wives disappeared into his hut, and the other women dispersed to bank the cooking fires or send their overwrought and excited children to bed. The hot winds of summer would make sleep uncomfortable for everyone, Kimi thought, lifting her eyes to study the outlines of treetops silhouetted against the darkening sky. And many of the women would not sleep at all because their husbands had joined Askook and the war party.

She slipped inside the dwelling she shared with a dozen other women and lay down upon her grass mat. The heavy, regular breathing of children filled the hut, but Kimi could not sleep. She should have been worried about Askook, for they were to be married at the celebration of the green corn ceremony in another month's time. After that, Kimi would move her meager belongings to the hut Askook shared with his parents and siblings.

She knew Askook desired her, for she had felt his eyes grow hungry when he looked her way, and the other women never hesitated to praise Askook for his courage, loyalty, and skill as a hunter. But though he possessed a rugged, masculine appeal and could throw a spear with the force of a cannon, Kimi's smile did not warm when he caught her eye, nor did her heart stir at his approach.

She had confided her reservations to the chief's eldest wife, and the esteemed woman had waved away Kimi's concerns. "Your heart will grow fond as the seasons pass," she promised, gazing fondly upon her grandchildren as they frolicked near the river's edge. "Your heart will grow fierce with love and longing. But these things take time."

Time had not lessened the ache of sorrow in Kimi's heart; how could it lead her to love a man for whom she had no feeling?

She sat up on her grass mat and beat her fists into the beaver pelt that pillowed her head. As she lay down again, the golden circle on the leather cord around her neck slipped from beneath her tunic and cast a beam of reflected moonlight upon the walls of the hut.

"Boldly, faithfully, successfully," she murmured in English, recalling the distant words of Reverend Whitaker. "But I cannot be bold, God, alone. And how can I be faithful when you have deserted me? And how can I measure success in this village? Our chief would say I should marry Askook and bear him children who will rise up to drive the Englishmen from the land. But in the house of one Englishman I was happy for a time."

She closed her eyes against the troubling memories and willed herself to sleep.

> **The canoe spun lazily across the water as she crouched inside. Fear knotted and writhed in her stomach because soft, silent, warm bodies were in the darkness of the boat with her. The air smelled of grass and humidity, and a hard wind blew the canoe across the water faster than any man could row. Kimi pressed her knuckles against her mouth to keep from crying.**
> **Suddenly the canoe struck a riverbank—**

Kimi sat up, gasping aloud in panic. Every nerve leaped and shuddered in relief when she looked around and realized that she was not in a boat, but in her own hut with the others of her tribe. It was nothing but a dream, the same nightmare she had had for as long as she could remember.

She lay back upon her bed and curled into a tight ball, her heart thumping against her rib cage. On this night, like many others, she would not sleep.

The two ministers slept as easily as if they had been born on the side of a riverbank, but Brody found it difficult to rest amid the rustling of wildlife and the shifting of shadows beyond the edge of the fire. He finally slid into a thin sleep as Fallon kept watch, but awoke abruptly at the touch of a hand on his shoulder.

"Soft, do not shout," Fallon said, his eyes scanning the shadows in the forest. "But you must wake, Brody."

"Is it my watch already?" Brody mumbled, struggling to throw off the heavy mantle of exhaustion.

"We will need another pair of eyes, I fear," Fallon said, cautiously creeping back to his place by the fire. "There is trouble afoot in the forest. I can smell it."

Brody lifted himself on one elbow and sniffed the air. Looking around, he saw nothing unusual. The moon reflected itself in full splendor upon the gently ruffled surface of the river, and the canoe rested easily upon the bank. The two ministers' bellies rose and fell rhythmically as they snored in the silence of the night. Nothing moved in the fire-tinted darkness.

"You are imagining things, my prince of the forest," Brody muttered, lowering himself again to the ground. "I hear nothing but the snoring of our two holy escorts."

"In that lies the problem," Fallon answered, his face pale, almost bloodless, against the darkness of the night. There was no look of the timid schoolmaster about him now. Determination lay in the jut of his chin; cunning and hard-bitten strength were etched into every feature of his face. "Where are the night sounds? They are hushed, for something treads in the forest."

Brody rested his head on his hand, listening. The air of the clearing seemed to vibrate softly in the rising heat from the fire, and the gentle waves of the river whispered as they brushed the overhanging shore. But Fallon was right. Throughout the night there had been bird calls and wild hootings and rustlings, but now a silence had settled upon the place, and the absence of greater sound had almost a physical density. Fear like the quick, chilling touch of a nightmare suddenly shot through him, and Brody sat up, shivering.

"We should wake the ministers."

Fallon paused. Tenseness and fear lay upon his face. "I will feel foolish if I am wrong," he said, a nervous edge in his voice, but he put out his hand and gently shook Reverend Whitaker's shoulder.

"Reverend, will you wake?"

The words were no sooner out of his mouth when the heavy silence exploded into evil shrieks and howls. The sounds came spiraling down from the forest, chilling Brody's blood with their awful intensity, then the leaves of the trees parted and the darkness filled up with the bodies, shields, and spears of savagely painted Indians, whose copper-colored torsos gleamed with malevolence in the red firelight.

Brody screamed and rose to run, but felt the copper tip of a spear suddenly bite the soft flesh beneath his chin. A warrior appeared before him, chattering wildly in an angry, foreign tongue while he applied pressure from the long spear aimed directly at Brody's throat. Brody raised his head and backed up against another Indian warrior, who caught his paralyzed arms and bound them tightly behind his back.

A whisper of absolute terror ran through him as he watched his comrades undergo similar treatment. Fallon tried for a moment to defend himself by brandishing the end of a burning log, but another warrior simply raised his bow and pointed an arrow at Fallon's chest. Fallon dropped the log and raised his hands, then was bound as quickly as the other three men.

The ministers, so abruptly roused from sleep, turned their protests into prayers as they were lined up and forced to follow a meandering trail through the woods. The clergymen walked in the front of the line, guarded by warriors on either side, and Brody turned his head long enough to whisper to Fallon, "I told you we should have brought soldiers!"

"If we had, we would be dead now," Fallon managed to reply before a brave slapped him silent.

▼▲▼▲▼ The war party returned at daybreak, and Kimi ignored the celebratory gathering in the center of the village as she rose from her bed. War parties came and went at the chief's whim, often bringing back captives from neighboring tribes who were either adopted into the clan, tortured, or branded as slaves. She had no stomach for the art of torture and death and little interest in other Indian tribes.

She walked to the river and splashed water on her face and hands. Shafts of bright sunlight fell through the clouds and she knew it would be another hot day. Seizing the opportunity of peace and quiet, she slipped from her leather tunic and waded into the water, relishing the feel of it on her skin. She floated on her back and kicked lazily for a minute, recalling the wonderful warmth of the summer days when she and Pocahontas had splashed together in the river.

Echoing from the palisade, the raucous noise from the village had evolved into the rhythmic song and dance of judgment, and Kimi knew that the prisoners, whoever they were, had stood before Opechancanough and heard his decision. Undoubtedly Askook stood at the chief's right hand, beaming with celebration and honor, and he would search the crowd to see if she approved of his victory. Sighing, she swam to shore, squeezed water from her thick braids, and donned her tunic again.

▼▲▼▲▼ Fallon stared at the man before him in a paralysis of astonishment. By heaven, how could this be the same Opechancanough who had sentenced him to death eleven years before? The years that had grown Fallon from a boy to a man did not seem to have marked the Indian at all. The chief stood as tall as ever, his dark eyes a stream of black gold above the white scar on his cheek, and his arms glistened with hard, distinct muscles. Now, however, the shock of hair that stood upright on his head was woven with many feathers, and a richly embroidered mantle hung upon his shoulders.

After only a quick glance at Fallon, Opechancanough focused his anger and distrust upon the two ministers. His eyes gleamed hard and cruel as he pronounced judgment in the Indian tongue, and though Fallon recognized the accent and sound, he could not follow the rapid words.

The people of the village roared with approval as the chief announced his verdict, and with a broad sweep of his arm he indicated Fallon and Brody as well. Rough hands grabbed all four men, and warriors herded them from the chief's dwelling to the center of the village.

Four stout poles had been thrust into the ground, one at each corner of the central fire. Rather than unloose the bonds that tied their hands behind them, the warriors lifted each man until his bound hands fell behind the top of the pole, then he was dropped so that he fell, helpless, to await judgment.

Hideous dancing figures whirled before Fallon, each seemingly intent upon his destruction. Little children, goaded by their mothers, rushed at him with clubs, which they swung effectively at his arms, knees, and stomach. One little girl, barely old enough to talk, fastened her mouth onto Fallon's hand and seemed determined to chew through his fingers. Brody screamed in panic and confusion as he met the same lot of punishing youngsters, and Fallon turned his face away from the sight of his friend. The great adventurer had met more danger than he had hoped to find within two days of landing in Virginia, and it was all Fallon's fault.

*Is it for this that you brought me home?* Fallon cried out in his heart, his eyes sweeping across the crowd for some reason to hope, some miracle of release. *I followed your will, God, and if you will that I perish here under the same sentence of death from which you saved me years ago, yet I will trust you. But Brody has done nothing to deserve this, nor have your two ministers.*

He leaned back against the heaviness of the pole and was filled with remembering as the dancing warriors lifted their voices in a high, thin song of triumph. The inhabitants of Ocanahonan had sung similar cadences, but theirs were songs of praise and thanks to God for a bountiful harvest and recovery from illness. And the converted Indians among them had sung songs upon their deathbeds, not the mournful, defiant heathen songs designed to impress death, but joyful, confident songs of children coming home to God.

Fallon closed his eyes against the pain of the falling blows and traveled back, picking up the strings of time. The words of a familiar song filled his head and he took a deep breath and began to sing:

> *"A mighty fortress is our God,*
> *A bulwark never failing.*
> *Our helper He amid the flood*
> *Of mortal ills prevailing. . . ."*

▼▲▼▲▼ Kimi padded softly around the standing circle of spectators, intending only to show her face to Askook for a moment, long enough to assure him that she had done her duty as his intended wife. But over the sound of the victorious chanting and the squeals of the excited children, a clear baritone voice rang out. The shock of the sound held her riveted to the ground. She knew the song, though she could not predict the words, but each phrase of the lyrics rang in her heart.

She whispered along with the singer, "For still our ancient foe . . . doth seek to work us woe. . . ."

Memories threatened to come crowding back like unwelcome guests, and Kimi pressed her lips together and shouldered her way through the crowd, determined to discover who had dared open the doors to her secret place of grief.


▼▲▼▲▼ "On earth is not his equal," Fallon finished the song, dimly aware that the noise around him had stilled. The silent warriors stood frozen in a circle around him, and for a moment even the children had stopped their blows. Expressions of startled delight lay upon their faces, and Fallon knew they would have responded in the same way if a doomed deer had suddenly begun to speak.

The ministers prayed softly from their places, and Brody's fearful whimpers cut through their whispers. Not a soul moved in the Indian camp till one young woman broke through the line of spectators and gazed at Fallon with chilling intentness. He lifted his eyes to hers in a mute plea for help and for an instant was startled by her beauty.

Opechancanough stepped forward from his place and motioned to his warriors. Battered and bruised, Fallon was lifted up and away from the torture pole and dragged to a large rock near the chief's hut. The crowd followed expectantly, and Fallon sighed in relief, knowing that the torture session had been cut short. Most tribes tortured condemned prisoners with unspeakable cruelty for hours before mercifully ending a captive's life, but for some reason Opechancanough seemed eager to be done with this dealing of death.

The priest muttered an incantation, and Fallon tossed a brief smile to Brody over the heads of his audience. "Do not fear," he called, forcing a note of triumph into his voice. "We'll be eating dinner at the Lord's table this noon!"

Opechancanough growled, and Fallon pulled against the restraining hands of his captors until he faced the chief. "To you, Opechancanough, I say this: The blood of Christians is seed; we will multiply whenever we are mown down by the forces of darkness. Do what you will, evil one, but you will not claim this victory!"

The dark light of anger gleamed in the chief's eye. He gestured to his warriors, who leapt forward and forced Fallon to his knees. He had time to scan the faces before him one last time and saw the beautiful girl again, her smoke-blue eyes wide and perturbed. Her hair hung wet upon her shoulders, as if she'd just come from the river, and a single ring of gold hung from a cord around her neck and gleamed against her damp skin.

Someone yanked his head to the side and pressed it down onto the rock. He did not resist, knowing the war club would soon descend. He closed his eyes, awaiting the final blow, then the windows of his memory flew open. The ring! Her blue eyes! It was not some unknown Indian girl who stood before him in the crowd—

"Gilda!" he screamed, struggling against the executioners who held him down. "Gilda!"

▼▲▼▲▼ Kimi trembled as the Englishman resisted death. He had gone willingly to the rock, and for a moment she had thought she would see Christian faith in action, a martyr's story worthy of those Reverend Whitaker used to tell. But then the man looked at her and screamed that strange name.

Gilda. Who was Gilda?

A black veil moved painfully at the back of her mind, and she resisted, but the memory of another man's head on the rock of execution edged her teeth. Her friend John Smith had once been in this place, and Pocahontas had leapt forward to save him. But like Pocahontas, John Smith had left her. Everyone she had ever loved had left her.

Two warriors on opposite sides of the rock picked up their heavy battle clubs. Two others held the prisoner in place. He continued to shout the name she refused to hear, and tears spilled from his eyes as his face twisted and scraped over the stone as he struggled in his efforts to reach someone.

Her hands clenched and unclenched at her side. The conjuror nodded to the warriors, and the heavy clubs swung into the air.

▼▲▼▲▼ Fallon closed his eyes and felt the wetness of his own tears upon his cheeks. He heard the swift intake of breath from the crowd and knew that the warriors stood ready to land the fatal blows. He shouted one final time: "Gilda!"

"Stop!"

Soft arms fell upon his head, cradling him from the death-blows. He breathed a heavy sigh of relief, not understanding what had happened, and a moment later someone pulled his blessed savior from him.

He opened his eyes and cautiously lifted his head. The girl who had to be Gilda stood before Opechancanough, who questioned her rapidly in the Indian tongue. She fired back answers with the insolence of youth, defiantly lifting her chin as if she possessed some kind of authority. Then Opechancanough leveled a charge and she paled and grew silent. Fallon felt his heart sink. Had his brash determination endangered Gilda, too?

But another warrior answered the silence following the chief's charge by stepping forward. This man gave the chief a terse comment for which Opechancanough had no answer. The chief finally held up his hands in an attitude of surrender, then gestured to Fallon, the girl, and the three waiting prisoners. While the tribe watched in stunned silence, Opechancanough dramatically folded his arms and turned his back on the scene.

The girl hurried to Fallon's side and put her hand under his elbow to help him to his feet. "Come, we must go away at once," she said in perfect English, untying the bonds that held his wrists. "Untie Reverend Buck and Reverend Whitaker, and I will unloose your friend. They must not linger in these lands, for the chief will not be merciful the second time you are brought before him."

"You know the ministers?" Fallon asked, amazed at the purity of her speech. He had not remembered the Algonquin dialect half so well.

"Of course," the girl snapped, striding rapidly toward Brody. "We must hurry."

He followed her, fascinated by the clean purity of her profile and the ethereal beauty of her eyes. He remembered Gilda as a golden, chubby child, but all traces of girlishness, immaturity, and baby fat had evaporated. Gilda had become a woman, and she moved before him as if she were totally unaware of her significance in his life.

"Gilda," he whispered, falling into step beside her as she advanced toward the place of torture. "I am Fallon Bailie. Do you not know me?"

Her gaze swept over him from head to toe and she did not smile as she answered. "I am Kimi of the Powhatan. I do not know you."

The circle of observers grew restless, probably eager for blood, Fallon thought, and he moved swiftly to loosen the bonds of the ministers. As he untied Reverend Whitaker, he could hear Brody blubbering his thanks as the girl cut his bonds with a dagger from her belt.

"What happened?" Whitaker whispered as Fallon released him. "I couldn't see over the crowd. Why are we free to go?"

"Because God works in mysterious ways," Fallon answered, his eyes fastened upon the girl called Kimi.

**Brody McRyan**

*For sufferance is the badge of all our tribe.*

*William Shakespeare,*
The Merchant of Venice

The crowd parted silently before them as Kimi led the way through the opening of the palisade. Her mind whirled in a series of disconnected thoughts as she fell into a quick, easy step along the trail that led through an open meadow and then to the river. The vivid memory of Pocahontas's rescue of John Smith had compelled her to save the copper-haired Englishman, but she had never dreamed that Opechancanough would challenge her.

"Why are you doing this?" the chief had asked, his eyes flashing as she left the side of the condemned prisoner.

"It is my right," she answered, her voice quavering despite her resolve. "Just as my sister once saved an Englishman, so I wish to spare this one."

"You have no rights here," Opechancanough replied, his words raw and angry in the morning stillness. "Your sister was the chief's daughter. You are nothing."

The earth had seemed to shift beneath her feet; the circle of onlookers swayed before her eyes. A trembling rose from deep inside her and moved steadily upward through her chest. She could not deny his words.

But Kitchi, son of Powhatan, had stepped out from the crowd. "She is my daughter," he said, placing his hands on his hips in a fierce, protective gesture. "She is blood of my blood and bone of my bone. I claim her as my own and give her the right to spare this prisoner and the others."

The chief pressed his lips together in silent fury, unable to dispute Kitchi's claim. Kimi stared at the warrior in a daze of confused gratitude, then Opechancanough jerked his head toward the warriors who waited with their battle clubs. They lifted the copper-haired man to his feet, and Opechancanough pronounced a new verdict: "Their lives are spared, but you must take them from the land of the Powhatan before the sun sets. They are yours, Woman-with-a-Secret. What will you do with them?"

"I will restore them to their people."

Sounds from the men who were now her responsibility returned her to the present. Behind her, the one who called himself Fallon grew breathless as he struggled to keep up. The golden-haired man walked silently with fear in his eyes, and the two ministers uttered quiet prayers of thanksgiving as they walked behind.

When they left the open field and entered the sanctuary of the forest, she paused to steal a backward glance toward the palisade. "They haven't followed, if that's what you're thinking," Fallon offered.

She turned on him in a flash of defensive spirit. "I did not think they would follow," she lied, angry that he had guessed her thoughts. "Maybe I wanted another look at the home I am leaving for your sake, Englishman!"

He blanched before her anger, and she whirled and led them through the woods in a steady jog. Before long, she had the satisfaction of hearing a wheezing cough from the stout Reverend Buck, and Fallon begged her to stop and rest.

She paused on the trail, a bit winded herself, and the ministers collapsed on the ground, closing their eyes against the summer heat. The golden-haired man sat on a fallen tree and hung his head between his knees. His forehead had been bloodied by a warrior's blows, and he walked with a limp.

"I pray you remember that we have not been long off the ship from England," Fallon said, leaning forward with his hands at his waist. "We cannot continue this pace."

"I should have left you to die on that rock if you cannot survive in the forest," she said, making an effort to steady her voice.

She breathed deeply through her nose so they would not guess how tired she was.

Fallon's red hair was stringy with sweat and his face as pale as paper, but his eyes seemed to probe her very soul. "Why did you save us?" came the unexpected question. "The chief was not happy with your interference."

"It was my right," she answered, sitting cross-legged on a clump of roots. "I once saw my sister save another condemned Englishman. It was her example that gave wings to my feet."

"Your sister?" Fallon sank to the ground beside her and stretched his long legs out before him. Through the torn edges of the leggings Kimi could see nasty purple bruises from the children's sticks.

"The daughter of the great chief who has left us was my sister," she answered, her voice husky as her throat tightened with memories.

"If you're a daughter of Powhatan," Fallon pressed, his forehead creased with apparent concern, "then why did the chief hesitate to grant your request? The other man had to intervene before Opechancanough relented."

Kimi pressed her lips together. This man was perceptive, she had to admit, but why did he care how she had saved him? "Anyone has a right to stop an execution if he or she will take responsibility for the captives," she said, bending the truth to fit an Englishman's limited understanding. "The chief questioned my wisdom. But Kitchi stepped forward and—"

"Kitchi?"

"Kitchi," she answered, frowning at him. "He is a brave warrior, and the chief could not refuse both of us." She cleared her countenance and painted on a mocking smile. "So now you and your friends owe me your lives. If we had remained in camp I could have adopted you, killed you, or made you my slaves. But since the chief admonished me to take you away—"

"You would not do any of those things," Fallon answered, again seeming to read her thoughts. He lay back upon the earth, pillowing his head in his crossed hands, and closed his eyes in a patch of dappled sunlight. Just when she thought he had fallen asleep, he opened one eye. "So your name means nothing to you?"

"Kimi? I am Woman-with-a-Secret. The chief gave me the name."

"I'm sure your secret is very interesting," Fallon murmured, his voice pitched low so that only she could hear. "But I knew you once by another name. As sure as I live, you are Gilda Colman, granddaughter of Jocelyn and Thomas Colman. You lived with your grandparents in the village called Ocanahonan—"

"I will not hear such nonsense!" The words rose from her on a wave of confused and crazily furious emotions, and she leapt to her feet and backed away from him. "I am Kimi of the Powhatan!"

"It is strange, then," Reverend Buck said, the corners of his eyes crinkling as he smiled at her, "that I knew you as Numees, sister of the maiden I married to John Rolfe. Come now, daughter, can you be thinking I'd forget you in only four years? You've become a lovely young woman, but there's no mistaking our blue-eyed Numees."

"Indeed not," Reverend Whitaker added, the light of recognition filling his eyes. "By heaven, I had nearly forgotten! But you were there in my classroom with Mistress Rebecca. You learned the catechisms even more readily than she, if I remember aright."

"Because, good sirs, she has known them from her childhood," Fallon said, standing. He extended his hand to her and looked fully into her eyes. "You are Gilda Colman. You were my childhood friend, and on the night Powhatan attacked Ocanahonan our parents gave me charge of both you and my brother, then sent us down the river. I cared for you until Powhatan's warriors raided the village where we had taken refuge. We were captured and carried away. Do you remember nothing of it? You have probably thought me dead these many years—"

A rush of bitter remembrance swept over her, and she threw up her hands as if to ward off a blow. She felt as though she had worn the mantle of grief for a long time, but had she donned it so early? To accept this man's words would be to embrace losses she could not recall.

"I am not Gilda," she whispered, turning from him. "And I am no longer Numees, for now I have no sister."

"I can prove who you are," Fallon went on relentlessly, stepping closer. "The circle of gold around your neck is a ring placed there by Jocelyn Colman, the woman you knew as mother. There is an inscription she often used to repeat, for her father sent her to Virginia with a single charge."

"I can bear witness to this," Reverend Whitaker interrupted, leaning forward in excitement. "I have seen the ring's inscription."

"With respect, sir, be silent," Fallon answered, casting the minister a warning glance. He came close enough for her to see concern radiating from the depths of his blue eyes—eyes so like hers—and her heart thudded like a drum when he reached out and took her hands. "Your charge for life, Gilda Colman, is written upon your heart as well as upon that ring: boldly, faithfully, successfully. Can you look at me and say that you do not recognize the truth in my words?"

His voice echoed in the stillness of the forest, drowning out the wild noises, and Kimi wanted to break free of his grip and pull the offending words from her ears. She was furious at the vulnerability she felt in his grasp, stunned that he knew the foreign words it had taken her years to understand, and mystified that God could have whirled her painful past round to meet her again.

"No!" she screamed, ripping her hands from his grip. "I will not believe you!" She turned to run, but the golden-haired man had risen behind her. He caught her as easily as she and Pocahontas had snagged butterflies in their nets of woven flax. She beat against his chest, weeping with frustration and sorrow, and he held her tight until her tears would come no more.

▼▲▼▲▼ Fallon was not surprised to discover that their canoe and supplies had disappeared from the place where they had been captured. He stood on the riverbank, wearily considering their options, and the others sank to the ground in exhaustion. Gilda had not spoken since her outburst in the forest, and now she walked away from the group and plucked several broad leaves from a shrub. After spreading the leaves on the ground near the water's edge, she lay down and turned her back on the knot of tired men.

"We should sleep here," Fallon remarked. "Truly, this is as good a place as any. If we are fortunate, another passing vessel will pick us up." He leveled the ashes of their previous fire with his boot. "I will build a fire and keep the first watch."

"Sleep here?" Brody asked, his face twisting into a startled expression of disapproval. "In the same cursed spot where the savages took us? What if they come back?"

"They won't come back," Reverend Whitaker answered, following Gilda's example by spreading leaves on the ground. "We've been ransomed, at least for this present time. And we have nothing they could want."

"What if they come for the girl?" Brody persisted.

"They won't," Fallon answered, venturing out of the clearing to gather wood. "She left by her own choice."

Not entirely convinced, Brody slumped against a tree, choosing to sleep upright, and Fallon gathered an armload of kindling, then lit it with the flint in his doublet pocket. When the fire burned steadily, he set a log into the midst of the flames. Keeping his eyes turned in the direction of the woods, he sat with his back to the river. Unbidden, his gaze fell upon the girl's slender form. His heart went out to her, for his news had brought her much anguish. In time she would reconsider his words, and when she did, how could she not be awed by the mighty working of God? Not only had he reunited the two of them, but God had used her to save Fallon from the devilish hand of Opechancanough.

More important, Fallon reflected grimly, God had prevailed against that particular devil's prophecy. Eleven years ago Opechancanough had looked into Fallon's frightened eyes and predicted that Gilda would forget the things of God and her family. Though she had forgotten much, the things of God had been engraved upon her heart, and the Almighty had seen fit to refresh the writing through men like the two ministers who slumbered even now around the fire.

And yet he sensed within her a certain pride, an instinctive defensiveness of all things Indian. It was only natural that she should feel so, he reasoned, since the Indians had reared her, but how could she defend the so-called wisdom of Opechancanough, the fiend who had incited Powhatan to destroy Ocanahonan and their parents?

Fallon felt his blood stir within him as he considered his own desire for vengeance. Because of Opechancanough's evil, he, too, had grown up as an orphan. Gilda was not the only one who had tasted bitter loneliness and grief. She had not suffered alone. And somewhere beneath these very stars, Noshi lived and waited for them to find him. Fallon prayed that his little brother had not suffered as much as he and Gilda.

*"Always take careful soundings, lad,"* a voice called in his memory as his eyes grew heavy. It was the voice of Christopher Newport as he navigated his way into the English Channel. *"For nothing ever stays the same."*

When sleep threatened to overtake him, he crawled forward and put his hand on Brody's shoulder. His friend's eyes flew open and his hand automatically closed around a large stick, but Fallon soothed him. "Nothing is amiss, Brody, but I must sleep. Can you take the second watch?"

"Yes," he answered, settling into the easy smile of his usual temperament. He crawled toward the fire, shaking leaves from his hair, and stretched out like an old dog on the ground. "You didn't tell me this sister of yours was so beautiful, Fallon," he teased, tossing a handful of kindling onto the fire. "'Pon my soul, if I had known she was so ravishing, I'd have suggested that we come to Virginia years ago. When she fell into my arms back there, it was all I could do—"

"She's not my sister, but she's in my care," Fallon answered, lying back upon the damp ground. "So you'll keep your thoughts away from her, Brody McRyan, or you'll have to reckon with me."

She was small again, for her thumb slid easily through the ring that hung about her neck. She clutched it in her hand, loving the soft coolness of the golden circle against her skin, and a light voice called from an English house of wattle and daub. "Gilda," the voice called, then a dark-haired woman appeared in one of the shuttered windows. "Where have you been? We have been worried about you."

The lady walked out of the house and gathered the child into her arms, swinging her in a circle as the girl laughed and nestled into the softness of the woman's embrace. Mother smelled of warmth and bread and honey. Her dark hair, soft as a rabbit's fur, curled into ring-lets at her temples and the nape of her neck.

"Your father wants you to find the boys," Mother said, planting the child's feet firmly on the ground. "Noshi and Fallon are down by the river."

Suddenly she stood at the river's edge, and the ring had shrunk again to its usual size. Two boys knelt in the soft sand, building houses of mud and sticks. One boy was dark-haired and honey-colored like herself; the other was tall, thin, and pale, with hair the color of burnished copper. It was Fallon, without a doubt, in the gangly throes of adolescence.

Fallon saw her and stood up, shading his eyes with his hand. "Who are you?" he asked, backing away from her. "I don't know you."

"I am Kimi," she said, moving toward him, but the name seemed to fill him with fear. He backed away, closer to the edge of the swirling river.

"I am Numees," she offered, smiling as she moved closer, but again he moved away. "I am Concheta, a stranger," she said, offering whatever names came to her mind. "Or you may call me Taima, woman of thunder."

With every name she offered he trembled and moved closer to the water until he teetered on the edge, his arms pinwheeling, and she felt something in her soul give way. "I am Gilda!" she cried, thrusting out her arms to catch him. "Father sent me to find you."

The ridge of soil beneath the boy's bare feet cracked and broke, but Gilda's hands caught his and pulled him to safety. He gave her a smile as bright as sunshine. "I thank you," he whispered, pillowing his head against her shoulder. "You have saved me."

Reality returned in a rush and Kimi sat up, as wide awake as if she'd just drunk a cup of the conjuror's strongest tea. Brody dozed by the fire, the two ministers snored steadily in the dusk of twilight, and Fallon lay motionless under an oak.

It was only another dream. For a moment she relaxed in relief—then was overwhelmed by a fierce pang of loss for the smiling woman and the boy who had nestled in her arms and whispered his gratitude.

The distance they had traveled in two days by canoe would take
at least four to recover on foot. Kimi was grateful that despite the
bruising beating they had endured at the hands of the children,
none of the men in her company proved to be of a complaining
nature. She had seen many Englishmen who shuddered at the
sight of snakes and grumbled about their bunions and sore feet
with every step, but Fallon, Brody, and the two ministers main-
tained her pace through the woods and made only casual conversation, when they talked at all.

Even so, their casual conversation revealed much. Brody, the
tall one with golden hair, asked Kimi if she had seen the veins of
gold reported to lie deep under the banks of the rivers. He shook
his head in regret when she said she had seen no gold save the
ring around her own neck. Later she heard him tell the ministers
that as soon as he was able, he would lead an expedition into the
interior to open those golden veins for England's share of the
riches the Spanish had been plundering for years.

Brody was observant, charming, and independent, she had to
admit, but now that they were well out of Opechancanough's immediate territory, he grew more brash than she thought wise. He
talked of the infallible escape plan he would have effected if
Fallon had been killed and bragged that the savages would
never have placed *his* head on the rock of execution, that he
would have died in battle before willingly kneeling before the
chief.

Fallon listened to Brody's blustering without rebuttal, and
Kimi wondered that he did not smack the younger man for his
impudence and be done with him. But Fallon bore his friend's

comments with no sign of ill humor, and Kimi decided that the
friendship between them must be very strong and deep indeed.

The two ministers spent most of their conversation with each
other, and once they asked Fallon what had brought him back to
Virginia. Fallon told them of his school in England and the London Company's request that one hundred boys be brought for
indenture. "So I came, hoping to find them good homes and
places of service," Fallon explained, tossing his words over his
shoulder as they hiked along the narrow trail. "But I was greatly
dismayed when I finally came ashore to find that the boys had
already been dispersed throughout the settlements."

The clergymen promised to help Fallon visit the settlements if
he wished to do so, and as she walked Kimi pondered the nature
of a man who would cross the great ocean to care for such a number of boys. Such a man would be patient and temperate and
true. He must of certain be honest, for children had the gift of
clear sight and knew when men were false-natured. So how,
then, could he tell her such a preposterous story about her childhood? And how had he known about the inscription of the ring?

Understanding dawned. Because Reverend Whitaker told
him, of course. And her dream? A lie unleashed by the story he'd
told her. But even as she offered these simple explanations,
another voice, buried deep within her, repeated Fallon's claims:
*As sure as I live, you are Gilda Colman.*

Her mind skated away from the unsolvable dilemma, and she
quickened her pace along the trail.

▼▲▼▲▼ They had not eaten in two days. As the darkness came on at sunset the air along the riverbank seemed to
vibrate softly in a great rush of noise. Kimi held up her hand,
stopping in her place, and Brody darted forward to question her.
"What is it?" he whispered, naked fear in his eyes.

Fallon gave the answer. "Dinner."

Without a word, Kimi pointed upward. Branches of the trees
above them sagged beneath the weight of an enormous flock of

roosting passenger pigeons. At short intervals a swarm launched themselves into the sky, blocked the lingering rays of sun, and returned to the trees, which rustled heavily with the bodies of the birds. Kimi had often seen the huge flocks; their migrations would sometimes take days to pass overhead.

"Your God has smiled upon us," she said, glancing over her shoulder to the two ministers. "We shall eat today and carry meat for tomorrow."

The gigantic flock had begun to settle down for the night, and their chirps and cries echoed eerily across the stillness of the water. Kimi motioned for the men behind her to stand still, then she looked at Fallon. "I will need your doublet," she whispered. Without hesitation he slipped it from his shoulders and handed it to her.

She walked quietly into the woods until she stood under a tree whose limbs sagged with the weight of the birds. Standing as motionless as a statue, she gave an abrupt whistle, and half a dozen birds flew to the ground to peer at her, cocking their heads as if she had spoken. She murmured to them in a low, soothing voice and, while they sat transfixed by the sound, she slipped the doublet over the closest bird, trapping him underneath.

"That's a very good trick," Brody called from where the men waited. "And that's about two mouthfuls for each of us."

Ignoring him, Kimi lifted the jacket and caught the bird's body in her hands, still soothing him. "Do not fear, little brother," she whispered, "for you will fly again."

She had always been awed by the beauty of the graceful birds. The creature who cooed beneath her hands was a male, brown with streaks of blue upon his body. His mate, a tall female with a beautiful cinnamon-rose colored breast, perched on a low branch and jeered at Kimi. "Patience, my sister," Kimi crooned, trapping the male beneath the doublet again so she could rip a strip of fabric from its lining. "Your mate will come home."

Quickly tying a loose knot in the fabric strip, she eased the bird's head out from under Fallon's coat and fastened the noose over the male's head, effectively blinding him. With the bird imprisoned beneath the heavy fabric, she uprooted a vine, stripped it of its leaves in one swift motion, and tied one end of the supple plant around the bird's foot. After looping the other end around a broken branch on a fallen log, she carefully lifted the doublet and backed away.

The hooded bird hopped uncertainly in the clearing, then beat his wings in distress. His cries and frantic signaling carried through the silent forest, and others of his flock descended to watch his agitated movements. When the birds covered the ground as thickly as a living carpet, Kimi turned in triumph toward the astounded men behind her. "Use your doublets to capture as many as you can," she whispered, tossing Fallon's torn coat back to him. "But do not hurt the hooded bird."

The men swarmed forward, cheering in their excitement, and the distracted birds flew into each other in a frantic attempt to flee. Each man caught at least three birds, and when their necks had been wrung, Kimi set the hooded pigeon free.

"By heaven, that was a good trick," Brody crowed with delight as Kimi led them back to the river, where they could roast their catch. "Why don't you come with me when I go inland? I could use a girl who knows her way in the wilderness."

She gave him no answer, but pointed to the place where they should build a fire.

▼▲▼▲▼ After a filling meal they stretched out in a clearing to sleep. Kimi sat with her eyes fixed upon the dancing fire, lost in thought, and shifted in annoyance when Fallon sat down beside her.

"You have saved our lives more than once," he said, his eyes sweeping over her with a tenderness no one save Pocahontas had ever shown her. "If we had not eaten, I doubt we would have had the strength to make it back to Jamestown." His forehead crinkled. "I used to know how to call the animals, but I have forgotten so much. . . ."

She did not know what he expected her to say, so she

remained quiet and stared into the fire. Her silence did not dampen his desire to talk. "I once took care of you, Gilda, though I doubt you remember it. You and Noshi were such little things. I fed you with eggs I found on the river, do you remember? I took care of you then, and I'll take care of you again when we get to Jamestown. After we find Noshi, if you want to go to England, we can, or if you want to live in Jamestown, we could do that, too—"

She recoiled from his words. "Go to England?" she said, her soul flooding with horror. "John Rolfe took my sister to England and she did not come back. Why would I want to go to such a place?"

Fallon shrugged. "I cry you mercy; if you don't want to go, we won't. It doesn't matter where we go. But I'm here to take care of you now, Gilda, just like I promised."

She stood and angrily brushed the dirt from her tunic. "I do not need your help. I am taking you to Jamestown as my chief commanded and then I will return to my village." She lifted her chin in defiance. "The chief has promised me to Askook, a fine warrior."

"Promised you?" Fallon's lips pursed suspiciously.

"I will become his wife."

"Oh no," Fallon answered, a smile playing briefly upon his face. "Your mother and father would never allow that. I can't permit it. If you marry at all, you must marry a Christian man."

"You mean an English man!"

"No." Fallon shook his head and smiled again as if her anger amused him. "I care not whether he be English or Indian or French. Even Spanish, if he is not a popish Catholic. But you and I are of Ocanahonan, and by the laws of that city, you must marry a believer in Christ. It is a principle of the Bible, God's Holy Word—"

"I am not of Ocanahonan!"

"Then what are you?" he asked, and the simple question caught her off guard.

Tears of frustration filled her eyes as she searched for an

answer. She was not of the English, nor was she truly of the Powhatan. Opechancanough had not trusted her, and by rescuing these men she had proved that she harbored tender feelings toward the English and their God. But an Englishman had taken Pocahontas and the baby, those she loved the most. . . .

"I belong to myself," she finally whispered, her eyes falling again on the devouring fire.

Fallon stood up, and his hands fell upon her shoulders. She caught her breath at his gentle touch and lifted her eyes to his. "You and I, Gilda, were born into a place where God, not an earthly king, established laws and justice," he said, his voice like a warm embrace in the chilly air. "We were born to people who measured men by the love in their hearts, not the color of their skin. In Ocanahonan, English and Indian worked and lived together. All were joined in a common service to God and their fellowman—"

"Ocanahonan was a cursed place." She spat the accusation toward him. "The priests say that town was destroyed by an act of the gods."

"No," Fallon persisted, his hands tightening upon her arms. "It was a beautiful, civilized city, and maybe it is the only place in the world where you and I will feel at home."

Home. A stab of hope pierced her heart at the word, and a sob escaped her. While with the Indians, she had crept every night into any hut whose inhabitants were willing to give her rest. At Jamestown she had stayed with Edith Rolfe only because Pocahontas had been welcomed there. She had never known a place where she was welcomed because she belonged there, and in the privacy of her heart she had never dared to dream that such a place could exist.

In a silent plea for understanding, she lifted her hands toward his shoulders, afraid to touch him, but he opened his arms to her. For a long moment she leaned against his sinewy length for support, then a warm wave of breath in her ear brought her back to reality. "You see," he whispered, "somewhere inside, you do remember."

She pulled away, thumbing tears away from her eyes. "You misread my weakness," she said, struggling to regain her dignity, "and my intention. Though you may have known me as a child—" she paused, the desire to stay at his side and fill in the gaps of her life warring with the urge to cast him off—"you do not know me now. I will see you safely to Jamestown, then I will return to my village and obey my chief's wishes."

"You'd marry a godless heathen?" The firelight magnified his horrified expression of disapproval. "You'd give your strength and beauty to one who does not deserve you—"

"Askook was clever and strong enough to capture you, wasn't he?" It was a throwaway accusation, but she'd hit home, for he snapped his mouth shut and left her by the fire without another word.

▼▲▼▲▼ With growing delight, Brody watched as Kimi and Fallon continued to spar with each other throughout the next day. On the remaining journey back to Jamestown they had little to say to one another save cutting remarks. When Fallon lost his footing on the slippery river trail and tumbled into the water, Kimi openly questioned why she had bothered to save such a hapless fool. Then she asked the ministers if they would think her a terrible sinner if she sold Fallon into slavery once they reached the fort.

The ministers laughed, albeit weakly, and for a moment Brody wondered if she expected some sort of payment for saving their lives. But as soon as Fallon pulled himself from the river she marched ahead without glancing back. Fallon did not answer her or offer an excuse, but his face flushed red and blotchy with anger as he followed her along the river trail.

Brody thought the girl—Gilda, Kimi, whatever she wanted to call herself—an absolute marvel. She was fluent in the English tongue as well as the Indian, knowledgeable and steady in the wilderness, and terribly clever about finding food, water, and shelter. She could probably earn a bountiful living as a scout or guide if she wanted to consider such a thing, but how much more pleasant it would be if she would accompany him as a wife!

Brody marveled that she had not married. She was yet young, probably not more than sixteen, yet her figure had ripened to a slim womanly fullness and her face shone like gold in the flickering light of their campfire. He had fallen asleep these past nights studying that face with its long, slender nose, high cheekbones, and lips like a thread of scarlet. And those eyes! They were bottomless pools of blue that seemed to look through rather than at him.

A heaven-sent walking miracle she was, and if Fallon couldn't see the girl's worth, he would marry her himself. Together they would find the mythic waterfalls where melon-sized gold nuggets waited in pools of sparkling water.

▼▲▼▲▼ They crept into Jamestown like defeated, weary refugees, and a crowd of soldiers and planters at the docks greeted Fallon and his companions with jeers and catcalls. "Well now, what's this?" one trader called as they walked up the riverbank toward the fort. "Where are your bags of gold, my friends?"

"Hey, schoolmaster," another man shouted. "It would appear the savages have given you a few lessons."

The back of Fallon's neck burned with humiliation, but he imagined that Brody felt worse than he did. Their plans to conquer Virginia had doubled back and slapped them in the face.

The ministers accepted the mocking comments with good grace, though Fallon suspected that they would blame their indignity on the two ignorant newcomers who had arranged the ill-fated trip into the wilderness. Only Gilda seemed unfazed by the mocking crowd. She carried herself with vigor and grace past the fort and the inn.

The ministers and Brody went inside the inn, but Fallon paused on the threshold. "Gilda, where will you go?"

"I am Kimi," she casually corrected him, tossing the words

over her shoulder. "And I have a place." She walked on, seemingly oblivious to the admiring glances of the men she passed. Fallon shook his head. He'd never known a woman with such an independent spirit—but then, he'd not known many women.

A short, squat man with a red and bulbous nose staggered out of the inn with a tankard of beer. He looked around, then gave Fallon a leery wink as he jerked his thumb toward Gilda's retreating form. "I know that one. She stayed at John Rolfe's house while he was married to that Indian woman."

"She wouldn't go there now," Fallon said, thinking aloud. "Master Rolfe lives at Henrico—"

The man guffawed. "John Rolfe lives mostly in his tobacco fields these days. His house is kept by his sister, a sour-faced witch who keeps a loaded musket handy lest a man come within twenty yards of the place."

Fallon's goodwill returned in a rush and he extended his hand to the man. "Excuse me, sir. Fallon Bailie, I am, and pleased to make your acquaintance. Maybe we have met before, for you look familiar to—"

"Tobias Harden," the man interrupted, extending a grubby paw. "Likewise." He burped slowly, gave Fallon a bleary smile, and patted his chest. "What brings you to these parts, young Master Bailie? If you don't mind my sayin' so, you look like you've been on the receivin' end of a whole lot of trouble."

Fallon glanced down at his dirty, torn clothes and managed a shamefaced grin. "Aye, so I do. My friends and I have just returned from the river."

"Are you a tobacco planter?" Harden's eyes narrowed suspiciously.

"No," Fallon answered, shaking his head. "I'm a schoolmaster."

Harden nearly choked on his beer. "Ha, ha, ha," he roared, slapping his leg as yellow foam dribbled down his chin. "That's a good joke. There isn't any school here, Master Bailie, so it is the devil's truth you are trying to sell me!"

Fallon shook his head again. "No, you misunderstand. I was

commissioned to bring a crew of students here to work in indentured service for a term."

The grin evaporated from Harden's face. "So you're the one!" he bellowed, staggering backward. "Brought me a load of worthless flesh, you did! I paid good tobacco for the bag o' bones you gave me, and I've got nothing good out o' him!"

"I don't know what you mean—," Fallon began, but Harden held up a thick finger and stomped to the side of the building. In a moment he returned, dragging a pitiful, pale form forward. "This!" Harden roared, dropping the small figure at Fallon's feet.

Stick-thin arms protruded from a torn and muddied shirt with unmistakable bootprints impressed upon the fabric. Fallon caught glimpses of a bruised face under the matted hair, and a soft moan passed through the urchin's lips as Harden spat on the pitiful bundle on the ground.

The small face tilted upward as the head rolled back, revealing the countenance in its entirety, and Fallon gasped as though he had been punched in the stomach. The scarecrow at his feet was Wart Clarence.

"Wart?" Fallon fell to his knees and pushed the mass of tangled hair from Wart's blackened eyes. The boy moaned again and clutched his stomach. Fallon felt a cold sweat break out upon his face and he shivered through fleeting nausea. He had never seen a boy so badly beaten, and Wart had been sick when they landed.

The boy had dreamed of a family and found a monster.

"What have you done to this child?" Fallon roared, standing. His fists clenched at his side. He had never hit another man in his life, but if ever there was an appropriate occasion to pummel a scoundrel, of certain this was one.

Harden's eyes squinted at the challenge in Fallon's words. With an easy motion he tossed his mug of beer away and hunched forward, rolling up his sleeves as he glared at Fallon. "Are you of a mind to be telling me what to do with me own property?" he shouted, moving sideways into the clearing past the boy's broken body. "I paid for that boy and haven't gotten a lick o' work out of him."

"He was sick!" Fallon yelled back. His arms wriggled out of his doublet as if they had a mind of their own. He flung his coat aside and crouched low in imitation of the other man.

The crowd inside the inn sensed the electric charge in the atmosphere and spilled out to watch the confrontation, shouting encouragement as they came. Fallon stole a quick glance and saw that Brody and one of the ministers knelt over Wart's bruised body. Brody's eyes lifted from the boy and caught Fallon's, then he nodded grimly.

A strange, cold excitement filled Fallon's head as he stared at his adversary. Harden's lips twisted slightly, then he lowered his shoulder and charged.

Fallon's weight was no match for the brute strength of the older man, and he went crashing back into a pile of wet canvas. The crowd roared and Harden whirled around to acknowledge their praise. Fallon struggled to his feet, his blood rising in a jet. He was down, but not out, for Wart's motionless form still lay like a pile of rags in the dirt. Enraged, Fallon lunged toward his opponent, who turned in the instant before impact and jammed his fist squarely into the pit of Fallon's stomach.

Fallon doubled over, unable to breathe. Harden backed away, brushing his hands together in a taunting gesture, then he squinted again and rushed forward, landing a knife-edged hand strike to the back of Fallon's neck. Colors exploded in Fallon's brain as he fell face first to the dusty ground, then through the din he heard Brody's strong voice: "Think you that I should join in, Fallon?"

"Yes," Fallon croaked into the dust. He heard Brody roar and the crowd shouted in approval as the fight continued with another contender.

Fallon closed his eyes in thankfulness as he struggled to catch his breath. When he was finally able to lift himself from the ground, he saw that Brody had Harden trapped with a hug from behind and was lifting the man up and down as if he could pound him into the ground. With his bloodlust still at a fever pitch, Fallon stumbled forward and drew back his clenched fist. "This is for the boy," he said, flecks of mingled saliva and blood spattering from his mouth to Harden's purpling face.

He smashed his fist into the man's jaw and felt the bones give.

▼▲▼▲▼ His body laced with pain, Fallon groaned.

"I'faith, you should have left it alone," Brody called from his bunk in the jail. "I had him under control. Why'd you have to hit him?"

"I didn't know I'd break my hand," Fallon moaned, eyeing his bruised and swollen fingers. "How was I to know the man has a head of granite?"

A footstep echoed outside the iron bars of their cell and in a moment the nasal voice of a guard cut through the gloom. "Are you two able to cease brawling in His Majesty's streets of Jamestown?"

"He had a good reason for brawling, haven't I said so?" Brody said, sitting up to face the soldier. He tossed the man one of the good-natured smiles that never failed to win him favor. "The child had been battered to a pulp and even now stands in danger of losing his life."

"Where is the boy?" Fallon said, struggling to sit up. "I don't care if you keep me in here, but the boy needs help. He was in a bad way when I last saw him—"

"We took the boy to Mistress Rolfe," the jailer replied, his keys jangling against the iron lock. With a click and a protesting screech of metal, the door swung open. "You are both free to go, but if you tangle with Tobias Harden again, you'll spend six months in our jail."

"Thank you," Brody said, slipping easily from the bed.

He paused to wait for Fallon, who rose gingerly from his cot. His ribs ached, his bones felt permanently misaligned, and his right hand was utterly useless. He moved carefully past the jailer and met the man's steady gaze with a timid smile. "Tell me this, at least," Fallon whispered confidentially, hugging his swollen hand to his chest. "Did I hurt that ruffian at all?"

The man covered his mouth with his hand to hide a reluctant grin. "No," he said finally, giving Fallon a glance of grudging admiration. "But you were the first man to try."

Fallon nodded and went out, finding a strange satisfaction in the answer.


▼▲▼▲▼ The late morning air was warm and burnished with sunlight, and a clear blue sky canopied the fort as Fallon and Brody walked from the jail. The actual fort enclosed about an acre of land, and within the enclosure stood a chapel, various storehouses, an armory, and a barracks for the men of King James's militia. The main gate faced the river to protect against enemy ships.

Fallon knew little about warfare, but it seemed to him that the place was well defended. The engineers had surrounded the palisade with a moat, and four small cannons were mounted upon bulwarks at each of the five corners. A line of muskets stood loaded and ready outside the armory, and Fallon was glad to leave the place, for it reminded him too much of the omnipresent danger from unpredictable savages.

"They'll of certain not see our like again," Brody said, laughing as they nodded farewell to the guards at the gates of the palisade. "What are you thinking that we should do now?"

"I know not," Fallon answered, pausing to survey the open clearing before him. "I am not fit for work with this injured hand, but we must work to eat, for my purse will not last long here."

"Aye."

The land before them sloped gently down to the riverfront, and the two men paused near the docks to ponder their future. To their right stood several buildings framed of rough pine and filled with a latticework of saplings and reeds. A crude plaster of mud and ground seashells covered the walls, and reed roof thatching kept out the rain. These were the public buildings: the inn, the tavern, the meetinghouse. One solitary brick church stood to their left, and further away, rising up from the green of summer growth, were private homes skirted with growing green tobacco fields.

"I have been thinking," Brody said, shrugging hesitantly. "You know I want to explore the wilderness. I know gold lies in the west, Fallon, and I want to find it."

"Indeed, how could I help but know it?" Fallon answered with an impenitent grin. "It is all you have talked about."

"But, truth to tell, I will need money to furnish an expedition, and I have none," Brody went on.

Fallon was about to offer his purse, but Brody cut him off with an abrupt lift of his hand. "I know what you're thinking and I'll not be taking your money, Fallon Bailie. I have decided instead to join the king's regiment for a term of six months. The pay is good, I'll be quartered at the fort, and maybe I can learn a wee bit from the traders who come in and out of this place. As you and I have already learned, it is too soon to go running off into the wilderness."

"Aye." Fallon agreed. They had been foolish to run into the woods immediately after landing in Virginia, but God had honored their earnestness, hadn't he? They had found Gilda, and maybe they could find Noshi as easily if they attempted a second journey.

*But,* an inner voice nagged, *what good has come of your venture? Gilda resents you now. How can you expect her to respect you and submit to your guidance when she has had to save, feed, and shelter you?*

Brody waited in silence to hear whether or not Fallon would join him with the regiment, but Fallon did not know what to say. "I know not what I shall do," he said finally, lifting his eyes to the east, where he could just see the watery ocean horizon. "I came to find Gilda and Noshi, and though I have found Gilda, my brother is still lost. And surely God would not have sent me all this way to see Gilda married to a heathen."

"Then marry her to me," Brody casually replied. "I will cherish her for you, Fallon, and I'm as God-fearing a man as any you might want to meet."

"Are you?" Fallon asked, giving his friend a lopsided grin. "You looked more like Goliath than David yesternoon when we fought that knave Harden."

Brody laughed, then fell silent as Fallon continued to consider his choices. "I have thought much about Wart," he finally said. "I was charged to take care of my students and bring them to safety and service in Virginia. Though they may have found service, they did not find safety. I think it may now be my duty to visit the plantations where they are and charge the planters with the good care of the boys."

"And if you encounter another like Tobias Harden?" Brody asked, crossing his burly arms. "Will you break your other hand?"

"No," Fallon answered, feeling his cheeks burn. "There must be a civil recourse. If a cruel master will not hear the admonitions of God to treat servants fairly, then I will appeal to the governor and to the king himself, if necessary. Perchance something can be done, and if I can be the instrument, I am willing."

Brody regarded him in silence, then uncrossed his arms and extended a hand. "I am glad to know you, Fallon Bailie," he said, grabbing his friend's uninjured hand and pumping it earnestly. "When we were boys, I thought you a prince. And now that we are men, I know you are."

Fallon waved away the compliment and stood to his feet. "So I suppose you will want to go now," he said, glancing back toward the tall walls of the fort. "The next time I see you, you'll be wearing the regimental red."

"And where will you be going?" Brody asked, concern shining in his eyes. "You are in no condition to travel far."

"I want to see Wart, and if Mistress Rolfe is running an infirmary, maybe she can tend to my hand as well," Fallon answered. He stepped back and saluted his friend. "Till we meet again, Brody McRyan."

▼▲▼▲▼ The third passerby pointed out the large, tidy-looking house kept by Mistress Edith Rolfe, and as Fallon opened the gate and walked up the flower-lined pathway he tried to ignore the hopeful voice in his head whispering that Gilda might be there. He could not sort through his feelings about her—he had found her and wanted to protect her, but she wanted no part of his protection and seemed to regret that she'd been found. If she wanted to go back to Opechancanough's village and marry that painted heathen brave, what right had he to stop her? But it would be better if she married a Christian. Though he had always imagined she would marry Noshi, if

Brody was willing to marry her, maybe he should urge her to consider that option. But she would have to prove willing to listen to him, and when they had parted, she had scarcely been willing to speak.

The door of the house swung open as he approached on the path, and a tall, solidly built woman leveled a musket at his chest. "State your name and business," she said firmly, her color-less lips flattening. "And know that I am willing to shoot any man that walks."

He lifted his arms in a "don't shoot" pose, and his injured hand throbbed as he raised it. "I am Fallon Bailie and I've come to see about Watford Clarence," he said. He jerked his head toward his hand. "And I'm injured myself."

The woman lifted her brows eloquently at the sight of him, then lowered the musket. "I have heard of you, Master Bailie," she said, her eyes flickering with a sort of reserve he couldn't place.

"Pray excuse me," Fallon said, slowly lowering his hands. "But I am seeking Mistress Rolfe."

"I am Mistress Rolfe," she said, standing the musket in the doorway. She folded her arms and leaned against the door frame as she swept appraising eyes over him. "I heard about the fight and your night in the jail. You are to be commended, sir, for defending a boy, but I cannot allow a strange man inside my house."

"He is no stranger," a soft voice interrupted, and a golden hand pulled the door open further. Fallon blinked in surprise when he saw Gilda, for she no longer wore the buckskin tunic of an Indian, but a delicately embroidered blouse and the elegant kirtle of an English lady. Her hair, still as dark and glossy as a crow's wing, lay piled in elegant curls atop her head, and her gaze fixed him in a blue-eyed vise.

"Is this—?" the mistress asked, and Gilda nodded. "Ah, then," Mistress Rolfe said, extending a hand of welcome to Fallon. "Come in, sir, and see for yourself how your student fares. The entire town has heard of your brawling in the streets, and though I've never been one to countenance street fighting, I have to admit that you saved the child."

Gilda moved away as Fallon came into the house and followed Edith through the roomy front hall. Wart lay in a small chamber that stood like an afterthought at the side of the structure. The room was heavily curtained and dimly lit, but he could see the small outline of a boy underneath a thin summer blanket.

"He had a fever when he was brought to us," Mistress Rolfe said as Fallon knelt by the boy's bed. "But the fever broke last night and Numees says he will be better soon."

"Numees?" Fallon asked, momentarily confused. Then he remembered. "You mean Gilda."

The woman shook her head slightly and touched her hand to her forehead. "Yes, she told me the story. It is difficult to believe, sir."

"It is total truth, I assure you," he answered, turning to Wart. He placed his left hand upon the boy's forehead, and Wart's thin eyelids flew open at his touch.

"Master Fallon," he whispered hoarsely through swollen and cracked lips. "Is it really you? I wondered if you'd come."

"Of course," Fallon whispered, forcing a smile even though the sight of bruises upon the boy's face made him want to break his other hand on Tobias Harden's jaw. "Sleep, Wart, and regain your strength. Then you shall be my assistant, for I have important work to do."

"I'd be happy to help you," Wart murmured, his eyes closing slowly. "But I fainted in the tobacco field and the master hit me. . . ."

Fallon waited until the boy resumed the heavy breathing of sleep, then he smiled his thanks at Mistress Rolfe. "My good woman, your medicine is marvelous," he said, rising to his feet. "With a little time, and a little food, the boy will be better than he was on the ship." Sheepishly, he pulled his bruised and swollen hand from inside his doublet. "And now I wonder if you have medicine that might help me?"

The woman grimaced at the sight, then she smiled and

crooked her finger at him as they left the chamber. "Numees—I mean Gilda—is the healer," she said, leading the way to the back room, which served as a kitchen. "If you want to be healed, sir, you will have to speak to her."

▼▲▼▲▼ Kimi saw Fallon's eyes darken with pain as she palpitated the bruised flesh, but he did not cry out. "The fingers are not broken, only the joints," she said, carefully lowering his hand to the table where he sat across from her. "I can give you an herb for the pain and tie your hand with a bandage so the inner flesh can knit together. But you must not use the hand for six weeks, nor should you remove the bandage."

"What about lice?" he asked, his eyes rising to hers like a scolded boy's. He grinned sheepishly. "They do itch terribly, you know, Gilda."

"Don't call me Gilda." Her voice was sharper than she'd intended, and she made a belated effort to smile.

"Then what shall I call you?"

"Nothing at all." She moved toward a drawer where Edith kept a spool of linen.

"But what if I know of one who would call you wife?"

She froze, the spool in her hand. What sort of monstrous joke was this? Fallon lowered his eyes as if embarrassed, but continued talking. "Brody himself told me that he would like to marry you. You are of age, and Brody is a fine Christian man. You wouldn't have to go back to Opechancanough's people, Gilda. I know you can't truly feel at home there."

She caught her breath. Home. That word again.

"So may I tell Brody you'll consider him?"

Distracted, she glanced back at Fallon. His blue eyes locked upon hers, and despite his pain he wore a firm smile.

She turned back to the spool and slowly unwound a length of linen. She'd been furious with him when she reached Edith's house, and only the woman's patient counsel had calmed her. Then they'd heard about the fight, and when the boy came, delirious with fever, he'd moaned only one name: Fallon. She couldn't deny that a man who would fight against impossible odds for the sake of a lowly child possessed honor and courage, but why did he feel he had the right to order her life?

She moved toward the table and grasped his hand, not caring if she caused him momentary pain. "And what will you do while Brody considers marriage to me?" she asked, pressing the edge of the linen under his thumb as she prepared to wrap his hand.

For the first time, Fallon looked away. "I came here with dual responsibilities. It was important that I find you and Noshi, but it was urgent that I administrate the positions of my students. I failed in my administration, for Wart is one of my boys. My heart breaks to think others may endure what he has suffered."

"What can you do about it?"

His blue eyes met hers again, and she found herself grudgingly admiring the steady glow of devotion that gleamed from them. "I can travel to the plantations and make certain that the boys are well treated," he said, wincing as she began to wrap the bandage. "If they are not, I'll appeal to the governor. There is no excuse for cruelty to indentured servants. A cruel master turns servants into slaves."

"I believe people would be more kind to slaves than to indentured servants," she said, slowly wrapping his hand. "In my tribe, slaves are valued property. Indentured servants, on the other hand, are worked by the English till they drop, for the masters intend to wring every ounce of energy from them until their contract expires."

"You know this to be true?"

"Everyone knows this," she said, shrugging.

"It is wrong for any man to abuse another in such a way," he said, his free hand rising in exclamation.

"You sound very sure of yourself."

"I am. I was an indentured servant for seven years."

She paused, reflecting upon this new nugget of information. She had neglected to consider his past, so centered had she been on her own. Maybe the past accounted for Fallon's concern for his students, for his unreasonable devotion to duty.

"And after you have given an account of your boys, what will you do?" She finished wrapping the bandage and pulled a wooden needle and thread from a pocket under a slit in her skirt.

"I will look for Noshi."

"And when you have found him?" Her needle bit into the fabric and pulled it taut.

"I suppose I will go home."

She stitched quickly, suddenly angry that she had wasted a quarter of an hour in conversation with him. He would go back to England without further thought for her if she married his friend Brody. So much for his glorious quest to find and protect her!

She gave herself a stern mental shake and rose from her stool, leaving the kitchen. She had been foolish to allow her heart to soften.

Charles City, October 1618
  To Thomas Smithson, Student
  The Royal Academy for Homeless Orphans, London:

Loving and kind brother Thomas,

This is to let you understand that I am in a most heavy
case by reason of the nature of the country. It causes me
much sickness such as the scurvy and the bloody flux
and diverse other diseases which make the body very
poor. And when we are sick, there is nothing to comfort
us, for since I came off the ship, I never ate anything but
peas and water gruel. As for deer or venison, I never
saw any since I came into this land. There is indeed
some fowl, but we are not allowed to go and get it, but
must work hard both early and late for a mess of water
gruel and a mouthful of bread and beef. A mouthful of
bread for a penny loaf must serve four men, which is
most pitiful.

  We live in fear of the Indians every hour. We are in
great danger, for our plantation is very weak by reason
of death and sickness of our company. We are but thirty-
two to fight against three thousand if the savages should
come, and the nearest help that we have is ten miles
from us. When the rogues overcame this place last, they
slew eighty persons.

  I have nothing to comfort me, nor is there anything to
be gotten here but sickness and death. But I have noth-

ing at all, no, not a shirt on my back, but two rags, nor no clothes, but one poor suit, nor but one pair of shoes, one pair of stockings, and one cap. My cloak was stolen by one of my own fellows, and to his dying hour he would not tell me what he did with it, but some of my fellows saw him receive butter and beef out of a ship, which my cloak no doubt paid for, so I have not a penny, nor a penny worth to help me to get either spice, or sugar, or strong waters, without which one cannot live here.

I am not half a quarter as strong as I was in England, and all is for want of victuals, for I do protest unto you that I have eaten more in a day at the academy than I have allowed me here for a week. The cook has given more than my day's allowance to a beggar at the door. And if Mr. Fallon Bailie had not relieved me, I should be in a poor case, but he is like the father we do not have.

Ofttimes we go up to Jamestown, for there lie all the ships that come to the land, and there they must deliver their goods. And when we went up to town as it may be on Monday at noon, we arrive there at night, and load the next day by noon, and go home in the afternoon, and unload, and then go away again in the night. We have nothing in all this but a little bread, so it is hard. But Master Bailie pitied me and found me a place to rest when I come up, and has given me bread. Oh, he is a very godly man, and will do anything for me, and he much marveled that you would consider indenturing yourself to come to Virginia as a servant to the London Company.

If you love me, make efforts to redeem me suddenly soon, for which I do entreat and beg. And if you cannot get the headmaster to redeem me for some little money, then for God's sake entreat some folks to lay out some little sum of money in cheese and butter and beef. I will deal truthfully with you before you send it out, and beg the profit to redeem me, and if I die before it comes, I

have entreated Master Bailie to send you the worth of it.
He has promised he will.

Good brother, do not forget me, but have mercy and
pity my miserable case. I know if you did but see me
you would weep. Wherefore, for God's sake, pity me.
The answer of this letter will be life or death to me, but
as for you, I pray you will not come to Virginia. And as
for me, perchance it is too late. But pray for Master
Fallon Bailie.

Your loving brother,
Richard Smithson

▼▲▼▲▼ Fallon knew nothing of Richard Smithson's letter nor the scores of others like it. Nor did he know that in the
winter of 1618 a rumor ignited in Jamestown and blazed its way
through the frontier plantations.

One master, or so the tale went, had so viciously beaten his
servant that a gentleman intervened and spent the night in the
jail for his efforts. But since that day that same princely gentleman had undertaken to seek out and destroy all cruel masters
who mistreated their servants.

Some claimed that the brave gentleman was a dishonored aristocrat, others described him as a simple tutor. Those on the most
distant plantations called him a phantom, a wraithlike pale creature who crept through the woods with the stealth of a savage
and the cunning of a panther. It was generally agreed that he
could take any form, so masters should take care and be wary
lest he appear unexpectedly.

Through the misery of illness, near-starvation, and loneliness,
indentured men and boys lifted their heads and looked with
hope gleaming in their eyes across the tobacco fields toward
each approaching stranger. In fear of retribution, masters found
themselves less quick to use the lash and more generous with
their servants' daily rations. And throughout the king's colony,
other reports and tales substantiated the first rumor so that the

news became common knowledge: Indentured servants now had an advocate.


▼▲▼▲▼ Kimi had truly thought to leave Jamestown after a short visit with Edith Rolfe, but she had stayed to tend the sick boy, and before he was well Fallon brought other boys to the house for her care. Most suffered from malnutrition, for the plantation owners planted tobacco to the exclusion of all nutritional crops, and the servants worked every day in the fields and had no time for hunting or fishing. Fortunately, John Rolfe managed his plantation more capably, and after Edith sent him a dispatch explaining their need for corn, squash, beans, and pumpkin, supplies came regularly to the small house at Jamestown from the estate at Henrico.

But many of the sick men and boys who appeared at Edith's house shivered with fever or suffered from the bloody flux. Despite Kimi's watchful eyes and potions of pulverized hemlock bark and sassafras, more than six died in November alone. She gritted her teeth and wept each time a soul slipped through her fingers, for in some perverse way she saw each boy Fallon brought to her as a challenge. Though still raw and unused to the wilderness he once had known so well, Fallon ventured without fear into the forest, risking his life to bring boys to her for healing. It was a devastating blow when she discovered that she could not always heal.

Yet, despite Fallon's frequent appearances at the Rolfe house, he did not often tarry to visit, and only rarely did he beg permission to sleep on a mattress in the front chamber. Perhaps, Kimi thought, he wished to avoid her. But despite her personal resistance to his force of will, she grudgingly admired his fortitude, for he persisted doggedly in his search for all of the eighty-eight boys he had escorted to Virginia. And through his efforts all indentured servants benefited, for if his student was undernourished, Fallon demanded better rations for all the servants. If a student bore the mark of the master's whip, Fallon threatened to haul the master before the governor.

When faced with Master Bailie's threats, most of the planters either agreed to make changes or simply told him to take the sick servants away. Thus Mistress Rolfe's house was slowly growing crowded with men and boys in need of attention. The large front keeping room was filled regularly with sick men, and Kimi's small chamber usually housed at least four boys, one against each wall. The large room, which had once served as a bedchamber for John and Rebecca Rolfe, had become a ward for the dying, and the marriage bed had long been stripped of its straw mattress and broken into kindling for the fire.

The kitchen was the only room that did not house the sick, and every night Kimi and Edith wrapped themselves in their cloaks and lay down to sleep on the hard-packed earthen floor. Whenever she awoke shivering with cold, Kimi would rise to put fresh logs on the keeping room fire. Thus on the coldest of nights she awoke four or five times as she worked to keep her sick boys warm.

She wasn't really sure when they had become her boys, but now they needed only to pass the threshold of her house for her to take them into her arms and heart as she tended their bodies. Edith joined in the effort gladly, happy to have a more productive role in the community, and ofttimes Brody came by the house to chop wood or help the women carry some of the heavier patients.

Kimi had thought of her heart as frozen in grief, but as she worked for her boys her emotions begin to thaw. Soon she felt great fondness for everyone who had anything to do with the healing house. Everyone, save one man. He alone remained outside the defensive circle of her affections. That man was Fallon Bailie himself.

▼▲▼▲▼ She woke the house with her screaming. Though darkness pressed down upon the kitchen, Edith sat up and grappled with the frantic girl. "It is all right," she shouted above Kimi's screams as the younger girl slapped her hands away. "You're having a nightmare."

Of a sudden the kitchen door flew open and Fallon's startled face appeared above a rushlight. "Name of a name!" he whispered, his speech heavy with sleep. His hair and nightshirt were rumpled, and he carried the light in one hand and a pistol in the other. "What has possessed her? I thought of certain that savages had come into the house."

"She has had another nightmare," Edith explained, taking a moment to tie her nightgown more securely at her neck. "And she will be upset for an hour or more. It's as though she doesn't know us after such a dream; she won't respond to anything I say."

"The Indians believe that spirits talk to them in dreams," Fallon said, lifting the light to brighten the scene before him.

"Well," Edith said, moving away from the girl, "if God is talking to her, she's not listening. She won't hear a word I say, either."

Fallon dropped the rushlight and pistol on the table, then knelt at Kimi's side. The girl was sitting upright, her dark hair flowing over her nightgown in a tumbled mass, but her face was blank and her eyes focused on some fright in her imagination.

Edith lay back down, pulling her blanket up to her chin. If Fallon wanted to deal with this bad dream, she was more than happy to let him.

"Gilda," he whispered, placing a hand on the girl's shoulder. "What did you see?"

A terrible keening moan sprang from the girl's lips, and from under her blanket Edith shivered at the sound.

"It is only a dream," Fallon murmured, and Kimi seemed to relax within the coaxing timbre of his voice. "Can you tell me about it?"

Kimi trembled and stared in hypnotized horror into the darkness. "A boat," she finally whispered in a little girl's voice, her hand crawling to the security of Fallon's arm. "I was in a boat. It was dark. And we hit the sand."

Fallon sank to the floor and slipped his arm around the stricken girl. "Were you alone?"

She shook her head. "No. But it was dark. And I had to get into the black water and walk. I was so frightened."

"Where did you go?"

"The wall." Her voice broke, and she buried her head in her hands, weeping. Through the dim shadows Edith saw Fallon give Kimi a look that was compassionate, troubled, and anxious.

"You saw a wall? A palisade?"

"I don't know," she wailed, throwing back her head. "I ran away. The wall came toward me, and I ran back to the water but it got deeper and deeper and I knew I could not swim. . . ."

Fallon made gentle shushing sounds as he pulled the weeping girl into his arms. After several minutes, Edith saw Kimi relax, then her eyes closed. Like a loving father, Fallon lowered Kimi to her pillow, then covered her with the crumpled quilt.

He stood, then his eyes met hers. "She does this often?"

"Often enough," Edith replied, propping her head on her hand. "In the morning, she'll remember nothing of it. But I can always tell when she's had a bad dream, for there'll be circles under her eyes."

He sat on the edge of the hearth. "Could something be responsible for her dreams? Losing a patient, maybe? A certain food?"

Edith shook her head, considering whether or not she should share her suspicions, then she blurted out the truth. "She has these dreams occasionally, to be sure, but she has the worst of them on the days you visit us, Master Fallon."

He blanched in surprise, then bit his lip and stood. "I'll leave the light burning," he said, then left her alone with the sleeping girl.

▼▲▼▲ The sharp December morning was wind-whipped and bitter cold, so when a knock sounded at the door Kimi hurried to answer it, afraid Fallon had been carrying a sick boy since dawn. After opening the door, she took a quick breath of utter astonishment when she recognized the finely dressed gentleman who stood before her: "Governor Argall!"

"I give you good morrow, mistress," he said, formally tipping his hat. "May I come in?"

She nodded in astonished silence and moved back so that the governor could pass into the room. She had never seen the man at such a close distance. He wore a fine silk doublet with what seemed an obscene amount of lace at his neck and wrists, and his breeches, gloves, and stockings looked warm and new. With a single fluid motion he untied and slung his cloak from his shoulders, handing it to her as if she should know what to do with it. She took it into her arms and marveled at its dense weight and warmth. Oh, to have blankets out of this lovely wool!

Edith came around the corner with a chamber pot in her hands and gave a timid squeak at the sight of such an esteemed personage in her keeping room. "Governor Argall!" she exclaimed, nearly dropping the porcelain pot at the governor's feet. She darted around the corner and hid the unmentionable object, then returned to the front hall. After curtseying lightly, she took the cloak from Kimi's arms and hung it expertly on a peg near the door.

"What brings you to us, Governor?" she asked, pinching her lower lip with her teeth. She fluttered her nervous hands toward a bench near the fireplace, and the governor sat down stiffly, his hands upon his knees.

"I heard that Fallon Bailie is expected here today," he said, moving his fingers restlessly as if he hated to be kept waiting. "I need a private audience with him."

"We never know when Master Bailie will appear," Edith said, running her hand over her hair. "It could be today, or tomorrow—"

"I have it on good authority that he has entered the city today," the governor barked, pulling back his shoulders. "Now, if you could be so good as to get me something to drink?"

"Right away, Governor," Edith answered, scurrying into the kitchen. "We have a wonderful peach cider put away."

After seeing that the governor was merely a man—and not a very impressive one—Kimi's trepidation vanished. She tiptoed quietly to the bench across from him and sat down, studying him intently. He had to be aware of her gaze, for his fingers continued their restless drumming against his bony knees, but he cleared his throat and took a sudden interest in the fire behind him.

There was something familiar about the man's graveled face and slicked-back hair, and Kimi double-checked her memory. "Governor Argall?" she whispered, more to herself than to the visitor. "Samuel Argall?"

"That's right," the man said, turning to her.

And then she remembered. He had been Captain Samuel Argall when she first met him aboard the *Treasurer,* and he had smiled and informed her and Pocahontas that they could not return to their tribe. He had not been harsh but seemed to think that the feelings of two Indian girls were of no importance whatsoever.

"What could you possibly have to do with Fallon Bailie?" she wondered aloud.

He looked at her then, and she noted an odd mingling of wariness and impatience in his eyes. "Excuse me," he said, aligning his face in a forbidding expression, "but I said I wanted a private conversation with Fallon Bailie."

A grudging smile played across her face, and she stood to go tend the quartet of sick boys in her room. *Talk to Fallon about whatever you want,* she thought. *But within the thin walls in this house, no conversation is truly private.*

▼▲▼▲▼ She heard Fallon's distinctive knock and the creak of the front door a few moments later. "Hallo, ladies," he called, his voice snapping with joy as he entered the house. "Know you what day it is? I'd nearly forgotten, but it is Christmas—"

His gay voice broke off suddenly and Kimi knew he had seen

the governor. Smiling at the boys in her care, she laid her finger across her lips and pressed her ear to the flimsy door that separated her from the keeping room.

"And a happy Christmas to you, Governor," Fallon said, speaking in a calm, neutral voice. "What brings you to this house?"

"Trouble," the governor growled. "Complaints. You are giving the planters a hard time, Fallon Bailie, and they are keeping me awake at night with their reports."

"Ah, the planters," Fallon replied easily, closing the door behind him. "A worrisome group they are, Governor; they think gardening is living on the edge of life. But what reports are these? I have brought sick boys to receive care, escorted lost men through the wilderness—"

"You know what reports," the governor snapped. "Since when is it a crime for a master to strike an insolent servant? Yet you would make it so. And how can planters feed their servants venison and milk when they are starving themselves?"

"I'm sure these things have been exaggerated," Fallon answered, his voice soft and eminently reasonable. "My charges, sir, have been concerned only with unjust and unwarranted punishment, not proper discipline. And never yet have I seen a plantation owner with the ghost of hunger in his eyes."

"Be that as it may, we are struggling, sir, to build a prosperous life for one and all in this colony. It is difficult enough to do so without your interference upon the part of men who have signed lawful indenture contracts modeled after those of our fatherland—"

"I am well aware of the system of indenture in England," Fallon answered crisply. "And though my master was not kind, he was not unreasonable. I survived despite his lack of feeling and kindness, and I wish to know of certain that my students will survive at least as well here in Virginia. I am not asking for extravagance, sir, but I demand that even indentured servants receive the justice due to every man created in the image of God."

A cold wind blew past the house with soft moans, then the bench creaked as the governor stood. Kimi knelt and pressed her eye to the keyhole in the iron lock.

"Very well," Governor Argall answered, standing before Fallon with his arms folded tight as a gate. "I have learned that you will not leave Virginia until you have found a boy reported to be missing among the Tripanik Indians. I am prepared to offer you an escort of twenty armed men, boats, and provisions enough to take you into Tripanik lands. Find the boy you seek and take him back to England with you. But you must begin your journey on the morrow or my offer is void."

Kimi stiffened as she held her breath. Surely Fallon would accept the governor's offer, for his work with his students was at best a halfway measure. They lost a boy for every two they saved, and there was no guarantee the boy they saved today would not be stricken with disease on the morrow.

She shivered. God would lead Fallon to Noshi as surely as he had found her, then the two brothers would go to England and leave her alone. They would be two sides of a triangle, forever missing the third piece because she could not embrace what Fallon had told her of her past.

"Thank you, sir, but I will find the boy I seek on my own terms."

She bit her thumb, unwilling to believe what she had heard.

"You are a fool, Fallon Bailie. There are men who would give their lives to leave this place."

"Then let them leave." Fallon waved his hand toward the empty mattresses stacked against the wall. "As you can see, I have work to do here."

The governor shook his head in stern disapproval, flung his cloak across his shoulders, and slammed his way out of the house.

▾▲▾▲▾ Disturbed by reports of unchristian and harsh behavior in the colony, Governor Samuel Argall decreed that all who failed to attend Sunday church service would be imprisoned in the guardhouse, "lying neck and heels in the corps of the guard the night following and be a slave the week following." He further ordered that dancing, fiddling, card playing, hunting, and fishing were forbidden on the Lord's Day—but nursing, if a life demanded it, was permitted.

Kimi could never recall going to church, so she looked forward to her first visit. The long, narrow chapel in the center of the clearing outside Jamestown fort was the only brick building in the settlement, and its tall tower lifted her eyes to the sky. With Mistress Rolfe firmly at her side, Kimi passed easily through the crowd of admiring men and took a seat upon a solid wooden bench at the front of the building.

Reverend Buck smiled at the women in greeting, then led his greatly expanded congregation in songs that rang familiarly in Kimi's mind. And when he read from the Bible she felt a warm glow spread from her heart to her face as his words rang over the assembled gathering:

"'I am the good shepherd: the good shepherd giveth his life for the sheep. But he that is an hireling, and not the shepherd, whose own the sheep are not, seeth the wolf coming, and leaveth the sheep, and fleeth: and the wolf catcheth them, and scattereth the sheep. The hireling fleeth, because he is an hireling, and careth not for the sheep. I am the good shepherd, and know my sheep, and am known of mine. As the Father knoweth me, even so know I the Father: and I lay down my life for the sheep. And other sheep I have, which are not of this fold: them also I must bring, and they shall hear my voice; and there shall be one fold, and one shepherd.'"

It was as if the voice of God spoke directly to her heart through the reverend, and of a sudden Kimi's mind blew open. God had sent Fallon as a shepherd; she and Noshi were the sheep to be found and guarded. Guilt washed over her, for she had long denied the truth of Fallon's words. But in the face of his dedication to his task and the purity of his goodness, she knew he had spoken and dealt with her truly.

Her hand trembled slightly as the congregation bowed their heads for prayer. The dark veil at the back of her mind ripped, and in that moment she knew it was useless to resist the truth. She was indeed Gilda Colman.

Bone-numbing cold gripped the low-lying settlement through-out the months of January and February, and though the wind rushed out to lash the settlers with the threat of snow in its breath, none fell. Not once in forty days did even a sliver of blue sky dare to peer through the heavenful of gray scud, and as Fallon's boys died in the healing house at Jamestown, Gilda felt her heart grow as gray as the sky.

One evening Fallon came to the house with news that the governor had pressed the ruling council to petition London for another hundred boys to work in the tobacco fields.

"No, Fallon," Gilda whispered, thinking of the stream of sick boys that surely would fill the house.

"The letter has already been sent and received," Fallon answered, watching her in a way that suddenly made her feel like some form of ministering angel. "I'm sorry, Gilda, but I have no influence with the governor—"

She put out a finger, wanting to touch it to his lips as she told him that she understood, but she could not move toward him. There was no look of the weak, confused schoolmaster about him now. Under the heavy fur mantle he wore a loose cotton shirt, and his Indian tattoos, so similar to hers, shadowed his wiry forearms as he rested them upon the table. A masculine force clung to him, a great presence born of certainty and experience.

In the beginning, she had been the wiser one. Now he was as much at home in her world as she was in his.

Intimidated by his confidence and concern, she shook her

head and turned back to the kitchen to help Edith bank the hearthfire.

▼▲▼▲▼ A week later, Governor Argall approached Fallon and Gilda as they left the church after the Sunday service. Fallon felt himself grow tense; after the governor's frank attempt to be rid of him, he was unsure what to expect from Argall.

"I am pleased to report," the governor said, smiling mechanically at both of them from beneath the rim of his hat, "that we have finally collected sufficient funds to establish a school for both English and Indian children. It will be established at Falling Creek, Master Bailie, and since you often travel that way I thought you'd like to know about it. George Thorpe, a devout English scholar, has come to direct the school, and we hope to instill and educate the savage children according to the same Christian principles that govern this colony."

From the corner of his eye Fallon saw Gilda stiffen, and he cast a quick glance at her face. All color had left her cheeks and her eyes glittered strangely.

"Well, sir," Fallon said, guessing her concern as he turned to the governor, "I hope you have consulted with the Indian werowances. I doubt that Opechancanough will take kindly to his children being taught in a Christian school. I believe he has a very devout hatred for all things having to do with our God."

"Why should he?" the governor replied, honest surprise on his face. "Pocahontas was Powhatan's daughter, yet she converted without a moment's hesitation."

"After you kidnapped her and held her prisoner aboard your ship," Gilda interrupted, her voice low and quiet. "By the time you sent the minister to us, Governor, she had fallen in love with John Rolfe. She would have done anything to stay with him."

The governor blanched. "Surely you are not saying that her conversion was insincere!"

"No," Gilda whispered. "But her motivation was strong. She had lived among the English and learned to love them. Opechancanough has no such motivation. No one has tried to live among his people and learn to love him."

The governor bristled visibly at her words. "Again, you folk insist upon giving me trouble," he muttered to no one in particular before stalking away.

"I'faith, now you've done it," Fallon said, resisting the impulse to squeeze her hand as the governor joined a circle of men and began to shout and gesticulate his opinions. "You've angered our honorable governor."

"I spoke the truth," she replied, walking steadily toward the house. "Aren't we supposed to speak nothing but the truth?"

"Yes," he answered, hurrying to keep up with her swift step. Even in the confining long English kirtle, she could still outpace him. "But what harm will it do if the governor and Master Thorpe establish their school? Maybe some good will come out of it."

"There are pitifully few English children here," Gilda pointed out, waving her arm toward the fort behind them. "And none at all at Falling Creek. The chief will see this for what it is, an attempt to take Indian children and make them bow to the English God. The governor wants to make them English."

"But shouldn't they worship the true God?"

She whirled to face him and pressed her finger to his chest. "Yes," she whispered, "for he is the truth. But you cannot force a man to accept truth by overpowering the hearts and minds of his children. Nothing will come of this school but trouble, Fallon, mark my words."

▼▲▼▲▼ Winter melted into spring; spring bloomed into summer. Of all the one hundred boys who had traveled to Virginia with Fallon in 1617, only Wart survived the year. And as Gilda had suspected he would, Fallon took on the cause of the entire servant population of Virginia, making regular visits to the various plantations and even investigating stories of ill-treated runaways who had hidden themselves in the Indian villages.

At each plantation and Indian town, Fallon inquired about the Tripaniks. Their villages lay south of the James River, and their hunters had not ventured northward in many years. Few of the soldiers, planters, or traders with whom Fallon talked could report dealings with Tripanik tribes. Once Fallon spoke with a captain of a Dutch ship who had traveled up the Chowan River and attempted to trade in Tripanik territory, but the Dutchman had found entire Indian villages wiped out by the dreaded small-pox.

"The disease is terribly painful," Fallon later explained to Gilda and Edith at dinner, not realizing that both women had stiffened at the mention of the disease that had killed Pocahontas. "They say the bravest warriors cut their own throats in order to die swiftly and surely. Others plunge themselves into icy rivers to ease the fever and take water into their lungs."

Though it pleased her little to hear these things, Gilda did not comment. Fallon's visits were so rare now that she hesitated to mention her aversion to certain topics. He had grown increasingly dear, and she did not want to bring him undue stress.

However, while Fallon's appearances at the ladies' dinner table grew more and more rare as he searched for Noshi, Brody's became common. Usually he came to help with hauling water or mending the roof and inevitably stayed for dinner or supper. Gilda knew the house was a welcome change from the rough quarters Brody shared with fifty other soldiers. After serving his six-month term, Brody had signed on for another half year, still planning to buy a boat and set out to find gold and the elusive northwest passage to India.

Edith cackled merrily at his dreams of adventure, urging him on, but Gilda usually listened to his boasting in silence, uncomfortably aware of Brody's interest in her. Though his admiring gaze gratified her and she held him in great affection, she could not imagine what she would do if he ever seriously proposed marriage or offered to take her from the house in Jamestown.

"Did you hear? Fallon is to be a voting member of the House of Burgesses," Brody announced at dinner one Sunday afternoon. His eyes met Gilda's over the table. "Martial law is to be replaced by English common law, and we're to have the same rights as His Majesty's subjects in England."

Gilda shook her head, unable to conceive of such abstract governmental concepts, but Brody and Edith lifted their glasses in a spontaneous toast. "To the General Assembly," Edith said, her pale cheeks glowing.

"To the governor and council," Brody answered, clinking his glass to Edith's. They turned expectantly toward Gilda, who obediently raised her glass to theirs. "To Fallon," she added weakly, mentioning the only name that sprang to her mind.

▼▲▼▲▼ The first session of the General Assembly of Virginia met from July thirtieth to August fourth in the choir section of the village church at Jamestown. The new governor, Sir George Yeardley, was present, as were John Rolfe and Reverend Richard Buck, who served as chaplain. Two burgesses, or representatives, from each plantation were also present, independently elected from the freemen who lived and worked at the plantations.

As part of the new council, Fallon took his seat next to the governor's secretary and winked at Wart, who remained in his shadow in case Fallon needed him. The session began as the burgesses stood for a prayer offered by Reverend Buck, then they took their seats and the credentials of each burgess were examined. Next on the agenda was the matter of relations with the Indians, which had worsened considerably in past months.

Several of the planters stood and raised their concerns about parties of raiding Indians, which had plundered or burned their fields in recent months. These planters, most of whom lived far out in the forests, wanted the authority to mount armed attacks of reprisal against the Indians, but Governor Yeardley vetoed the idea. "No injury or oppression shall be wrought against the natives," he said, leaning forward in his seat. "We shall not give their king any justification to raise a hand against us."

Fallon pressed his lips together. Governor Yeardley surely was an intuitive man, for he had apparently sensed what Fallon had known all along: Opechancanough was not the easily placated man Powhatan had been. The present chief of the Powhatan tribe waited only for an excuse to attack the English.

"There is one additional matter of business before we adjourn," the secretary announced on the fifth and hottest day of their meeting.

"What's that?" the governor growled, fanning himself with a crinkled sheet of parchment.

"It pertains, sir, to the matter of, ah—women."

One of the burgesses cheered, and Fallon grinned as the mood lightened. "The plantation can never flourish till families be planted and the respect of wives and children fix the people on the soil," the secretary went on. "While it is not known whether men or women be more necessary for a colony's success, it is of certain that few are women here."

In no mood for debate, the governor stood to his feet. "I do so move," Governor Yeardley said, his face dripping with perspiration as he leaned forward, "that we write to the London Company and petition for women."

"Aye! Aye!" the crowd cheered.

"Any other business, Secretary?" the governor barked.

"None, sir."

"Then this meeting is adjourned."

▼▲▼▲▼ The *Mary Elizabeth* docked again at Jamestown in September 1619, and this time Fallon was prepared when the shallops began to bring boatloads of boys ashore. With the governor's full blessing and authority, Fallon, Brody, and Wart supervised the purchase of boys for indentured service. The sick boys were not immediately assigned, but were sent to Mistress Rolfe's house to regain their strength and health, and no master against whom Fallon had filed a complaint in the previous year was allowed to purchase a boy's contract. As Wart examined the boys and asked them about their particular skills, Fallon recorded each contract in a ledger, and brawny Brody stood on the dock with his arms folded and sized up the planters. All in all, it was an efficient arrangement, and after two weeks, the seventy-six boys who had survived the voyage had been set to work. Reverend Archer and the London Company had even agreed to pay Fallon and his men a nominal fee for agenting the students' services.

"I think we handled things well, if you don't mind me saying so," Brody said as he and Fallon relaxed in the tavern room after settling the indenture accounts. "It was nothing at all like last month."

"No," Fallon said, shaking his head. The month before, a Dutch ship captained by a man called Jope had brought a group of twenty black men and women to the docks for sale into indentured service. Startled by the dark complexions of the Negroes, the planters refused to bargain for them. Finally Governor Yeardley and the merchant Abraham Piersey bought them, paying for the group with provisions. The blacks now lived in Jamestown—eight with Piersey's household and twelve with the governor's.

"Would you ever buy one?" Brody asked, staring at the tabletop as if he pondered a difficult question.

"A black servant?"

"No," Brody laughed, blushing. "A bride. There's a notice posted in the fort. For two hundred pounds of tobacco a man may choose a virgin bride from a ship the London Company's sending. Truth to tell, they say a bevy of beauties will sail from England in the spring."

Fallon tapped his pen against the table and rested his chin in his hand, the idea of taking a wife swirling through his head.

"A bride, eh? In truth, I haven't given marriage much thought," he said, slanting Brody a rueful smile.

*Liar!* a voice within him cried out, but he ignored it determinedly, focusing instead on his friend. Obviously, Brody was anxious to marry, but it was possible he didn't have the full two hundred pounds. Plus there were other expenses to consider. Once Brody had a bride he'd have to house and feed her.

"I'll put up half of the money," Fallon said, looking again at his ledger, "if you've got the other half."

"I've got it," Brody said, his eyes suddenly bright. "I know a planter who'll sell us tobacco cheap, and we'll have two hundred pounds in two days."

"When does the boat come in?" Fallon asked absently, studying his accounts—but the image dancing before his eyes was not ledger lines and figures. From out of nowhere, the image of Gilda's lovely face had risen to float across the paper, mesmerizing him.

"Can I be predicting the sea?" Brody shrugged. "But, Fallon—"

"What?" He lowered the paper to the table and turned his eyes from the empty space that had vibrated with Gilda's likeness. No matter how much he longed for her, she did not want him.

"Which of us takes the bride? It isn't right or moral for a woman to have two husbands."

The corner of Fallon's mouth twitched as he suppressed a smile and looked over at his friend. "No, it isn't. Well, Brody, I guess we'll just see which of us needs marrying the most when the ship arrives. Agreed?"

Brody slapped the table in delight. "Agreed!"


▼▲▼▲▼ The growing settlement at Jamestown endured another blast of winter, and Edith Rolfe's house at Jamestown became an unofficial hospital of sorts for the entire settlement. Many men recovered their health and strength beneath the comforting hands of Edith, Gilda, or Wart, and others were dispatched to heaven, escorted by Fallon's fervent prayers.

Gilda was glad to see spring come. The winter had been difficult, with scores of lives lost, and she had wondered whether spring and health would ever return. But the scent of gradually greening earth filled the house, and the sea breeze blew warm with the promise of sun and summer. Men's spirits revived in sunshine, she noticed, and often she helped carry weak men into the yard to lie in the invigorating rays of light.

One morning she stood at the window, gazing wistfully at the sky as the wind herded scribbles of clouds over the horizon. "Come with me, Gilda, for a walk on the shore," Brody called, smiling at her as he came up the path to the house. "It is too pretty to be staying inside, if you take me meaning."

"I'm coming," she called, her spirits rising at the thought of a carefree walk by the water. She tossed her shawl over one shoulder and sped through the door. Brody gently took her arm as they walked to the shore, and she liked the way his protective touch made her feel. After two years of service in the regiment at Jamestown fort, Brody had developed a good reputation for himself. At twenty-four, he was well favored and more than passing handsome with a pleasant face, a good pair of shoulders, the thickest arms she'd ever seen, and an easy, open manner. He had put off his red uniform for good, he told Gilda, and now he wore brown breeches of leather and an open-collared shirt of linen that suited his carefree attitude.

"So I've saved my wages, and I could depart for my journey within a month," he said, sunshine breaking across his face. "But I won't go alone."

"Indeed, you've always talked about the dozen men you'll hire to carry home your gold," she said, laughing up at him. "How will you choose this fortunate few?"

"Men are cheap and plentiful in this town, but it is not men I'm waiting for," he said, stopping suddenly on the shore. He stood before her with the confidence of a healthy young man who has never been hurt, and for a moment her heart twisted. She knew what he wanted to say and with everything in her she hoped he wouldn't say it.

She shifted uneasily. "We should be getting back now," she said, not sure how to lead him away from the question that burned in his eyes. "Wart has his hands full with the sick at the house—"

"Wait." His voice was quiet—and stubborn. She steeled her nerves to hear him out. "I'll be wanting to leave Jamestown," he said simply, holding his hands behind his back, "but I won't be going without a wife."

"Well, I've heard that the Virginia Company plans to bring a shipload of women very soon—"

"I know." He ran his hands through his hair in a detached motion. "Fallon and I have pooled our money to buy a bride because we're both thinking it is our duty to help settle this place with families. But I don't want an English maiden, Gilda. I want you."

She scarcely heard the last part of his declaration, so stunned was she by the news that Fallon was among the men waiting for the ship of brides. The scheme had been launched back at the first meeting of the General Assembly a year before, and the planters had steadily been setting aside tobacco to purchase what were promised to be "sweet and tractable English virgins."

"And did you think you would share a woman?" she snapped, furious questions rising in her head like bees from a disturbed hive.

"No! Have I said such a thing? I'll be wanting to marry you, Gilda—it was my plan from the first—but I wouldn't be here if not for Fallon, and since he promised to give me your hand, I thought it only fair to help him secure a bride of his own."

"He . . . promised to give you my hand?" Slowly she forced the words out. "What right has he to make such a promise? I am not his daughter, nor his sister, nor his possession. And you, Brody McRyan, think you I will jump for joy because you want to marry me? Then in truth, sir, you should think again!"

He backed away, honestly startled by her sudden angry declaration. "Gilda," he said, raking his hair again, "be sensible. Fallon said you should marry a Christian man, which I am, and I'm two years younger than he, so I'm closer to your age. Besides, we're friends, aren't we?"

"Are we?" she replied bitingly, crossing her arms.

"We are, mind you," he said calmly, stepping closer. "We have worked together, played together, laughed and cried. . . . I'faith, you saved my life, so my life is naturally yours." He gave a short laugh. "Gilda, Fallon and I just want to see you happy."

It was as though a rock had fallen through her heart. She looked away from him toward the distant sea as she felt herself slipping into a devouring gulf of despair. That cursed English superiority had reared its head again, though she had hoped never to hear it from the lips of Fallon and Brody: *We want to make you happy, we know what is best, leave your Indian ways and follow our example.*

"Gilda," Brody pressed, his warm hand gripping her upper arm, "do you remember the day when you saved us from Opechancanough? There in the woods, you cried in my arms."

"I remember," she whispered, not daring to look at him.

"Don't you see?" he went on, his voice strengthening, "ever since that day I've wanted to marry you. I don't want a bride from England, I want you! I'm waiting for you, Gilda, and when you are ready to come inland with me, we'll set out and find whatever treasures this country has to offer!"

She forced herself to look at him despite the pain that raked at her heart. His eyes shone with such longing and sincerity that she could not bring herself to speak the truth. Better to avoid it, ignore it, make an excuse. "I can't leave, Brody," she finally whispered. "There's my work with the sick—"

"Edith and Wart can handle it. You've taught Edith everything you know about medicine, anyway; haven't I said so? And I hear an English physician is coming on the next ship."

"But Fallon needs me; he's so busy with his travels and his work on the council."

"Fallon told me to take you away. How old are you, Gilda, seventeen? You should have married long ago. Fallon wants to be married, but until you are settled and happy—"

"Fallon wants a sweet and tractable English wife," she broke in, her voice hard and brittle in her ears. "And I am of certain not cut of that cloth."

Brody shrugged. "You are all that I want, and more. Marry

me, Gilda, and come away with me. We can go next month, next week, or even on the morrow. Just say the word."

She wanted to clap her hands over her ears; her chest and belly burned with hurt and rage. Fallon had told Brody to take her away. He still ordered her life as though she were five years old. Despite all she had done for and with him over the past year, he preferred to make a life with some ignorant English girl who would melt in the heat of a Virginia summer and faint at the sight of blood. *But his English children would be fair skinned and red haired,* a mocking voice from within told her, *and no trace of Indian blood would come near them.*

The fires within her exploded and in an instant of decision and she threw herself into Brody's arms and pulled his head to hers for a rough kiss that left him gasping for breath. The wind blew her hair across her face when she pulled away, and she smiled in rueful gratitude because Brody would not see the storm in her eyes. He reached for her again, but she put out a hand and, whirling in the wind, raced away and left him on the beach.

# Gilda

*If you love, you will suffer,*
*and if you do not love,*
*you do not know the meaning of a Christian life.*

*Agatha Christie,* An Autobiography

Because Jamestown served mainly as a transfer post for immigrants who arrived from across the sea, less than one hundred people had permanent residences at the settlement. Fallon certainly never considered building or finding a permanent place to live on the peninsula. When his work called him to the port, he usually divided his time between Edith Rolfe's house and the keeping room of the Jamestown tavern. He did not enjoy the uncouth bustle of the tavern's public room, but ofttimes he found himself too distracted to think clearly at Edith's house. Gilda's voice, her smile, even the warm scent of her filled every room, and Fallon found the brawling drunks and foreigners at the tavern far easier to ignore than the effect Gilda had on his weary senses.

He wasn't certain when he began to love her. He thought perhaps he had always considered her his own. First she had been a responsibility, then a maddening frustration, and then a delight. But over the course of the past year he had seen her courage, her determination, her strength . . . and he had realized that, with every fiber of his being, he wanted her by his side throughout life. He wanted her to mother his children, to walk at his side, to hold his hand at the wearisome end of day, to let him hold her when she, too, was weary.

He couldn't imagine coming to Jamestown without finding her in Edith Rolfe's house. With every mile he journeyed away from Jamestown, he felt his soul empty, only to be filled up again as he traveled back to the fort—and Gilda. He thought perhaps that Edith had divined his feelings, for more than once she had met him at the door saying simply, "You'll find her outside, Master Fallon." And no matter how weary his feet, he had fairly flown to Gilda's side, ostensibly to talk over his progress. In reality, he longed—no, *needed*—to feast his eyes and ears and heart upon the sight and sense of her, to drink in every word and thought she might utter, to watch the emotions as they washed over her face, to warm to the fire in her eyes.

But still she treated him like a meddlesome older brother, often chiding him for his protectiveness. Why couldn't she see that his life depended upon protecting her? It was for her that he honed his hunting skills, that he worked to gain respect among both Indian and English. It was to her healing hands that he brought his sick boys, that she might touch them with the life she had brought to him.

The child he had loved had grown into the woman he adored—and yet he could not speak of his devotion, for she still thought of herself as Kimi, Woman-with-a-Secret, hiding behind the walls of some untold pain.

He had just finished his dinner of peas and loblolly, a common dish of cornmeal mixed with water, when Brody sauntered into the public room and caught Fallon's eye. He approached with the air of a conquering hero, pulling back a stool and straddling it. "Well," he said, the grooves beside his mouth deepening into a full smile that was at once lazy, complacent, and smug. "She's all yours."

"Who?" Fallon had been about to consider a brickmaker's proposal to enlarge Edith's house, but he set the parchment aside as he looked at his friend. "Who's all mine?"

"I've been to see Gilda," Brody went on, leaning confidently on the table. "And I've talked to her—"

Brody paused and grinned wickedly across the table as adrenaline quickened Fallon's heartbeat. What in the world had Brody said to her?

"Yes, I surrender my claim here and now," Brody said, slapping the table in his eagerness. "Forget me part in the venture— the prize is yours, me friend. Claim the first English beauty that catches your eye, for the bride shall belong to you, and I'll not quibble about it. Gilda has agreed to marry me."

Fallon felt his flesh contract as if a chill wind had blown over him. His foolish hopes had been nothing but fantasies to make life bearable. He took a deep breath, overwhelmed by the sickening sensation of his life plunging downward.

It was right that Gilda should marry Brody; with the possible exception of Noshi, of certain no man alive would be a better husband for her. Fallon shook his head, pushing away the pain tearing at his heart, ruefully accepting the knowledge that he had been caught up an illusion. Gilda did not need him.

He forced himself to smile in congratulations and lowered his eyes to the table. "What did you tell her?" he asked, smoothing the emotions that threatened to erupt in his voice. "I thought she intended to return to the Indian village to marry her warrior."

"No," Brody answered, laughing. "Truth to tell, I believe she's forgotten all about him. I told her that things would be changing now that I was ready to leave, and that you had put up money for one of the English girls—"

"You told her that?"

"Of course." Brody's face shone as innocent as a child's. "And naturally I said that I didn't care about the English girls, for I wanted her. And then she kissed me—"

"I see," Fallon interrupted, clearing his throat. He picked up the brickmaker's proposal and pretended to read, but after a moment he put it down and looked at Brody again. "You know, Brody, I thought *you* wanted an English bride. If you wanted Gilda, why didn't you declare your intentions long before this?"

"I wasn't ready," Brody answered, frowning as if the question had offended him. "And I told you months ago that I wanted to marry Gilda. It is only natural that I should be wanting to marry her, being that she's an Indian. She knows her way through the woods—"

"If it is an Indian guide you want, you could hire one of the scouts for a pound of copper and a few beads. He'd be a lot less trouble than that girl."

Brody's gaze fixed on Fallon with a knowing look. "She's never lit into me the way she does you. And, if you take me meaning, I think she's rather fond of me."

"Fond of you?" Fallon whispered, hearing an edge of desperation in his voice. "Don't you think love should play a part in something as serious as the holy ordinance of marriage?"

"I'll love Gilda more than you'll love the total stranger you are taking off the boat," Brody retorted. Fallon's face flushed, and he suddenly realized he was risking Gilda's welfare. If he continued to bait Brody, the younger man would likely abandon the idea of marriage, and Gilda needed a good Christian husband. Marrying her to Brody was better than having her return to a heathen warrior, and as surely as the sun would rise on the morrow, she would never consent to marry Fallon.

"You are right, of course," Fallon said, making an effort to gain control of his feelings. "I'm sorry, Brody, it's just that I see her as a younger sister, and naturally I want the very best for her."

"Well, you can be certain I'll take care of her," Brody said, his good humor restored. He crossed his ankle upon his knee and called out to the tavernkeeper, "Two jugs of the best o' whatever you got for me and Fallon here! Right away!"

The bewhiskered tavernkeeper nodded and scurried to his storeroom. "Well, have patience with her nightmares and take care to keep a light burning," Fallon said, tearing his eyes from the joy in Brody's face. "She's waked the house more than once with her cries."

"There'll be no nightmares when I'm sleeping by her side," Brody said, nodding confidently.

"And dandelions make her sneeze," Fallon added quietly. "Once, when we were children, I gave her one and she pressed it to her nose and inhaled—" Fallon shook himself out of his reverie and smiled in embarrassment—"Anyway, she sneezed for a week and her mother fussed at me for longer than that."

"No dandelions," Brody promised.

Fallon studied the paper in his hand a minute more, then

slapped it down upon the table and leaned closer toward Brody. "Whatever you do," he said, his voice heavy with dread, "keep her away from Opechancanough. She cannot see the danger there, but I know him, Brody, and he is the devil's own instrument. The savages say he is immortal."

"Come now," Brody burst out, shocked. "You can't be believin' that!"

"I know not." Fallon shook his head. "I don't know if God would allow such a thing, but Opechancanough is far more powerful today than he was when he ordered my execution thirteen years ago. Watch him, Brody, and keep Gilda away from him."

Brody made the sign of a cross over his heart and lifted his right hand as if taking a vow. "I swear it. Now, Fallon, will you hush and let me enjoy thoughts of me marriage?"

Fallon waved his hands in a gesture of surrender. "I have said enough," he said, picking up the parchment again. *And I am resigned to being caught in a web of my own weaving,* he thought bleakly. After a moment, he looked up. "When is the blessed event to take place?"

"I don't know," Brody answered, frowning. "She didn't say."

"Well, what *did* she say?" Fallon pressed, pretending an offhanded interest while he skimmed the proposal before him. "Maybe I can divine something from her words. Did she say, 'Yes, as soon as possible I'll marry you' or some similar thing?"

"No," Brody answered, his frown deepening. "She didn't say yea or no. She just kissed me, then ran away."

Fallon lifted his eyes to Brody's. "No answer? Just a kiss?"

"A kiss is a bonny good answer," Brody retorted, his lower lip jutting forward in the stubborn expression Fallon knew well. "You don't kiss a man unless you intend to marry him."

"Maybe you're right," Fallon said, scratching his chin. The tavernkeeper brought two tankards of warm beer, and Brody lifted one in a celebratory toast. "To Gilda and me, and you and your wee English bride," he said.

Reluctantly, Fallon lifted his mug to join the toast. "To my bride and yours."

▼▲▼▲ Edith's spring flowers frilled themselves in the late afternoon sun as Fallon approached the house. He paused outside the fence when he saw Gilda sitting on a bench by the front door. She leaned against the house, her eyes closed, tendrils of dark hair brushed against her throat. She wore a simple blouse and a long English skirt, but she had pulled the skirt up over her knees in an effort to feel the sun's warmth on her legs.

Fallon averted his eyes from the tempting sight, and with the silent movements of an Indian he jumped the fence and crept near. He had hoped to surprise her, but her blue eyes flew open as his shadow crossed her face.

He had rehearsed his opening comments so that no unexpected emotions might trip his tongue. "I hear congratulations are in order," he said, removing his hat. "Brody tells me that you two are to be married."

"It would appear so," she answered, lowering her eyes as she appeared to study her hands. "I understand that you are to be married, too."

"It would appear so," he said, then laughed at the echo of her words. He shifted his weight, as awkward as a schoolboy, then gestured toward the bench. "Do you mind if I sit awhile? We have so little time to talk these days."

She did not answer, but slid to make room for him. He sat next to her, uncomfortably aware of the pressure of her arm against his. He thought he could sense the texture of her soft skin even through the rough linen of his doublet, and the sensation distracted him. By heaven, maybe it ~~was~~ time he got married and found a wife of his own.

"What did you want to talk about?" she asked, turning those blue eyes fully upon him.

He crossed his legs and frowned, trying to maintain the posture befitting the elder brother of a future bride. "Well, if you are going to be leaving here, I wondered if Mistress Rolfe is willing to continue caring for the sick and wounded. Brody assures me that you've taught her all you know of healing."

"She knows more than I do now," Gilda answered, turning

her face to the street. "The younger boys see her as a mother and thrive under her care."

"So you won't mind leaving, then?"

Her face was inscrutable as she looked at him. "When it is time to leave, I'll know."

A companionable silence fell between them, and Fallon folded his hands to overcome the urge to hold one of hers. "We've been together some time now," he said, nodding to acknowledge the friendly wave of a man passing by the house. "I thank God that he brought me to you so soon after my arrival. It would seem he has worked his purpose in our lives."

"Are our lives nearly done?" Gilda asked, a smile in her voice. "Can he not continue to work?"

"Yes, of course, I just meant that our time—yours and mine—would seem to be done."

He glanced sideways to see if she would look at him, but she kept her eyes on the front gate, and her expression did not change. From inside the house, Fallon heard Edith call for Wart to bring her a cup of sassafras tea, and a moment later Wart grumbled past the open window.

"Have you given up the search for Noshi?" Gilda asked suddenly, tilting her head to look at him. "You have been so persistent, Fallon, I cannot imagine that you will settle down with a wife and plant tobacco."

"I will go where God sends me," he answered, lazily stretching his legs out in front of him. "And I have strong faith that Noshi will be found. But on his last journey south Reverend Buck learned that the Tripanik tribe has been annihilated by the pox. Entire villages have been wiped out, so where do I begin to search? Lately I have begun to pray that God would bring Noshi to me as surely as he led me to you."

A soft laugh escaped Gilda's lips. "Prayer! How can you pray such a thing? If I have learned anything about this great God of ours, Fallon, it is that he does what he wants, when he wants to do it. What good are our prayers? I prayed that my sister would return to me, and she did not. I prayed that I would be able to enjoy her son, but John Rolfe left him in England. If what you have told me is true, our parents were murdered even as they bowed on their knees in prayer. So what is the use in praying? Prayer does not change God."

Fallon shifted on the bench to turn toward her. "Ofttimes we pray and ask amiss—"

"No!" she cut him off. "I have prayed with tears over the bodies of innocent boys in this house, and yet they have died in agony. How can a prayer for the sick be selfish? Despite my prayers to the true God, more men have died here in this house than ever died in our Indian villages, where conjurors pray to the spirits of the sun and wind."

"Gilda, you are speaking blasphemy."

"No, I am not." Her voice cracked with weariness. "I believe in the true God who created heaven and earth, and I always have! And my prayer is pure before him. But I have suffered, Fallon, more than you, and I have prayed with all my heart and soul for—"

Her flood of words stopped abruptly and she lowered her head as if she were suddenly exhausted. "My prayers have not changed the face of our angry God," she whispered, tears tangling in her lashes. "I have tried to walk rightly before him and yet still he punishes me."

"God is not punishing you," Fallon answered. Suddenly he wanted to kiss the tears from her eyes, but he could not. She was not his. Restraining his raging impulses, he slipped his arm around her shoulders in a gesture of brotherly concern. "He has blessed you, though you cannot see it. When you marry Brody, a fine Christian man, he will take you from this place of death and disease—"

"And you?" she whispered, lowering her head to his shoulder.

"I will be a friend closer than a brother," he said, breathing in the sweet scent of her hair. He rested his cheek upon the tumbled, silken mass, then pressed his lips to it and smiled when she nestled closer. "If you only knew, Gilda, how deeply your name is carved upon my heart! You would not worry about the future, for just as God brought me to you when you needed a brother, now he has brought Brody to you for a husband."

She seemed to stiffen under his arm, and he released her from the embrace as she pulled away. Hurt coursed through him, but he dismissed it—even as he dismissed the odd sense that he was somehow bereft, that his arms were achingly empty without her. *Fool!* he told himself, *she is an engaged woman now. How would you like it if your betrothed were seen leaning on another man in public?*

Not one bit, his heart answered. If Gilda were his betrothed, he would want her entirely to himself and not be willing to share her with another man, no matter how innocent that relationship!

Fallon picked up his hat and stood. "Do not stop praying, Gilda," he said, bending down to search her face.

She avoided his eyes and would not answer.

▾▴▾▴▾ By 1620, English and Dutch vessels landed regularly at Jamestown, but when the fabled and long-awaited ship of brides anchored off the docks, a cheer echoed along the streets, and runners raced to the far-flung plantations. "Fetch your bride in two days' time," the runners called as they hurried throughout the settlements. "Bring your warrants to the secretary's office."

At his favorite table in the tavern's public room, Fallon worried between his fingers the slip of paper entitling him to a bride. Brody had been more than generous to provide half of the amount necessary to purchase the warrant of entitlement, but Fallon had the uneasy feeling that Brody had given the money only to rid himself of a rival for Gilda's affection. Still, Brody's contribution had been significant, for not only did the warrant guarantee Fallon a wife, but by means of the headright, which authorized anyone to claim fifty acres of land for each individual whom he brought into Virginia, Fallon would soon be a propertied man.

Brody, of course, had no interest in acreage or planting, but Fallon was sorely tempted by the thought of venturing forth to found his own settlement. There he would build a house, then plant tobacco and enough food to feed his workers and run a school for the proper education of children. He shifted in his chair, distracted by thoughts of a sturdy village like Ocanahonan, where Indian and Englishmen would be free to follow God's purpose for their lives. He knew such a place could exist, for he had been born in such a village. And with Gilda and Noshi at his side, such a place could exist again.

Reality cut through his dream like a scalpel. Gilda would not be by his side. The woman whose arrival would provide his fifty acres was yet a stranger; an intriguing, unsettling image in his imagination.

▼▲▼▲▼ Edith had gone to the fort to dose a dozen ailing soldiers, so Gilda left Wart in charge of the house while she slipped out the front gate and joined the crowd that streamed toward the docks. Earlier she had resolved to stay away, telling herself that she cared not one whit about the woman Fallon might choose to be his wife, but an inordinate and devouring curiosity would not let her rest. Like the others of Jamestown, she hurried to the river's edge to see what sort of women the London Company had managed to procure for the desperately lonely men of Jamestown.

On any other day Gilda or even Edith would not have been able to walk through the settlement without attracting every male glance and at least a dozen ribald or admiring comments. But today she moved among the planters and merchants as if she were invisible, for every eye had fastened onto the galleon at anchor in the river.

At least fifty freshly shaven and bathed men waited in a line upon the dock, each clutching a slip of parchment. The governor's secretary waited with the first man in line, and though she stood on tiptoe and craned her neck, Gilda could see no sign of Fallon in the line, nor was he in the curious crowd of servants,

Indians, and traders who had come to observe the festive parade of ladies.

A cry rose from the men on the shore, and she looked up as a shallop, heavily laded with colorful passengers, appeared from behind the ship. The women aboard squealed with each scend of the rough water, and the oarsmen grinned in delight as they brought their treasure to shore. Gilda frowned. If these simple creatures carried on so because of the motion of a sturdy shallop, how would they fare in a delicately balanced canoe?

The shallop pulled alongside the dock, and the crowd on shore pressed forward in anticipation. Gilda wanted to walk away, so great was her disgust at the fawning attitude of the men around her, but curiosity would not let her leave.

A dozen hands were extended to the first woman who climbed from the boat to the dock, and the crowd fell back with an audible gasp of surprise when the newcomer turned to survey her new community. All thoughts of derision left Gilda's mind, for never in her life had she seen an Englishwoman in the full blaze of adornment.

She had never imagined that such an abundance of ribbon and fabric could be worn by one person, and yet each approaching woman seemed determined to outdo her companions. Out of the shallop came a dozen virgin brides-to-be, dressed in pleated skirts jutting out from their tiny waists as if their hips were monstrously wide. Lace edged every hem and garnished two dozen cuffs and split sleeves. Pearls glistened from ropes around their necks, and several ladies wore pearl buttons that began at the neckline and continued down to the front edge of their dresses. Each woman's petal-pink complexion was framed by a monstrously large collar that rose stiffly behind her head, and if that weren't enough, each bride wore a heavily plumed hat. As their feathery fans fluttered in the hot ocean breeze, Gilda thought they looked like fragile butterflies upon the dock.

"All right," the secretary boomed once the first boatload of women stood safely upon the dock. "Which twelve gentlemen will vie for these first twelve ladies? Gentlemen, approach the lady of your choice, and ladies, if he doesn't please you, kindly defer and wait for the next man."

The first dozen men in line upon the dock suddenly fell as silent as awkward schoolboys, and the raucous crowd on the beach roared in delight. "Take the bonny brunette, Ned," someone cried out. "And ask her if she's got a sister!"

Gilda lifted her chin, disturbed at the scene before her. While they were certainly dressed to attract attention, the women on the dock were not young, and most of their painted faces bore the look of hard experience. One woman brazenly advanced toward the men, her lips set in a crimson sneer, and the man at the head of the line backed away from her so suddenly that he fell into the river. While the men on shore roared with laughter, the second man in line extended his hand to her, surrendered his warrant to the secretary, and waved to his cheering comrades as he led his bride off the dock toward the church, where the minister waited to pronounce them man and wife.

"I didn't think I'd see you here."

The voice spoke in her ear and Gilda looked up to see Brody next to her, an expression of concern on his face. "Don't you think you should wait at the house? Truth to tell, this isn't a safe place for a woman. What if one of these men decides to take you home with him?"

"I'm not for sale," she replied lightly, turning to go. But she paused at the sight of the warrant in Brody's hand.

"Ah, this," he said, noticing her startled expression. "And you are wondering if I'm planning on taking two wives. No. Fallon sent me down here to have a look around. He's coming later."

"He is." Her voice was flat in her own ears and she made a weak attempt to smile. "Well, the ladies are dressed well enough. There's enough fabric in one of those skirts to outfit the women of an entire Indian village."

Brody lifted his head to scan the docks, and Gilda noticed that the scene held as much fascination for him as it had for her. "You are right," he said finally, still watching as another shallop prepared to unload its female cargo. "Fallon will not have an easy time of choosing amongst so many beauties."

She left him gawking in the crowd.

▼▲▼▲▼ Brody watched until only a dozen unclaimed women remained. These brides, who had not yet been spoken for, were consoled by the secretary, who assured them that many of the planters had not yet had time to travel to Jamestown from their prosperous estates. "They will be given a week," the secretary said, his beard bobbing vigorously against his doublet as he sought to assuage their ruffled feelings. "Then you will be free to accept the attentions and proposals of any of our other fine citizens of Virginia."

Properly mollified, the brides followed the secretary off the dock, and the observing crowd on the shore parted like the Red Sea as they passed through. Brody watched with his mouth open as they rustled past in gleaming silk and taffeta, then he turned and sprinted toward the public house where he knew he'd find Fallon.

Fallon was hunched over a book of records and scarcely looked up when Brody burst in upon him. "Name of a name, why do you sit here?" Brody demanded, leaning on the table. "I saw them, Fallon, and they're beautiful! Not exactly young, I'll warrant, but this morning I saw redheads, and blondes, and brunettes with eyes to make a man's bones melt."

"I'm not interested," Fallon answered, turning a page in the book before him. He dipped his pen in an inkwell and made a notation on the page while Brody stuttered in amazement.

"Not interested? There's a woman and fifty acres of whatever land you choose waiting out there! How can you say you are not interested?"

"I'm not, that's all," Fallon answered. He put down his pen and looked up at Brody. "I've been thinking about it, and praying, and I don't think I can marry a woman just to gain fifty acres."

"Then marry her because she's soft and gentle and has what every man needs," Brody whispered intently. He pulled up a stool and crouched on it, his face inches away from Fallon's. "Listen, me friend, this celibate life we're living here isn't exactly natural, you know. It isn't God's plan for man nor beast. Now I've given you half of the warrant we hold, and you worked hard for the other half, so how can you let it go to waste? Go out there and claim a bride!"

Fallon sat with battleship solidity and picked up his pen. "I told you, Brody, I'm not interested."

Brody slapped his hand on the table in exasperation and crossed his legs, thinking. Months ago Fallon had been more than interested, even eager, to marry, but something had happened in the interim period. Suddenly, in a breathless instant of understanding, he knew the truth.

"Name of a name," he muttered slowly, fixing Fallon with his gaze. "You are in love with Gilda."

Fallon flinched ever so slightly, then he smiled and toyed with the feather quill in his hand. "I care for her deeply, you know that," he said, his voice calm and eminently reasonable. "But she hates me, so how could I possibly love her?"

"She doesn't hate you," Brody answered, suddenly plagued by dark suspicions. "Maybe she dislikes you—"

"Well, you see how it is, then," Fallon said, lifting his hand in a theatrical gesture. "How can a man love someone who resists his every thought and word? No, Brody, I do not love Gilda, except fondly, as a sister. I give her to you with my blessing. And for now, I am not interested in taking a wife. There is too much to be done here in Jamestown for me to leave and become a planter." He frowned and leaned forward, lowering his voice. "Did you know that some in the council are actually talking of selling men as chattel slaves?"

"Slaves?" Brody crinkled his forehead. "How is that different from selling men as we do now?"

"Indentured service is a choice and only lasts for a certain time," Fallon said, closing the book that rested on the table.

"And then the master is required to establish the servant in his new life of freedom. But slavery, Brody, is for life, and the slave has no choice in the matter! I can't imagine that the assembly would ever allow such a thing in Virginia."

"Well—" Brody was about to argue that many of the prisoners sent from England to serve life sentences upon the plantations were virtual slaves already, but he was interrupted when a man burst into the public room.

"A massacre!" the man shouted, his face red with exertion. "Four days ago at Falling Creek! All are killed but one!"

Brody and Fallon exchanged a meaningful glance, then followed the other men to the fort.

The story, brought by a lone survivor who had hidden in a barrel of corn, was brief and horrible. George Thorpe, the gentle scholar who had come to direct the school for Indian and English children, had initiated a friendship with the great chief Opechan-canough. In order to demonstrate his trust, Thorpe allowed Opechancanough free access to all the grounds of the school at Falling Creek and had even built the chief an English house at Henrico. While Thorpe was congratulating himself on the suc-cess of his peacemaking venture, Opechancanough spied out every corner of the settlement and school at Falling Creek as the Indians and English worked together in the fields and forests.

"Master Thorpe," the frightened survivor panted, his eyes roll-ing wildly in his fright, "even ignored the law forbidding mus-kets to the savages. Opechancanough was given a musket for hunting, and it was with that gun that he blew a hole in Master Thorpe's head."

A strange whispering moved through the air, like the trembling breaths of a hundred simultaneous astonishments. "Shall we not avenge these deaths?" one man in the crowd yelled, his hand upon the pistol in his belt. "Or will we wait until Opechancanough comes to take us as well?"

The crowd broke forth in confused babble, each man arguing with his neighbor, until Governor George Yeardley shot his pistol in the air. As silence and the acrid smell of gunpowder fell upon the group, the governor lifted his hand to address the mob. "We will take a party of armed men to the village of Opechanca-nough," he said, his brows rushing together in a brooding knot over his eyes. "We have a treaty of peace with the chief, and until we know why the peace was broken I will not attack his people."

A roaring shout of disapproval met this pronouncement, but the governor stepped down and shouldered his way through the crowd. Yeardley's secretary followed, slinking timidly behind in the wake of the frightened and distrustful looks directed at the governor.

Brody turned to Fallon and gave him a twisted smile. "So since you are not taking a wife, how about joining the governor as part of the militia?"

"No," Fallon answered, turning toward Mistress Rolfe's house. A confusing rush of anticipation and dread whirled inside him. "I have the feeling I'll be needed here."

▼▲▼▲▼ Gilda was surprised later that evening when Governor Yeardley himself escorted the hysterical survivor of Falling Creek to the house. News of the massacre had traveled like a firestorm through the settlement, and she greeted the governor quietly and pointed toward an empty mattress for the terrified and exhausted survivor. The man shrank from her at first, his face set in a look of startled wariness, but she soothed him in perfect English and told him he had nothing to fear.

After settling the man and giving him an herb potion to help him sleep, she entered the kitchen and found Fallon in conversation with Edith. "How fares your new patient?" Fallon asked, giving her a polite smile. "He seemed unhurt, just scared."

"He is exhausted and hungry, and he needs a bath," Gilda said, picking up a bucket of water near the fireplace. "His body is strong, but the healing of his mind will take time. He has seen things he did not expect to see."

"Let me help you," Fallon said, coming to take the heavy bucket from her. She allowed him to carry it and led the way to the man's bedside. Fallon put the bucket on the floor, and she dipped a clean cloth into the water, wrung it out, and proceeded to wipe a week's accumulation of dirt from the unconscious man's face and hands.

"His name is Jack Traylor," she said simply, working expertly with the cloth while Fallon unbuttoned the man's soiled jerkin. "He has only been in Virginia for a few months. He was not prepared for the realities of warfare."

"The realities of savage warfare, you mean," Fallon answered, lifting the man's shoulders so Gilda could slip the jerkin from the man's back.

She bit back angry words and reproved him with a stern glance. "Indian warfare is no more savage than English," she said, tossing the lice-laden jerkin onto the floor. "And the Indian way is much more truthful."

"How can you say that?" Fallon asked, kneeling to face her across the man's body. "Opechancanough has promised peace betwixt our peoples, yet he has attacked and killed godly men who sought to educate his children—"

"Opechancanough sought to defend his children from the Englishmen's crafty intrusion," Gilda answered, her temper flaring. "The English promise peace, but then they teach Indian children to deny the Indian way of life. They win hearts through subtlety and trickery and make Indian warriors drunk so they can steal furs and grain!"

"Where have you heard these things?" Fallon snapped, reaching for her hand. He caught it and held it tight. "You have listened too much to Opechancanough."

"You have not listened to him at all! He is old, Fallon, and wise. His scouts have been north where the French give strong waters to warriors, who drink themselves crazy with it. Opechancanough has been south, where the Spanish made slaves of the Indians more civilized than they."

"He is a liar. He denies God and has led you astray."

"He knows more about the holy book than you, Fallon. And though he now denies God, he once walked in the holy way. Something changed his heart, but if we are patient and try to understand him, we can bring his heart back to the truth—"

"It is folly to think such a thing!" Fallon said, thrusting her hand away from him as if she had suddenly turned into the hated chief himself. "He is a plague, Gilda, an evil spirit, a cursed creature, and we would do well to be rid of him!"

"He is of my people!" Gilda answered, sinking to the floor. She curled her hands to her breast. "He is the only person who still lives that was a part of my childhood. He is my uncle. He is part of me, Fallon, and if you hate him, you must hate me also."

"Gilda, I don't hate—"

"Yes, you do."

She felt the chasm between them like an open wound. After a moment, Fallon shuffled to his feet and left the room. When she was sure he had gone, Gilda wept, burying her head in the mattress where Jack Traylor lay.

▼▲▼▲▼ Governor Yeardley set out for Weromacomico at dawn the next day and returned a week later. He had visited Opechancanough himself, he reported, and the attack on Falling Creek had been committed by another tribe, not the Powhatan. Opechancanough personally guaranteed that the peace between his people and the English would continue to stand. "This he said to me," the governor told the audience assembled outside the walls of the Jamestown fort, "that the sky should sooner fall than the peace be broken on his part, and that he has given order to all his people to give no offense. He desires the like from us."

"What of the witness?" a harsh voice called from the crowd. "The survivor himself saw Opechancanough kill Master Thorpe."

The governor allowed his stone face to crack into a pose of compassionate humanity. "The man we saw last week is not of sound mind. We cannot risk the peace on account of his rantings."

"You mean it is not politic to believe him!" another voice accused, but Governor Yeardley lifted his hands in dismissal, then moved inside the fort.

Still fearful and hungry for blood, the disgruntled crowd dispersed, and Gilda noticed that more than one pair of eyes turned toward her in distrust. Unfortunately, since Jamestown was a city of transients, few in the crowd knew her as a longtime resident, and her dark skin and hair drew immediate attention. The new brides proved to be especially skittish since hearing of the tragedy at Falling Creek. Most were vocal and loudly determined that they would not venture to their wilderness plantations unless something was done to neutralize the threat of the Indians.

So in the days that followed the attack upon Falling Creek, three Indian hunters were captured on the river and hanged in the city square, but by whom no one knew. A fortnight later an Indian family was found lying in the dust outside the fort; even the throats of the children had been cut. The bodies remained in the hot sun for hours until Fallon and Wart retrieved them for burial.

*Fallon can say nothing about Indian savagery now,* Gilda thought after hearing about the murdered family.

These evidences of English brutality sickened Gilda far more than the harsh looks she endured whenever she walked through the settlement. But her defining moment of truth came one Sunday at church. The narrow building was crowded and buzzed pleasantly with the whispers of brides eager to make themselves right with God before journeying into the wilderness with their new husbands. Gilda noticed several suspicious sidelong glances when she and Edith entered, but she held her head high as she led Edith to an empty bench. She could not help but notice that Brody did not choose to sit behind her as was his custom. In an odd moment of distraction, Gilda wished that Fallon had come, but he was visiting a plantation at Charles City.

After the benediction, Gilda remained to chat for a moment with Reverend Buck, then slipped through the doorway with Edith. Looking up, she was surprised to see that many in the crowd of worshipers, both men and women, had lined up in a gauntlet of sorts outside the church.

"Maybe we should wait," Edith said, pulling on Gilda's arm.

"We're in no hurry to return home, Gilda, and if we wait a moment—"

"No," Gilda answered, staring at the pale, pinched faces before her.

Edith visibly shrank back. "I can't do it," she whimpered, wringing her hands. "The Lord knows I bear enough scorn for being plain, so I can't walk through that crowd with you. I just can't."

Gilda gave her a dry, one-sided smile. "Then stay here." With a quick intake of breath like someone about to plunge into icy water, she wrapped her dignity about her and walked through the double lines.

An ocean of contempt engulfed her. "Stay away from the house of God, you murdering savage!" one of the women hissed, and another tossed her head forward and spat upon Gilda's cheek before letting loose a stream of foul invective.

Verbal insults, growled threats, and at least three stones were hurled at her, but Gilda held her head high as befitted an Indian princess and walked steadily home.

▼▲▼▲▼ Back in Mistress Rolfe's house, Gilda took a damp cloth and washed her face, let down her hair, and slipped out of the simple bodice, kirtle, and petticoat she had worn to church. Leaving them in a pile on the floor of her small chamber, she went to her trunk and lifted out the buckskin tunic she had worn into town so many moons before. She rubbed her hands over it, relishing its supple smoothness, then slipped it over her head.

Sitting on the floor, she crossed her legs and ran her hand expertly over her scalp, parting her hair into two sections. Her fingers automatically plaited her dark hair into two braids while she sat before the shuttered window and thought.

Edith crept into the house in the quiet of the afternoon and left Gilda alone, of certain too ashamed to face her. Wart respected her closed door and stayed away. Brody did not come to the house at all, and in the arctic emptiness of her soul Gilda felt vaguely grateful for the quiet.

Brody finally appeared at sunset, and as he knocked on the front door of the house Gilda padded to the window in her bare feet. Pushing the shutter open, she lifted herself up and out. Moving as soundlessly as a shadow while the dark came on, she crept across the courtyard and had nearly reached the gate when a hand closed around her upper arm. She stifled a scream.

"Where do you think you are going?"

Fallon. He was the only one, other than she, who had been taught to prowl silently in the darkness. She closed her eyes, wishing him away.

"I heard about what happened at the church, Gilda. I'm sorry I wasn't with you."

"Go home, Fallon. You said you would go home to England, so why are you still here?"

"England has never been my home." He pulled her around to face him, and she stiffened in rebellion. "You are being a child."

"Am I?" Her eyes flew open. "Did we not speak of English and Indian brutality?" she asked, blazing up at him. "Which have we seen thus far? Have I, an Indian, spat upon any of the pitiful men that have sought help in this house? Have I reviled them for the diseases they picked up from loose women in the Caribbean or threatened them with death because they look upon me with lust in their hearts? No, Fallon, I have not. And yet, though I have sought to treat them with the kindness God expects of his children, today I have suffered far worse than the innocent family who lay in the dust of Jamestown this week. They are now in merciful heaven, while I am left to suffer the torment of the enlightened English who lift their hands to God one minute and hurl stones at Indians in the next."

"They are wrong, Gilda, so why will you let them drive you away? Opechancanough has no answers for you—"

She swung her arm wildly, flinging off his grip, and Brody suddenly appeared from out of the house, his form a huge shadow in the yellow rectangle of light thrown through the open door. "Thank God you found her, Fallon. Edith and I had just checked her room—"

"The canary has fled the cage, Brody, and thought to run away unheeded," Fallon answered, his face strangely empty of emotion.

"Run away?" Brody gazed at her with the naiveté of a child. "Whatever for, Gilda? I heard there was a bit of unpleasantness at church—"

"Where were you, Brody?" Fallon interrupted him in a stern voice.

For a moment Brody stammered, then he lifted a hand in explanation. "I had to speak to the governor's secretary about an important matter. I was on the far side of the church and had no idea what was happening." His blue eyes focused on hers. "Gilda, you can't be thinking to leave. You promised to marry me."

"I made no such promise," she said, noting a look of surprise on Fallon's face.

"But you didn't say no," Brody said, shaking his finger playfully. "Come, lass, we can forget all this. It is only a bit of trouble that will blow over like a bad storm. Now go back inside, put on your pretty dress, and let's have supper."

"No." She took a step toward the gate.

"Fallon," Brody's voice carried a pleading tone. "You talk to her. Make her stay."

Gilda lifted her chin reflexively. Fallon would command her to go inside, ordering her life as he always did, and though she wanted desperately to leave this place and its rivers of anguish, she knew she would stay if he asked her to. Because he alone could convince her that things would be better.

But Fallon shook his head, and for the first time since she had known him, he refused to tell her what to do. After a long moment in which her heart yearned for him to ask her to remain, he looked toward the ground and idly moved a mound of earth with his moccasin. "It is her choice to make," he said, more to Brody than to her. "She is not mine to command."

She stared at him, stunned for a moment, then tossed her head, the victor at last in their war of wills. Fallon opened the gate for her as Brody blustered in protest. She did not look back, but moved away through the darkness and soon broke into a run, breathing heavily as tears rained down her cheeks. She had finally broken free of Fallon Bailie's self-ordained control of her life. Why, then, had she never been more unhappy?

▼▲▼▲▼ Fallon shut out the sound of Brody's complaining and walked toward the house. He sank onto the bench he and Gilda had shared so short a time ago, and Brody left to find his supper in the public house, slamming the gate as he stalked away.

Leaning forward, Fallon wearily rested his face in his hands as he studied the rectangle of light from inside the house, where Edith and Wart bickered companionably. He had finally done it. He had set Gilda free, hoping she would be unable to leave, but she had flown away as surely as a caged bird who glimpses the blue bowl of sky for the first time. Had he been wrong to insist she belonged at Jamestown? She said she had suffered; had he taken her so for granted that he was blind to her unhappiness?

But he had suffered, too. He understood the ache she felt over the loss of those she loved. He, too, had suffered loss: his beloved parents, Noshi, and Captain Newport had disappeared from his life. Loneliness had become an aching hollow within him; he felt empty, a man without a past. And the only person who could help him validate it, who could assure him his memories were indeed true, had just walked out of his life.

It seemed to him that he had loved Gilda all his life, that he had not ended a day without thinking of her well-being and praying for her happiness. But she had never seen him as other than an elder brother, and an interfering one at that. Fallon had been painfully aware of this. Because he loved her he had never spoken of his true feelings, fearful that the resulting awkwardness would cause her to withdraw even her friendship.

Because he loved her he had never allowed himself to imagine her arms solid and strong around him. . . .

He abruptly checked his thoughts, for the woman who could take away the brooding hurt he struggled to hide had just vanished into the darkness. Would he ever see her again?

He found no answers in the vast and endless plain of evening, and after a long while he went into the house and asked Mistress Rolfe if she would allow him a few hours' sleep on an unoccupied mattress.

The dark docks rang with the noisy shouts of drunken sailors, so Gilda slipped quietly through the night to the river's edge. In the shadows of a screen of shrubbery she eased herself into the black waters, then side-stroked across the river until she reached the far shore. Her leather dress clung wetly to her, causing her to shiver in the cool evening air, and she realized with some surprise that she had grown accustomed to the warmth and comfort of an English house. Now it was time to unlearn comfort and adjust to life as an Indian. Again.

A well-worn path led away from a nearby clearing. Gilda avoided it and ran to the shelter of a thick bush with needlelike branches. She slipped below the lowest limbs and lay on the silken comfort of fallen needles, pillowing her head on her hands. She slept fitfully, waking as the sun rose, and sprinted out of her hiding place for the deeper security and shelter of the trees. Once she stood under a dense forest canopy, she brushed dirt from her damp clothing and allowed her survival skills to surface.

The virgin forest on this side of the river stood as a green fortress around her. She forced herself to look through the forest instead of at it, and cocked her head to hear what sort of life might be afoot in the wilderness. The gnarled root of an oak showed its dark power as it pushed up earth before her, and the early morning shadows shifted like stalking gray cats who seemed to whisper, "We will take you back, daughter of the Powhatan. We welcome you home."

With the sure grace of a forest creature she pressed forward into the woods, and within a quarter of an hour she discovered a deer trail that led westward. She followed it eagerly, her eyes and ears acting as sentries. *I am Indian,* she thought, the refrain repeating in her mind as her feet slipped over the moist earth of the forest floor, *I am of the land.*

*But you are English, too,* a voice deep within reminded her, *and as much at home in the healing house as you once were in the woods. Your eyes are the color of the spring sky, and your heart yearns toward a pale, copper-haired man who will never see you as more than a child. You worship his God; you understand his thoughts. In this you will forever be different.*

She moved steadily through the dense vegetation, stopping periodically to listen for sounds of anyone following. Would Fallon come after her? She had been honestly surprised when he had allowed her to go; something within her even now hoped he would follow and beg her to return to Jamestown. But no footsteps sounded behind her. Could he have grown so weary of fighting her stubborn resistance that he no longer cared?

She picked up a dead branch on the trail and swung it lazily between two trees where a fist-sized spider hung motionless. Such an action was careless; to an experienced scout it would mark her path as surely as if she had hacked out a trail with a sword. If anyone from Jamestown chose to follow, it would be easy enough to find her.

She walked in silence for hours, but no one followed. Perverse thoughts stormed her mind. Didn't Fallon worry about her at all? He wouldn't send Wart or even Brody out into the forest alone, but, despite all his talk about protecting her, he had allowed her to go. Maybe he had at last come to see that she was a strong woman who did not need his protection. Or maybe he had thought she would grow so hungry and frightened she would return to Jamestown.

As the sun dipped toward the western horizon, Gilda found a dry spot and cleared brush away from a sizable circle to make sure no snakes lingered nearby. She thought about laying a fire, but the effort seemed like too much work for so warm a night. Exhausted, she lay down under the trees.

She had been gone from Jamestown for twenty-four hours, and Fallon had not come for her. He did not care. She buried her face in the crook of her arm and refused to give in to the tears that pricked at her eyes. Somehow his indifference hurt her far more than his anger ever had.

▼▲▼▲▼ With an effort, Fallon tore his thoughts away from Gilda and directed his attention toward the visiting planter. Master John Rolfe sat with Brody, Wart, and Edith at the large table in the kitchen. A fire crackled under the dinner pot, and Wart sniffed the delightful mingled aromas appreciatively while Rolfe discussed the business and profit of tobacco and its effect on the burgeoning population of the colony.

"The population in Jamestown will forever be transitory, I fear," he said, pausing to sip the steaming cup of herbal tea Edith had forced upon him. He looked up at Fallon, then gave his sister an affectionate smile. "That is why I am taking my new bride to the house in Henrico."

"Your new bride!" Edith gasped, slapping her hand against her plump cheek. "What news is this?"

Rolfe smiled modestly and tapped his long fingers against the rim of his cup. "I'm to marry Jane, the daughter of Captain William Pierce, within the month. I'm planning to take her out to Henrico, but I wanted you to know that I have deeded this house to you, Edith. It is yours now, though I'm hoping you'll continue to maintain it as a hospital."

Rolfe's eyes met Fallon's, and the planter nodded in appreciation. "I am not unaware, sir, of the work you have done to improve the roughshod lives of the men who land here. Your success has been noticed, I assure you."

"Is it success when four out of five men don't survive their first year?" Fallon asked, lifting an eyebrow.

"It is success when you consider the hardships of this place," Rolfe answered, suddenly unsmiling. His eyes hardened. "The merchants continue to overcrowd the ships, and the men who arrive here every week are in worse shape than the blokes the week before. Betwixt the decks a man can hardly catch his breath by reason of the stink in the air, and our men fall sick and poison their fellows. The voyage, poor food, foul water, cold, and dampness all contribute to debilitating those pitiful souls in the hold."

"The ships are horrible," Fallon admitted, "but Jamestown could use improvements, too. Housing is poor, and bad air rises from the marshlands and swamps. The plague of mosquitoes every summer cannot do the men good, and rats consume more corn than do the men."

"Yet here at this house, you have managed to save many of the men who fall ill," Rolfe pointed out. "You have done better than the governor's English doctor. I pray you, tell me. What is your secret?"

Edith waved her hand in a genteel gesture. "I feel, gentlemen, as did Gilda, that the men here do not die from diseases of the body, but of the mind."

"What do you mean?" Rolfe asked, leaning back to look at his sister.

The young lady's tired face looked middle-aged as she gently inclined her head. "They have no wives or mothers here, no family life, and they have heard this place overpraised in England. Ofttimes they are harshly treated by their masters, they fall ill, and when they lie down in sickness, nobody but Fallon comes to help them, and he cannot be everywhere at once. They starve, good sirs, as much for simple love and affection as for food and medicine."

"And so you . . . ," Rolfe prodded.

"Gilda and I prayed for their souls as well as their bodies," she answered, slouching forward as she leaned against her hand. "We laughed with them and listened to their stories. We asked about their mothers and sweethearts back home. And when they recovered, if they recovered, we bade them remember to pray and not give up hope, for their time of service would soon be finished."

Fallon cupped his chin in his hand, thinking. He had been content to find ill-used men and bring them to the house with nary a thought of how Gilda and Edith had accomplished the wonders of healing. He had supposed that the women dosed their patients with Indian herbs and remedies, but he had no idea their cures had involved body, soul, and spirit.

How would they continue without Gilda? It was true that Edith and Wart could keep on with their work, but Mistress Rolfe did not have Gilda's charm and vitality. Besides, Wart was nearing manhood and would of certain want to find a place of his own, maybe even take a wife. No, the hospital could not remain open forever. Without Gilda, it would fall into disrepair and disuse, and soon be nothing but an empty shell.

Just like Fallon's heart.

By heaven, he missed her! Stubborn little fool that she was, she would never know what it had cost him to allow her to walk away. Fallon wanted to imagine her wandering on one of the river trails, tired and hungry, but he knew she was more than capable of finding food and her way back to Opechancanough's village.

At the thought of the chief, a pang of bitter pain shot through Fallon. So the old devil had won at last. The chief's taunting prediction that Gilda would turn from the true God and become one of the Powhatan had of certain come to pass. Though she hadn't yet begun to worship the heathen spirits, Opechancanough had won her loyalty. And loyalty, in the end, proved the measure of a heart.

Fallon clenched his fist under the table. If he had a chance, he'd yet live to see Opechancanough defeated.

▼▲▼▲ Five days after leaving Jamestown, Gilda entered Weromacomico. The guards at the gate stared at her with expressions of stone, and women looked up from their cooking fires and whispered to one another as she passed. Young children blinked curiously at her, then ran to their mothers. She had been away for two full years; it was no surprise that they did not recognize her.

Gilda knew she must immediately present herself to the great chief. If he refused to welcome her, she would no longer have a place in the world. The English despised her. If the Indians cast her off as well . . .

She found Opechancanough in his dwelling, surrounded by his council of elders and priests. She entered and bowed her head before him and opened her hands to show that she had brought nothing with her from the English village.

The power in Opechancanough's face had not lessened, and he stared at her with a combination of defiance and curiosity. "And so, Woman-with-a-Secret," he said in the Algonquin tongue, his voice rumbling through the stillness of the dwelling, "you have come back to us with open hands. But what is in your heart?"

She forced herself to look up and meet his gaze. "Willingness and submission," she said, taking pains to hide the heartache that threatened to erupt in her voice. "I have come back to the Powhatan, my people, and will do whatever my chief asks of me. I will marry Askook or another warrior, and I will bear children for the Powhatan—"

The chief held up his hand and she obediently fell silent. "Is there nothing else in your heart?" he asked, speaking in English so that his elders could not understand. "What of the English God? Does his image still dwell there?"

Gilda hung her head. "My God is a spirit; he has no image," she whispered. "And I am still Kimi, Woman-with-a-Secret. I cannot tear the English God from my heart, for he will remain as long as it beats."

The chief's eyes flared suddenly, then dulled to black holes in his granite face. "Our gods will cleanse your heart," he proclaimed in the Indian tongue. "You will spend three days fasting in the ceremonial sweat lodge. After three days, you will be taken to the women's hut on the bank of the river, there to stay until the moon returns to the full shape it will have tonight."

"And after that?" she whispered, knowing she risked his wrath by questioning him further.

The dark eyes gleamed, as indecipherable as water. "The spirits of wind and fire and earth will tell me what to do with you."

▼▲▼▲▼ Outside the protective walls of the palisade, the ceremonial sweat lodge stood in solitary remoteness far from the noise and bustle of village life. Built of a framework of slender wooden poles covered with buckskin and an outer layer of heavy furs, the low, squat lodge was designed to cleanse a soul and body through perspiration and prayer.

Gilda could not recall a woman ever using the sweat lodge, but when the conjuror summoned her she followed him to the structure and crawled inside the opening. The lodge was empty but for a pile of steaming rocks set on glowing logs in the center of the room. Outside, the conjuror began a nasal chant as a heavy leather flap closed off the doorway.

One of the women poured water through a small opening at the center of the domed roof, and steam rose from the heated rocks. Gilda shimmied out of her tunic and took shallow breaths to accustom herself to the stifling warmth of the enclosed space. She knew women sat outside to watch and listen, and they would not allow the fire to die down, nor the rocks to cool.

Gilda crossed her legs and closed her eyes as water droplets began to trickle over her skin and down her back. Moving as if in a dream, she loosened her braids and combed her hair with her fingers till it slipped like a soft tide over her shoulders and absorbed the water that poured forth from her skin.

The chief was wise to order this. Here she could cleanse her heart and mind of all traces of Fallon and the life she had left behind. Here she could speak every unspoken word she had ever thought in his presence, and she would say her farewells to Edith and Wart and Brody until no more words remained to be said. Here she would tell Fallon how she resented his taking

charge of her life and his overprotectiveness, then she would con-
fess that she admired his compassion, persistence, and devotion.

And when all her strength had ebbed away, when nothing
remained in her but the most basic of emotions, she would tell
Fallon that she loved him and let the words vanish without consequence into the steam of the sweat lodge. And at the end of
three days, when her heart was empty, her body purified, and
her mind clear, she would be free of Fallon Bailie and all things
English.

▾▲▾▲▾ The women pulled her out of the sweat lodge
on the morning of the fourth day, and Gilda was wholly taken
aback to find that autumn had turned her bitterly cold breath
upon the valley during Gilda's time of confinement. Shivering
with weakness and the unexpected briskness, she did not speak
as the women pulled a new tunic of buckskin over her head and
piled a thick bearskin around her shoulders. After slipping her
feet into new moccasins, the women pointed Gilda toward
another hut that stood on the banks of the river. Gilda knew this
hut well—it was the ceremonial hut where women were
required to live apart from the village during the time of their
bloody cycle or during childbirth.

She shook off the women's supporting hands and stumbled
determinedly toward the hut. She had not eaten since leaving
Jamestown, but her body had defeated the arching pangs of hunger in her first two days of solitude. The hunger had been easy to
conquer; not so the thoughts of her other life.

She stooped to crawl inside the women's hut and noticed with
an odd sort of grateful detachment that the women had not forgotten to provide her with food. A wooden bowl steamed with
hominy, and a small cake of corn bread lay upon a broad leaf.
One of the women had followed and stood outside the hut, peering curiously inside. Gilda nodded her thanks.

She picked up the cake of bread and nibbled at the crusty
edge. Her days in the sweat lodge were a painful blur of tears,

pain, and suffering, but now her mind felt as cool and clear as spring water. With no effort at all, the words to the daily morning prayer she had recited with Edith leapt into her mind: "Make a joyful noise unto the Lord, all ye lands. Serve the Lord with gladness: come before his presence with singing. Know ye that the Lord he is God: it is he that hath made us, and not we ourselves; we are his people, and the sheep of his pasture. Enter into his gates with thanksgiving, and into his courts with praise: be thankful unto him, and bless his name. For the Lord is good; his mercy is everlasting; and his truth endureth to all generations. Glory be to the Father, and to the Son, and to the Holy Ghost; as it was in the beginning, is now, and ever shall be: world without end. Amen."

Outside the hut, yellow sun-shot leaves arched over the path to the river, and the river itself seemed to be dusted with ash-orange tones by the fading light of autumn. From far away came the sounds of children laughing as they splashed in the chilly waters, and Gilda leaned upon the backrest in the hut and smiled. Life was simple in the Indian village: Women cooked and sewed clothing and looked after children and pleased their men. When necessary, they defended their homes or used their wiles to help trap food during the lean winter months. And during the time of their uncleanness, they came to this hut to ponder the ways of their sex and give thanks to the gods who had either gifted them with fertility or spared them from another mouth to feed.

If the chief married Gilda to one of his warriors, maybe she would be with child the next time she came to this hut. The thought made her shiver, and Gilda mentally braced herself as the image of Fallon inevitably rose from the depths of her imagination to shake a reproving finger at the notion. But Fallon was no longer a part of her life, and his frown of disapproval had no sway over her heart.

Gilda finished her breakfast and pulled her sleeping mat outside. She would lie like an Indian on the earth and enjoy the woods. She was a Powhatan; she was Kimi, Woman-with-a-

Secret, until the chief decreed otherwise. Her life would ever be spent with her tribe. Sleep came nudging in among her thoughts.

She dreamed of the familiar canoe upon a narrow river that moved swiftly into the west. She was not alone in the boat, for a protective presence overshadowed her, and finally the canoe beached itself outside a palisaded city. Gilda splashed through the water toward the gate, but a voice called, "No! This way!" and a freckled, tattooed arm directed her toward a small hole underneath the timbered wall.

The dark space under the palisade gaped like a yawning mouth, and a new kind of fear shook her body from toe to hair, twisting her mouth in a spasm of terror. She let out a tiny whine of mounting dread as sounds leapt over the wall: savage war whoops, the terrible ringing cash of steel upon steel, the rising screams of women.

"Go!" the voice shouted behind her, and Gilda whirled around to protest. A young version of Fallon stood beside her, his handsome features dead-white against the gleam of his coppery hair. "Gilda," he said, kneeling beside her so that his eyes were level with her own, "you have to go beneath the wall. And you must do it now."

She trembled, turning slowly, and the dark void beneath the palisade gaped at her like Opechancanough's black eyes. "I won't go," she screamed, turning again and flinging herself into Fallon's arms. But he pushed her away, and before her eyes his face shifted and hardened into maturity. Suddenly his eyes narrowed in the same pained, wounded expression he had worn when she left him outside Edith's house.

"You have to go," he said, firmly pushing her away.

"No!" she screamed, desperation filling her. "No!"

Wakefulness hit her like a punch in the stomach. She sat up, breathless, and saw that several children on the riverbank had turned toward her in surprise. Struggling to mask her panic, she painted on a warm smile and called out a greeting, then urged them on to their play. When they shrugged and moved away, she rolled over onto her elbows and hung her head in mortification.

Despite the rigors and harsh discipline of the sweat lodge, her nightmares had not vanished. Despite her prayers and good intentions, Fallon still haunted her. And so did the dark dream, which came now even in the stark light of day.

▼▲▼▲▼ She did not dream of the river again, nor of Fallon, during the time of her solitude. At the month's end, she stood before Opechancanough and proclaimed her readiness to reenter the tribe. When the chief squinted as if he would deny her petition, she rolled up the sleeves of her tunic and pointed to the fine marks of the tattoo upon her forearms.

"These scratches declare me to be a daughter of the great chiefs of the Powhatan," she said, blithely ignoring the sudden silence in the hut as the elders watched her challenge the great chief's hesitation. "Deny this mark, if you can, my uncle!"

Two of the elders leaned toward each other to consult in hoarse whispers, but Opechancanough sat stiffly upon his mat and said nothing. After a moment of stately deliberation, he raised his ceremonial pipe to his lips and inhaled deeply.

Gilda relaxed slightly. The pipe was a bid for time, nothing more. The great chief wanted to occupy his hands with smoking while his mind raced to more important matters. The chief passed the pipe to the priest who sat at his right hand. The priest inhaled and passed it to the next elder. Around the circle the pipe went, while Gilda stood in the center of the men and waited patiently.

"What is it you want, dear daughter?" Opechancanough asked when the pipe had returned to him. His voice was formal, and she knew the endearment was not meant to be taken literally.

"I want to live with my people, the Powhatan. I want to take a husband and bear children."

Opechancanough closed his eyes and nodded. "How many years are you?"

Gilda blinked, surprised by his question. "I have passed seventeen summers."

The werowance looked at his conjuror. "She will still be young enough to bear children in another year," he said, knocking the ashes of the pipe onto the floor.

"Yes," the conjuror agreed. Opechancanough glanced at the other elders, who nodded in unison.

The dark eyes settled on her again, and Gilda knew he did not yet fully trust her. "You may live and work with your people," he said, "but you will not marry until next year. When you have passed eighteen summers you may approach and ask for a husband."

Grateful that he had not cast her out, Gilda bowed and backed out of the chief's dwelling.


▼▲▼▲▼ Despite Gilda's resolutions, it was impossible not to miss the healing house at Jamestown during the cold winter months. Though that house had not been plush, life in the Indian community was decidedly harsh. Gilda worked all day with the women, storing and preparing food, and spent hours bending over the stone-lined firepits as she cooked steaming pottages of vegetables and venison. Occasionally she was called by the conjurors to help with healing, and while they chanted and blew smoke over the sick patient, Gilda quietly lifted prayers to the only God she knew.

She kept to herself as much as possible, aware that most of the women and many of the warriors were suspicious of her sudden reappearance. The children, as always, were wary of her blue eyes and scattered at her approach like leaves before an angry wind. But she did what was expected of her without comment or complaint, knowing that in faithful service alone could she convince Opechancanough that she was worthy to resume her rightful place in the clan.

Her nightmares did not trouble her in the Powhatan village, for she rarely rested well enough to dream. Each night, blind with fatigue, she crawled into the crowded hut where she had been grudgingly welcomed. A thick cloud of smoke hovered at the top of the domed structure, making it impossible to stand up and breathe at the same time, and though a fire burned constantly at the center of the dwelling, both moonlight and the bitter breath of winter came in through a thousand cracks in the thatched walls and roof. If she was fortunate enough to sleep near the fire, whichever side of her body faced the flames roasted as she slept. On most nights, though, she tried to ignore the sleeper who pressed against her and huddled into her blankets as her teeth chattered.

When a heavy snow fell in January, the children used it to build an insulating wall around each hut. The warmth of the fires inside soon turned the snow into ice, and under the magic workings of winter the huts glistened like Edith's clear crystal teacups turned upside down.

Thoughts of Edith made Gilda's throat ache with regret. She couldn't deny that she had abandoned Edith and Wart to a difficult work. If, as Opechancanough insisted, clothed men were continuing to pour into Jamestown and the surrounding areas, then the healing house was certain to be crowded.

Memories of the house often filled her with a longing to turn back, but by sheer force of will Gilda concentrated on the work before her and thrust recollections of Edith, Wart, and Brody from her mind. She was not English, she was a Powhatan. Her tattoos indicated her lineage, despite the symbol of the cross within them, and she would make her home forever with the Indians.

If only she could forget Fallon.

▼▲▼▲▼ Fallon splayed his legs to maintain his balance as the ship rocked in the rough water off the docks of James-town. "Twenty men are left below," the captain said, jerking his thumb toward the narrow stairs that led to the filthy area below deck. "I unloaded a hundred men at Elizabeth City, and a hun-dred-fifty here at Jamestown. But the lot remaining are too far gone to be bought by anybody; none of the planters upriver would take 'em. So I asks you, Master Bailie, what I am sup-posed to do? By the sword of St. Denis, I'm of certain not about to take the poxy lot back to England!"

"That won't be necessary," Fallon said, deliberately taking a deep breath of fresh air before descending the companionway. "That's why we have a hospital."

Each time Fallon entered a ship he thought he was witnessing the most pitiful conditions known to man, but each galleon of late had been far worse than the one before. In months past the labor merchants had taken to crowding increasing numbers of passengers into holds designed solely for inhuman cargo, and Fallon now found even women and children crammed into tor-turous spaces too small to sustain life for any length of time.

The horrible odors of raw sewage, vomit, and assorted filth assailed him as he began his descent, but he halted when the cap-tain tugged on his sleeve. Grateful for a moment to delay his errand, Fallon looked up.

"Whatever happened to that beautiful young miss who used to tend folks in that house of yours?" the captain asked. "She tended me herself the time I was down with scurvy last sum-mer."

"Gilda," Fallon said, looking away from the captain's yel-lowed eyes. For a moment he imagined her face in a ruffled cat's-paw on the sea, then he smiled ruefully and turned again to the seaman. "She's been gone for nearly a year. She's gone inland, and I don't think she'll be returning to the house."

"More's the pity," the captain answered, shaking his head. "But she'll be busy if she's still wanting to take care of the sick. The savages are all dying of the pox, you know."

"No," Fallon answered, a dark premonition holding him on the stairs. "I didn't know. There is sickness in the Powhatan villages?"

"Aye," the captain answered, his heavy cheeks falling in worried folds over his collar. "Hardly an Indian to be found in the woods or in the smaller villages. They lie sick and dying on the ground by the river or in the shallows where they drown trying to ease their fever."

Fallon swallowed against the unfamiliar constriction in his throat and forced himself to continue on down the stairs.

▼▲▼▲▼ In the late summer Gilda approached the chief with another request to marry, and two months later he sent for her.

"You have done well, little sister," Opechancanough said, giving her a restrained smile. "The women in your hut speak highly of you. And you have passed eighteen years."

"Yes," she whispered, wondering if he would finally keep his word.

The chief leaned forward, the firelight giving his face a ghostly aspect. "It pleases me to grant your request." He lifted his hand toward a tall warrior seated behind him. "Anakausuen is a fine worker," he said, scanning her face for signs of resistance. "He has watched you and agrees to take you as his wife. You will live in his village."

Gilda stepped back, momentarily stung. She had seen the warrior enter the village days before, but she had never imagined that Opechancanough might send her to one of the other villages. Some were far away, a month's journey from Jamestown even by canoe.

Anakausuen stood and came toward her; she met his appraising eyes with her own. The chief's choice had the clear, unlined face of a youth, and muscles bulged and slid under his bronze-red skin as he crossed his arms and studied her. He wore a warrior's breechcloth about his waist and a fur mantle over his

broad back; rough black hair tumbled past his shoulders. Indomi-
table pride was chiseled into his handsome face, and Gilda suddenly realized that Anakausuen did not look like the type of
man who would allow thoughts of another to fill his wife's head.
Good.

"Our chief is wise," she murmured to Opechancanough. She
bowed to her affianced husband as tradition demanded, then left
the chief's dwelling. They would not actually be married until
her husband led her into his hut, and she was not sure when
they would leave for his village. But by insisting upon her rights
to create a family within the Powhatan tribe, she knew she had
done the thing most likely to keep her thoughts forever from
Fallon Bailie.

Anakausuen and his men had come to Opechancanough's village to trade, so Gilda bundled her share of supplies and goods upon her back as she joined the group of half a dozen men who left Weromacomico. Her intended husband said little to her on the three-day journey to the village of Ramushonnouk, nor did he move to touch her as the party lay down to sleep at night by the comforting light of a campfire.

They entered Ramushonnouk on the morning of the fourth day, and Gilda realized with pleased surprise that her future husband was a highly respected warrior. Friends greeted him with eager embraces, women blushed and twittered when he approached, and children scampered and squealed for his attention like puppies eager for a juicy bone. Again, the goodness of Opechancanough had proven Fallon wrong, for he would not have given her such a worthy husband unless he held her in esteem and affection.

Distracted by the sights around her, Gilda followed in the wake of Anakausuen's retinue and nearly bumped into his broad back when he stopped in front of a hut. The children giggled at her confusion, and suddenly Gilda realized that Anakausuen had turned because this dwelling was his. It was time for them to join in marriage.

She blushed to the roots of her hair and let the pack fall from her back. Two women lifted it eagerly away and brought it to Anakausuen, who untied the leather bindings and unwrapped the fur bundle. From it he pulled forth a knife in a handsome leather sheaf and a string of bright yellow beads.

Almost reverently Anakausuen lifted the beads and gravely

slipped them over Gilda's head. "I take you to be my wife," he announced in an awed, husky whisper. The surrounding warriors shouted their approval, and Gilda tried to inject enthusiasm into her smile as she gave the expected response: "I accept you as my husband."

Then Anakausuen lifted the grass mat that served as the door to the hut and pulled Gilda inside.

▾▴▾▴▾ It was no mystery what married men and women did to enjoy each other, for Gilda had lived most of her life in a community where up to twenty people bedded down in a single hut. She did not doubt that Reverend Buck would be horrified to realize how open the Indians were in expressing their marital pleasures, but Gilda had discovered the great gulf that existed between English pronouncements and English actions. While they congratulated themselves on their recently deceased virgin queen and pledged to honor the precepts of Christian morality, most of the men aboard ships from the Caribbean arrived infested with venereal diseases and vermin that had never been seen among the people of the Powhatan.

She and her husband stood alone in this hut, however, and Anakausuen stared at her, his eyes glinting with pure masculine interest. He raked her with a fiercely possessive look, then put out a tentative finger and touched the bridge of her nose. Tenderly, gently, he moved his finger across the wings of her nostrils and over her cheek, then down to her lips.

She bent her head humbly before him and tried to rein in her rebellious mind. Why did she think of Fallon now?

Her husband stepped closer, cradling her head in his hand as he kissed her cheek and forehead and eyes and lips. A protest sprang to her lips but she bit it back.

*This is what you wanted, an Indian husband. This is the life you have chosen.*

His hand crept up the wide fullness of her sleeve, and the warmth of his palm against her shoulder seemed to send fire though every nerve in her body. Bending down, he lightly pressed his lips to hers, and suddenly Gilda realized that the warmth of his body had risen not from passion, but fever.

"Anakausuen," she whispered, placing her hands on his shoulder and gently pushing him away. "You are ill."

He mumbled and reached for her again, but she propelled him down to the furs piled on the floor, pressing her hand against his burning forehead. "Name of a name, what a fever is this!" He did not resist her ministration, but sighed in relief and closed his eyes as she soothed his skin with her cool hands. "I will fetch water and herbs," she said, whispering in his ear. "I am a good healer, my husband. I will make you well."

He said nothing, but drifted away in weariness. Gilda slipped through the doorway to beg the village conjuror for the medicines she needed.

▼▲▼▲▼ Anakausuen was not the only warrior affected with fever. Many others fell ill that same day, and their stubborn fevers would not break despite the frantic chanting of the conjuror and the cups of tea Gilda held to their lips. On the third day of fever, Gilda stiffened in horror when she looked at the strong body of her husband and saw that his bronzed skin had erupted in small red spots. Great wailing came from other huts as entire families were affected, and the conjuror danced himself into exhaustion as he pleaded with the gods of wind, rain, and fire to send healing to his people.

Gilda prayed to her God, too, as on the sixth day the small red spots grew into angry, pus-filled blisters. Her robust husband, who could doubtless walk through burning coals without flinching, wailed in misery as he thrashed upon the furs she had spread under him. Every inch of his body was affected with the painful boils, particularly his hands and feet. He could not walk, nor could he handle any object without extreme pain. There was no comfortable position in which he could rest, no fur soft enough to ease his suffering.

One by one, others of the village came down with fever and the spots until only Gilda and a few of the children remained free from illness. Gilda directed the children to help her move the sick into two adjacent huts—one for women, one for men—then she sent the healthy children to a third hut, away from contagion. She nursed the feeble as best she could, then sat and prayed for her patients as Edith had taught her: "Hear me, Almighty and most merciful God and Savior; extend thy accustomed goodness to these who are grieved with sickness. Sanctify, I beseech thee, this thy fatherly concern to them; that the sense of their weakness may add seriousness to their repentance: That, if it be thy good pleasure to restore them to their former health, they may lead the residue of their life in thy fear and to thy glory."

Once, after she finished praying, the village werowance broke into miserable screeching and cursed her for coming to Ramushonnouk. For more than an hour he raved about the evil of her blue eyes and the affliction of sickness she had brought upon them all. When he finally fell silent, Gilda looked at him and in a ghastly moment of recognition saw that he was dead. There was no one to embalm the chief's body, no one to mourn him. Gilda pulled the corpse outside, wrapped it in buckskin, and waited for the next to die.

The older people died first, then the babies. On the twelfth day of her vigil she noticed that Anakausuen's blisters had begun to crust and heal, and she held every hope that he would recover. But a cry from the women's hut called her away from his side, and she hurried there in time to recite a prayer for an old woman who struggled for her life's last breaths:

"O Father of mercies and God of all comfort, our only help in time of need," Gilda prayed, the memorized words automatically springing to her lips. "We fly unto thee for succor in behalf of this thy servant, here lying under thy hand in great weakness of body. Look graciously upon her, O Lord; and the more the outward man decayeth, strengthen her, we beseech thee, so much the more continually with thy grace and Holy Spirit in the inner man. Give her unfeigned repentance for all the errors of her life past, and steadfast faith in thy son Jesus; that her sins may be done away by thy mercy, and her pardon sealed in heaven, before she go hence and be no more seen."

The woman exhaled and did not breathe again. Gilda lay her fingers upon the two blistered eyelids and closed the dark eyes forever.

While the other women's miaowing wails of sorrow tore through her heart, Gilda pulled four dead women out of the hut and lay them with the body of the chief. Wearily, she paused and leaned against a tree to consider her plight. Had God brought her out from the English to destroy her own people? She could not deny that the sickness had begun in the very hour that Anakausuen took her to be his wife. Had God cursed her for marrying a so-called heathen? Was the failure of her healing gifts part of a harsh God's penance?

"You must come." One of the children tugged on her skirt and pointed toward the men's hut. With a helpless wave of her hands, Gilda followed the little boy to Anakausuen's sprawled body. A pool of blood, not yet congealed, bloomed in a small puddle beneath his proud head. The English knife lay in his hand.

In a moment of atavistic horror, Gilda realized what had happened. Too proud to struggle under the pain, her husband had cut his own throat.


▾▲▾▲▾ Weeping silently, Gilda removed the knife from the hut, then dragged the body of Anakausuen to the others. With curt words and sharp gestures she directed the children to bring wood and the belongings of the dead; these were placed on and around the wrapped bodies, and they lit the first funeral pyre.

It would not be the last.

She made the children stand behind her as the fire blazed, and the horrible smell of burning flesh and hair filled the air as the tongues of fire leapt and danced in the orange-tinted darkness. When the flames had died down, Gilda sent the children to sleep in their hut. Tomorrow she would send them far away to another village where the killing strength of death's arm did not summon every woman and warrior.

Someone called weakly from the women's hut, but Gilda did not answer. What could she do? Nothing. She had suffered in the past at the hand of God, but never had she been surrounded by such pain that she had to close her heart and mind to it lest she go insane.

Her worthy husband lay blackened in death; her new village was a cesspit of disease; her dreams and hopes nothing but ashes in the funeral firepit.

She lay down on the ground in front of the fire and watched the gleaming embers until sleep claimed her.

▼▲▼▲▼ Three men and two women remained alive at the end of the second week. Gilda thought the men might recover, as long as they did not resist the pain so violently that they exhausted their strength. She prayed for a long time over one warrior, a young man who had not spoken since staggering into the hut two weeks before. He lay quietly, his body ravaged by the pox, his eyes closed, but once or twice she thought she saw his lips struggle to form words as she prayed "and in the name of the Father, and the Son, and the—"

"Holy Ghost."

She gasped, amazed that he should know those English words. Leaning forward, she studied him closely. His skin was bronzed in color, his hair dark and worn like the others of this village, his face composed of straight lines and clean features. Despite the disease, she could tell that his body possessed the slenderness and strength of youth, but his arms and shoulders were tattooed with the mark of a tribe she did not recognize. She studied the tattoo. An *x* was drawn within it . . . or was it a cross?

She whispered to him in the Algonquin tongue: "Are you

awake?" His eyes flew open, and Gilda felt a chill shock at the sight of them. Green, they were, the color of the river in summer when plants grow near to the surface, of the forest after summer rains. Gilda had never seen green eyes in the face of an Indian.

"How did you learn of the Holy Ghost?" she whispered, tenderly resting her hand upon his flaming chest. "The English name of God?"

He made a weak effort to smile and lifted his shoulder in what passed for a shrug. "I do not know," he answered, his voice laced with suffering.

"You finished my prayer to the true God," she said, settling back to observe him more closely. He was past the worst of the sickness. His skin was crusted with the blisters, though not one inch of his body had been spared from pain. "What is your name?" she asked.

Apparently even speaking was painful, for he grimaced with the effort. "Nosh," he answered finally.

"And have you lived always with this tribe?"

"Yes," he murmured, and though Gilda pressed him further, he would not speak again. Wary of causing him undue pain, she left him to rest.

That night Gilda stood beneath a black sky, icy with a wash of brilliant stars, and wondered why the Creator God had added another facet to her suffering. The youth in the hut was of certain Fallon's brother, for Nosh was an adult version of the name Noshi. Despite her prayers, he would die like the others. If she ever saw Fallon again, she would have to tell him that she had brought disease to the village of his beloved brother. Fallon's love would turn to loathing, and he would rue the day he had ever boarded the great winged ship that returned him to this land of death and destruction.

The next day she prayed again over Nosh and heard him whisper his thanks. The other two warriors, sensing that they had little strength left, began the undulating wails of their death songs, determined to show death that they faced him without fear. Nosh, however, continued to breathe deeply and evenly.

Because her prayers seemed to bring him comfort, Gilda stayed by his side throughout the day and offered every quotation from Mistress Rolfe's *Book of Common Prayer* that she could remember.

At length the two warriors grew silent and stiffened, and Nosh's breathing slowed. Gilda took his hand and pressed it to her cheek as tears began to flow, and the green eyes opened again and smiled up at her.

"Numees," he whispered, and she understood what he meant: sister.

"Yes," she answered, pressing her lips into his palm with an affection she had not felt even for her dying husband. "Tell me, if you can, does the name Fallon mean anything to you?"

The ghost of a smile played across Nosh's face. "Yes," he answered, his voice rasping. "My dead brother."

Gilda's eyes flooded with tears. Why had God gifted Nosh with memories while she had none? But it wasn't important now; she had to tell him that Fallon had not died.

"Fallon is alive; he is with the English," she said, bending closer. "He has been searching for you, but he thought you lived with the Tripaniks. He is at Jamestown, and when you are better I will take you to him."

Nosh struggled to catch his breath as mingled expressions of eagerness and fear crossed his face. "Opechancanough will attack the English soon," he whispered, holding her with a steady gaze. "You must warn my brother. Jamestown will be destroyed; everything English will be wiped from the land."

"That's impossible," Gilda said, smoothly raking his hair from his sweaty forehead. She forced a smile. "One tribe cannot rid the land of the English—"

"All the Powhatan tribes," Nosh broke in, his eyes darkening. "Every warrior will fight. Every English will die. It is settled."

Gilda's smile faded as the full import of his words hit her. No wonder Opechancanough sent her far away! He suspected that she would not support an uprising against the English. To prevent her from warning them as Pocahontas had often done, he had sent her away with a worthy husband so she would not suspect that she did not remain in his favor. She flinched, stunned and saddened by her own gullibility.

"When will this attack take place?" she asked, frantic, but Nosh's eyes had closed and he could no longer hear her.

▼▲▼▲▼ Nosh roused himself briefly the next day, and his green eyes locked on hers as Gilda washed the suppurating sores on his flesh. "You are Gilda," he said simply, as if the truth had just occurred to him. "You still wear the ring."

"Yes," she answered, a smile softening her lips. "I understand that we are old friends."

His lips curved into a smile that did not reach his eyes. "Gilda, I am ready to die."

A sob caught at her throat, but his eyes held hers and she understood what he wanted. Not for him a death song, but a prayer, the prayer of faith for those who followed the true God, the Father of Jesus Christ.

Gilda put down the soft washcloth and held Nosh's swollen hands in her own. "Almighty God," she prayed, keeping her eyes locked on her patient's face, "I humbly commend the soul of this thy servant, my dear brother, into thy hands, as into the hands of a faithful Creator and most merciful Savior; most humbly beseeching thee, that it may be precious in thy sight. Wash it, I pray thee, in the blood of that immaculate Lamb that was slain to take away the sins of the world, that it may be presented pure and without spot before thee. Amen."

Leaning over Nosh, she murmured a question: "Believe you in God?"

His parched lips cracked open: "I believe in God the Father, who made me and all the world."

"And in the Son?"

"I believe in God the Son, who has redeemed me and all mankind."

"And in the Holy Ghost?"

"Who sanctifieth me and all the elect people of God."

"Then go in peace, my brother." Leaning forward, she pressed her lips to his.

▼▲▼▲▼ Nosh did not speak again, but died on the second day of Gilda's own fever. She used her remaining strength to place his body with the others before lighting the pyre. Enervated by the stress of nursing and the fever that raged through her body, she slumped to the ground and watched the flames rise and claim the last of her people.

The black smoke climbed to the low-hanging clouds and then curled in upon itself like a dark and angry flower as Gilda closed her eyes in weariness. It was finished. She had done all she could do, and there was no one left.

Fallon's patience had nearly evaporated when he finally found Brody in the public house. Brody sat with his feet propped up on the table and a mug in his hand, and Fallon came forward and gave his friend a killing look.

"What?" Brody asked, his eyes widening innocently. "What'd I do?"

"It is what you didn't do," Fallon answered, pulling up a stool. "You were supposed to burn off the corn shucks of Mistress Rolfe's field today, but spring will be upon us before you get your sorry carcass out to take care of it."

"Faith, I'll do it in a wee bit," Brody said, waving his mug carelessly. "What's the rush?"

"I want to get things straightened away at the house," Fallon said, frowning at the sheaf of papers he pulled from his doublet. "There's a ship just arrived at the docks, and undoubtedly there'll be a new lot of men to care for. And that field has to be made ready for the spring planting, and Wart needs a new pair of shoes from the cobbler. There's precious little money to take care of everything, and yet I think we should—" He broke off suddenly.

"What?" Brody asked, his eyes gleaming with sudden interest. He thumped his feet to the floor and leaned over the table. "You've got that spark in your eye, Fallon. Are you thinking we should journey upriver?"

"It has been over a year since Gilda left us," Fallon said, running his finger idly over the surface of the table. "Lately I've felt that maybe a trip to Weromacomico would be in order. Just to be

sure, mind you—" he pointed a finger at Brody—"just to be sure
all is well with her."

"You are worried about the little vixen," Brody said, his eyes
squinting with amusement.

"No," Fallon protested, shaking his head. "Just concerned,
like a brother. She is too outspoken for her own good and too
rash in her decisions. I just want to make certain that she's well."

"It is fine by me," Brody said, slamming his mug on the table.
"I'd rather journey into the outland than work in the fields any
day."

"There's only one thing," Fallon said, pulling a tattered parchment from the sheaf of papers in his hand. "We'll need goods if
we're going to trade with the Indians, and we haven't the money
for copper and trinkets right now. We have only this."

He pushed the bride warrant across the table and held his
breath until Brody shrugged. "I don't want an English bride,"
Brody said. "Haven't I said so more than once?"

"I wanted to be sure you hadn't changed your mind. I don't
want one either." Fallon sighed in relief. "Then it is settled. We'll
offer the warrant to a merchant. Surely it is still worth two hundred pounds of tobacco."

"At least," Brody said, his eyes flashing with the first real
interest Fallon had seen in months. "When do we leave?"

"As soon as we barter our goods," Fallon answered, smiling.
"And as soon as you burn off Mistress Rolfe's field."

▼▲▼▲▼ The warrant was as good as gold, the merchant told Fallon, and in exchange for it he received a cask of
beads and copper trinkets, several copper pots, a half dozen blankets, and an assortment of knives and axes. The merchant had
long been in the business of equipping men for trade with the
Indians, and he even threw in a canoe when Fallon insisted that
a bride was of certain worth more than a load of hard goods.

Fallon made sure that Wart and Edith were well equipped to
handle the hospital while he and Brody were away, then they

loaded the canoe and turned it into the James River. Brody rode
at the front, paddling energetically, and Fallon sat at the back,
steadying the canoe as they followed the blinding dazzle of the
sun's path on the quiet water.

It seemed a lifetime ago that they had traveled in just this way
up the river. On that first excursion with the two ministers they
had been clothed almost visibly in naïveté and inexperience.
After nearly losing their lives at the hands of the savages, they
had returned home empty-handed but for Gilda. Fallon smiled
at the memory. Worth the risk, that trip was—as was this one.

They traveled mostly in silence, though Brody often whistled
with the excitement of the journey. Fallon wondered whether his
friend was excited to be seeking the adventure he had long
craved or if he looked forward to finding Gilda and pressing his
suit with her again. Brody was always restless for fresh horizons,
but whether he sought them in the wilderness or in Gilda's arms,
Fallon could not tell.

▼▲▼▲▼ Through the day and night they traveled,
sleeping in fitful naps in the canoe. Eager for adventure, Brody
seemed grateful for Fallon's sense of urgency, but with each mile
Fallon felt his apprehension and anxiety increase. He couldn't
explain it, but since hearing of the illness among the Indians,
he'd felt compelled to make this trip. He was only sorry he'd put
it off this long.

The river itself seemed strangely quiet as they journeyed westward. They passed a few English boats, whose crews saluted
them and drifted by without comment, but the usual Indian
scouts and traders did not appear. Nervous flutterings pricked
Fallon's heart as they moved further upstream into savage lands.

His heart was actually pounding when they landed near
Weromacomico. They beached the canoe, then shouldered their
goods and followed the trail toward Opechancanough's village.
Brody talked and joked while they walked, obviously in high
spirits, but Fallon peered through the undergrowth for signs of

life. He had the uneasy feeling that a hundred eyes watched them, but no one shouted a warning and no spears parted the evergreens to threaten them.

Finally they approached the gates of the town, and a group of women welcomed them noisily, pointing and jabbering at the various pots and goods that hung from the bundles on their backs. "Soon," Fallon told them. "After we talk with Opechancanough."

The women led them into the village, and Fallon saw Opechancanough's warriors standing like posts throughout the settlement, their arms hanging rigidly at their sides as if they waited for a sign or signal that had not come. He was about to say something to Brody about the grim aspect of the warriors' faces when a woman pointed him into the hut where the great chief waited.

Fallon and Brody stooped to enter and found the great chief sitting with his arms crossed. Again Fallon was struck by the ageless qualities of the chief's face and body. He had not changed since the day he had taunted Fallon with death so many years before. The gruesome scar still gleamed white against his bronzed cheek; a shadowy sneer still hovered about his thin mouth.

"We have come to trade, great chief," Fallon said, hoping Opechancanough would not recognize him. "And to inquire about a woman called Kimi."

Opechancanough's face darkened, and Fallon realized in that instant that the chief remembered more than enough to rekindle his anger. "You were told never to come back here," he thundered in English, his hand reaching forward as if to strangle them. "You came with the men of God!"

"We have come alone now," Fallon answered, hanging his head in what he hoped was a properly respectful attitude. "We have not come with the ministers. We seek only the girl. She is a friend, and we have brought gifts to her and her people."

Opechancanough stared at Fallon with deadly concentration, then his face cracked into a twisted smile. "The woman you speak of has gone to Ramushonnouk," he said, nodding gravely. "Her husband has taken her there."

"Her husband?" Fallon said, cutting a look from the chief to Brody. He should have known. She was more than old enough to be married and probably eager to love a warrior who was everything Fallon was not.

"Yes," the chief answered, folding his arms again. "The village is a three-day journey to the south."

"Three days?" Brody groaned. "Fallon, we'll never make it carrying all this stuff—"

Without another word, Fallon slipped the bundle of goods from his shoulders and presented it to Opechancanough. "We thank you," he said, pulling Brody's bundle from his back. "And we give these to honor you."

Opechancanough nodded and accepted the gifts with an inscrutable expression. Brody opened his mouth as if to speak, but fell silent when Fallon shot him a warning glance. They left the chief's house and the village, then followed the southern trail away from the river.

"Why'd you have to give him everything?" Brody complained once they were away from the prying eyes and ears of the Powhatan. "We could have used some of those goods for trading along the way—"

"We are not traders," Fallon answered, quickening his pace as the inner voice urged him to hurry. "We had to leave behind anything that would slow us down."

"Why are you in such a hurry to find Gilda and her husband?" Brody called, a taunting note in his voice as Fallon pushed ahead. "She won't like you barging in on her. She'll be mad as a cat, so why are you wanting to find her?"

"Only God knows," Fallon answered, not caring if Brody kept up.

▾▴▾▴▾ When the two Englishmen had gone, Opechancanough allowed his counselors and priests to look through the bundles. They exclaimed with great joy over the axes and knives and placed the beads and copper pots outside the hut for the women. Each elder took a blanket for himself, but Opechancanough sat before the display of treasures and stared moodily into the darkening twilight.

"Why did you allow the clothed men to go?" the priest asked, his new blanket securely around his shoulders. "You could have killed them and still you would have had the goods."

"The time is not yet right for killing," Opechancanough answered softly, his eyes fastened on the shining blades of the knives before him. "That time will come when the Englishmen believe they dwell in safety. We must act in love and peace until the hour comes to drive the English from the land."

He leaned forward and picked up one of the knives. It seemed alive in his hand, and it bit through his flesh as he ran his palm over it. Opechancanough held his hand aloft for his elders to see, and they watched in silence as a thin red line appeared as if by magic, then swelled and began to drip blood.

"When the time is right, thus shall the English be, cut and bleeding," Opechancanough said. He ran his tongue over the blood, tasting his planned revenge, as his elders threw back their heads in a triumphant war cry.

▼▲▼▲▼ Fallon and Brody wandered in the cold and leafless woods for five days, stumbling upon two different Indian villages before they finally found the palisade that surrounded Ramushonnouk. An eerie silence hung over the place—the quiet of night shadows that seemed strangely out of place in the middle of the day.

No guards stood at the palisade gate, no cook fires lofted smoke into the wide blue sky. Fallon gave Brody an uneasy glance as they approached, and a suddenly cold wind brushed the back of his neck and lifted goosebumps along his arms. His scalp tingled beneath his cap when he saw buzzards circling above the village.

They passed through the open gates, and a pair of thin, growling dogs loped into their path. Brody picked up a stick and tossed it in their direction, and the dogs took flight immediately.

The circle of huts stood silent and empty within the palisade. A blanket hung from a bare tree and flapped forlornly in the wind. Somewhere a dog whined. A stack of clay pots waited for the women near abandoned, cold firepits, and two deerskins had been stretched upon frames that wobbled unsteadily as if ghosts tested the tautness of the supports.

Fallon quickened his pace toward the center of the village where the central fire should have been burning. A mound of ashes and charred remains lay cold in the firepit, and he felt his gorge rise when he recognized the twisted shapes of human corpses. He brought his hand before his eyes to block the sight.

"What has happened here?" Brody asked in an aching voice Fallon scarcely recognized. "A massacre? An enemy tribe?"

Fallon looked around at the empty dwellings. "No enemy would burn the dead," he said, pausing to peer into one of the huts. The place was empty save for a pile of grass mats and bowls in one corner of the room. There was no sign of bloodshed, no rotting corpses, no evidence of treachery. But where was Gilda? Would he have to sort through the blackened bodies in the firepit to find her?

A small brown dog lurched into his path and paused to gaze at Fallon with mournful eyes, then sat down and threw back his head, howling pitifully. Fallon extended his fingers and made a soft clucking sound. "What can you tell me, pup?" he asked, as the dog slowly came forward. "What has happened here?"

The dog placed his head on Fallon's hand trustingly, then suddenly jerked away and rushed toward a pair of curs who were slinking toward one of the huts. The curs growled and bared their teeth for an instant, then retreated under the small dog's fierce defensive posture. The brown dog barked again, then slipped into the hut and disappeared from sight.

"Do you suppose she's got pups in there?" Brody asked, staring after the dog.

Fallon didn't answer, but sprinted toward the hut. A body lay just inside in the doorway with a blanket loosely wrapped around the head and shoulders. It was a woman, Fallon realized as he drew nearer, and he held his breath for a moment as he lifted the blanket.

"Father God, I cry you mercy!" he whispered when he saw the circle of gold at the woman's neck. It was Gilda who lay there, but he would not have known her at all. Her eyes were closed, and her golden skin marred by angry, oozing pustules that combined to bloat her facial features beyond recognition. Her limbs had swollen as well, though from her parched lips and dry skin Fallon doubted that she had found food or water in days. Her skin carried the flush of fever, but her lips were blue with cold.

"What is it?" Brody asked from a distance, uncertainty and fear ringing in his voice.

"It is Gilda," Fallon called over his shoulder. Brody started forward and Fallon flung up his hand. "Stay back! It is the pox. You should go back to Jamestown, Brody, and warn the others not to venture southward. I had heard that several Indian villages were infected."

Brody shifted his weight uneasily as if uncertain that he should go, but Fallon turned the full intensity of his gaze upon him. "You can do nothing for me here, Brody, so go back to Jamestown. If you get to the river, a merchant ship will pick you up. You will be safe. If Opechancanough wanted us dead, we'd never have made it this far."

He knelt by Gilda's side and lifted her head into his arms. She felt weightless in his grasp, but he thanked God that she still breathed.

"Are you quite sure I should go?" Brody called.

"Yes," Fallon said, looking up as quick-moving shadows of clouds skimmed over the empty village. "Don't feel that you have to stay. I don't know that she'll make it, and I—"

He paused. How did he tell Brody that he might not return to Jamestown? If Gilda died, he would never be able to spend another day in the settlement whose citizens had ignored her unfailing compassion and spat upon her. He had not been there to protect her from their hateful ignorance, and in his blindness he had allowed her to leave. Dear heaven, he'd opened the gate and practically told her to return to the savages. She'd left safety only to come to this. . . .

He cleared his throat. "Go back to Jamestown, Brody, and take care of Edith and Wart. Don't send help and don't worry. But pray for us."

Brody nodded and hurried away, his shoulders relaxing in the posture of relief. When he had gone, Fallon lifted Gilda and carried her from the village of death.

# Opechancanough

*The heart knoweth his own bitterness;*
*and a stranger doth not intermeddle with his joy.*

*Proverbs 14:10*

A well-worn trail curved outside the palisade, and Fallon fol-
lowed it, certain it would lead to water. The air around him
seemed as lifeless as the deserted village, the winter light melancholy and filled with shadows. Gilda groaned once in his arms,
and the sound startled him so that he almost lost his footing. He
could scarce believe that life still remained in a body so ravaged
by disease.

About a quarter mile down the trail he caught sight of a meandering stream at the bottom of a gully, and he stepped carefully
down the steep embankment toward the healing water below.

Gilda's flesh burned beneath his hands, so he found a shallow
spot and laid her in the cold stream. She gasped when the chilly
rivulets poured over her skin, and he cupped his hands and
splashed more water over her limbs. With the professional
detachment he'd developed while working with the sick and
injured, he removed her stained garment and tenderly wiped her
oozing flesh with a soft pad of moss.

As he poured water across Gilda's parched lips, her eyes flew
open and she looked straight at him. "I am here to take care of
you," he whispered, smoothing her damp hair from her forehead. "It is your turn to rest, Gilda."

When her fevered body at last began to shiver, he wrapped
her in a blanket and laid her beneath a shelter he had fashioned
by stringing his cloak between two trees. He would not take her
back to the village. He had seen enough sickness aboard
crowded ships to know that through some mischief of devilry
contagion could lurk in physical spaces.

He scooped a narrow crevice into the soil beneath the shelter and placed Gilda into the slender space, knowing the earth would cool the fevered warmth of her body. Over the crevice he threw another blanket, then he lay down upon the edge of the covering, shielding her body with his own as sun departed and the dark winter winds blew harsh and cold.

▼▲▼▲▼ The next day Fallon left Gilda sleeping and scouted about the area. Further up the steep hill he found a rocky overhang that formed a small cave. The cavern was not large, barely deep enough to shelter a sleeping man, but it would afford protection from the wind and rain. After checking on Gilda again, he retrieved furs, clean blankets, and a pot from Ramushonnouk. Inside the cave he fashioned a bed from a length of blankets covered with rabbit skins, the softest fur he could imagine for Gilda to lie upon. Then he carried her from her earthen cradle to the cave, and over her he placed a heavy bear-skin.

The second, third, and fourth days passed as a blur of pain and struggle. Each morning Fallon carried Gilda to the cooling waters of the stream and sponged her ravaged skin. She screamed at the icy touch of the waters, and begged in Algonquin and English for death to come and relieve her of her misery. At other times she lifted her eyes to the barren sky and demanded to know why God had chosen to afflict her since birth, since she had done nothing to offend him. Fallon did not answer her rash charges, knowing that she spoke in the delirium of fever. She seemed not to know who held her and cared for her.

Each morning, after the waters of the stream had cooled her inflamed skin, Fallon carried her back to the cave, then poked around in the rocks to find food. The rattlesnakes of Virginia did not appreciate being disturbed in the middle of winter, but Fallon managed to trap three. With a forked stick he pinned their writhing heads and, using a sharpened stone for a knife, beheaded them with a clean stroke. After slitting the belly and removing the innards, Fallon skinned the animals, then shred-

ded the meat into thin slivers. Because she was still too weak to
eat herself, he chewed Gilda's meat for her, then slipped it inside
her mouth and offered water until she swallowed.

Often she would stir beneath him in the night, her fever raging, and once she opened her eyes in a bright flash of recognition. "Give me your knife, Fallon," she demanded, her hot breath
striking him in the face like a physical blow. "Why does God
make me endure this? What sin have I committed? I tried to save
them all, but they died in my arms. . . ."

Her words ebbed away as did her strength, and Fallon lifted
her weightless body and struggled down the hill to the stream to
cool her fever once again.


▼▲▼▲▼ He felt like shouting with joy on the morning
when he awoke and Gilda had no fever. Lifting the bearskin, he
saw that the sores on her arms and chest had begun to crust, so
he did not take her to the river lest he disturb the healing process. Her eyes opened at some point while he examined her, and
he flushed when he realized that she had been watching him.

"Good morrow," he said, feeling his cheeks burn. He dropped
the bearskin over her body to preserve her modesty. "You are better today. I'll go down to the stream and bring up some water—"

"Fallon." Her voice was little more than a whisper, and he
leaned forward to listen. "Are they all dead?"

He paused, wondering what to tell her, then he nodded. Her
eyes closed in defeat as her chin quivered. "Noshi . . . ," she said,
tears wetting her lashes.

"Noshi will wait for us," Fallon said, efficiently rearranging
her bed. "You must get well before we look for him."

"No," she protested, and her ice-blue eyes met his again. "He
is dead. He died despite my prayers."

"You are not well," Fallon said, forcing a smile. "You only
think you saw him. Indeed, many times I have imagined his face
in every warrior I see—"

"Let me die," she whispered again, and with a great effort she lifted her scarred hand to grasp the edge of his coat. "Life is a journey toward death, so let me pass to the other side. Leave me, Fallon, and I will follow Noshi—"

"Shhh, rest now," Fallon answered, gently lowering his hand across her eyes. Obediently, her eyes closed and a moment later she was asleep.

But her words echoed in his mind as he searched for food, and he wondered what she had meant.

▼▲▼▲▼ Now that Gilda's body had determined to mend, Fallon was forced to reenter the ghost village to search for stores of substantial food. He found the community's winter provisions, buried pots of ground corn and dried beans, and was able to cook adequate meals for the recovering invalid and his own appetite. But he refused to return Gilda to the village where she had endured the nightmare of disease. Part of him idly wondered if his reluctance sprang from a desire to help her forget the man who had been her husband. Had she loved him?

A mocking voice inside insisted on answers, so one afternoon he decided to discover the truth. As he sprinted up the hill with a bowl of boiled squash and pumpkin, he was glad to see that she was awake and waiting for him. He had combed and cleaned her hair with dried herbs and sewn her a new buckskin dress from the softened hides he'd found in the village. Though her skin still bore the ravages of the disease, the pustules had begun to heal. She looked surprisingly pretty.

She demurely smiled her thanks as he approached, and he wondered if she was more grateful for the food or for his help. As he lay the bowl beside her, he gathered the courage to voice his questions.

"At Ramushonnouk," he said, offering her a wooden spoon from his pocket, "did you live with a husband?"

She accepted the spoon, but her eyes flew to his in a question. "How did you know?"

Fallon sank onto a blanket beside her bed in the cave and

made an effort to shrug as if the matter were of no more than casual interest. "Opechancanough told us you had married. Did you . . . ," he paused, the words forming reluctantly on his tongue. "Did you love this man you married?"

A faint smile played upon her lips before she lifted her eyes to his. "He was a brave and comely warrior. Opechancanough did me great honor by choosing him as my husband."

"So you loved him, then." Fallon wondered why he had ever imagined that she had not. She had always loved all things Indian, why not a warrior? It was folly to ever consider that she might hold anything more than affection for him, for he was too rigid, too stern, too English to suit her.

"I scarcely knew Anakausuen," she answered, dipping the flat spoon into the bowl. "He took ill with the fever and was one of the first to die." She paused to scratch her arms. "Name of a name, Fallon, can you find an ointment to stop this itching? I will scratch my skin off if it continues."

"You are better," he said, grinning at her, his good nature restored. "You are complaining again."

"No," she said, suddenly serious. She leaned toward him, and her nearness made Fallon's heart pound. "I have news, Fallon, that will be hard for you to hear."

"Say it." He braced himself for the worst. *She is in love with Brody; she is with child; she is—*

"I found Noshi."

He pulled away, realizing that she was completely lucid and telling the truth. "Noshi?" The word came from his soul like a prayer.

She nodded, and her eyes darkened with pain. "He lived in Ramushonnouk all his life; he was never sold into slavery as you feared. The pox had nearly taken him when I found him, but he knew me, Fallon, and he remembered you."

Fallon lowered his head to his knees, overcome by the knowledge too bittersweet to fathom. Noshi was dead, but he had remembered. Another of Opechancanough's prophecies had failed, for some kind soul had disobeyed the order to sell the boy into slavery and had instead raised him as a Powhatan.

"He bade me tell you that Opechancanough has ordered the extermination of the English," Gilda went on, pressing her hands to her forehead as though the news pained her. "He did not know when the attack would come. But he bade me warn you."

"He remembered me?" Fallon asked, looking at her through a blurred haze of tears. "Did he know I was searching for him?"

Gilda nodded. "He also remembered the one true God," she said, lowering her voice. "As death approached, he did not cry out in a death song like the others, but bade me pray for him. I put his body onto the burial pyre with the others and sent his soul to heaven."

For an instant an indescribable wave of jealousy overwhelmed Fallon, for Gilda, not he, had been the one to find and shelter Noshi! But God, in his great mercy, had let Noshi know that Fallon cared. It was enough, knowing that.

Gilda tugged gently on his sleeve. "I have prayed that you would not hate me," she said, genuine tears shining in her eyes. "I tried to save him. I tried to save all of them. But the fever would not leave and I could not feed and tend them all. In the end, I was the only one left. I brought the disease upon them and I wanted to die, too. I do not know why God did not let me die—"

"You didn't bring the disease," Fallon said, reaching for her hand. He gave it a comforting squeeze. "We have seen the disease of late in men aboard ship, and it strikes them two weeks after they have been exposed to another with the pox. The people of this village were stricken long before you came, Gilda. You are not to blame for their deaths."

She stared at his face, into his eyes, and he could tell by the way her haunted eyes shone with relief that she believed him. He pulled her into his arms for a gentle embrace, then lifted the bearskin so she could lie down and rest. Surprisingly pliant, she obeyed and soon fell asleep.

Sleep would not come to Fallon, though, and he sat motionless for a long time, pondering the threat of an Indian attack and wondering why God had not spared Noshi long enough for Fallon to find him.

▼▲▼▲▼ Though heavy sleep still fogged her mind, Gilda sensed a change in the atmosphere and awoke. A gloomy gray fog seemed to thicken and congeal in the cave around her as gusts of bitterly cold wind blew past the opening of the cavern and worried the skeletal branches of the trees. The atmosphere was heavy with impending rain, and ghostly mists whirled and danced over the hillside like phantoms from the conjuror's tales.

"Fallon!" she screamed, the hard fist of fear growing in her stomach. "Fallon!"

The wind snatched her voice and carried it away, but soon Fallon appeared below her on the hill, his skin pale in the fading afternoon light and his hair tangled by the wind. He carried a pile of furs from the village.

"Where were you?" she called, her nerves at a full stretch. "You should not have left without telling me!"

"I had to bury them," Fallon answered, dropping the furs outside the mouth of the cavern. "All of them, since I couldn't tell which one was Noshi. And then the wind freshened, so I gathered more furs. We've a storm coming on, but I think we'll be fine here as long as—"

Without warning, a sharp crack shot through the wild hooting of the wind. A weak branch from one of the leggy trees ripped loose and hurled from the sky overhead. Fallon instinctively flinched, but the branch cracked across his head and shoulders. He crumpled beneath the blow without a sound.

"Fallon!" Gilda shrieked, crawling forward. He lay ten feet beyond the cave, as pale as snow but for a bright red trickle that ran from a cut on his forehead. She knelt beside him, feeling for the pulse of life at his throat, then clasped her hands together in an attitude of prayer. "Dear God, what more will you do to me?"

she cried as the bawling winds mocked her. "Will you take even Fallon?"

As if in answer, rain began to fall, a dense slanting rush of thick drops that slapped sharp as a lance against her tender skin. Weeping, she tried to drag Fallon into the shelter of the cave, but the ground turned to mud beneath her feet and she did not have the strength to pull him through the mire. Finally, she managed to move one of the furs from the pile Fallon had dropped and covered him where he lay. Lifting his head into her lap, she held a lump of wet clay to the cut on his head. "I will not let you take this one," she told the angry heaven as she used her arms to shelter him from the rain. "Not today. You can take my life, God, but you'll not take his."

A blast of cold air rushed from the east, and a howling gust lifted the heavy fur and tossed it down the hill as easily as if it had been made of summer linen. Thoroughly soaked, Gilda lifted her face toward the roiling darkness above the slashing rain. "Take my life, now!" she shouted, lifting her clenched hands.

Deliberately ignoring all the polite and refined prayers she had learned from Edith Rolfe, she let the anger and venom in her heart pour out in the storm: "You have made me suffer all my life. You took Pocahontas and the baby; you took Noshi. You covered me with boils and took whatever beauty I possessed. You made me an orphan and a widow. You made me neither Indian nor English. In this very hour you have struck Fallon and you'll take him, too, so take me instead and be done with me! Kill me, God, for I'm tired of fighting with you!"

Lightning cracked the skies apart in answer, and thunder rumbled over the hillside while Gilda waited. The storm continued to blow its foul winds and strangling rain, but no thunderbolt from heaven struck, nor did the slippery earth open up to devour her.

Fallon's head was heavy and cold in her lap. Tears flowed down her cheeks as she caressed his wet and wounded face. Why had he ever come to find her? He would have been far happier as a respectable and prosperous schoolmaster in England. He had risked his life time after time on account of a promise made years ago and forgotten by everyone but himself.

"And now you will die with me," she whispered, her teeth chattering in the cold. "And all is for naught." Tears of regret streamed down her face. "Why has God done this to you? Why did he not keep you safe? What has he gained in wasting your life?"

The gale increased from warning winds to a great roaring current of air, and Gilda huddled over Fallon's still form and wept for the lost years of happiness he might have had, for his wasted effort on her behalf. Her mind wandered back, picking up the strings of time, recalling Fallon at her side at the Jamestown house, upon the road as they walked from church, within the woods. Then, just when she thought she could not bear another memory, she recalled his voice reading from the Holy Scriptures as he had sat with her and Edith around the dinner table: " *'Yea, I have loved thee with an everlasting love: therefore with lovingkindness have I drawn thee. . . . And I will very gladly spend and be spent for you; though the more abundantly I love you, the less I be loved.' "*

She opened her mouth in a soundless cry as the Spirit of God opened her heart to the truth. The answer was so obvious! Why hadn't she seen it before? Fallon loved her; he had spent his love upon her though she hadn't seen it, had steadfastly resisted it. . . .

God, in his everlasting love and patience, had sent Fallon to save her life, to draw her back to Himself, and though she had resisted Fallon—resisted God—in her time of greatest need, the almighty Father had not struck her down. He had only sent Fallon after her, again and again.

*"I have loved thee with an everlasting love."* The wondrous truth washed over her, sweeping her with clarity and understanding. Opechancanough was wrong! God did listen, he did answer, he did care. For her. Always for her.

Of a sudden Gilda knew that God didn't want her death. He wanted her life. Her surrender.

The muddy ground beneath her knees became the only solid

reality in a shifting world, and Gilda sat motionless as her heart absorbed the truth she had been too proud to understand. She had mistook God's blessings for curses, fortifying her heart in prideful resistance against every loss. Anakausuen had taken his own life rather than face the anguish of the pox; she, too, had yearned for death, holding herself aloof from God's plan and provision for her deliverance.

The rain slackened, the winds calmed, and Gilda shifted automatically to shelter Fallon as her mind riffled through the memories of years past. From the beginning she had resisted men . . . *anyone* . . . who had sought to command her life. She had accepted God's authority in nature and in the affairs of the English. But she had never surrendered her self-will and pride to the Almighty's molding hand. And oh, what a will she had! She winced as she thought of the occasions when she had glared defiantly at John Rolfe, Reverend Whitaker, Reverend Buck, Brody, and especially Fallon. God had given Fallon a deathless love for her, and she had rejected him from the first day he had dared to display his selfless, protective love.

Just as she had rejected God's care. She saw now, clearly, that never had she experienced a loss without a reciprocal gain. God had not taken from her! Indeed, he had provided someone to care for her at each critical stage of her life, and she had been too proud and headstrong to acknowledge his sheltering hand.

She had prided herself on her healing gifts and noble sacrifices, but now her cheeks burned in shame when she considered how Fallon had watched over and cared for her even under the sting of her indifference and scorn.

The wind blew the remnants of rain from the trees, and Gilda looked up. The night had passed, and dawn was spreading a faint, pink light over the eastern horizon. The rains had stopped. Beside her, Fallon stirred, and Gilda breathed a prayer of gratitude for his life.

Fallon groaned, suddenly conscious both of a dull pain in his
head and the fact that he was freezing. His coat, shirt, and
breeches were heavy with water, and mud pulled at his arm
when he raised it to feel the knot throbbing under the hair plas-
tered to his forehead.

He opened his eyes. The sky was clear and blue above him,
the trees black, wet, and still. A bearskin covered him, and he
pushed it away and tried to sit up as his head swam.

He blinked unsteadily. Gilda sat not far away, her face
upturned toward the warmth of the rising sun. Her eyes were
closed and her lips moved soundlessly as if she were praying,
and he hesitated to disturb her. But the air snapped with cold,
and her hair hung dark and wet down her back—

"I will have to nurse you again if you do not stay warm,
Gilda."

Her eyes widened joyously at the sound of his voice and she
flew to him. "Fallon!" she cried, wrapping her arms about his
neck as she planted a happy kiss upon his cheek. "I'm so glad
you are all right! I was afraid you'd die until I realized—"

"It is only a lump," he said, grinning sheepishly as he wondered if he were dreaming. "I've had worse."

"I know." Her smile softened as if she knew a secret, and her
arms relaxed on his shoulders. Fallon blinked at her. Indeed, she
was flesh and blood, and no dream—but Fallon marveled at the
change in her. Her eyes shone with peace and a quiet confidence,
and she seemed infinitely softer than he had ever seen her before.
Had illness wrought this change in her?

"I tried to drag you into the cave," she said, lowering her eyes modestly as she slipped her arms from him. "You should go there now and maybe we can light a fire to keep warm."

He nodded, then struggled to his unsteady feet as she pulled the bearskin from him and followed him to the cavern. The blow to his head had drained him more than he realized, for he fell upon her pile of furs as bright colors exploded in his brain and blocked his vision. "Maybe the fire can wait," he said, closing his eyes.

He felt her slide the bearskin over him, and after a moment he opened his eyes again. She stood before him, bedraggled, scarred, and thin, but her eyes glowed with inner fire as she watched him.

"You are cold, too," he said, turning onto his side and lifting the edge of the bearskin. "You will not get well if you do not stay warm."

She did not resist his invitation, but snuggled against him, wrapping her arms about his waist. He lowered the heavy fur over them both, then carefully positioned his free arm on top of the bearskin. When he heard her sigh contentedly, he wondered if her fever had returned and brought delirium with it.

"Are you well?" he asked, placing his hand upon her forehead. "No fever?"

"None," she murmured happily, resting her forehead against his chin.

"And no pain? No itching?"

"None," she said, tilting her head back to smile at him. "You have saved my life, Fallon Bailie."

"We are even then," he said, trying to position his arm again so he would not inadvertently touch her in an inappropriate way. "You saved mine once, remember?"

"I remember," she said, tightening her grip around his waist. "But it is I who forever will be in your debt. And according to the tradition of my tribe, you can adopt me, make me your slave, kill me, or send me away. But before you do any of these, I want you to know—"

She broke off, and Fallon looked into her eyes. "What?"

She smiled and ran her fingers to his cheek. "I think I began to love you the moment I heard you singing at the torture pole, do you remember? I wondered what sort of Englishman would be brave enough to sing in the face of death. And the song itself seemed familiar in a way."

"It was a song of Ocanahonan," he murmured, stunned at her words. "A hymn."

She nodded. "It was then I knew I could not let you die. But I could not accept your story about my parents, and I could not stand the thought of someone to order and command my life." She flushed and lowered her eyes. "I suppose Pocahontas and I were more than a little spoiled."

"So you hated me," Fallon finished. "I knew you did, and I knew just as surely that you would be lost if you stayed under Opechancanough's influence. His hate will devour him one day, and I feared it would consume you, too. When we were children, Gilda, he taunted me with the prediction that you and Noshi would worship heathen spirits, and that you would grow to forget the true God."

"His soul is sour with bitterness," she said. "And though I would not admit it, I enjoyed life at Jamestown. Edith and I had become close friends while I lived at her house with Pocahontas, and I was secretly glad that you brought me out of the woods. But you kept trying to marry me to Brody, while hinting that you wanted an English bride—"

"I never said such a thing," Fallon interrupted, lightly pressing a finger across her lips.

She thought for a moment, then nodded. "Perhaps Brody put words in your mouth," she allowed, smiling shyly. "But though I wanted to be close to you, you pulled away."

"I truly thought you'd be happier with Brody or Noshi."

"No." She shook her head. "I wanted more than anything for you to want me as a wife, but you never said a word. And then when you opened the gate and allowed me to leave, I thought you'd never care."

"I cared more than you will ever know," Fallon whispered,

the memory of his hurt passing through him like an unwelcome chill. "And I hoped you'd choose to stay."

She sighed, resting her forehead against his. After a moment she spoke again. "I tried to forget you. In everything, even in marrying a warrior, I tried. But God had other plans. And last night, when it appeared that I would lose you forever, I realized that with each trial of my life, I grew angrier at God. I'd be as sour and bitter as Opechancanough unless—"

"Unless what?"

"Unless I relinquished my pride. And in the rain and the storm I knelt and endured the sweet agony of surrender. It was the strangest feeling, Fallon; painful, because I was giving up my life, but wonderful because I could rest in the assurance that God would hold it for me."

Her eyes were mirror brilliant, and she stopped as her chin quivered. When she began to speak again, he was stunned by the sound of tears in her voice. "Know this, Fallon Bailie: I love you with all my heart and soul. God has been good to send you to me."

His heart reacted immediately to her words and the expression in her eyes, and embers he had thought dead and buried suddenly burst into flame at the core of his being. Long-suppressed emotions roughened his voice when he finally was able to speak. "I don't need a child, or a slave, and I've worked too hard to preserve your life to take it now," he said, a little in awe of the woman who filled his arms. "As for sending you away, I've done that one time too many. What other choices does a man of honor have when he saves a maiden's life?"

"Only one," she whispered, her hands slipping up to lock in his hair. He thought she would speak the words he longed to hear, but her gaze suddenly shifted and the light vanished from her eyes. She brought her hands down and covered them beneath the fur.

"What?" he asked, sensing her distress.

"I forgot." She refused to look at him. "Oh, Fallon, must our battles leave us so scarred? If only I had given you my heart when I still had some measure of beauty—"

"Think you that I care about this?" he asked, lifting her wounded hand in his. He pressed her palm against his cheek, parting her clenched fingers. "Or this?" He took her other hand and pressed it to his heart. "Your beauty has always come from within, Gilda. You are caring and compassionate, warm and womanly. It was for you that God made me."

The sun broke into her eyes as he spoke, and she smiled as she curled her fingers around his hands. "Then marry me," she whispered.

"Now?" he chuckled, trying to still the wild pounding of his heart.

"Now," she answered, her eyes shining toward him. "Before God, in this forest chapel. The Almighty knows our hearts and our intent. And I am yours, Fallon, until death parts us and we meet again in heaven."

Without hesitation he tossed back the bearskin and rose to his knees, pulling her up with him. With their hands clasped together, Fallon lowered his forehead to hers. "Almighty Father God," he prayed, lifting his thoughts heavenward even as his hands grasped the most precious earthly being he had ever known, "we consecrate ourselves to you this day. May the marriage of our hearts and souls accomplish more as one than we ever could as two."

He opened his eyes then, and despite the chill of the winter air his body flushed with warmth as Gilda looked up at him.

"Fallon Bailie, before God I surrender my heart and soul and body to you," she said, swaying toward him. "Leaving all others, I will cleave only unto you."

"Gilda Colman," he answered, tremors of rapture catching in his throat, "I accept you as my wife and offer my heart and soul and body in return. I will love you, protect you, and honor you until we join again before God in heaven."

He paused, lost in the wonder of her warmth, and felt his heart skip when she laughed softly. "And God has pronounced us man and wife," she murmured, tightening her hands around his. "And Reverend Buck can do it officially when we next see him."

"God's opinion is more binding than Reverend Buck's," Fallon answered, opening his arms to the warm and welcoming embrace of his wife. The sweet pounding of her heart made him shift closer to her, and the light touch of her lips against his throat unfurled streamers of sensations that hitherto he had only imagined.

▼▲▼▲▼ In the midst of the storm Gilda had thought she would never be warm again, but now she felt like a bird drifting through shafts of sun-brightened air. She snuggled into the warmth of Fallon's arms, desperately wishing that this hour would last forever.

Fallon's lips brushed her forehead, and he sat up in silence, his flesh pale against the darkness of the furs that covered them. She feathered her hands over his back, tempting him to stay, but he turned and kissed her, then resolutely stood up. "If what Noshi told you was true, I have to return to Jamestown," he said, slipping quickly into his shirt and coat. "Everyone at Jamestown thinks the peace with Opechancanough will hold. They will not be prepared for an attack."

"I will go with you," she said, sitting up. "I can't let you go alone. If Opechancanough's scouts tell him that you are out to warn the English—"

"He won't know," Fallon retorted, mischief gleaming in his eyes. "You forget, wife, that I am quite a scout myself. I'll be a passing shadow in the forest, and no Powhatan will see me. With any luck I'll be picked up on the river and will arrive at Jamestown within the week."

Worry jagged through her like a thunderbolt. "You would leave me here?"

In answer, Fallon sank onto the pile of furs and kissed her cheek. "You are not yet strong enough to travel, my love," he said, his breath warm in her ear. "Stay here in the cave. There are enough provisions for a few days, and I'll send help from one of the outlying settlements." He pulled back and caressed her with his eyes. "I won't leave my wife unprotected, and this is the safest place for you now."

Like an awakening giant, anger burst forth from a place of hiding within her. "You can't go!" she cried, wrapping her hands around his arm. "We have just found each other, Fallon, and we don't need the others! Forget them and stay with me!"

He pulled away, a wounded expression in his eyes. "You would have me leave Edith, Wart, and Brody to the mercy of Opechancanough?"

"Wouldn't they leave you?" she asked, not caring that her words were bitter and reckless. "Why are you here alone, Fallon? Where are your comrades? Where is your fast friend, Brody? Did he turn and run back to Jamestown at the first sign of trouble?"

Fallon didn't answer, and Gilda knew she had hit upon a truth. She took a deep breath and went on: "They have God to protect them, the same God who has brought us together. Last night, in the storm, I saw that I needed to surrender to God, and I did. And for the first time, I was able to surrender to you. Now that I have, I love you more than life itself. Would you risk your life and our happiness to warn stiff-necked people who aren't going to listen?"

"They will listen," Fallon answered stubbornly. He pulled a deerskin from the cave and tossed it over his shoulder. "I must go. I swear to you that I will return."

She watched, disbelieving, as he tossed a handful of dried corn and peas into a leather pouch and tied it around his waist. "You truly intend to leave me," she whispered, more a statement than a question.

"I cry you mercy," he whispered, begging for understanding. "I must!" He knelt beside her as if he would kiss her again, but Gilda turned her head away. After a moment, he spoke in a ragged voice: "Know this, Gilda, that I love you more than my life, but I cannot love you more than God! I will return to you, I swear it. But God has answered my prayers in leading me to you and Noshi, and he demands that I care for his people. The English must be warned, and for some reason, God has given me the responsibility to do it. There is no one else."

"Then take me with you."

"No. You are not as strong as you think."

His hand fell upon her head, imploring her to turn and kiss him farewell, but she stubbornly kept her face averted until she heard him stand and move away. The wet, dead leaves of winter muffled his footsteps as he moved down the hill toward the stream, and Gilda choked on the words that would have called him back. Part of her wanted to scream that she would be gone when he returned, that he would never find her, that he had used her heartlessly.

But as the sounds of his movement grew fainter, she knew that his leaving was inevitable. Fallon was a protector by nature, an honorable and godly man, and he could no more stay away from those who needed help than she could imagine life without him.

She curled up into a ball on the bearskin that still smelled faintly of Fallon. Last night she had promised God that she would surrender her self-will. She had not expected her decision to be tested so soon.

▼▲▼▲▼ With every step his feet took northward, Fallon's heart retreated southward until he was ready to race back to the cave and crawl in to Gilda and never come out again. He could happily live and die within her arms, without ever seeing another Englishman or Indian for the rest of his days. But every time he thought of turning back, the faces of Wart and Edith Rolfe flashed across his mind. His feet doggedly carried him forward until he spotted a column of smoke rising from a stand of trees in the distance.

He approached cautiously, fearing he had stumbled onto a Powhatan village, but over the rim of a hill he spied the timber fencing of an English settlement. More than twenty-three hundred colonists lived now in Virginia, and new plantations sprang up like weeds across the wilderness. Three stout wattle-and-daub houses lay in the center of this cleared field, and a handful of men were splitting wood outside one of the buildings.

They stared at him in frank curiosity when Fallon approached and raised his hand in greeting. "I seek your master or mistress," he said simply, and a gangly youth with a blotchy face jerked a dirty thumb toward the largest of the houses.

Fallon ran his hands through his hair to smooth his disheveled appearance, then knocked at the house. A thin, pale woman opened the door and blinked in surprise at the sight of him. "I give you good day, madam," Fallon said, nodding slightly. "I have news for the master and mistress of the plantation."

"I'm the mistress," she said, retreating slightly behind the door. "What news have you?"

Fallon gave her a careful look. She was one of those women who had reached middle age too soon, with taut skin held by a severe bun at the nape of her neck. She wore a decent though faded dress, probably the one she had worn off the boat, and when Fallon shifted his weight she shrank back like a hound that winces whenever his master raises a hand. Her eyes darted nervously past Fallon as though she expected trouble at any moment.

"Your plantation is not far from the place where I left my wife," Fallon said, smiling to put her at ease. "She is too weak to travel, and is resting in a cave a few miles south of the stream that cuts through this property. I'd be very grateful if your husband could send someone to care for her. She's recovered, but I dared not press her on this journey and I wasn't sure what settlements were in this area—"

"Why are you talking to my wife?"

Fallon felt a sharp pang of recognition and whirled toward the harsh voice. Tobias Harden stood behind him, squatter than ever, with the same bulbous nose and rheumy complexion. His pale green eyes glittered with hatred as he glared up at Fallon.

Fallon held up a hand and backed away. "I mean no trouble, sir, I've only come with a warning. I have news that Opechancanough plans to attack all the English settlements soon, so you should take your people and go into Jamestown until the threat is over."

"Leave my land?" Harden threw back his head in a loud guffaw. "You already stole one man from me, and now you want to take my land!"

"Tobias, please," the woman whispered, and Harden clenched his fist and frowned in her direction. With a whimper, she closed the door and disappeared from sight.

"I am not a planter," Fallon said, striving to maintain his dignity. "And I didn't steal a man, but cared for the half-dead boy you left in the street. In this, though, the danger is real, Master Harden, and you'd do well to heed my words. The Powhatan—"

"—are friendly," Harden answered, sneering. He pointed toward the skinned and gutted carcass of a deer hanging from a tree. "I've been trading with them for months. I give them worthless junk, and they do my hunting for me. So I know you are full of lies, and I'll give you two minutes to get off my land before I get my musket."

"There's another matter of some import," Fallon said, retreating before the hateful glow in Harden's eyes. "I left my—"

Harden went inside the house and slammed the door in answer, and Fallon slipped to the side of the building and caught a glimpse of the woman through the window. She looked at him and pointed emphatically toward the fence, and Fallon knew Tobias meant business. "My wife," he mouthed the words. "Will you help my wife?"

She nodded, then waved her hands frantically as Tobias slammed out the door. Fallon darted behind the house and ran for the fence.

▼▲▼▲▼ Tobias circled the settlement, his fist wrapped firmly around his musket, until he was sure the young troublemaker had gone. The man had some gall, appearing from out of the woods and demanding that they leave their land! Truth to tell, he probably had a company of ruffians hidden in the trees. If Tobias had been foolish enough to fall for that ruse, like as not he would come home to find an empty barn, an empty house, and somebody else living on his property.

Megan flinched when he slammed the door, and he glared at her before propping his musket against the wall and taking a seat by the board where his dinner waited. "You were talking to him before I came up," he said, ladling his thick pottage with the wooden spoon she had carefully handed him. "What were you two talking about?"

"Nothing of import," she stammered, averting her eyes. "It was only what he told you—"

"No," he said, clenching his free hand into a fist. "He said something about a woman. I heard the word *she*. What woman?"

Megan paled, but sank to her stool opposite him. "His wife," she said, her voice flat and expressionless. "He said his wife is nearby."

"And why would he be telling you that?" Tobias growled, still glaring at her. "You aren't likely to be dropping in for a cup of tea, are you?"

She shook her head fearfully, and when she did not speak, he slammed his fist down upon the table so suddenly that she jumped. "His wife is sick," she blurted out, wringing her hands. "He left her in a cave upstream, and he wanted to know if we'd help her."

"Sick, eh?" Tobias felt himself grinning. Turnabout was fair play, and maybe it was time for him to play the part of do-gooder. Since that redheaded upstart prided himself on rescuing sick servants, maybe he would pay a visit to the man's sick wife. After all, the knave lived in Jamestown and probably had his pick of the young beauties that arrived regularly aboard the ships.

"We'll find her," he said, attacking the bowl of pottage before him. He felt Megan's stunned silence across the table and looked up at his wife with a smile. "I owe that young man a favor," he said, wiping his lips on the back of his shirtsleeve. "We'll go right away, afore dark. We can't be leaving a young lady alone in the woods, now can we?"

Gilda heard the thrashing sounds and retreated into the darkness at the back of the cave. It was not Fallon approaching, for the intruders moved too clumsily and made too much noise. They also moved unsteadily, as if they were not sure what lay ahead.

"Up there!" she heard a rough voice call in English, and she recoiled against the wall at her back and knew she had made a mistake. She should have hidden in the rocks above where she would have had the opportunity to flee, but she had cut off all escape routes by seeking the shelter of the cave.

Cold terror lay in the pit of her stomach as she hid under the heavy bearskin. She knew she should not be frightened, for Fallon had promised to send help or return for her himself, but a vague premonition held her in the grip of fear. The sounds of movement came closer, and her panic increased when the voices fell to a whisper.

A tired-looking Englishwoman appeared in the mouth of the cave, and Gilda felt her uneasiness subside somewhat. The woman tilted her head when their eyes met, and she extended her hand with a tentative smile. "Come," she said simply, motioning forward, but Gilda hesitated.

"Your husband has red hair, does he not?" the woman asked, gesturing again. "He sent us to help you."

Gilda slowly rose to her feet. The woman looked at her with a mixture of fascination and concern, and Gilda stepped carefully forward to meet her. When at last they stood face-to-face, the lady smiled and clasped her hands primly in front of her. "I'm Megan," she said, glancing over her shoulder toward someone who remained out of sight. "And that's me husband."

Gilda stepped completely out of the cave to see the man, but she had barely taken his measure when his rough hand whirled her around and clapped over her mouth. "By heaven, the troublemaker took one of the savages to wife," a voice snarled in her ear as iron arms held her tight. A gust of the man's rancid odor assaulted her nostrils. "It is all clear to me now. He hoped we'd leave our land so he and his savage friends could raid the place."

"Tobias, don't," Megan pleaded, honest fear in her face. "If he meant us harm, why would he tell me about his wife?"

"Because he's a fool," the man answered, and Gilda struggled in his grip only to feel his arms tighten around her. He laughed. "Look at his taste in women! He's taken a dirty, flea-bitten savage when he could have had his pick from among the English ladies."

Gilda felt her head spin as the man began to drag her away. She clawed and scratched and kicked, but her weakness could not match his strength.

"Tobias, what do you think you are doing?" Megan screamed, her cries echoing in the silence of the winter woods as she followed. "Tobias!"

"Shut up, woman!" the man roared, his muscular arm squeezing the air from Gilda's lungs as he pulled her down the hill. She caught a glimpse of winter sky spiderwebbed by the dead, dark branches of the trees, then the world went black.

▼▲▼▲▼ The barn where she woke smelled of hay, manure, wetness, and rot. Her hands had been tied together with a length of rope, and her bare ankles were enclosed in iron manacles fastened to a sturdy ring upon the wall. Gilda shook her head to throw off the lingering wisps of sleep. Surely this was but a new variety of nightmare, for Fallon had promised to send help!

The small wooden door of the barn opened, and a stream of bright winter daylight entered the room before the door closed again. The woman, Megan, entered, carrying a bowl of gruel. A small loaf of bread lay under her arm, and she placed both the bowl and the bread before Gilda, then stepped away and thrust her hands behind her back. "I'm sorry," she said, her voice breaking as she looked directly at Gilda for the first time. "I meant to help you. I had no idea Tobias would do this. . . ."

Gilda said nothing, but lifted her bound hands. The woman nodded and came forward, kneeling in the sour straw as she untied the leather strips that held her. "I'm sorry. Tobias did it. He is convinced that Indians know how to vanish like the wind, and he said he didn't want to take any chances. He made all the other servants sleep outside last night and—" She lowered her eyes and blushed. "Nobody's violated you, if you are wondering about that. Tobias saw the marks of pox upon your arms in the lamplight, and that scared him away."

"Thank God," Gilda murmured, and the woman's head jerked upward in surprise.

"You speak English?"

"I am English," Gilda answered, rubbing her sore wrists. "I have lived in Jamestown for many years."

"But your hair, and your dress," the woman stammered. "Coming upon you in the woods like that, in that Indian cave—"

"I am also Powhatan," Gilda answered, eyeing the woman steadily. "A kinswoman of the great Opechancanough. Your husband takes a great risk in holding me thus, for the chief will demand your husband's head once he hears of what he has done."

Megan paled and hurried from the barn, and Gilda smoothed a smile of triumph from her face. If Tobias was reasonable, he'd release her, and she would travel slowly, saving her strength, until she reached Jamestown and Fallon. Once they were reunited she didn't care where they went, as long as they were together.

The metal bracelets on her ankles clinked together as she crossed her legs and began to eat.

▼▲▼▲ Fallon pressed northward until he reached the James River. He considered swimming across to Henrico but knew the frigid water could kill him more quickly than an Indian arrow. Finally he made a small raft by lashing sections of fallen trees together and used his hands to guide the raft through the current.

Though he was welcomed and fed at the Henrico settlement, his message of an impending Indian attack fell on deaf ears. The directors of the corporation, who had taken great pains to restore the peace with the Indians since the massacre at Falling Creek, did not want to hear disquieting rumors.

Fallon nevertheless pressed on to Charles City, where his message was openly scorned. The deputy governor of that settlement even made Fallon repeat his warnings before a group of visiting Powhatan traders. The savages listened to his charges without comment, then turned and flatly told the deputy that Fallon was lying. "Of course he is," the governor said, smiling broadly at his guests. "And do not be concerned about the peace. It will hold, God willing, and this man will be hanged if he dares utter another seditious word."

Shaking his head in contempt, Fallon left Charles City and moved eastward to Jamestown.


▼▲▼▲ Gilda discovered that she had underestimated the courage and daring of Tobias Harden. Megan repeated Gilda's news and threat to her husband, and Tobias regarded Gilda thoughtfully for two days, then disappeared. While the master was away, Gilda endured the unwanted attention of a dozen of Harden's indentured servants, who had returned to sleep in the barn. Though they kept a careful distance from her due to the scabs that still dotted her face and flesh, they taunted her with ribald suggestions that kept her forever on guard and prevented the deep, healing sleep she desperately needed.

On the fifth day of her confinement, Tobias opened wide the door of the barn, and Gilda blinked in the unaccustomed brightness. Three Powhatan warriors followed Harden into the building, and they regarded Gilda with impassive eyes as Tobias rapidly explained that he hadn't meant to offend the great chief by imprisoning the girl, but she was likely to run away if not kept chained. "Wouldn't the chief like to have her back?" Tobias asked, smiling as he bobbed his head before his guests. "And isn't her safe return worth a deer, maybe two?"

The Indians spoke to each other in low voices, but after a moment they nodded to Harden, who produced a key from his pocket and removed the iron bracelets from Gilda's ankles. She stood, determined not to show her fear before this most despicable of men, and walked toward the warriors with her chin high.

"Come," she told them in Algonquin. "The great chief Opechancanough will want to see me."

▼▲▼▲▼ The great chief did not want to see her when she reached Weromacomico, and Kitchi himself blocked the way to the chief's dwelling. "Your uncle will see you later," he told Gilda, an oddly appraising look in his eye. "You are to wait."

So Gilda joined the other women in their daily work, blending seamlessly into village life while she waited upon the chief's pleasure. Day by day she noticed that the marks of her disease lessened, and by the fourth day after her arrival, her skin had been restored to health.

It was on that day that Kitchi came out of Opechancanough's hut and motioned to her. She handed the ladle with which she had been stirring a stew to another woman, then smoothed her hair and brushed her hands on her tunic. It was time to face her uncle with the truth. She could no longer deny that he was a liar and untrustworthy—how had Fallon put it?—the very devil himself.

She stooped to enter the hut, then stood before the werowance and the circle of elders as she had so many times before. But this time no curiosity or affection gleamed in Opechancanough's coal black eyes. The elders regarded her impassively, and the conjuror's yellowed face squinted up at her in fearful suspicion.

"The copper-haired man has been telling the English that I plan to attack them," the chief said, wasting no time with formalities. "My scouts tell me that every day he moves toward the rising sun to warn the English."

"He speaks the truth," Gilda answered, lifting her chin. "You know that he speaks truly. You hate the English. You always have. And now you would put a dagger in the hand you have extended in peace."

His eyes seemed to see the tight place of anxiety in her heart. "You speak as though you know my mind, Woman-with-a-Secret," he said, his voice smooth with killing casualness. "Yet you are young, and I have lived for seventy-eight summers."

"They say death is afraid of you because you have the heart of a lion," Gilda answered, her eyes moving into the darkness of his. "But they are wrong. Death comes to every man, and it will come to you if you pursue this path of hate."

The conjuror hissed and rattled the gourd in his hand, but Opechancanough laughed, a menacing giggle that lifted the hairs on her arm. "Death will not come to me," he said, the whites of his eyes flashing toward her. "But it will visit you, little sister, if the English stand ready when I take up the war club against them. And it will claim the copper-haired man when we find him."

So Opechancanough's warriors were searching for him. Fallon would need every bit of his cunning and the strength of her prayers to elude the scouts.

The chief lifted a bony finger and pointed it toward her in judgment, then looked around the circle at the listening elders. "Kimi will remain in a hut of this village until spring," he said solemnly, while the elders nodded in agreement. "She stands condemned, for every warrior at Ramushonnouk is dead, including her husband Anakausuen. The children have spoken of a blue-eyed woman who brought sickness upon the village."

"How do we know she will not bring sickness upon us?" one elder asked.

As if in answer, the conjuror rattled his gourd in Gilda's direction and tossed a handful of powder into the glowing fire in the center of the hut. The powder erupted into a yellow smoke, then the conjuror smiled and turned to the elder who had spoken. "Our power is greater than this sickness," he said, flashing a malevolent smile toward Gilda. "This village will not be stricken."

Opechancanough looked directly at Gilda. "The gods will grant you life only if we are victorious over the English. When they are all dead, you may resume your place in our tribe as a healer. If they stand ready for our attack because of the copper-haired man's warning, you will die."

"Your gods are no match for the true God," Gilda called defiantly as two warriors stood to take her away. "And though the forces of darkness align with you, great uncle, the Creator God will have his way."

"Your God will not save your life if I decide to take it," Opechancanough answered, smiling in cruel confidence.

The warriors grasped her arms to carry her from the chief's hut, but Gilda jerked free and stilled them with a forbidding stare. Then she turned back to her uncle. "My life belongs to my God, and he can take it if he chooses," she said, her voice like iron in the stillness of the smoky hut. "But the victory will be his, great chief, no matter what happens."

Opechancanough picked up his war pipe. "We will see when the time comes," he said. "We wait only for a sign."


▼▲▼▲▼ At Jamestown, an Elizabeth City planter named Morgan loaded his canoes with trinkets for trade with the Indians and whistled sharply to the savage he'd hired as a guide. The guide was known to the Indians as Nemattanow, but Morgan had taken to calling the surly warrior by a simpler name. "Hurry up, Jack-of-the-Feathers," he said, smiling as he settled into his canoe. "For that's what I'll call you from now on. You can't be expecting me to learn all that Indian gibberish, can you?"

Morgan adjusted the angle of the jaunty cap he'd recently purchased from a sea captain who'd been bartering a cargo of new fashions from England. Made of red velvet with an ostrich feather set at a debonair angle at the side, the cap was unusually warm and one of a kind. The other planters in Elizabeth City joked that they could see Morgan coming from a mile away when he wore that hat, and Morgan liked anything that set him apart from the others.

Leaving Jack to paddle expertly at the rear of the canoe, Morgan leaned back upon his sacks of goods and propped his feet up on a barrel. They were moving into the chilly wind from the sea, and the Englishman hugged himself tightly into his fur coat. Glancing over his shoulder, he noticed that the stone-faced Indian at the back of the boat never even flinched in the cold, despite the fact that he wore only a pair of leather breeches and a deerskin draped around his shoulders.

"Pick up the pace, Jack, or I'll flog you after supper," Morgan called carelessly as he pulled the cap forward over his eyes. "I want to make Elizabeth City afore dark."

▼▲▼▲▼ The silent knife bit into the plump planter's neck, and after a quivering moment Morgan lay dead in the boat, still reclining like a fool among his bags of treasure. Nemattanow sheathed his blade and sprang from the canoe into the shallows, pausing only for an instant. The red velvet cap gleamed in the fading light, and without thinking, the Indian lifted the hat from the dead man's head and placed it upon his own.

Humming in satisfaction, Nemattanow pulled out his knife one last time, cut a long stroke across his own chest, and allowed the running river waters to wipe the blade clean before returning the knife to its leather sheaf. Then he found the trail to the settlement at Elizabeth City and rehearsed the story he would tell.

▼▲▼▲▼ John Crosby, Morgan's chief servant, saw the hat coming long before he recognized the man who wore it, and the hearth fire was burning brightly by the time Jack-of-the-Feathers told his tale of woe to Morgan's startled family. "We were set upon by alien warriors, probably Mohegan," Jack told Morgan's household. "The master is dead in the canoe, unless the savages have taken him away."

Crosby told one of the younger boys to tend the fierce-looking slash across Jack's chest while he and several others lit torches and set out to the riverbank. Before dawn they had returned with their master's pale body on a litter.

"His throat was cut as neatly as if he'd been sleeping," one man barked, flinging the words of accusation in Jack's face. "If you were attacked by the Mohegan, why weren't the goods stolen?"

"There were no arrows," another man pointed out. "Not a single arrow in the boat, in the master, or in the water."

"The canoe had snagged upon a limb," Crosby explained, carefully observing the effects of these charges upon the Indian's countenance. "Your story might have worked, Jack, but for that. Our master lay in the canoe as if someone cut his throat while he slept, and here you wear his hat. You'll have to come with us to Jamestown for questioning by the governor."

Jack-of-the-Feathers's eyes darted right and left, then he bolted forward in an attempt to run for his life. The servants charged him, his blade flashed from out of its sheath, and in the confusion a musket fired.

Crosby stepped back in alarm as the acrid cloud of smoke lifted. Jack bled from a neat circular wound in his chest and managed three steps toward the door before collapsing in the keeping room of Morgan's house. Since the doctor and the governor lived miles away in Jamestown, Crosby gave the order to load Jack-of-the-Feathers into his late master's canoe for transport upstream.

Jack died before reaching the fort. John Crosby told the authorities about Morgan's murder as calmly as he could, but the news of Nemattanow's murderous treachery and subsequent death coincided with the wild ravings of Fallon Bailie, a man who had hitherto been a well-respected citizen of Jamestown. Bailie had been insisting that Opechancanough had determined and planned an attack to wipe the English from Virginia. No one believed his fantastic story, but now that Jack-of-the-Feathers had been executed without a trial, the English waited with trepidation to see how the great chief might respond.

▼▲▼▲▼ The English did not send runners to the chief, for news traveled like the wind down the banks of the Powhatan and Pamunkey Rivers. Within twelve hours the bad tidings had reached the great chief of the Powhatan, and Opechancanough listened to the account of Nemattanow's death without comment. He had never been fond of that headstrong and murderous warrior, but the dark gods had been good to send Nemattanow into the other world at this time. It was the sign for which he had been waiting.

Opechancanough immediately dictated two messages. The first, to be carried by the swiftest runners, was to the current governor of Jamestown, Sir Francis Wyatt. "Notify the governor," Opechancanough said, nodding gravely at his messengers, "that Nemattanow, being but one man, should be no occasion of a breach of the peace. Again I say that the sky should sooner fall than the peace be broken on my part, and I have given order to all my people to give no offense to the English."

When the first runners had been dispatched, the great chief picked up the war pipe and lighted it from the sacred fire that burned in the center of the village. "Send scouts to every village allied with the tribes of the Powhatan," he said, his voice booming like thunder over the assembled crowd. "Tell the Chickahominies, the Powhatan, and those who have waited with us: At the eighth hour of the morning in three days' time, we will attack the English throughout our land and spare not a man, woman, or child. We will arise as one, slaughtering, burning, destroying all the works of English hands. The winged ships are forever bringing new people, and the time has come to drive them forever from this place."

His people stood in silence, hanging upon his words, and a smile crawled to the chief's lips and curved itself like a snake. "The day I have chosen is the one the English call Good Friday, for it is the day they say their God died. It shall then be a good day indeed, for they can follow their God to death!"

Warriors cheered, and the frenzied dances of war began with the women and children while the young men sprinted out of the palisade to spread the news. Satisfied, Opechancanough folded his arms and looked over his city, where three hundred warriors would soon arm themselves for battle. There were a hundred such villages in the land of the Powhatan, and soon three thousand would march against the English. As long as the English governor rested in the easy promise of peace, Opechanca-nough's victory would be assured.

"What say you now?" He threw the words at the black sky of night, bitterly remembering the dark-clothed holy men who had stolen him from the land of his youth. "You, whom they call the true God, will you rise up against me? If you do, I will cut you down as easily as I killed the friars long ago."

From the raging campfire, boiling clouds of smoke lifted into the air to block the bright stars above. Opechancanough threw back his head and let loose with a war cry that startled even his own people.

Fallon found the people of Jamestown more receptive to his warning of war after the incident with Jack-of-the-Feathers, but within twenty-four hours the message of peace from Opechancanough had arrived. The same men who had grown pale under Fallon's warning now laughed in his face.

"The great chief is afraid of us," they said, drinking freely in the taverns while they planned the large, widely spaced plantations they would build on Indian land. "He cannot stop us now, and he will do nothing to break the peace."

Indians moved freely throughout Jamestown and seemed to share the English contempt for Fallon's message. On Wednesday night, the evening of the twentieth of March, he fell onto an empty straw mattress at Edith Rolfe's house and groaned in exhaustion. He had much to tell Edith, Wart, and Brody about Gilda, but since arriving at the settlement he had spent all his time attempting to spread the warning to which no one would listen. Even Brody, who had never doubted Fallon before, turned an incredulous expression upon his friend and told him he'd been too long in the sun.

"You need a rest," Brody said, pinching Fallon's arm as he lay on the mattress in the front chamber. "Look at you! I'faith, you are skin and bones. I'm thinking you'll need to stay here awhile and let Mistress Rolfe fatten you up."

"I can't stay," Fallon said, pushing himself into a sitting position. "I left Gilda in the woods. I have to go back for her."

"She's alive?" Brody asked, his face alight with honest joy. "Name of a name, Fallon, I was afraid to ask, for she was half dead when we found her. Indeed, I thought you'd be dead of the pox, too."

"I didn't get it," Fallon said, looking at his hands as if he expected to see blisters there. "And Gilda recovered. God was good to me." He looked up at Brody and searched his friend's face. "Gilda and I are married, Brody. We pledged ourselves to one another."

"Go on!" Brody said, wonder in his voice. "You tamed that wild cat?"

Fallon grinned and raked his fingers through his hair. "Not a bit! She's as feisty as ever, but she was too ill to travel. I didn't want to leave her, but I had little choice. Now I've got to get back. But I had to warn you, Brody, about the Powhatan. They are coming. Maybe not today, or tomorrow, but they're going to come, no matter what Opechancanough says."

"We can fight off a hundred Indians," Brody said, shrugging. "It will be no trouble."

"Not a hundred, thousands," Fallon insisted. "It is a conspiracy of the first order."

Brody broke out into a guffaw. "Indians don't cooperate. It isn't in their nature, haven't you seen it? There are too many chiefs, each more proud than he has a right to be."

"You wait and see," Fallon answered, stretching out upon the mattress. His eyelids were heavy, and the grief of leaving Gilda throbbed dully in his heart. It was an effort to keep his mind from wandering into dark possibilities and thoughts of what could happen to her, but he'd go crazy if he allowed himself to think too much.

"Just be ready," he whispered, sinking slowly into sleep.

▼▲▼▲▼ The Indians who visited Jamestown spoke baby English around their English friends and slipped into the quiet tones of Algonquin when alone. Many lived permanently in Jamestown, and these were visited by the members of the woodland tribes in the early hours of Thursday morning. Even

Chanco, the thirteen-year-old godson of Richard Pace, an English planter who lived across the river from the Jamestown settlement, received a visitor from his tribe. Chanco listened intently as the warrior instructed him to murder his master at eight o'clock on the morrow.

Chanco carried his terrible secret throughout the day and took it with him to bed that evening. But as echoes of his kind master's heartfelt bedtime prayers rang in his ears, Chanco rose from his mattress and woke Richard Pace.

Pace listened to the story, then threw on his clothes and leapt into his boat, rowing like a madman across the chopping waters of the James. He pounded on the gate of the Jamestown fort until he was admitted by a sleepy guard. After hearing Pace's rendition of Chanco's testimony, the governor woke the militia and soldiers hastily distributed muskets from the armory. Soldiers ran quietly through the night to the nearby houses, waking the inhabitants and rousing them to action. Women and children hurried to the fort while their menfolk armed themselves with muskets, knives, axes, and spades. Any boy old enough to fling a brickbat was encouraged to stand and help defend his home.

Fallon heard pounding on the door of Mistress Rolfe's house and instantly quit his sleep. He admitted the messenger, listened to the man's intense murmur, then woke Edith, Wart, and Brody. The patients who were too weak to walk had to be carried to the fort, and Fallon pulled out the litters, which of certain would have to do double duty on this terrible night.

Through the remaining hours of darkness they worked, then Fallon left Wart and Edith at the fort as he and Brody slipped back to the house in the time of half-light before sunrise. They would defend the place as best they could and carry the fight into the streets. But there would be no element of surprise to confound the English, for the citizens of Jamestown had at last decided to heed Fallon's warning.

▼▲▼▲▼ On the twenty-second morning of March in 1622, a blurred and bloodred sun rose and lightened the horizon east of Jamestown. Inside the fort, soldiers gripped their muskets and checked their ammunition for the hundredth time. In the outlying houses men wiped sweaty hands upon their breeches and shivered in the frosty morning air.

Across the western valley of Virginia, the retreating moon seemed bent on hurrying from one dark cloud to another as the warriors of the Powhatan shifted in their positions. Most carried quivers of specially prepared arrows upon their backs and war clubs in their hands; others clutched weapons that their English friends had given them for hunting. Outside Henrico, Elizabeth City, Charles City, and Jamestown the warriors crouched at their posts with one eye cocked toward the sun as they waited for the angle of the eighth hour.

The citizens of every settlement but Jamestown rose and went about their business as usual, and at eight o'clock the slaughter began. At Henrico, a war club crushed John Rolfe's skull through an open window as he sat at breakfast to read his devotions. Bursting into the foundry outside the settlement, the Indians immediately killed the mill master and his men and threw the machinery into the creek.

The planters' houses were set aflame, and men, women, and children, both masters and servants, were killed as they ran in confusion from the carnage. Pillars of smoke rose one by one from the widely scattered English settlements, and before an hour had passed, more than three hundred fifty English lay dead in the Virginian forests.

Opechancanough's plan of genocide would have succeeded if not for Jamestown. Forewarned and ready, the Englishmen and women of that city successfully defended several Indian sallies by land and water. As muskets roared and cannon boomed, the savage invaders withdrew under the cover of the dense forest and retreated to await word from their chief.

▼▲▼▲▼ The night drew down like a black cowl as Fallon and Brody waited at the house for another attack, and Fallon's stretched nerves jangled when the silence was shattered by Edith's voice at the front gate. "Don't shoot, boys; it's only me and Wart," she called, stepping into the dim rectangle of light that streamed from the open window. "Open up the door—I've brought you supper. I'd wager you haven't eaten all day."

"Truth to tell, woman, are you crazy?" Brody said, jumping up to help her bring in a basket of supplies. "Edith, it's folly to move about out there in the dark. We don't know who might be lurking—"

"Jamestown is safe," Wart interrupted, warming his hands before the fire. "There's been no sign of a warring savage since this morning. And every Indian in Jamestown has been imprisoned save for Master Pace's boy, Chanco."

"The day's true hero," Brody said, tossing Edith a relieved smile. "I'm thinking we ought to erect a statue in his honor."

"That's well done, but I've brought supper for all," Edith said, moving toward the kitchen. "This day has been a horror, but with a good meal in our bellies we'll all sleep more soundly."

Wart followed her like an obedient puppy, but Brody paused when Fallon did not move from the window. "Aren't you coming?" Brody asked, his eyes narrowing in concern. "I'faith, Fallon, you can't be thinking—"

"If the streets are safe enough for Edith to come home, it's time for me to leave," Fallon said, propping his musket against the wall. He moved toward the door and took a long cloak from a peg in the wall. "Gilda's somewhere out there, Brody. If she was in one of the other settlements—" His throat closed around the words, and Brody grasped his arm.

"Don't think so, Fallon. She's a smart girl, and an Indian."

"All the more reason for me to find her," Fallon said, his voice grim as he slipped the cloak over his shoulders. "The English will begin a war of their own tomorrow, you can be sure of it. The days of peace are done, and anyone with dark hair will be a moving target."

He opened the door and stepped out into the night air. A quiet inner voice nudged him out of his musings and told him that this would be the last time he would visit the healing house. Brody must have sensed Fallon's feeling, for he followed through the open door and stood in the thin stream of light that cast a gentle glow upon the path. "Go with God, then, me friend," Brody said, his voice husky.

"Take care of Wart and Mistress Rolfe," Fallon said, reaching out to clasp his friend's hand. "You know, Brody, you ought to marry Edith and still the gossiping tongues of this town."

"Maybe I will," Brody answered, smiling. "She's a bonny lass, to me way of thinking." He cleared his throat. "Give Gilda me love when you find her. And you *will* find her, Fallon."

"Aye," Fallon whispered, releasing Brody's hand. A flicker of a smile rose at the edges of his mouth, then died out as he mentally said farewell to Edith and Wart, two precious people he might never see again. Then he turned his back on the small house where a single brave lantern steadily pushed at the gloom of Jamestown.

▼▲▼▲▼ The Englishmen who gave their lives in the defense of Jamestown lay respectfully covered in a corner of the fort. But at least thirty dead Indians lay exposed in the shimmer of moonlight on the riverbank, a warning to others who might consider a midnight raid.

The river gravel crunched under Fallon's boots, and instantly half a dozen men materialized from out of the shadows. The muskets at their shoulders were aimed at his head.

"Do not fire!" he called, lifting his hands.

"What are you doing out here, fool?" one of the guards called, lowering his musket only an inch. "Go home where you belong. We don't know who is in yonder woods."

"I need a boat," Fallon said, carefully lowering his arms. "My wife is stranded upriver, and I'm worried about her. I only came here to warn the governor."

"That's Bailie," another of the men said, lowering his musket altogether. "He was in the public house, telling us about the attack. We all thought he was crazy."

"How'd you know?" the tallest guard asked, keeping his musket cleanly in line with Fallon's eyes. "How chummy are you with the savages?"

"No more friendly than anyone else," Fallon pointed out. "I'd wager half the men in this place have had dealings with the Indians in the past month."

"Yet none of them knew about the attack," the tall man called, his voice brimming with suspicion. The other guards, who had begun to relax, suddenly hefted their muskets again.

"My wife is a Powhatan," Fallon said, making an effort to smile. "But her loyalties are with the English. She, like Chanco, told me to warn the folk at Jamestown. So if you will let me pass, I'll be able to tell her that all is well with you."

"If your wife is an Indian," the big man said, spitting the words slowly, "she's under a death sentence. Governor Wyatt has already prepared the papers. Tomorrow we begin our revenge on the Powhatan and Chickahominy tribes. The documents say we can seize their crops, burn their villages, and kill every last one of 'em, just like they killed the English today."

"That is not right!" Fallon protested, backing slowly toward the water. "Though Opechancanough did wrong, still we have no right to kill the innocent!"

"Come away from the water," the guard ordered, gesturing with the end of his musket. "And put your hands on your head. We'll not have you warning the Indians like you tried to warn us."

Fallon slowly extended his hands upward, then locked them upon his head. The men circled round to come between him and the water, and Fallon seized the moment to make a dash for the river.

"He's away!" one man shouted, and Fallon closed his eyes and dove just as the muskets roared and bullets whispered by him in the night.

Fallon stayed under the freezing water for as long as he dared, then surfaced to gasp for breath. "There he is!" another voice cried, and bullets tore holes in the water as he dove and frantically propelled himself upriver against the current. Again he came up for air, and the musket fire repeated. The noise and movement attracted the attention of Indians hidden on the far bank, and arrows fell in a whistling cloud around Fallon, reaching even to the Englishmen on the opposite bank. The English guards fired at random targets, then ran for cover as they dragged two fallen comrades back to the safety of the fort.

Drained of all will and thought, Fallon wrapped his arms over a floating log and hung motionless in the water. The current propelled him downstream, back toward Jamestown, and his tired legs managed to kick so that he and the log moved steadily westward as quickly as he dared without attracting attention from the dark savages who hovered unseen in the woods.

▼▲▼▲▼ In the hut at Weromacomico, Gilda raised her head expectantly as the old woman brought a bowl of hominy. "Eat," the woman urged, her voice coarse with age. "The warriors celebrate. Our chief has won a great victory."

Gilda hid a thick swallow in her throat and turned away as as she ruefully accepted the terrible knowledge. Despite his noble intentions, Fallon had not reached the English in time to warn them. Maybe he had not reached Jamestown at all, for she suspected that Opechancanough had sent scouts through the woods to strike her husband down in the midst of his journey. If the English were defeated, surely Fallon was dead.

She realized that the old woman watched her carefully, so Gilda pasted on a warm smile and dipped her fingers into the hominy as if she were eager to join in the celebration. After the old crone nodded in satisfaction and left, Gilda flung the offending food off her fingers and hugged her knees to her, burying her head in her arms.

The hunger to leave gnawed at her heart, but where would

she go? The English were defeated, and Fallon was gone. She would gladly follow him and Noshi into heaven, but she did not know if she had the courage or the right to take her own life. A month ago she might have done it, but at the hillside cave she had surrendered her life to another, and it was no longer hers to take.

She only knew with pulse-pounding certainty that she could not stay in Opechancanough's village. She had once considered him a kinsman and admired his strength of purpose, but no more. Again she acknowledged that Fallon was right. Opechan-canough was a devil, for he had looked into the heart of the same God she loved and rejected the goodness he found there.

The sounds of revelry and drums began to permeate the hut, and Gilda stood up, amazed at the dreamlike lunacy of it all. She bent low and crept out of the house. There was no guard at the door, no woman to screech for the warriors, no children to scream at her approach.

Opechancanough had said she would die if the English were prepared. And though she saw no sign of the chief, she knew that the warriors who danced around the fire now had clearly been successful. She was free.

Without another thought, she turned on her heel and walked from the campfire, out of the palisade, and into the forest. There was only one place she now considered home. She would go there and wait for the voice of God to speak again.

At daybreak Fallon woke in the mud at the river's edge. His fingers and toes were blue with cold, but he was grateful to be alive and uninjured. Orange mud coated him from his head to his feet, and he managed a sardonic grin—it was excellent camouflage, no matter that he hadn't planned it. Rising carefully, he crouched along the riverbank and followed it westward for three days, eating greens and small fish from the river to sustain his strength.

Like ghostly shrouds, clouds of smoke from burning settlements hung over the river valley, but whether the smoke rose from destroyed English or Indian villages Fallon could not tell. More than once he saw dead bodies flow past him in the river current, but not a single canoe or shallop cruised past him. If any of the English in the outlying settlements had survived, he knew it would be folly to travel upon the open river. They would likely make their way to Jamestown through the woods.

The moon nervously hid her face in fog when Fallon first approached the settlement where he had met Tobias Harden. All that remained of what had been a prosperous plantation was a blackened chimney and a burned fence. In the courtyard Fallon found the twisted remains of two men in leg-irons, and near the chimney lay the charred corpse of a woman, her face frozen for eternity in a paroxysm of terror. But the woman was not Gilda, of that he was certain.

Pain and frustration walked with him through the ashes of his dreams. He had hoped to find Gilda here, but instead only death and destruction had awaited him. Where could he find her now?

His eyes stung from the fine layer of ash that coated everything in sight, and his muscles ached. Too tired to think, Fallon

slumped to the ground under a scorched tree and rested his head
on his knees while he waited for the sun to rise. Back in the hillside cave, Gilda curled into her bed of furs and dreamed.

> She was small and in a canoe traveling west
> on a river that flowed east. Noshi lay beside her,
> his green eyes shining in trust, and behind Noshi
> she could see that Fallon's long and lanky body
> was tense with responsibility.
>
> The canoe gently beached itself on a sandbar,
> and Gilda peered over the edge of the boat. A
> palisade rose before her in the semidarkness,
> and a small opening under the wall beckoned
> toward her. "That's it," Fallon said, his voice
> high pitched and reedy with youth. "That's
> where we have to go."
>
> She slipped out of the canoe and splashed
> toward shore, then paused and put her finger
> into her mouth as she looked up at the tall tim-
> bers of the palisade. They towered over her,
> making her feel slight and insignificant, but
> then Fallon's warm hand engulfed her smaller
> one. "I'll help you," he said, pulling her closer
> to the opening. "Just go through."
>
> Gilda stopped, for odd wind-borne sounds
> came to her: agonized screams, the thunder of
> muskets, the low moans of suffering. Fallon's
> face clouded with disappointment when she
> would not follow, then Noshi appeared at her
> shoulder, his eyes level with her own. "I'll go
> first," he said, stepping toward the hole. "I'll
> go to the other side and pull you through."
>
> Gilda watched in amazement as Noshi dove
> toward the hole. Wriggling like a rabbit, his
> head disappeared and a moment later his body

followed. His voice called joyously through the opening: "Come on, Gilda! Don't wait!"

She looked toward Fallon, ready to falter again, but he stepped back and crossed his arms. "I won't tell you what to do," he said, his voice deepening to that of a man. "You must decide."

The roar of absolute silence engulfed the other sounds, and Gilda stepped forward and knelt near the edge of the crevice. She could not see what lay beyond the wall, only a few pebbles in the narrow passageway. She considered putting her feet into the opening first, but knew she could not maneuver in such an awkward position. She had to dive head first, totally committing herself, or do nothing.

Taking a deep breath, she lay flat on her belly, pressed her face to the dirt, and shimmied forward. She kicked and wriggled her hands as if she swam through mud. And after her first thrust she saw nothing, but as she pushed and kicked again, strong hands caught her, and suddenly she was through the opening and inside the palisade. Standing before her were two couples: an English couple, both brown-haired, tall, and thin, and another couple who had wrapped Noshi in an eager embrace.

The brown-haired woman came forward and opened her arms. "Gilda, darling," she said, her eyes shining with love. "We knew you would come."

"We knew you would understand," the man said, nodding formally though a smile played upon his handsome features. "We taught you things that can never be forgotten."

"About God," Gilda whispered, fingering the circle of gold at her throat.

"Yes," the woman whispered, touching her finger to the ring. "And about love."

The woman drew Gilda into an embrace, and she reveled in the warmth of it. She clasped her own childishly chubby arms around the woman's neck and turned to see Fallon embracing a red-haired woman who stood with a tall, majestic warrior at her side. Unbidden, their names surfaced in her mind. *Audrey. Rowtag.*

She turned again toward the dark-haired woman. "Mama?" she asked, and the lady nodded slowly, her eyes bright with tears. "Papa?" Gilda asked, turning to the man.

"Yes," he answered, coming to stand beside her. "We have always been so to you."

Gilda buried her face in the woman's shoulder and held her tight. "God has taken me," she whispered in relief, her voice muffled by the thick fur the woman wore on her shoulders. "I am dead, and so are Fallon and Noshi. This must be heaven."

She stirred in sleep and murmured the lovely phrase again. "This must be heaven."

Suddenly the comfortable warmth of the woman's embrace evaporated, and Gilda's arms closed upon empty air.

"It is only heaven if you and I are together," a masculine voice said, cutting through her dream, and Gilda opened her eyes, fully awake. Fallon stood before her in the glory of sunrise, her fur blanket in his hand, his face caked with mud. Yet he was the most beautiful, precious thing she had ever seen, and she leapt to her feet and threw herself into his arms.

▼▲▼▲▼ The force of her welcome rocked Fallon back on his feet, but she was warm and alive in his embrace. He blinked back tears of gratitude and relief as he folded her close.

"I thought you were dead," she said, her voice a low murmur in his ear. "The warriors at Opechancanough's village danced to celebrate their victory, and then I dreamed—I saw them all, Fallon: Mama and Papa, Audrey and Rowtag and Noshi—"

"You saw them?" He pulled back, his eyes scanning her face. He'd never mentioned his parents' names to her. "What did you see?"

"It was my old dream," she said, laughing as she brought her hands to her cheeks. "Name of a name, it's as though I was just there! We were in the canoe, but I wasn't afraid because I knew you and Noshi were with me. And we beached on the riverbank, and we walked to the palisade. I didn't want to crawl under the wall, but Noshi went first. And then I followed, and I saw Mama and Papa and your parents—"

Her eyes darkened in love, and she reached out, tangling her hand in his hair. "Your mother had red hair, too," she whispered, smiling. "And Noshi's green eyes were hers."

Emotions tumbled in Fallon's heart so that he could not speak. He nodded wordlessly.

"And I hugged my mama and papa, and I knew everything would be all right. But I thought you were dead because I saw you there, too."

"You and I are alive," he said, slipping his arms around her. "It was not heaven you visited, but your past. You are of the English and the Indians, Gilda, but more than that, you are of Ocanahonan."

Her head sank against his chest as she considered his words, and he gingerly ran his fingers through her thick hair.

"You are right," she whispered after a moment. She turned her head and smiled up at him. "Are you always right, my husband?"

"Usually," Fallon answered, grinning, then the light in his eyes dimmed with sadness. "But not everyone is quick to believe me. At Charles City and Henrico I did my best to warn the planters, but no one would listen. Until Jamestown. An Indian boy confirmed my story and the settlement was alerted in time.

Opechancanough's victory was not complete, Gilda. Our friends are safe and well."

"God be praised," she whispered. "I know now that I was wrong to oppose your going to them. It was selfish and prideful of me to argue with you."

"My heart resisted every step that took me away," he confessed, his gaze focusing on her lips. "I'll never leave you again."

Surrendering to the crush of feelings that drew them together, his mouth moved over hers with exquisite tenderness.

"You are freezing," she whispered when they finally parted. "And tired, too, no doubt."

"No," he whispered, flushing as a rush of warmth flashed over him. "I am happy to be with you. Only God knows how much I have missed you, Gilda. I feared that you were at Harden's plantation and had been killed in the attack—"

"I was there, for a time," she said, her hand pressed against the strong drumbeat of his heart. "But that traitor traded me to Opechancanough like a sack of beads. The chief held me prisoner for a while—"

"And you gave him such grief that he will be delighted to find you gone," he said, smiling tenderly.

"Fallon Bailie," she scolded, tilting her head back to look up at him. "You sound as if you are sorry you found me."

"Never," he answered, his lips trailing a path along the side of her cheek. "If I had to search to the ends of the earth, I would do so to find you." He relaxed and enjoyed the soft feel of her in his arms as he kissed her, then he paused and settled his hands about her waist with easy familiarity. "We have much to consider, love," he said. "The English revenge upon the Indians will make Opechancanough's attack pale in comparison. The militia at Jamestown is already planning raids of reprisal. No Indian will be safe in an English settlement for a long time."

"Neither can we make a home among the Powhatan," she answered, looking at him with something very fragile in her eyes. "Opechancanough knows it was you who warned those at Jamestown."

They stood looking at each other as the meaning of their words took hold. They had no place to go.

Guilt poured over Fallon as he considered the thought. "I never meant to take you from your people," he said, overwhelmed by memories of the loneliness he'd felt while at the school for homeless orphans. He knew the anguish of being alone, and yet he had taken her, irrevocably, from both worlds in which she had found a place. "I never realized how I might hurt you—"

"You have never done anything to hurt me," she stopped him, cradling his head in her hands. "I am no longer of the Powhatan. I am bone of your bone, Fallon Bailie, and flesh of your flesh. My home is in you, and the sky should sooner fall than I would leave your side." She lifted a hand and gestured toward the canopy of forest around them. "Maybe it is God's call for us to make our own home, with our own children."

The thought was comforting, something to hold on to. "Think you so?" he asked, feeling his heart turn over as her eyes shone toward him in love.

"Yes," she answered, her expression seeming to fill the woods with light. "And I know where we should go. The place where we began, the city where Englishmen and Indians lived together with respect and love for the true God."

"Ocanahonan?" His eyes clouded with hazy sadness. "But there is nothing left, Gilda; it was destroyed years ago."

"There is much left," she whispered, taking his hands. She gave him an abashed smile. "There are two survivors, a man and a woman who believe they should boldly, faithfully, and successfully venture forth into the new world. If these two go in God's blessing and grace, who can stand against them?"

"A man and a woman," he echoed, his reservations vanishing in the space of a heartbeat. He pressed his finger to the circle of gold at her throat, the ring God had used to bring them together again over the space of years.

"A husband and his wife," she corrected. She gave him a shy glance and led him into the cave, then knelt on the pile of furs and lifted her fingertips until they brushed his hand. Her touch send a wave of warmth along his pulses. Fallon smiled at his bride, then lifted the heavy bearskin to shield them from the breath of the wind.

▼▲▼▲▼ In the next week Fallon and Gilda collected supplies from the abandoned village, then repaired a canoe they had found hidden at a point where the small stream below their cave deepened. According to Fallon's calculations, the creek would join with other south-flowing waters and eventually widen into the Chowan River. It would be along the banks of the Chowan that they would find the ruined walls of the village once called Ocanahonan.

As the colors of sunrise painted a new day, Gilda settled herself into the front of the canoe and watched a pair of cardinals court each other among the branches of trees overhanging the water. Behind her, Fallon paddled expertly and hummed a tune that harmonized with distant chords of memory in her heart. He had doffed his English coat and wore a pair of supple leather breeches and a shirt made from the softest buckskin Gilda could find at Ramushonnouk.

She ran her thumb over the gold ring circling her finger and smiled in the calm strength of knowledge. Fallon had slipped it onto her hand last night, telling her that the ring would symbolize their marriage and his unending love.

But it meant so much more. When she looked within the clouded surface of the gold band she could see the reflection of her mother and father, of Fallon's parents, of Noshi and Pocahontas. Boldly, faithfully, successfully, they had surrendered their lives and hopes to God, and she had forever been changed by their faith. She and Fallon would follow their example, and trust God with the future.

Flooded with the wonderful sense of going home, she leaned back upon a bundle of provisions and felt the first rays of morning touch her face.

And the river carried them away.

# REFERENCE LIST

If you are interested in further study of Jamestown, Pocahontas, or the Powhatan tribes, consider the following books, which the author used in her research for this novel.

Bridenbaugh, Carl, 1980. *Jamestown*. New York: Oxford University Press.

Chartier, Roger, ed., 1989. *A History of Private Life, Volume III: Passions of the Renaissance*. Cambridge, MA: Belknap Press.

Fishwick, Marshall W., 1965. *Jamestown, First English Colony*. New York: American Heritage Publishing Company, Inc.

Grant, Bruce, 1989. *Concise Encyclopedia of the American Indian*. New York: Whip Books.

Hawke, David Freeman, 1989. *Everyday Life in Early America*. New York: Harper and Row.

Jacobs, Wilbur R., 1972. *Dispossessing the American Indian*. New York: Charles Scribner's Sons.

Marcus, Robert D., and David Burner, eds., 1989. *America Firsthand, Volume I: Settlement to Reconstruction*. New York: St. Martin's Press.

Meadows, Denis, 1961. *Five Remarkable Englishmen*. New York: The Devin-Adair Company.

Millar, John F., 1978. *American Ships of the Colonial and Revolutionary Period*. New York: W. W. Norton & Company.

Noll, Mark A., 1992. *A History of Christianity in the United States and Canada*. Grand Rapids, Mich.: William B. Eerdmans Publishing Company.

Quinn, David Beers and Alison M. Quinn, eds., 1982. *The First Colonists: Documents on the Planting of the First English Settlements in North America 1584-1590*. Raleigh: North Carolina Department of Cultural Resources.

White, Jon Manchip, 1979. *Everyday Life of the American Indian*. New York: Indian Head Books.

# EPILOGUE

The lives of Fallon and Gilda, keepers of the ring, continued in a distant part of the country, but the war between the English of Jamestown and Opechancanough persisted for many more years.

Opechancanough's attack upon the English is now considered by many to be the most brilliantly conceived, planned, and executed uprising in the history of the American Indians. For several months after that Good Friday in 1622, Opechancanough believed that he had won a major victory, even urging the king of the Potomac Indians to wipe out a trading party upon his river. Opechancanough assured this chief that "before the end of two moons there should not be an Englishman" in all their countries.

But the retaliation of the English was fierce and relentless. More Indians were killed in 1622 than had been killed in all the years combined between the founding of Jamestown and Opechancanough's massacre. From August 1622 until 1632, the English war of revenge continued until the Indians were forced out of the peninsula between the James and York Rivers. Because they were forced from their villages and fields, more Indians died of starvation during those years than at the hands of the English.

The final act of the great chief's war took place in Jamestown in 1644, when the one-hundred-year-old Opechancanough, finally taken captive, was paraded down the street and shot in the back by an English soldier.